PRIZE STORIES
1995
THE O. HENRY
AWARDS

PRIZE STORIES

1·9·9·5

·THE·

O. HENRY

AWARDS

◆

*Edited and with
an Introduction by*

William Abrahams

DOUBLEDAY

NEW YORK LONDON TORONTO SYDNEY AUCKLAND

PUBLISHED BY DOUBLEDAY
a division of Bantam Doubleday Dell Publishing Group, Inc.
1540 Broadway, New York, New York 10036

DOUBLEDAY and the portrayal of an anchor with a dolphin
are trademarks of Doubleday,
a division of Bantam Doubleday Dell Publishing Group, Inc.

Library of Congress Cataloging-in-Publication Data
Prize stories. 1947–
New York, N.Y., Doubleday.
v. 22 cm.
Annual.
The O. Henry awards.
None published 1952–53.
Continues: O. Henry memorial award prize stories.
1. Short stories, American—Collected works.
PZ1.011   813'.01'08—dc19   21-9372
                                                        MARC-S

ISBN: 0-385-47671-X
ISBN: 0-385-47672-8 (pbk.)

April 1995

1   3   5   7   9   10   8   6   4   2

First Edition

CONTENTS

PUBLISHER'S NOTE

This volume is the seventy-fifth in the O. Henry Memorial Award series, and the twenty-ninth to be edited by William Abrahams.

* * *

In 1918, the Society of Arts and Sciences met to vote upon a monument to the master of the short story: O. Henry. They decided that this memorial should be in the form of two prizes for the best short stories published by American authors in American magazines during the year 1919. From this beginning, the memorial developed into an annual anthology of outstanding short stories by American authors, published, with the exception of the years 1952 and 1953, by Doubleday.

Blanche Colton Williams, one of the founders of the awards, was editor from 1919 to 1932; Harry Hansen from 1933 to 1940; Herschel Brickell from 1941 to 1951. The annual collection did not appear in 1952 and 1953, when the continuity of the series was interrupted by the death of Herschel Brickell. Paul Engle was editor from 1954 to 1959, with Hanson Martin coeditor in the years 1954 to 1960; Mary Stegner in 1960; Richard Poirier from 1961 to 1966, with assistance from and coeditorship with William Abrahams from 1964 to 1966. William Abrahams became editor of the series in 1967.

In 1970, Doubleday published under Mr. Abrahams's editorship *Fifty Years of the American Short Story*, and in 1981, *Prize*

Stories of the Seventies. Both are collections of stories selected from this series.

The stories chosen for this volume were published in the period from the summer of 1993 to the summer of 1994. A list of the magazines consulted appears at the back of the book. The choice of stories and selection of prizewinners are exclusively the responsibility of the editor. Biographical material is based on information provided by the contributors and obtained from standard works of reference.

INTRODUCTION

Prize Stories 1995 is the seventy-fifth volume in the O. Henry Awards series, which was launched in 1919. Here in its entirety, save for a decorative and quite indecipherable colophon, is the title page of the first volume:

O. HENRY MEMORIAL AWARD

PRIZE STORIES
1919

CHOSEN BY THE SOCIETY OF
ARTS AND SCIENCES

WITH AN INTRODUCTION
BY
BLANCHE COLTON WILLIAMS

Garden City, New York
DOUBLEDAY, PAGE & COMPANY
1920

That page, encountered now, has something of the flavor of a faded historical document. "O. Henry Memorial Award" (singular) has been simultaneously expanded and compressed to "The

O. Henry Awards" (plural). The Society of Arts and Sciences no longer exists. Nor does Blanche Colton Williams, nor Doubleday, Page & Company, which underwent a succession of metamorphoses, becoming Doubleday, Doran, and then, as it has been for many years now, simply Doubleday.

In her introduction, which has an historical flavor of its own, Ms. Colton Williams explained how the Award came about:

> On April 18, 1918, the Society of Arts and Sciences of New York City paid tribute to the memory of William Sydney Porter at a dinner in honour if his genius. [He had died in 1910.] In the ball-room of the Hotel McAlpin there gathered, at the speakers' table, a score of writers, editors and publishers who had been associated with O. Henry during the time he lived in Manhattan; in the audience, many others who had known him, and hundreds yet who loved his short stories.
>
> Enthusiasm, both immediate and lasting, indicated to the Managing Director of the Society, Mr. John F. Tucker, that he might progress hopefully toward an ideal he had, for some time, envisioned. The goal lay in the establishing of a memorial to the author who had transmuted realistic New York into romantic Baghdad-by-the-Subway.
>
> When, therefore, in December, 1918, Mr. Tucker called a committee for the purpose of considering such a memorial, he met a glad response. The first question, "What form shall the monument assume?" drew tentative suggestions of a needle in Gramercy Square, or a tablet affixed to the corner of O. Henry's home in West Twenty-sixth Street. But things of iron and stone, cold and dead, would incongruously commemorate the dynamic power that moved the hearts of living men and women, "the master pharmacist of joy and pain," who dispensed "sadness tinctured with a smile and laughter that dissolves in tears."

Hence and thence: Prize Stories. The present volume contains twenty-two stories from fifteen magazines. Two of these magazines, *The Atlantic Monthly* and *Harper's Magazine,* were also represented in the 1919 collection—a welcome and rare instance of continuity. I say "rare" because it is change, not continuity, that has been the dominating characteristic of the history of the world since 1919. Change: the changes effected by history, by science, by politics, by manners, morals and mores, and so inevitably on for seventy-five years, and thus, inevitably, to change in the world of the story.

Writers of fiction are not journalists or historians recording and interpreting "real events" in a "real world," but they are inescapably a part of that world, and consciously or not, they respond to it in what they write. Even when there is a deliberate attempt to escape from reality into fantasy of one kind or another, the actual world is felt as an invisible though persistent presence. But beyond the changes of subject matter and minute particulars that have offered themselves to writers—what the story is about—there are the evolving changes in style and form—how the story is written.

When this series was launched in 1919, it is now clear to us as it would not have been to Ms. Colton Williams, that the genteel tradition of the short story in America was entering its decline. The modern story—essentially as we know it, with its roots in Chekhov and Joyce—was soon to emerge in the 1920s with the appearance of such newcomers as Sherwood Anderson, William Faulkner, Scott Fitzgerald, and Ernest Hemingway—perhaps the single most influential writer of stories in these seventy-five years. Modified and responding to the changes in the public world and private sensibility, the modern story has continued virtually to the present. If, as some suggest, it has given way since the mid-1980s to postmodernism, the kinship is still unmistakable, and whatever postmodernism has brought us, it has not been a return to the genteel tradition. If I were to generalize about the stories in this present collection, I would say that they are remarkably free of deference to dogmatic programs, but each pursues its own vision of what the story should be. I am quite willing to admit that my taste in assembling this year's stories is eclectic. But that, after all, is what the collection was meant to be from its very beginning.

Once again, special thanks to Arabella Meyer at Anchor Books for her assistance.

—William Abrahams

PRIZE STORIES

1995

THE O. HENRY

AWARDS

Cornelia Nixon

THE WOMEN COME AND GO

One quarter of her waking life had gone to practicing the violin, but when her teacher entered her in a national audition, Margy was surprised to make it to the finals, and didn't bother checking the results. The teacher had to track her down at home to tell her that she'd won. Margy knew it was a fluke, but within a month she was invited everywhere to play (to Tanglewood, to Aspen, with the Boston Symphony); and at her school in the Back Bay, where she'd always had to practice straight through lunch, ignored by everyone, suddenly she had so much cachet that the most sought-after girls were seeking her. Ann was generally acknowledged the most beautiful girl in school, and beautiful in a way that made other girls feel awe: she was perfect in the natural state, like Grace Kelly before she met the prince, only better, since she'd never bleached her hair or worn lipstick. She had a nunlike aura, and wore expensive modest clothes, the kind that most girls' mothers picked for them and they refused to wear. Even the Huntington uniform looked good on her. Calluses did not grow on her toes. Whatever she said was considered wise. She liked to quote from Hermann Hesse, Kahlil Gibran, and other sources of deathless wisdom.

"Just sit on your bed and think," she said. Hushing to listen, girls went home and sat on their beds.

And with Ann came Elizabeth, her lifelong acolyte. Their mothers were friends, former debutantes who had married the wrong men, and now lived in a neighborhood much faded from its former glory, instead of in three-story mansions out in Brookline or in Lexington. Elizabeth dressed like Ann, even vied with her a little in the neatness of her gestures, the propriety of her shoes. But she didn't have the face, or the hair or the skin, and no one stopped to listen when she talked, unless it was about Ann.

"As Ann said to me last night," she might begin, through a din of girlish voices, and suddenly a hush would fall.

Then in their junior year they took on Margy, who was related to no debutantes, whose hair was impossible, maggot-white and curled as tight as Velcro in tiny fetal snarls, who was always fidgeting and humming and dancing with her boney legs whenever she wasn't playing violin—but who learned fast, and soon the three of them were gliding modestly around the school, discussing Robert Lowell or Sylvia Plath, looking benignly (but silently) at the other girls. Ann and Elizabeth would listen to Margy practice during lunch, and after school they all walked home with Ann (who lived only a block away, on "hardly passionate Marlborough") or out in every weather to the Esplanade, where they would grieve together privately, for the divorce of Elizabeth's parents, and the death of Margy's mother when she was only twelve, and the last cruel thing that Ann's had said to her.

"Could it be then that this was life?" Ann quietly intoned one brilliant winter day beside the Charles, the sky Delft blue, the river frozen blistering white. "Was there no safety? No learning by heart of the ways of the world? No guide, no shelter, but all was miracle, and leaping from the pinnacle of a tower into air?"

In their senior year, they read Camus in French and took on existential responsibility, marching gravely, all in black, with a hundred-thousand others up and down the major avenues, to protest the bombing of North Vietnam. Margy started quoting from the things she'd read, but without Ann's authority: she might just mutter quietly, so no one else could actually hear, "Quick eyes gone under earth's lid," or *"Il faut imaginer Sisyphe heureux."* On her birthday in November, Elizabeth and Ann gave her a locket with their three initials in a triangle, and for Christmas they all gave each other books, disapproved together of their family celebrations, and went to midnight mass at Holy Cross, for the music, and to appall their parents, none of whom were Catholic or in danger of becoming so. Away from Huntington they were more free, and sometimes standing on street corners, waiting to cross in the winter sun, Ann and Elizabeth might fall in with Margy's dance, gently snapping fingers, tapping feet. Crazed with success, she once vamped off a curb into the path of a careening cab, but they yanked her back in time.

Margy was happy to be their friend, though she knew that she was not like Ann. She had calluses not only on her toes but on every finger of both hands, and had once had a hickey on her neck. She got it from a pianist named Gary Slade, on whom she'd had a crush, until the night he tried to make her fish the car keys from his underpants. She had walked home that night, and never been alone with any guy since then, but still she went on having similar effects on other boys and men. The chorus master at her music school was a handsome man, but he was past her father's age, and if she looked at him it was only on obligatory Saturdays, singing husky alto in the second row. But at the last school picnic out to Marblehead, he'd gotten her off by herself, both of them in bathing suits, not fifty yards from where her father stood—and, running a pool cue through his toes, had said, "You know that I want to make love to you," as if she were accustomed to hearing words like that, when she was just sixteen and had been kissed exactly once, by Gary Slade.

She'd never mentioned these events to Elizabeth and Ann—in fact she would have died on the rack before she did. But once she told her father about Gary Slade, in vague theoretical terms, as if it were simply something that she'd heard, to see whose fault he thought it was. Her father was an architect, and he liked theoretical problems, though preferably the geometrical kind. He was willing to talk about anything, however, after dinner, when he'd had a few martinis just before.

"Well, now," he said, running one boney hand across his hair, which sprang up in a solid hedge as his hand passed, curled like Margy's, only slightly red. "That would depend on how she got into the car, now, wouldn't it?" If she had kissed the man and led him on, then it was her fault too. He thought in general women were too quick to speak of rape. Leaning with one elbow on the table, he held the other hand out in the air, and looked at it.

"When a gal shows up at the precinct and says that she's been raped, they make her hold a hand out, and check to see if it's trembling. Because if it is, it means she had an orgasm, and it wasn't rape."

He glanced at Margy, looked away, fair cheeks flushing clear red.

"Of course sometimes it is." He grinned, as if he knew he shouldn't say what he was going to next. He gave her a bold look. "But when it does happen, when it can't be stopped—why not just relax, and enjoy?"

In January of their senior year, Ann was elected queen of the winter festival at a boys' school across town, by guys she'd mainly never met, and Margy and Elizabeth went with her as her court, flanking her at the hockey match, triple-dating to the ball that night. Ann chose as her escort Gary Slade, who was still the best-looking young man they knew, while Margy (having no one else to ask) went with his little brother Jason, with whom she'd shared a violin teacher since they were six.

And the night of the ball she rode in Gary's car as if she'd never seen it before. She didn't have to talk to him, or even much to Jason—she was really there with Elizabeth and Ann, as they were there with her. Gary had to stand for hours by the throne the boys had made for Ann, while she sat silent and expressionless, in a white ball gown and rhinestone crown, bearing the stares of all those eyes. When the ball was over, they asked to be delivered back to Ann's, where they dismissed their escorts at the curb (Gary trailing after Ann forlornly, saying, "Can I call you soon?") and went in to drink hot chocolate, while Margy pranced in her long skirt from room to room, too excited to sit down.

"Gary should be falling on his sword by now," Elizabeth noted, smiling down into her mug.

Lifting her lovely head, Ann seemed to consider an object far away. "Gary? Oh, Gary will be fine. He'll get married and buy a house and have five children of his own, and become a sixty-year-old smiling public man."

Margy was fidgeting nearby. Suddenly she felt bold. "The women come and go," she said. "Talking of Michelangelo." And then, with special glee, "I do not think that they will sing to me."

Ann laughed, and kissed her cheek. She put a record on, and they all began to dance, to "Let It Bleed" and "Love in Vain" and "You can't always get what you want, but if you try sometime you just might find you get what you need," until they had calmed down enough to sleep, Elizabeth with Ann in her canopy bed, Margy on a cot down at the foot.

Margy started reading through her father's library, leatherbound classics hardly touched by anyone, and after sampling here and there she settled on the Sigmund Freuds, which were small and dense and rewarding even in small bites, and therefore suitable for reading in the moments when she wasn't practicing. She read Dora, Anna O., *Civilization and Its Discontents*. She took to peppering her talk with Freudian remarks.

"I have cathected to those shoes," she'd say. "The economics of my libido may require a chili dog." Or, "Time to catastrophize about that test."

One week she was excused from classes in the afternoons to rehearse with the Boston Symphony, and as she waited for the T at Arlington, she read that if a woman dreams her daughter is run over by a train, that means she wants to go to bed with the man who once gave her flowers as she got onto a train. She was about to turn the page, when she felt a hard stare from a few feet off. Pretending to read on, she tapped out the timing of the Paganini she was going to play, against one edge of the book, as if deeply engrossed.

The staring did not stop. Annoyed, she glanced that way, and recognized the new girl in her class at Huntington. Rachel had arrived only that year, a tall dark awkward girl with huge black eyes, who stared at everyone as if she found them very strange, and slightly amusing. Imitating Ann's most unrevealing face, Margy gave her a brief nod and returned to her book, which was the most effective of the small polite rejections she and Ann and Elizabeth practiced every day on other girls at school.

Rachel moved closer, staring like a baby over its mother's

shoulder. She read the spine on Margy's book. Her voice squeaked in amazement.

"Are you holding that right-side up?"

Margy finished the sentence, and looked at her. Rachel's uniform was entirely disguised by a black leather jacket and beret, her hair whacked off around the earlobes. But her face was fresh and artless as a two-year-old's.

"Insulting people in train stations is a sign of unresolved dilemmas in the inner life."

Rachel chuckled, watching her. "And what about the virgin goddess, does she read books too?"

Margy pretended not to know who she could mean, narrowing her eyes at her. "Why aren't you in school?"

Rachel whipped out a pass and twirled it in the air.

"Legal as milk," she said, but grinning in a way that made it clear she wasn't going to the dentist after all. She had a sick friend at B.U., and how could she leave her there alone, pining for a cool hand on her brow?

"Freud used to operate on people's noses," Rachel calmly said. "To clear up their sexual hangups. He thought if you put your fingers in your purse you were playing with yourself. He was a little bit hung up on cock, and thought the rest of us were too."

Margy rode with her to Copley, slightly stunned. On the platform, changing trains, she glanced back at the one she had just left, and there was Rachel pressed against the glass, eager as a puppy locked inside a car.

She introduced her to Elizabeth and Ann, and soon Rachel started showing up at lunch, refusing to fade off as other girls had learned to do. She even followed on their private walks, stalking behind them with her long unhurried gait.

"What about me?" she would actually cry, throwing her arms out wide, as they tried to walk away.

She introduced them to new lore, Simone de Beauvoir and *The Story of O* and *The Tibetan Book of the Dead*, and gradually to other things. Rachel had lived in Paris and L.A. and Israel, but now her parents had moved into Beacon Hill, a few blocks from the house where Margy'd always lived, and she took to turning up on Sunday afternoons, to listen to her play and go for walks and tell her things that would have made her mother's hair stand up. Already Rachel had a lot of friends, older women living on their own, who had fed her marvelous meals, peyote buds and grass, and taught her unimaginable acts in bed. She kept her fingernails cut to the quick, so that they could not wound. She said she could do anything a man could do, only better, because she was a girl too.

"There's nothing nicer than getting ready for bed," she said, "knowing there's a girl in there waiting for you."

Margy listened, thrilled and shocked. She began to look back with new eyes on certain things she'd done herself. The summer after her mother died, a rash of slumber parties had gone through her neighborhood, with girls she hardly knew at Huntington. But Margy went to every one, and when the lights were out they'd played a secret game. Bedded in their sleeping bags on some girl's living-room rug, they'd touched each other's breasts, circling incipient nipples with light fingertips, until the hostess said to switch, and then the one you had just touched would do the same to you. They did it as a dare, to prove that they were brave, and they would have all dropped dead to learn that it had anything to do with sex—though the boldest girls, who had invented it, played an advanced form of the game, removing pajama pants and circling fingertips on a certain sensitive spot. Torture, they called that.

"Who were they?" Rachel squeaked, dropping to her knees on the Common, clutching Margy's coat. It was early spring, the air cold and sweet, and they were loitering after a rally against the bombing of Cambodia. "Please please, pretty please. Tell me. Are they still at Huntington?"

Most of them were, but Margy said they had all moved away. Rachel sank her hands into the pockets of her leather jacket, slouching morosely down the path.

"Why do I never meet girls like that? I just meet little virgin straights. Not that you aren't cute, of course," she said, and tousled Margy's hair.

Margy assumed that Ann knew nothing of Rachel's other life, and that it would be best to keep it to herself. Then one Sunday she called Ann's, and Ann's mother said that she and Rachel had gone out. Another time she stopped by, on her way home from music school, and found Rachel cooking in the kitchen with Ann's mother. Ann's mother was formal and remote and tall, a suntanned woman in yachting clothes, who smoked and watched you without smiling while you spoke. Margy was afraid to say a word to her, and she had always called her Mrs. Church. But in the kitchen she was laughing, deep and slow, stabbing a spoon into a pot, while Rachel watched her, hands on hips.

"Betsy! Not like that!" Rachel cried, and tried to wrestle the spoon away from her, both of them laughing like maniacs.

Margy stood chuckling in the kitchen doorway. Mrs. Church whirled at the sound, face sobering at once.

"Oh, hello, Margaret. Annie's in her room, I think."

Margy stood on one foot, smiling, but they did not go on. Dutifully she went to look for Ann, as peals of giggles echoed from the kitchen walls.

That spring, Margy fell in love. Yale was taking women now, and her father'd asked her to apply, since he went there, and to try it for at least a year instead of Juilliard—and to help convince her, he arranged for her to meet the son of a new partner in his firm, who was finishing at Yale and would be entering the law school in the fall. Henry Bergstrom was handsome and sandy-haired like Gary Slade, but soft-spoken and grownup and kind, with broad shoulders and a narrow waist and one chipped tooth that gave his grin a boyish charm. He was from New York City, had lived in Texas and Brazil, his family having only recently relocated to Boston, and he was a fan of *carnaval* and soccer as well as football and World War II. His voice thrilled her, deep and faintly drawled, but abrupt and furtive when he was moved.

"Where have you been?" he would say quickly on the phone, as if in pain, when she'd been practicing too long. But in person he might hold out an ice-cream cone too high, focus his eyes above her head and gravely search for her. The Brazilians had a dozen words for "shorty" and "little kid," along with maybe a hundred each for "pester," "scram," and anything to do with sex, though he wouldn't tell her what they were.

"Hey, *pixote*, what's it to you," he would say when she asked, or call her *tico-tico, catatau*.

He took her to the symphony, where he listened with shining eyes, turning at the end to say he'd rather hear her play. She gave a solo recital in June, and he sat up straight and rapt beside her dad.

"Pretty good for a *pixote,*" he whispered in her ear, standing by protectively as Ann and Elizabeth and Rachel all surged up to kiss her cheek. He drove a powder-blue MG, and Rachel called him Ken, after the boyfriend of the Barbie doll.

"Is *Ken* coming up this weekend *again?*" she'd say, staring with outraged onyx eyes.

Margy got into Yale, and agreed to give it a try. Henry came home to Boston for the summer, worked for his dad, and she saw him almost every night. They went to hear the Pops, and to restaurants a few times, then settled into eating with her father or his parents, and after dinner going for a walk. Henry didn't really like to go out at night.

"When I'm married, I won't go anywhere at all," he said, blue eyes warm. "I'll have my own fun at home."

The last thing every night before he left, in the car or on her porch or in her living room, he'd lean close and kiss her a few times, always stopping before she wanted to. Once he pulled her down onto his parents' couch, stopped as if switched off, and apologized. On the way home, he talked about the beauty of *carnaval,* how all rules were suspended there ("Don't you ever go to one," he said, grinning hard, gripping her hand). But a few nights later in the car he slid one hand up her side, where he could feel a little of her breast—stinging her so unexpectedly with want, that tears spilled from the corners of her eyes.

"I may have to sign up for a nose-job soon," she said one sultry afternoon, twirling on a swing in a park near Rachel's house. Ann was at the Vineyard with her family, and Rachel moped on the next swing, rolling a joint in her lap.

"That is, if things go on this way."

Pulling down her heavy black sunglasses, Rachel regarded her with some alarm. "You wouldn't. Not with *Ken?*"

Margy tipped her head back toward the ground, viewing the world from upside-down. "That's who it's done with," she pointed out. "By virgin straights. The Kens of this world."

Rachel pushed her sunglasses back up over her eyes, and looked inscrutable.

"Not necessarily," she finally said, and gave one fleeting grin, though she would not explain.

In August Henry's parents left for their summer place down on Long Island, and Henry lingered on alone. At first they pretended nothing had changed, eating at Margy's, taking walks. Then one night he made dinner for some friends from Yale, at his parents' house in Brookline, and invited Margy too. The friends were a couple, tall gazelle-like blonds who almost looked alike, both living with their parents for the summer, and happy to be out of their sight.

They all drank gin and tonic before Henry's manly fare (steak and potatoes and oversalted salad), and then the gazelles disappeared, into Henry's bedroom, it turned out, with his warbooks and his model planes. Margy and Henry climbed up to the widow's walk on the third floor, where they could watch the city lights reflected on the river in the summer dusk, Margy in a dress that tied behind the neck and almost nothing else, Henry in a seersucker jacket. She was quivering lightly, not from cold, and when he ran his fingers down the bare skin of her back, she turned and started kissing him.

Startled, his eyes opened wide—and then he seized her like a tortured man. Moments later they were in his parents' bed, pressing together through their clothes until she lost all sense of being in a room, or even in a body of her own, apart from his. Then he stopped. Fingers in the tight curls at her scalp, he shook her face from side to side.

"Negativo, pixote," he said, and left the room.

Henry left to join his parents in Wading River, and suddenly her life went blank. She called her friends, but already they seemed remote. She hadn't seen them often over the summer, and Elizabeth and Ann had had a fight, though neither would say why. ("It's me," Rachel explained. "Elizabeth is jealous of the time I spend with Ann.") Margy saw Ann a few times, but never alone, no matter what they planned: when she arrived, Rachel would be with her, grinning and relaxed and full of little jokes. They were both staying home, Ann to go to Radcliffe and Rachel to B.U., and Rachel seemed almost to live at Ann's place now. Her clothes were hung on chairs in Ann's room, and once

Margy found her lying on the canopy bed, an arm across her eyes.

"Ann needs support right now," Rachel explained, when Margy asked her what was going on. Since they'd left Huntington, Ann's mother had started a campaign, telling her she was spoiled and self-centered, and other cruel, unnecessary remarks.

"Last year, when your friends found you so charming," Betsy'd lately said, in reference to the winter festival. Ann's eyes were always shining with leashed tears, and Rachel hovered close to her, one hand on her shoulder, staring at anyone who came near.

"Oh, for God's *sake*," Margy said one hot night in Cambridge, as they were walking toward a party full of Rachel's friends. "People's mothers *say* things like that. It's just the ordinary coin of mother-daughter economics. You're lucky that you have a mom at all."

Rachel's mouth fell open as if she'd fired a gun. Clutching Ann's shoulders, she steered her away. Later she cornered Margy at the party, in a throng of loud and happy older women. ("Lay off, she's straight," Rachel kept saying, as they stopped to stare.)

"You don't know," she said quietly, watching Margy with a light in her black eyes. "You just don't know. *Comprends-tu?*"

Henry wrote to Margy, in a big angular hand on heavy paper, about his father's need to win at golf, and where they'd sailed that day, and how much he thought of her. Once he said remembering how she'd kissed him on the widow's walk that night was driving him insane—but he didn't trust letters, so he'd say no more. Except he hoped that he could see her the moment she got to Yale, in fact he would be waiting in her college yard.

The night before she left, Ann stopped by with Rachel to give her a blank book with a dove-gray linen cover, for a journal while she was away, and Rachel gave her a God's Eye she had made. Ann was wearing Rachel's leather jacket, clutched around her tightly with both hands. She gazed at Margy with her beautiful clear eyes.

"You are coming to a place where two roads diverge, and taking the one less traveled by." She touched Margy's hand.

"We understand each other, don't we, Margy? No matter what happens."

Margy followed them out to the street and watched them walk away. In the dark, their heads inclined in toward each other, till their silhouettes converged.

Her father drove her to New Haven, delivered her to his old college, and took her on a campus tour, pointing out the design of each quadrangle. Then he was gone, and Henry was there, in his seersucker jacket, fingers clenched around her arm.

"Can we go now?" he said quietly, hardly moving his lips.

It was Indian summer out, hot sun with an autumn drowsiness, and Henry had the top down on the MGB. Quickly crossing town, he raced south. The wind was too loud in the car for talk, but Margy knew where they were going now. She had on a simple sheath of rose linen that Ann had helped her to pick out, her hair restrained in a ribbon the same shade. But as they crossed the bridge onto Long Island in late sun, the wind teased out the ribbon and her hair burst free, with a ripple of pleasure along the scalp.

He had her back soon after breakfast, though she'd missed the freshman dinner in her college and had failed to sleep in her bed. Calhoun was full of southerners, from Georgia and Virginia and the Carolinas, and they were all just trooping off in tennis whites, or to try out for some *a cappella* group, as she made her way upstairs, trembling slightly and trying to look blasé. At the last second, when the pain was most intense, she had tried to pull away. But Henry went on saying "Just relax" into her ear, and soon she lay still listening to him sleep, with a feeling she didn't recognize, like floating in a warm bath, with an undertow of fear.

In the morning he had quickly pulled a pillow across the bloodstain on the sheet, as if she shouldn't see that, when she had already seen it in the bathroom twice, in the middle of the night and again after the second time, when he woke her at first light, his lean hairless chest quivering before her eyes like a wall she had to climb. Driving back, he didn't say a word—the law school had already started, and he had to be in class. But he kissed her tenderly, by Calhoun gate in the open car, and said he would be there to pick her up on Friday afternoon.

She took long meditative showers, spent whole days in the practice rooms, and only joined her fellow frosh in class. On Fridays Henry drove her out to Wading River, where the house was always packed now with his friends, who played tackle on the beach and drank all night, and she was only alone with him in the sandy bed. With a football in his arms he was unexpectedly exuberant, and she watched him from a beach-chair in the autumn sun, trying to write something profound to Rachel and Ann. They'd sent her two postcards, one from a small hotel in Provincetown. ("All quite legitimate, you understand," Rachel's part had said. "Searching the beach for pebbles you may have sent. Now is the time to buy a kite.") But Margy had nothing to say that she could trust to letters now, so she watched Henry steal the ball, and laugh and cheat and leap across his fallen friends with lean tan legs, and streak across the sand to score.

The weather changed, dry leaves crackling in the wind at night. The first cold week, she did not hear from Henry, and on Saturday she called his rooms, where his suitemate said he had gone home to Boston. Margy was concerned. Of course she knew that men could change, from the days of Gary Slade—but the last time she'd seen Henry, he was more tender than before, and held her hand on the long drive back to Yale.

Monday night, on her way home from the practice rooms, she stopped by the law-school dorm, where he was studying. He seemed surprised but glad, and pulled her in protectively.

"Everything all right?" he said, ushering her quickly into his room, shutting the door. "Nothing wrong?"

They talked politely, sitting on the bed, his lawbooks lit up on the desk. He did not explain why he went home to Boston, and she didn't ask. When she rose to go, he said goodbye at the door and watched her leave—then strode behind her down the gleaming brown expanse of hall.

"Don't go," he said, clutching her arm and looking at the floor. "Please stay, all right?"

She couldn't sleep in his narrow bed, and she got up late to walk back through the cold clear night. That weekend she practiced all the daylight hours, avoiding telephones. But when she went back to Calhoun at night, there were no messages for her. She called Henry's rooms, pretending to have a French accent.

"Boston," his suitemate said.

"Ah, *bon*," she said, and did not call again.

Henry wrote her a careful letter, saying he had made a mistake and wasn't ready to be serious yet, but asking her to let him know if she ever needed anything from him. Margy wrote four versions of a letter back, outraged, pleading, miserable, abject, and tore them up. Finally she sent a postcard with a view of Wading River (bought to send to Rachel and Ann), saying she was always glad to hear from him but didn't think she would be needing anything. He sent her a biography of Freud, which she had already read ("From your friend, Henry," it said inside) and a yard of rose-colored ribbon, to replace the one she'd lost while riding in his car. Once she saw him on Elm Street, idling in traffic as the snow fell on the cloth top of his car. Honking and waving, he half emerged—but she saluted with her violin, and hurried off against the traffic, so he couldn't follow her.

Sleet was rattling on the windows as if hurled from fists, on the day she started to throw up. She tried to make it stop, lying on her bed in the hot blasts from the heating ducts, as Rachel's God's Eye twirled above. It was ridiculous, it was impossible. Henry had been so cautious, breaking open little hard blue plastic cases, exactly like the ones she'd seen once in her father's dresser drawer when her mother was alive, and dropping them beneath the bed as he put their contents on. The night she'd visited his room, she crouched to count the empties in the silvery light, and there were at least a dozen more than he had used that night—though it was hard to tell, of course, how old they were.

She went to class and could not hear a word. She could not play the violin, or remember why she'd ever wanted to. The nausea surrounded her, six inches of rancid blubber through which she had to breathe. She threw up in the daytime, in the evening, in the middle of the night. She told herself to just relax —morning sickness is all in the woman's head, Freud said. She ate a crust of hard French bread, and saw it unchanged moments after in the white cup of the toilet bowl.

She found a doctor down in Bridgeport, where she wouldn't run into anyone from Yale. The man she picked had chosen his profession because the forceps used at his own birth had damaged a nerve in his face, causing his forehead to hang down across his eyes, while his mouth pulled to one side. Yes, he had good news for her, he said—Mrs. Henry Bergstrom, she had called herself, and lied about her age. Alone with him when the nurse had left, she mentioned that they weren't quite married yet. The doctor may have given her a kindly look, though it was hard to tell.

"Don't be upset if something happens to it," he said, lips flapping loose around the sounds. "It's not because it's out of wedlock or anything like that. It's not your fault."

Margy nodded, and started to weep quietly. Moments later she was on the sidewalk in cold sun, with the recommended diet in her purse, and Mrs. Henry Bergstrom's next appointment card.

She'd be a famous violinist, live in a garret with the child. It would be a purse-size child, round and pink, a girl, never growing any bigger or needing anything, and it would ride on Margy's chest while she played the major concert stages of the world. She would wear flowered dresses, cut severely—bought in France—with black berets and leather jackets. She would smoke fat cigarettes through vermillion lips, drink liqueur from a small glass. And one day, in a cafe on the Boul' Mich', or in Nice, or in her dressing room in Rome, Henry would track her down. He'd send his card backstage, and she would send it back. She'd look the other way in the cafe.

"*Mais non, monsieur,*" she'd say. "*Nous nous ne connaissons pas. Excusez moi.*"

For Thanksgiving she had to fly to Florida with her father and pretend to eat some of the thirty pounds of turkey her grandmother made, and throw up in the bathroom of the tiny oceanview apartment with the fan on and the water running. Back at Yale, she learned that she had failed midterm exams (equipped with the vast wasteland of all she hadn't read), and packed to leave for Christmas break.

Rachel met her train. Sauntering down the platform, thumbs hooked into black jeans, she looked very young in a new black motorcycle jacket with silver chains. But her stare was just the same.

"They're engaged," she said, with a tragic face.

Margy kissed her on both cheeks, said what? and who? and even laughed. She felt a little better, having not thrown up almost all day.

Rachel hung suspended, watching her. Slowly a look of wonder, almost delight, broke on her face. Stepping closer, she took tender hold of Margy's head.

"Oh, baby. Don't you know anything yet?"

It had started in the summer, Rachel said, when she and Ann first went to bed. They'd been in love since spring—she and Ann, that is—and Rachel was spending all her time at Ann's by then. Ann never wanted her to leave, but at first they didn't get near the bed. They'd sit on the floor in her room, and talk until they fell asleep, right where they were. Ann couldn't face it, what it meant, or do more than kiss Rachel on the cheek.

"She was just a little virgin straight," Rachel explained. "Like you, only worse. She thought that girls who went to bed with girls would end up riding Harley-Davidsons and stomping around in big dyke boots. It wasn't possible for the queen of the winter festival."

Then suddenly it was, and they'd been lovers now for months, every night in the canopy bed. It was the most intense thing in her life—and in Ann's. One night they'd been making love for hours when she touched Ann's back, and it was wet.

"That does it," Rachel'd told her then. "No matter what, you can't go saying you're a virgin now."

Things were good then for a while. They took some little trips. ("You lied to me on that postcard," Margy pointed out, and Rachel shook her head. "I promised her," she said.) Ann was jealous of her other friends, and accused Rachel of not loving her—while she, Ann, was in love for life. But Rachel reassured her, and then things were all right. Even Betsy laid off Ann.

"Betsy thinks I'm good for her," Rachel said, and grinned. "She likes the way Ann shares her toys with me." Of course Betsy had no idea what was going on, it wasn't in her lexicon. But she liked Rachel, they got along. And Rachel learned to head her off, when she was going after Ann.

Then one night in the fall, Ann announced that she was going out, and Henry showed up at the door. He took her out to eat, and to a play, and to the symphony.

"They went *out?*" Margy cried, but Rachel only looked at her. Out, and home to meet his parents too. It was a bulldozer through their happy life. He started calling every night from Yale—Ann would take it in her parents' room and close the door. She started quoting him. He said that men should always be gentle to all women, and he was sorry it had not worked out with Margy—but that they had parted friends. This was the time in their lives that counted most, he said, when the steps they took would determine all the rest, and it was important to be circumspect. Ann agreed, and every weekend circumspectly she went out with Henry, and came home to sleep with Rachel.

"So now she's wearing this big Texas diamond, that used to belong to his grandmother. And all she does is cry. He brings her home, and she gets in bed with me and starts to cry. She cries while we make love, and then cries in her sleep. In the morning she gets up to try on her trousseau, and puts on sunglasses so Betsy won't see, but they just dam up the tears, till she's got this pool behind them on her cheeks. She's just afraid, and she knows it, but that doesn't mean a thing. They've got the guest list all made out. She's going to marry him in June."

Margy took the T to Cambridge, looked for Rachel's friends. She found the one who'd had the party, a big-breasted woman in a tee-shirt with short rough hair, who offered to make tea, or lunch, or roll a joint. Yes, she could tell Margy where to go, and no, she wouldn't mention it to Rachel if she didn't want her to. But was she sure?

"It's not a nice thing to go through," she said, as she followed Margy out onto the landing, carrying a large gray cat. "Don't do it by yourself, baby."

Margy thanked her, put the number in her purse, but did not make the call. First, she needed to understand. She needed to see Ann one more time, from a distance, preferably—maybe that would be safe. Maybe then the thing that happened when you looked at her would not, and she would understand, why all their lives arranged themselves Ann's way, as if they were the notes, and she was the melody.

Christmas eve, Margy played chess with her father, which he had taught her as a child, but she was too sick to concentrate, and he won both games. Humming happily, he went off to bed, and she sat waiting in the ornate living room, still decorated in her mother's taste, Persian rugs and heavy velvet drapes and lamps held up by enslaved caryatids ("early sado-masochist," as Rachel'd labeled it). When she could hear nothing but the antique clocks, ticking out of sync, she eased her coat out of the closet, and the bolt out of the door.

Flagging a cab was easier than she'd supposed, with the neighbors all returning home, and she was early for the service at Holy Cross. The cathedral was already nearly full, rows churning with genuflection, kneeling, crossing, touching lips, and she took up a position to one side, beneath a statue of the Virgin, plaster fingers open downward as if beckoning the crowd to climb up into her arms. In an organ loft somewhere above, someone was playing Bach's most schmaltzy fugue, hamming it up with big vibrato on the bass, while in the aisles people streamed both ways, like refugees from war, out toward the doors and in for midnight mass. Their coats were black and brown and muddy green, with sober scarves and hats, and when Ann's head emerged beneath the outer arch, hair glowing like ripe wheat and freshly cut to brush the shoulders of her camel-hair coat, she seemed to light the air around for several feet.

Margy pressed back closer to the wall—she hadn't forgotten how beautiful Ann was, but memory could never quite live up to her. Henry's shoulders framed her head, wide and straight in a navy overcoat, with Rachel tall as he was next to him, looking strangely wrong in a lace collar, wool coat and heels. None of them had time to glance across the nave. Rachel was clowning for Henry, rolling her eyes and gesturing with her hands, and he gave a grim smile, looking handsome but harassed, as he stepped up to take Ann's hand. Rachel moved to her far side, and together they maneuvered to a spot behind the final row of pews.

Now all three stood, Rachel and Henry crowded close on either side of Ann, bantering above her head, while she looked docile as a child, and lost. Henry had a firm grip on her hand,

and he kept it well displayed, curled against his chest or resting on the pew in front or in his other fist. Ann's other hand was out of sight, but Rachel's arm pressed close to hers, and both their hands plunged down behind the pew, as still as if they'd turned to stone.

Ann leaned back her head, looking high up toward the ceiling, a parted sea of water shining in her eyes. She said something to distract the other two, and all three of them looked up, as if they could see something descending from above. In a moment, other people near them looked up too.

The Bach swelled to an end, and the crowd pressed in, packing all the spaces on the floor. Forging a path back through stiff overcoats, miasmas of perfume, Margy stepped out to the cold pure night. She'd seen enough, and as she hurried up the avenue, alive with pinpoint lights, Salvation Army bells and taxis rushing through the slush, the city opened up around her, smaller than before, while she felt strangely huge, as if she were parading through the air like the Macy's Mickey-Mouse balloon. A thousand windows lit up small and bright, no bigger than the hollows in a honeycomb, and for a moment she could almost see inside, into the thousand tiny rooms, where figures crossed, and smiled, hiding their hurts, and wanting the wrong things, and spending long nights in their beds alone.

John J. Clayton

TALKING TO CHARLIE

Divorced

It begins as the old story, I've told so many stories of divorce and pain: six months back, David Kahn read by accident the wrong letter, and it was as if he'd already known, as if he finally had to open the door to the closet where the monster squatted. His wife in love with somebody, somebody brilliant, supervisor of her cases as a therapist. This guy also happened to be David's tennis partner. And in a rage, as if surprised, as if betrayed, as if such a thing had never entered his mind, he packed up, moved to a motel, drank—and fell apart.

The usual divorce story, dismal, of pain and humiliation, his family broken, ahh, you could write it yourself. Then Kahn takes a leave from his high-powered job—selling mainframes and networks for corporations—drops everything, to live the winter like a monk at his cottage in Truro, on Cape Cod.

Why is he leaving? Revulsion, he'd tell you, for the whole *megillah*. Secretly, he's in panic for his life. And maybe, too, he knows, could even tell you, he's leaving out of spite; he's punishing Sarah. All these years, he's been a Good Provider. While she became the intellectual, the PhD psychologist, he provided. Let somebody else do the providing.

But there's more to it. There's this. He isn't willing to be bullied anymore by the vague dream of making it, sick of working so hard—working not just to succeed but to make himself worthy in his own eyes, or really in his dead father's eyes—ghost father from childhood. What he really wants, David, is just to clear the books, to live an honorable life.

In my story he stops drinking, gets into shape. In Truro, early spring, he plants a garden: it makes him happy, on knees in old jeans, to break up the cold, sandy soil with garden fork, mix in bags of peat moss, top soil, manure. Occupational therapy.

Big chest, heavy shoulders—funny to think of a guy like him on his knees with a young plant between his fingers, planting, then patting down the soil. A big man, David played high school football, went to Deerfield Academy for a thirteenth year on football scholarship. Though it was baseball he'd played really well—he was offered a chance to try out for pro ball. A lot of guys still take him for an athlete with his big frame and heavy neck. But since the time in the hospital for his back, he feels like a sandcastle against an incoming tide, like the way his chest has started to slip and sink. Bags under his eyes, and the skin between eyelids and eyebrows beginning to go limp; hair graying and the gray strands lightening, growing light as smoke, angel hair—silly when it isn't combed into place.

The gardening calms him, the beach runs clean out his head. He doesn't think so much about Sarah and Nick. Gulls and terns and the spastic little sandpipers rise up as he lumbers their way. He watches for seaweed hiding glass or shells that could cut his feet. But soon his mind falls away, the watching happens without him. A dream is how it feels. And now he begins to get peculiar intimations, as he's chopping onions, say, that everything has happened beyond his willing. Intimations that these past months of pain, the dream-maker, dream-writer, knew all along where David was going.

Climbing to the top of the dunes, he can see more than a mile of beach. Cracking explosions of surf—small charges going off together all along the beach—and then the hiss of water rushing to the high tide line.

It scares him a little, becoming aware of this . . . presence, this dreamer of David's own life. His scriptwriter. Night of a full moon, and David wonders whose hands he's in. If, just maybe, the hands might be tender, holding him, not dangling him like a puppet but holding, and he could relax and let the guy take over.

The point is, David says to himself, that if there's a script beyond my making, he, the scriptwriter, has never *not* been in charge. It was illusion, that I, David Kahn, was accomplishing anything with my struggling. I enacted, I never acted. My whole life, the dream provided a script. That's it, exactly, he thinks, as he hunts driftwood for his evening fire.

And so, walking the dunes, David becomes aware of this presence he's joined to as if there were an invisible filament carrying messages between them. He talks to the presence. It's a little like the times he used to talk to God. His mother would take him to the synagogue after his father left for work Saturday morning and he'd get sleepy and ride the waves of the old men's chantings. He didn't mind staying. But when she recited the Kaddish for her mother and father, she made him leave. Why? Was it superstition that she herself would die if he were there when she remembered a parent? Or did she not want him to see her weep? When he came back, he found her eyes red. Was she crying for her parents—or for her failure of a life? And he, unable to change her life or be her life, he stood in the marble lobby talking to God.

Now he talks to nobody, to the sky. He ought to be talking to Charlie, negotiating with Charlie Bausch, his immediate boss and his mentor at Data Management, to go back to work. Sooner or later, he'll need the money. And he'll need the work.

I tell about David, this man struggling then letting go of the need to struggle. He's ruined his days and nights trying to be worthy. Now he knows, it's this trying that is the problem, his belief in his sickness that is his sickness, the belief that his life is in his hands. And feeling now that his tense hands on the wheel give only an illusion of control—like "driving" a roller-coaster car—ahh, he lets go.

And now, magically, the story wants to move towards restoration: his family restored to him. I can feel that kind of story humming in his head. I can sense it in my own prose, sense my tenderness for David. Peaceful, he'll return to Boston, win back his wife—as if he's getting into shape for *her*—and enter a new life.

I don't trust this story.

He imagines himself at peace, imagines himself *into* peace. I write wanting—who wouldn't?—that peace for myself. The story is my own prayer to let go. To put myself in God's hand. I've never been able to let go, to quiet myself. Peace? You wish, buddy. You wish. Still, the story is true; I've felt the way David feels; there are times you float above the issues that have been clinging to you like a thick web; you know, deeply, that you've spun the web yourself, and it's not even real, it's a hologram, you can step through it and away anytime you feel like it. You needed the web. For what?—for something. I remember I sat once with a friend and felt touched by the sunlight, greenly irridescent through the plants at the window, and I didn't have to do a thing, nothing, just *be*. But a feeling like that, it comes, it goes, it's not final—New Life—God knows.

So David *wishes* it were his new life. I've wished it for him. In a sense, I'm the dreamer he's thinking about. And I'm imagining a dreamer dreaming *me*. I understand why they're so seductive, David's imaginings: they let me see the scripts of the culture as God. No need then for a ride into the dark.

But I have to take courage and ride whatever words I can find down into the dark at the bottom of the dark. I take to my heart the old myth, everybody's old thumping heart-hunger turned myth, that there be a quest. Saying that, I see myself with a paper sword on a horse made out of words. I must want to mock this quest, its pretentiousness. But that mockery is like the dog at the mouth of darkness. One more thing to get past.

Riding down into the dark, not up towards the light. But believing in the light, that the light is there, crusted over, a pulsing jewel down at the bottom of the dark, hidden to keep the searcher safe—its danger is its core; it's nothing if not dangerous; hidden also to keep the jewel itself safe, keep it from being ruined by the wrong finder.

I'm talking about the wrong finder within my own ruined self, the fat one, the exploiter, willing to turn anything into grub. The point of the hardship in the quest is to force the self to burn in a refiner's fire, so that the soul that finds the pulsing jewel is worthy of receiving it, will make good use of it. As I pray I may be, pray I will make.

.   .   .

And so I find my story changing. I'm telling you not about
David's falling-away of self but of his longing to *believe* that he
can disentangle himself from himself by himself, can ride the
tails of some holy Presence. How can he, anymore than I can?
But the quiet is something good. He stands, thick-bodied ex-
jock, winded from his morning run, at the highest point of the
dunes in Truro, looking like a god over the world south towards
Wellfleet, the world north towards Provincetown, beach and
ocean spread out eighty feet below him, and he doesn't need to
make a single business call or smile a single business smile.

And the feeling he had just a few weeks before—that his
whole life was over, this fabrication of marriage and family
fallen like a house of cards, that it would be a relief to jerk the
wheel of his BMW just slightly, ah, just the least bit—why, that
feeling seems now as if it belonged to somebody else. He,
David, is the actor who played that role, suffered through those
pages in the script, and now he's inside his own skin, open to
the next scene that's handed him before the shooting.

Last night I dreamed I was at an AA meeting, it was called that
in the dream, but the room was filled with the wrecked, with
hopeless alcoholics, not recovering alcoholics, and I, though not
in my awake life a drinker, was on my knees in prayer, saying
"I can't do it alone, I'm in Your hands." And that's it: different
as I am from David, I long the same longing, to reshape my clay.
But I can't do it alone, David can't do it alone.

Not completely alone, David goes to the next town, to Wellfleet, for dinner, sits at a bar drinking seltzer and watching the
Celtics. He talks trades, injuries, coaching, with some of the
regulars. But that's not people you work with or live with. If I'm
going to imagine him into peace, and so imagine my own peace,
it will have to come because he works or lives or prays peace-
fully with other people. Then who? Maybe a woman he meets?
—but no—he did that when he was first separated.

He remembers the turmoil after he found out about Sarah, the
nights of no sleep in the expensive motel, the drinking, the
wreck he needed to become in order to dramatize and therefore
feel some control over the pain. And then that terrible night in

New York when he went to bed with a lovely woman, too young for him, thirty years old, a lawyer, thinking he was fooling them all, the gods of middle age, making a sneaky end run into a second youth without mortgage or two A.M. squabbles or back problems. Wild man again. Carol could save him. They made the bed rock.

But then he was awake and it was three-thirty in a morning in an unfamiliar New York apartment, and he was sick as hell, head thumping, mouth dry, not saved, a scared sick man of forty-five is what he was, in a strange bed, a stranger's bed. Tiptoing into this stranger's kitchen, he drank orange juice out of a foreign glass at three in the morning.

So suppose it's a man at the bar he meets, big guy with red hair who asks him to help him out a couple of weeks, help him build an addition, kind of work David did summers when he was at college, and David, who'd earned a hundred thousand, hundred and twenty thousand a year plus stock options selling computer systems, likes the idea of working with his hands again, framing a building, putting in windows.

So he puts off talking to Charlie, Charlie Bausch, his boss. He works with this refugee from the sixties, thick red hair halfway down to his shoulders. Terry has a Masters from Michigan in archeology but makes his living now as a carpenter.

The next week, he works with Terry on an addition that has to be finished this spring. By Thursday, they have it framed and sheathed. End of each day, he comes home aching, ragged, old jeans and workshirt musky with sweat, dusty with sawdust. Rock and roll in his head from the tinny radio that's always blasting under the whine of the circular saw. Maybe he'll live this way. He's surprised how much he cares to do a good job; surprised how much he remembers. He isn't surprised that Terry can keep working full-steam a lot longer than he can.

But sometimes, hefting two-by-fours, measuring and cutting, hammering, sweating, he realizes his body has taken over, he's home-free, humming along on cruise control, something like that. This is nothing to do with *listening*. It's this presence, expressing itself through his hands, his shoulders. He's riding the waves. Secretly, he thinks that working with two-by-fours will help him find the jewel hidden in the dirt. For years he's been a

luftmench, a man living in the air, living by phone and by phoni-
ness, making money—just numbers—nothing you can touch. So
now, as he measures and planes, he is enacting a metaphor, a
ritual, making a new David.

David hammers out a ritual, imagines himself changed by the
ritual he's hammered out. But David is still David, nothing to be
done. He's a rough, kind-hearted, lonely man, tired of pretending that he likes lugging two-by-fours all day. And he knows
that if he came out here to live, he'd turn Terry's catch-as-catch-
can operation into a serious construction business, he'd wind up
selling houses instead of computers. Why bother? But the work
has been good for him.

One night David looks into the mirror and sees less flab
around his face, his body firm, old jock returning to jockdom.
The sadness is still there in the bags under his eyes, sadness that
he's lived the wrong life—his whole life he's worked like a horse
to feel like a human being. But the peculiar understanding has
calmed him—or the calming *is* the understanding: that not only
does he live his life—he's been lived by it.

With this understanding, he returns to Boston quieted. No
more boozing, no more catting around to show he still has the
stuff. And with this quiet his new life begins.

Only begins: he has to find the way to the dark at the bottom
of the dark, where long ago he buried someone with his true
face, shining. Once in a while he has a glimpse of the face he
buried long ago, as I have of my own self at the bottom of myself. Maybe it's easier for David, for he has less to lose. That's
the point of being stripped naked, like Lear on the heath. Maybe
I envy.

If I knew how to imagine David going on from there, finding the
jewel, changing in the soul, maybe I'd know how to make my
own peace. But back in Brookline, in the apartment he finds not
a mile from the old house, he feels less peaceful and more alone.
The lovely quiet of the dunes, the sense that he was held in the
hand of that benign Presence—it's hard to get it back. There's no
ocean to sing to him, and sometimes he wonders, was it just a
trick of consciousness, his imaginings of a presence supporting
him, being spoken by his life?

He thinks about work, about talking to Charlie. Sitting at a deli on Beacon Street and poking through the want-ads in the *Globe,* he finds the good jobs not all that different from his work at Data Management. Why lose what he's built? Why lose colleagues he cares about? He's watched their kids grow up.

I'm listening on headphones to the music of Thomas Tallis, mid-sixteenth-century English composer, choral music of peace and harmony, written at a time of chaos, struggle, murder, torture, poverty, and oppression. Well, what time hasn't been like that? Tallis was composing within a tradition, even while he was changing it. And underpinning the tradition was a separate world, a world of the spirit, on which he could stand while the world around him was full of murder. Where can David stand?

There are times he stands on a street corner on his way to pick up Beth at school and watches a couple of MTA cars glide by down Beacon, and suddenly he feels a hollow rush in his belly, as if he were riding a roller coaster. And he realizes there's a piece of himself standing high up above Beacon Street, looking down from a high haven.

Every other weekend, he sees Beth and Noah from Friday afternoon until Monday night. Sarah, who has a full case load and then works at the Boston Institute for Psychotherapy some evenings, is grateful for the help. The weekends he doesn't have them, they're with him two midweek nights. When the kids complain about all the changing, they begin to spend alternate weeks—one week with Sarah, one with David.

Now, half the time a single parent, he's got to think about making dinner for them every night, think about whether they have clean clothes for the morning. He's got to have their friends over and drive them home. Now he sees what it is to be a father.

Slow, patient, a yoga of steadiness and devotion. This is a story I trust and understand. A person changes by doing the laundry on a daily basis, by picking up the kids at school and taking them to gymnastics. This is the work. No mysteries.

But David resists this story. His new life feels full of mysteries. Something's happening I don't understand, a trick of consciousness, maybe, but it lets him float above his pain. I've always thought that the dark body, of which the person you look at in the mirror is merely an emanation, had to be restored in battle. You have to wrestle for the prize. Deny and deny until you can't deny and your face is rubbed bloody into the dirt; then, raw, burnished, it shines with darkness. But as he gets used to being back, and being with the kids, David doesn't do battle: doesn't go back to work or into therapy. He hangs out; he wanders. He finds himself in a city with . . . reduced gravity. He doesn't need, the way he used to, to be weighed down, doesn't need his pain. He thinks, It's still there, the pain. Just not so much *mine*.

He takes long walks through Boston, feeling the strangeness of not working. And the part of him that's free of gravity and in touch with something beyond himself, that part begins to occupy his shoes. At this rate, he says, I'll never wear my shoes out. Someone leads, he follows, perfect dancer.

Sitting over a cup of decaf listening to Miles Davis after the kids are asleep, he gets a sudden urge to call Sarah. He doesn't call—afraid she'll take it wrong, as a sign of his longing. And he's doing all right. That same night, *she* calls, needing to talk. Can we meet? Sure, he says, I'd like that.

Is she, he wonders, going to insist on couples' therapy? Sarah is one tough insister. Well, he's not eager, but willing. He makes a mental note not to make fun of therapy, therapists, psychology in general. He and Sarah will have to be especially careful of one another's bruised places. David goes to a barber, he buys a new suit, dove gray, he's like a bridegroom getting ready for a wedding. Looking into the mirror, if he doesn't peer too closely, he likes what he sees—a ruddy, strong man in his prime. A little beefy, okay—and crude for a woman like Sarah; still, women go for him. And okay—there's the wounds: terrible, humiliating nights like the night in Bermuda when (they were making love), looking into her eyes, he saw she wasn't at home. Not even a message machine on. He ended that night alone, talking to himself in an outdoor hot tub. Marriage! The wounds and, worse, the bruises. Why else is it that before marriage and kids, we can meet each other and dance together with words, everything is tender music; then we marry and can't buy a ticket to the dance hall?

But driving Sarah to a really good little French restaurant they both used to like, slipping the little BMW between lanes like a great jockey maneuvering a thoroughbred, he feels optimistic. He tells her how nice the garden in Truro is turning out, and she asks about those lovely words: *hollyhocks, columbine, delphinium.*

In a dark corner of the restaurant, he sits across the table with its checkered tablecloth and sips wine and leans his chin on his hands and his elbows on the table and grins like a fool at Sarah, listening to her story about Noah at gymnastics. This woman, he says to himself, so beautiful to me even now, Jewish Indian with her olive complexion and prominent nose, the heavy, lovely breasts I see with my hands' eye, and black hair curly and turbulent no matter what she does to tame it.

He sees her face now and it becomes her face at the instant after she'd given birth to Beth, and her hair, oh, was stringy, her skin bloated and her eyes giddy with joy. He'd been crying too, crying for the newborn they lost two years before, crying with relief that this time it would be okay, the birth okay, Beth was going to live.

"You're looking good," he says. "Been working out, I bet."

"Not much. You look really good yourself."

This woman, he says to himself, she's still my life. His eyes mist, he blows his nose in his table napkin, then remembers how she hates to see him do that. He laughs to make it a gag.

"So," he says after they order, "you called the meeting. You need a new computer or what? Kidding, kidding— Hey, tell me, how are we doing with the kids? Pretty good, I think."

"Really, really good," she said. "It's some change. God. You remember, Davie—I'm not saying this to start anything, but— when you were home you were never home."

"I know, I know," he says.

"You were always somewhere else, always at the office, on the phone all weekend."

"You're right, you're absolutely right."

"Really, I'm happy about it—especially for Noah. He's been needing a father bad."

"I don't think I ever realized, so help me God. The kids, they've been a lot to me these past months." Been *everything*, he would have said, been my script—but he wants to come on like a man of strength, a grownup.

"Well, it's wonderful, Davie."

"See? I can learn, Sarah. I guess I'm never going to talk about French feminist psychoanalysts, but I can learn about being a father. Maybe a husband."

She sips her wine, he's afraid to put his hand on hers. "So what do you think?" he whispers.

It takes her time to catch up to him. Then she's there, and she drops her eyes. "Oh. David, I'm a fool," she says.

"No, no—"

"Listen, you don't understand," she says. "I'm really sorry. I mean that's not why I wanted us to talk."

"Okay. Okay. That's okay." He holds up his hands, palms out in surrender.

"No—I'm sorry. I wanted you to know—I wanted to say it face to face—I might get married again," she says. "I'm probably getting married, Davie. Married to Nick. So . . . we need to begin proceedings, you and me."

There's a hollow rush in his belly, and he breathes in a deep breath and his eyes lift involuntarily into the ceiling. Only he can't lift up into a safe haven above himself, looking down on the poor sufferer. He *is* the sufferer. He's falling through a hole.

"Sure," he says. "My lawyer and your lawyer. We'll get a letter of agreement ready." Falling through a hole—or it's like his real life is a train leaving the station without him. He smiles his salesman smile and wants to drink his wine but he's afraid the glass will be shaky in his hand. At the same time, another piece of him is thinking shrewdly that if she needs an agreement so quickly, then okay, good, he'll come out of this with more than his shirt. Is she afraid, he wonders, that too long a delay and Nick might back off? Could Nick do a thing like that, the prick? He finds himself feeling protective, like a father worrying that his daughter might get hurt by a suitor. It must be a cover-up feeling, he thinks. He must be full of rage. Down and down and down he looks for it, for the rage, but all he feels is protective and full of grief and afraid she'll see. He says, "Don't worry, Sarah. I'll get my guy on it right away."

.   .   .

The only way he can keep from drinking now is to work out hard. He does Nautilus, takes a daily swim. The worse he feels, the more he needs the discipline. His life has imploded into a core of pain. There's nothing in him to resist gravity, to lift himself up above himself. He dances to no strange tune. His *story* collapses, and with it the David who wasn't burdened by his life, the David who enacted a dream, a script he'd been handed. It's no script. All morning he sits, like stone, like one of those meteorites in the planetarium—hot rock melted into dense, cold stone, pure weight—sits over coffee and fingers his lower lip and looks up his stocks in the *Globe*.

This isn't what he had in mind. It's the wrong story. He's supposed to have suffered and become a changed soul with a new life. *This* grief seems a waste. There are ways to use grief, taught for thousands of years, but none of them David knows. Alone, the soul, awash in grief until half-drowned, grasps any rock it already knows. Change it wants, though still—still to be somehow familiar to itself. Maybe what is being asked instead is that the soul let go, that it become a sea creature; and it would rather die than grow gills or turn dolphin, so strange! Instead, it will pretend to change, like Proteus, the Old Man of the Sea. Wrestle with him, Odysseus was told; don't let him go no matter how he seems to change form. David, not knowing how to wrestle, sits and fingers his lower lip.

Mired in pain, maybe it's a good thing he has to begin thinking of money. He's just another guy in Massachusetts out of work. He's got money put away for the kids' education, money in an annuity, but he's been cashing in CDs and Treasury notes, and it doesn't feel so romantic, so life-renewing, as it did at the beach. He can't keep stringing Data Management along, they won't hold his position open forever. Finally, he has to go back to DM and talk to Charlie Bausch. Driving out to 128, just as if this were a year ago and nothing had gone down, he finds himself lifting out of himself, high up above the BMW, above Route 9, and he looks down on a guy who couldn't make a new life or fix up the old one, a guy who was broken the way everybody gets broken.

Everybody, everybody, it's like being popped onto the board

of a pinball machine and—whew!—missing the holes, one, two, three. Hey!—You don't die in somebody's war or gas chamber, you don't get cancer or AIDS, your kids don't Godforbid get childhood leukemia, you don't wind up in a dead-end job and some roach-infested apartment in Chelsea, but the board is slanted, and sooner or later—wait—there'll be a hole for you.

DM feels strange to him, maybe most strange because nobody seems to notice anything unusual about his being back. He waves at Ed McKitterick, at Ginny Shepherd with the lovely doe eyes—all these years he's wanted just to touch her face and to bless her. He keeps walking, successful-salesman grin stuck on his face.

Sales works out of an open-plan office, half a football field of space, columns at regular intervals but cubicles every which way, a maze of cubicles. As he threads his usual path, he hears a guffaw. Stephen Anapulsky bursts out of his cubicle laughing, Sid Langdorf out of *his*—

"That clown he turned the messages on my screen upside down, the clown!"

His office is still untouched, the drawers still stuffed with his papers, with old snapshots of the kids. He writes a note to the custodian: PLEASE CLEAN UP. THANKS! And he heads for his meeting with Charlie Bausch.

Too heavy still, though he's lost maybe thirty pounds, Charlie carries his weight like a tired old sailor lugging a duffle. He limps a little, but David's always thought of it as a royal swagger. As if there's something dignified in the way Charlie Bausch hefts the extra weight and the tired bones.

They've never really become friends, but for fifteen years, now, Charlie Bausch has been his mentor in the company. I made some success, where did I take it but to Charlie? Old salesman himself, Charlie taught him shrewdness, and often, middle of a sales presentation, David finds Charlie inhabiting his body, finds himself mellowing down, slowing his gestures, slowing his voice like a record going from 45 rpm to 33, down to Charlie's courteous gravel tones. I think what he does is he gets clients into a kind of hypnotic trance, a place where they feel so comfortable that they're open to persuasion.

Especially since Charlie's heart attack a few years ago, David has found his own heart open to him. The guy can get a little boring, but boring isn't so bad. If Charlie can't stop talking about the international bond market or about his granddaughter in Phoenix, what the hell.

He looks puffy and dark under the eyes, Charlie.

They talk, as they have a couple of times over the phone, about the sales that David left unfinished. "You know about Polaroid coming through," Charlie says. "That commission is yours, you know." Then Charlie tilts way back in his chair, feet go up, pencil between his two forefingers like a bridge over a precipice—a posture that means, *I'm gonna philosophize, Dave;* that really means, *I'm gonna sell you something.*

"Dave," he says, "I can understand a guy going through confused times, he goes off and puts himself together. I respect that. A retreat's a great thing. The Catholics are no dopes, they've been successful a long time with this retreat business."

"You've been very kind to me, Charlie."

"Kind? I've been grooming you. You know that. I don't want to see you lose it all. Forget the Catholics. Think of it this way," Charlie says, his voice slowing down and, like the voice on a tape recorder, dropping into a lower register. "You got knocked around the first half, so you rested in the locker room. Now you suit up . . . You used to play fullback, am I right?—you get back on the field and you play to win."

"But suppose," David says, falling into the slow melancholy of Charlie Bausch's talk, "suppose you don't care about the game, suppose it's the wrong game?"

"Dave, listen, listen, Dave: it's the only game in town."

David considers this. He wishes he could ask Charlie why it was a game worth playing, but Charlie doesn't have answers like that. Besides, David knows it's a ritual, this talk. There's really no need to convince him of anything, he walked in here convinced that he has no other option. Just walking in, no matter how kind Charlie is, has got to feel like a defeat.

"The way I see it," Charlie says in a kind of singsong, "everything got sour for you when Sarah kicked you out. Your work, whatever. Are you kidding me? If you really hated your work, you couldn't do the job you do. Am I right? Tell me, 'You're right, Charlie.' "

"You *are* right, Charlie. I'm a salesman."

"I know I'm right. How many times you win the special parking place, Salesman of the Month? For Christsakes, you practically owned the slot. You're a better salesman than I ever was."

"That's bullshit."

"But you're forty-five years old, maybe it's time to get you out of the trenches. Like me. Okay, here's my offer. Regional Sales Manager is opening up. You want it?"

David looks into Charlie's tired eyes and solemnly nods.

"Surprised you, huh? See, the only way I could sell your goddamn desertion to the big guys, I said, 'Kahn is sniffing out a management position.' They came through. We'll talk details another time," Charlie says, voice lifting. "Let's you and me go get some dessert to celebrate. To hell with the cholesterol."

David drives Beth and Noah down to Truro. They're lucky: it's a sunny Friday afternoon and promises to be sunny all weekend. Late June. Cape light. A few of the tulips are still blooming, waving in the wind, making the old house look as if somebody lives there, it's not a summer rental. A pioneer columbine is flowering, and the bleeding heart is fuller than it has a right to be this first year. Look, look. To humor his dad, Noah looks and sighs ironically at the way his dad makes him look at things; Beth sniffs a tulip and comes away disappointed.

They carry in suitcases and groceries, soon they're hiking the sand trail over the dunes to the beach. Noah adores David's cellular phone. "Can we take it along? Will it work from the beach?"

"Can I call Mommy and she can listen to the ocean?" Beth wants to know.

"We'll try." David hooks it on the belt of his jeans.

At ten, Noah isn't too old to be excited about his dad's new job. He asks, "Will you be on the road a lot?"

"Less than I used to. The money's less, too . . . Beth?—Careful of the prickers on the bushes, Beth."

"How come?" Noah asks. "You'll be top guy."

"But I'm not out there as much doing the selling and pulling down the big commissions. You know what commissions are?"

Noah nods. Beth says, "What are commissions?" But before

he has to answer, she sees a rabbit and runs after it, yelling "Bunny, bunny, bunny!"

"Still, it'll be better, Noah. There's stock options. And I'll have more time with you and Beth."

"No-eee, No-eee!" Beth calls, her name for her brother since she could speak at all. "Find me, No-eee."

"Regional Manager! *Yes!*" Noah says, doing a victory dance for his father.

"I'll tell you the God's honest truth," his father says. "I wouldn't be disappointed if you did something else entirely."

"Like what?"

"Like . . . anything. What can you imagine yourself doing?"

Noah, not wanting to think, runs off through the scrub oak and squat pine of the outer Cape. He pretends to search for Beth.

When David gets to the top of a high dune, he finds a strong offshore wind that drives through his zipper and down his neck. He can lean into the wind; it holds him up. And he closes his eyes and imagines he's hang-gliding, all two hundred pounds of him floating on this wind. He hears Beth's singsong and Noah's shout.

And his elbow bumps the cellular phone, so he imagines it's ringing, because how else *can* he get in touch these days? The presence he'd listened to, it hasn't been present, maybe he's been too busy, moving into his new office, making calls, making meetings, making a living if not exactly a life. So it makes crazy sense to him, that if he wants to get in touch again, it should be with this phone.

When it rings, wherever he is, it connects him to his ordinary world, there's no getting away from it anywhere anymore. So he imagines a different ring, oh, it's like little bells, and looking around to make sure the kids aren't in sight, he takes the phone off his belt and says, "David Kahn here." But there's no voice from some other end. "I know," he whispers over the rush of wind, "that even when I hear nothing, I'm saying what you're telling me and doing what you'd have me do. Isn't that right?"

"What, Daddy?" Beth's there; she holds onto his leg.

"I'm just pretend-talking . . . Hello, hello," he says into the phone, "you want to talk to Bev? *Bev*—I don't know anyone by that name. Sorry."

"Beth, it's for *me,* I'm Beth."

"Oh, it's *Beth* you want. Well, here."

"Hello," Beth says, taking the phone. "Well, I'd love to come to your party . . . All right . . . They want to speak to you."

David takes the phone. "Oh, I see. Well, we will," he says to the phone. And to Beth he says, "Dance. They said we have to dance." Still holding the phone, David dances his daughter at the top of the dune, round and round, oom-pah-pah, as if he's got no choice; and in the middle of the dance he feels it coming back, the connection, the presence, as if he's a fish at the end of an invisible line, and he's so into his dance he doesn't know Noah's there till the kid says, "Who're you talking to, Dad? You talking to Mom?"

"No," David says, phone to his ear, "I'm talking to Charlie, just talking to Charlie."

Because it's the same, he thinks, as long as you do the dance. David dances, and me, I watch him do his dance, while I do my own, hoping that I can hear the music, and that, at least for a while, David's dance can take me home.

Elizabeth Hardwick

SHOT: A NEW YORK STORY

She, Zona, went along the avenues of the East Side of Manhattan, turned up the brownstone side streets of the Seventies and the Nineties on the way to the houses of her group. Once there, she would iron shirts, untangle the vacuum, and at times would be called to put on her black uniform and pass the smoked salmon curling on squares of pumpernickel at cocktail parties. Occasionally, one of the group might see Zona racing up Madison Avenue in the late evening, passing swiftly by the windows where the dresses and scarves and jewelry stood or lay immobile in the anxious night glitter of the high-priced. Zona would, of course, be making her way home, although not one of her people was certain just where that home might be. Somewhere in the grainy, indivisible out-there: area code 718, and what did that signify—the Bronx, Queens? She was tall, very thin; in her black coat, her thick black hair topping her black face, she seemed to be flying with the migratory certainty of some wide-winged black bird.

Her rushing movements were also noticeable about the house. She flew with the dust cloth—swish, swish, swish over the tabletops and a swipe at the windowsills; a splash here and there in the sink; a dash to recover the coat of a not quite sober cocktail guest. Yet, for all this interesting quickness of hand and foot, she was imperturbable, courteous, not given to chatter. And she was impressive; yes, impressive—that was said about Zona. A bit of the nunnery about her, black virgin from some sandy Christian village on the Ivory Coast. So you might say, in a stretch.

A decorator; a partner in an old-print shop; a flute player, female; and a retired classics professor, who liked to sit reading in a wheelchair. To him, Zona would say: Up, up, move, move, and he might spring to his feet or he might not. Such was Zona's group. She had been passed along to them by some forgotten homesteader, perhaps the now dead photographer from *Life*, who took her picture and used it in a spread on Somalia. These random dwellers did not see much of each other, but each had passed through the sponge of Manhattan, where even a more or less reclusive person like the professor had a bulky address book filled with friends, relatives, window-washers, foot doctors, whatever—a tattered memorial with so many weird scratches and revisions it might have been in Sanskrit.

It was at the decorator's apartment that the messenger first stopped. Tony's was a place on the first floor of a brownstone in the Seventies—a more or less rent-controlled arrangement, since the owner, an old lady, did not want to sell and did not want to fix anything: a standoff. Except for leaks and such matters, Tony was content to do up his own place in his own manner. And a neat number it was, if always in transition, since he bought at auction, tarted the stuff up with a bit of fabric, and sold to his clients, when he had clients. Freelance, that's what he was. A roving knight available for hire. But, even if his sofa had disappeared, Tony had his rosy walls in a six-coat glaze, and a handsome Englishy telescope that stood in a corner, a tôle chandelier done in a leaf design of faded greens and reds, and lots of things here and there. But not too many.

It was near the end of a nice autumn day when his doorbell rang. Lovely September air, and gather it while ye may, for tomorrow in New York a smoky heat could move across the two rivers and hang heavy as leather on your eyebrows. Tony, at the sound of the bell, looked through the peephole and saw before him a young black face, not very black, almost yellow. His mind rushed to accommodate the vision, and, talking to himself, even doing a little dance, he went through his inner dialogue. Ring the bell, open the door. You-have-got-to-be-kidding. This is New York, fella. . . . And so on. Nevertheless, curiosity had its power, and when a finger from the great city touched the bell once more, Tony called out in as surly and as confident a tone as he could summon, What's up?

There was a pause, and the young caller answered in a fading voice. He said: *From Zona.*

Whoa. Come again. Not in a million years could anyone make up the name of Zona and present it on Tony's doorstep under a rare blue-pink sky. Tony looked again through the opening. From Zona was wearing a tangerine-colored jacket, he noticed. Not bad. The latchkey lay near at hand, and with it in his pocket Tony stepped out on the stoop, closing the door behind him, and there they were, the two of them.

The young man shifted uneasily and it fell to Tony to proceed like a busy interpreter at court. From Zona, are you? And there was a nod. Zona? Now here's a coincidence. I had a few friends in the other night. Not many—about six, nothing special. But I could have used a little class in the presentation, you know how it is, and that made me think of Zona right away, but no answer from her. Tony took in the handsome, young, light-skinned face, with its black, black eyes and black, black oily curls. So what is your errand?

Zona passed away. That was the message from the slim youth, about fifteen in Tony's arithmetic.

Zona passed away. You mean dead?

Passed away, the young man repeated, leaving Tony to meet the challenge of whatever was in order—information, emotion? I call that downright horrible news, he said. Such a wonderful person, a gem of a person, Zona. You sure have my sympathy, for what it's worth.

And then, as they stood on the steps, Tony now braced on the iron railing, a car alarm went off. A loud, oppressive, rhythmical whine, urging, Help, help! When at last it came to an abrupt, electronic end, Tony said: Be my witness. There's not a soul on that side of the street, not a soul when it went off and not a soul there now.

It's like the wind sets them off, the boy offered.

Very good, Tony said. Very good. They remind me of a

screaming brat, spoiled, nothing wrong, just wanting attention. Something like that. Rotten, screeching Dodge or Plymouth or whatever it is.

The young man gave a hesitant smile before settling back into silence.

Well, business is business, and Tony gathered himself together and asked with true sweetness: What can I do for you, sir?

We're not able to make arrangements for Zona. The young man shifted and brought his doleful countenance up to meet Tony's eyes, with their flashing curiosity blinking bright in the pleasant sun.

Tony held fast to the railing. I want very much to do something for Zona, he said. And he found himself adding, like a parson, Zona who did so much for us.

The afternoon was retreating; schoolboys and schoolgirls, women with groceries, nurses with prams. Family life and double-parked maintenance trucks of electricians, pipe fitters, floor sanders taking off for the boroughs. Such sad news you have brought to my door, Tony said. And unfortunately I cannot meet the news as I would like. Consolation, all that. I don't have any cash around just now. . . . Maybe I could write you a check somehow or send something later.

Checks are hard to handle, the caller said, to which Tony replied with emphasis: *You are telling me.*

In truth, Tony didn't have any money. As he often expressed it: I don't have any money to speak of, and have you ever thought what a silly phrase that "to speak of" is? Tony didn't have any money. What he had were debts, piling up as they always did, month after month after month. Nothing ever seemed to place him ahead. Ahead? Not even in balance. When he got paid for a job or sold something, by the time the payment came through he owed most of it.

He borrowed from his friends, had borrowed from his sister until that source dried up in a ferocious finale. When reproached or reminded of a default, Tony was something grand to see and to hear. He attacked the lender and carried on with tremendous effrontery, often weeping in his rage. I don't need you to tell me that I owe you money. Don't you think I know that? Do I have to sit here and tell you that damned money is on my mind day and night? And then, in a change of pace, he would crumble, or appear to do so. Listen, I've been having a really rough time. Just now. This wonderful United States economy is in a god-awful mess. Right down there in the mud, as I see it. Or haven't you had reason to notice? You have no idea what borrowing is like, Tony would go on in an aggrieved tone. I hope you never have to go through it yourself, believe me. Borrowing from friends is the worst of it. Sheer hell on earth. Better Con Ed and the phone company after you every day, better than a friend out there waiting . . . With the utilities and all that, there are thousands in the same shitty hole. Those companies don't know you, wouldn't know you on the street, thank God. But with pals, it's torture on the rack.

Take it easy, Tony. Calm down. Everything will work out—and such was the end of that bit of troublesome arrears. Settled.

Autumn leaves lay in damp clumps along the curbs. Some of them still struggling to be yellow and red as they fell from far-away trees and were somehow carried into the treeless streets. Thinking of autumn leaves brought Tony's mind to the first vodka of the evening. It was time to step back through the door with its polished brass knocker in the shape of a lion's head. Time for his little bar alcove and zinc sink encased in pine, his American Back Porch period; time to get ice from the Sub-Zero, High-Tech period. It was time to relax, watch the evening news and, after that, "Hard Copy" or "A Current Affair." But the lovers didn't know *the wife was waiting!* That sort of problem.

Poor Zona, he said. I'd give the old eyeteeth to help you out. I really would, believe me. I know what you folks are going through, but things are a little tight with me at this point in time. That is, right now.

Tony was from Memphis. It had long been understood by him and his world in New York that he had a special sort of down-home, churchgoing way with black people. Perhaps he did, with his loquacity, curiosity, good humor—when he wasn't in a rage. There were, indeed, some occasions when he was more "Southern" than others.

The financial aspect of the transaction on the stoop in the East Seventies seemed to have blown away to rest elsewhere, like the leaves. This resolution, if you could call it that, left Tony free to ask: What's your name, fella?

My name is Carlos.

Carlos, is it? A bit out of the way to my ear. But then I don't know just where Zona got her name, either. And you might ask how I come to be Tony, like an Italian. Never laid eyes on one till I was your age.

That went by without interference, and Tony prepared for a retreat. Zona was a fine person, a special individual. Kind of a lady in her bearing. Of the old school, as they say. And how old was she? No time for that now. Time for the zinc-sink folly. He directed Carlos to another of Zona's group when he saw the young man looking at what appeared to be a list.

Check out Joseph, he said. But don't turn up before seven. He works. As a goodbye offering for Carlos, Tony went into his act, accent and all. Joseph's a good ole boy. And, just between us, he's got pigs at the trough, chickens scootin' round the yard, hay in the barn, and preserves in the cellar. Definitely not hungry, if you get my drift.

Carlos bowed his head and made his way down the stoop. Now, Tony wondered, just what was I going on about? Carlos, not even Southern, for God's sake. But, Southern or not, he called out to the disappearing tangerine back, God bless!

Inside, double-locked, vodka in hand, he rang up Joseph and gave a synopsis and foretold the boy's visit.

What did Zona die of? Joseph wanted to know.

Don't ask me. Just passed away.

At seven-fifteen the elevator man called Joseph's apartment and said that a young man named Zona wanted to be brought up, and Joseph said, Bring him up. It was an awful moment at the door, with the young man saying, Zona passed away.

Yes, I know. Tony rang me. It's very sad news indeed. I've known Zona for fifteen years. A long time for New York, I guess.

Joseph worked in a distinguished print shop on Madison Avenue, a shop owned by a distinguished dealer, a Jewish refugee from Germany. Joseph himself was a second-generation Jewish refugee from Germany. He had been brought up in America by his parents, who left Germany in the mid-nineteen-thirties, went first to England and then to New York. They left with some of their family money, and in New York the father became a successful accountant and the mother trained with Karen Horney and went into practice as a therapist. The parents died and did not leave Joseph penniless, even if what had seemed a lot in the nineteen-seventies didn't seem much at all now.

He had studied history and French at the University of Michigan in Ann Arbor, a happy place for him, which confirmed his parents' notion that young persons of foreign birth should experience the country outside New York. Several years after graduation, he married a Michigan girl and they came to the city, where he learned the old-print business from the Master. It was not long before the Michigan girl found life too old-print—too German and all that. For Joseph the marriage seemed mysteriously to dissolve, but his bride used the word "disintegrate" with unflattering fervor. She took some of Joseph's inheritance and left Joseph with his natural sentimentality and diffidence increased. She left him also in some way frightened, even though cheerfulness was his outward aspect and went handily with his stocky, plumpish figure.

Joseph was wearing a black suit, a shirt of blue stripes, and a black tie. Business wear, except that he was in his socks. The therapeutic walk of twenty blocks up Madison Avenue had taken its toll on his feet, as he explained to Carlos. He invited the young man into a study off the living room, where there was a large desk. Here Joseph planned to talk to Carlos and to write out a check in honor of Zona. Of course it was a difficult meeting, since Joseph lacked Tony's chattering, dominating intimacy with every cat and dog and beggar (Sorry, man, out of change) on the street.

Please be at ease. Uh, Carlos, isn't it? Be at ease, Joseph said. And he sent the young man to sink into an old leather chair. Here in this dark cubicle, with the desk taking up most of the space and books on the floor, Joseph switched on the lights dug into the ceiling. Under the not entirely friendly illumination, the face of Carlos was a warm, light brown, the color of certain packing envelopes. With his eyes a swim of black and his oily black curls, Carlos looked like a figure in a crowded painting of some vivid historical scene, a face peering over the gleaming shoulders of white bodies, a face whose presence would need to be interpreted by scholars. Joseph found himself lost in this for a moment or two but could not name the painting, if any, that he was trying to recall.

No, no, he said. This is going too fast. No hurry, no hurry. He led Carlos into the kitchen and brought forth a bottle of Pellegrino. They took their glasses and Joseph had the idea of showing Carlos around the flat. In a mournful voice, he said: Carlos, this was Zona's place.

The apartment was on the overstuffed side, like Joseph himself. It had been *done* by Tony, and that was the cause of their meeting. Tony's contributions were window drapery that rolled up in a scalloped pattern, a sofa in something that looked like tapestry and ended in a band of fringe around the bottom— those and the recessed ceiling lights. For the rest, there was a mahogany dining table, with six heavy high-backed chairs spread around the three rooms. The bedroom had a suite done in an ivory color with a lot of gilt on its various components, a dated bunch of pieces coldly reigning amidst the glossy white walls.

While the apartment was being renovated, Joseph had announced that he didn't intend to buy any large pieces, because he had his mother's things in storage. Tony rolled his eyes and said: A catastrophe lies ahead. And, not long after, he came face to face with the accumulation of objects as heavy and strong, and spread around as helplessly, as old, dull-eyed mammoths. Tony blew a smoke ring at Joseph and exclaimed: I wouldn't believe it. It's wonderful. Park Avenue Early Jewish!

He wanted everything sent off to Tepper's auction house. Estate sale, Joseph. Estate sale. Joseph was taken with a fit of sentimental stubbornness, and most of the loot remained. Sometimes, when friends came around, he would smile, wave his arm about, and say, Here you have it. Early Jewish. Of course, he had his prints, his library, his silver, some old clocks. And he had Zona, whom he seldom saw, but whose presence in his life was treasured. Her hours, once a week, with a single gentleman out of the house, unlike the freelance Tony, were whatever suited her. Sometimes Joseph was at home in the late afternoon and they collided. Rapid, graceful, and courteous, she filled him with the most pleasurable emotions. The wastebaskets were emptied, the sheets on the ivory-and-gilt bed changed, a few shirts, not his best, ironed. There was that, but even more it was the years, the alliance, the black bird herself.

He directed Carlos back to the room with the desk and, hesitating, uncertain of his ground, he said: Tell me what happened to Zona. That is, if you don't mind.

Zona was shot, Carlos said, lowering his gaze to the wrinkled kilim on the floor.

Joseph drank from the water glass. Then he put it down and pressed his plump hands together. Shot. What a miserable ending for Zona. Such a—what shall I say about her? In truth, Joseph did not have words to describe Zona. He often felt: I love Zona. But that did not appear to be an appropriate expression somehow. For love, although fearful of the details, he asked: Who shot Zona?

Carlos said: Mister Joseph, they haven't got him yet. The one who did it.

You mean on the street? Just like that?

It was with the driver. Her livery driver.

Livery driver?

The driver with the car who drove her around to her places, brought her into town in the morning and met her at their corner and drove her home. For a long time, it's been. Some years, the arrangement. Martin was his name.

Joseph said: Martin shot Zona?

Carlos looked at him with a curious, long glance, a look of impatience, as if he could not believe Joseph did not comprehend what he knew so well himself. Carefully, he said: Martin didn't shoot Zona. She always sat in front with him. They were both shot.

Joseph, near to a sob, said: You must mean a robbery or something like that.

That's what it was. A fare that came in on the car radio. Got in the back seat and that was it.

There it was. It was time for Joseph to ask, What can I do for Zona? Carlos said they were having trouble with the arrangements, and when Joseph got his pen to write a check, Carlos

said, Checks are hard. We don't have any banks especially. Any
that know us. So, in the end, Joseph found two hundred dollars
and Carlos rose to leave. I'll take it to her sister.

Whose sister?

Zona's sister. My mother. And in the gloom he was escorted
to the elevator and went down to the street, where now rain
splashed and wind blew.

Joseph phoned Tony and said, Shot. And Tony said, Shot?
Wouldn't you just know it?

Joseph said, There's a sister.

Whose sister?

Zona's sister. That's who we're talking about, right? The sister
is the mother of Carlos. It's horrible to think of Zona gone like
that. From the back seat.

Tony said, What back seat? But Joseph declined. Nothing,
Tony, nothing. Just shot.

Tony said: History of this goddam city—at least a footnote to
the history of these fucking times. The whole place is a firing
range, up and down and across.

Joseph said: Zona's not a footnote to me. I loved Zona.

Didn't we all? came back over the wire.

The next morning, Carlos arrived at a town house on East
Ninety-first Street, the house of Cynthia, the flute player. The
door was ajar and noise could be heard inside—voices, a phonograph, a telephone ringing and answered. Carlos pushed the
bell button and waited next to a stone urn of faltering gerani-
ums. After a time, a young girl, about his age, called out for
Granny, and after a minute or two here came Cynthia in a
smock. This time the opening line was: I'm Carlos. From Zona.

How nice. Come in, come in. You are welcome here.

There were boots and umbrellas in the hallway, coats hanging
on pegs, newspapers stacked for recycling—quite a busy entrance, you'd have to say.

Carlos was led into the front parlor, where there was a piano,
along with bookcases, two-seater sofas, and a big, lumpy armchair by the window, to which he was directed. Cynthia drew a
chair very near to him, and her greenish, amiable eyes gazed
into his liquid black ones and at last she said: I missed Zona this

week. You know—Carlos, is it?—that I consider it very brave of Zona to set foot into my jungle. An army couldn't handle it. You can see that, I'm sure. But Zona found things to do, and I am much in her debt.

Carlos looked aside. Zona passed away, he said.

Cynthia sat up straight as a rod in her chair and looked up at the ceiling for a long time. At last she said: I wasn't prepared for this. Passed on from this life, Zona. Just like that.

Zona passed away, he repeated, and Cynthia seemed lost in contemplation, meditation of some kind. Oh, oh, passed away. I'm sorry. I'm sorry. I hope it was an easy death. An easy passage after a hard, honorable life.

Carlos said: No, Ma'am. It wasn't easy. Zona was shot.

Cynthia drew her chair nearer, brought her golden-gray head so close that Carlos tilted his black curls back a bit. Then Cynthia placed her long fingers on his hand and drew his other brown hand over her own so that they were in a clasp like that practiced in progressive churches. Shot, you say. More than the heart can bear.

Cynthia grew up in Baltimore, went to the Curtis Institute, in Philadelphia, had a three-week summer session in Paris with Rampal, and in her younger years had played for a time in the Baltimore Symphony Orchestra. Then she came with her husband and daughter to New York and bought the house on Ninety-first Street. Thirty-nine thousand it cost then, she would say. Only that. The money had come from the closing of her grandfather's Baltimore business, a handsome store where well-to-do women could buy dresses, coats and satin lingerie, cologne and face powder. Three floors in a fine downtown brick building, clerks long in service, and seamstresses with pins in their mouths while making alterations. Ours was a *select* business, she would say with an ironical lilt and the special tone of Unitarian modesty. It was very well known and much respected in the community. To be that, you had to be somewhat cool to ordinary people. You didn't want them to look at things and then go pale at the price. But the doors were welcoming to one and all on the Day After the Fourth of July Sale. A yearly excitement it was, people in line at seven in the morning.

Releasing the hand of Carlos, Cynthia said: Tell me what you

and your family have been going through. She passed him a
damp cookie and a cat entered the room and settled on his lap.
Carlos ate the cookie and stroked the cat. Looking hard at
Cynthia, he said in a tone of apology: You see, I never met any
of the people Zona worked for before this happened. I don't
know just what they might want to hear.

I want to hear what you can bear to tell, Cynthia said.

In a breathless rush, Carlos told about the livery car that had
taken Zona back and forth to her work, about the passenger
who got in from the radio call and hadn't been caught yet. And
he added that his mother, Zona's sister, would have come round
to the people but she was home crying herself crazy.

I will attend Zona's funeral, Cynthia said. I want to be there.
For me, it would be an honor. And it occurs to me that if you
wish I might play a little music. Something suitable, of course.

Carlos raised his hand to interrupt. It was time to complete
his errand: We haven't been able to make the arrangements for
Zona.

Cynthia said at this point: Funeral arrangements cost much
more than they need to. I read a book about that—although
I didn't need to be informed about the ways of such institu-
tions.

Carlos, a diver at the tip of the board, fixed his glance on
Cynthia's bright head of white hair, with the brown streaks
turning golden. He said: She's been there a week while we
couldn't make the arrangements. They put them in the ground,
like in a field, they say.

Been where?

With the city down where they keep them. If you can't make
the arrangements to transfer, they put them—

Oh, Cynthia said. You mean Potter's Field?

Carlos said: That sounds like it.

The granddaughter who had opened the door came into the
room and introductions were made. As she was going out, she
said to Carlos: You're cute.

This young person is in a state of bereavement, Cynthia called
to the girl. And she added: Neither of my grandchildren is musical. They can't sing "Adeste Fideles" in tune. A deprivation.

Pigeons rested on the sills of the long, handsome, smeary windows still divided into the original panes and now interrupted only by a rusty air-conditioner. I can't take it all in, Cynthia said. I would like to know what Zona's family needs.

What we want, Ma'am, he said, what we want is a coffin on a train, and a few of us family will go down and have her buried in Opelika.

Opelika? Where is that?

Alabama. Zona's town.

Opelika, Alabama. What a pretty name.

The ground down there's paid for, Carlos explained.

Cynthia drew a pencil from the pocket of her smock, found a pad, and began to write on it. I have probably waited too long to sell this house, she said. The prices are falling fast—the darkness deepening, as the hymn goes.

Cynthia and her chamber-music group occasionally held concerts in this house, and at one of those Joseph had brought Tony along. Tony, when the invitation came, said: I might have guessed you'd go for that, Joseph. German.

During the wine and cheese, inferior quality indeed, Tony approached Cynthia and in an excited mode informed her: You are sitting on a million bucks here—if not exactly in mint condition. He noted the panelling, the high ceilings, and the matching fireplaces of decorated marble on the first floor. Assets you have here. A million for sure, at the bottom.

Tony was floating like a sturdy little boat on the waters of the house market. A million for the property and another mil *at least* to do it up. They're terrorists, these buyers. They like to gut the place, break down walls, even move the staircase so they can put a powder room under it. Space, dear lady, that's the ticket. Space is what you have to sell.

Of course, Cynthia stayed on. The house, the space, was all she had to leave her daughter, the way things looked. She rented rooms to students, gave lessons, while lamenting that the lesson-takers were mostly girls and few strong enough for the instrument. In these rooms now she was contemplating life and death with Carlos. It was calculated that a thousand dollars was needed to rescue Zona. And there was the problem with cashing checks, and just two days before they would, down there at the city, before they would—

Please, please, Carlos. Don't speak of it. More than the heart can bear.

Cynthia's finances were more than a little murky. Her husband, when they moved to New York, had worked for a publishing group that put out *Family Days*. Perhaps he got a bit overloaded on that, and he squared the circle, so to speak, and shifted to *Liberty*, when that magazine was around. He also shifted to an ignorant girl in the mail room. Cynthia was left to provide for her daughter, who quit Barnard College in her freshman year, took up with a boy from Columbia, and went up to New Hampshire with him to pursue carpentry and to produce two daughters. Cynthia had bits of trust funds from the old Baltimore emporium, from a childless uncle, and from her father, who declined the clothing business and went into a small local bank, not very successfully. He raised his nice, musical daughter, who ended up on the flute.

At last, toward noon, with the temperamental city sun shining one minute and disappearing the next, as if turning a corner, Cynthia found a sweater and put her arm through the arm of Carlos, and the odd tandem made its way down Lexington Avenue to the Chemical Bank. Inside the bank, the odd tandem became an alarming couple; Carlos like a thief avoiding eye contact with the teller, a young Indian woman in a sari, and Cynthia, in an old gentlewoman's untidy fluster, withdrawing a thousand dollars in fifties and twenties.

They stood outside in humbling confusion until the money in two envelopes was passed into the hands of Carlos. Off in a gallop to the subway and to do the paperwork down there where they were impatiently holding the body of Zona. Alert the River Jordan Twenty-Four-Hour Funeral Service. And at last meet the train rolling down to Washington, D.C.; there a crunching change of cars, a wait, before wheeling through state after state, through West Virginia, passing the memory of the prehistoric Mound Builders and the rusting scaffolds of the anthracite-coal counties. On to the point of the Chattanooga Campaign, down to the grass and myrtle of the cemetery lying in the Alabama autumn. Journey's end.

Adios, Carlos. Au revoir, Zona. Rest in peace in Opelika.

Cynthia recounted the dire circumstances to Joseph, who said,

I loved Zona. A great hole in my life, this is. It's like planting a field of seeds and none of them coming up. In a manner of speaking.

Cynthia said: Nothing for Planned Parenthood this year. But no matter, no matter.

Tony, informed, said: They love funerals.

Padgett Powell

TRICK OR TREAT

On her way to the grocery store, to which she could walk, in celebration of which she often wore lizard-skin cowboy boots and other excesses of dress for a daily trip to buy food for a family, Mrs. Hollingsworth recited, "It loves me, it loves me not. I love *it*, I love it not—" until she was interrupted by a child behind a picket fence next to the sidewalk.

"What are you talking about, lady?" This came equably from a round freckled face just above the sharpened pickets, all of which suggested briefly an uncarved, unlit pumpkin speaking to her.

"The South," Mrs. Hollingsworth said to the pumpkin face, which she presumed, not altogether comfortably, was a portrait of innocence. The child was, in fact, a portrait of insolence and had wanted to say not "What are you talking about, lady?" but "Hey, lady, how about some pussy?" For weeks he had watched her walk in costumes to and from the store and he had prodigious twelve-year-old need.

"The south?" he asked. "What's that?"

"This," Mrs. Hollingsworth said, indicating with her arm the trees and air and houses and suspiring history and ennui and corruption and meanness and bottomland and chivalric humanism and people who are smart about money and people who don't have a clue and heroism and stray pets around them.

"Have you lost your mind?" the boy asked.

Mrs. Hollingsworth, to whom the proposition was tenable, said, "Grow up," and walked on.

The child was left there in a rage of early tumescence, kicking himself for insulting the object of his waking and sleeping lusts. The back of his T-shirt, which Mrs. Hollingsworth had not seen, said JUST BLOW ME, ostensibly in promotion of a brand of bubble gum. He had had the wit not to let his parents see the shirt and knew, almost, what it meant. He had intended asking Mrs. Hollingsworth how about some pussy and then turning his back to her. It would have worked, he was sure.

The child had no way of knowing that it *would* probably have worked. Mrs. Hollingsworth had three children, one older than her suitor, and had been happily married for fifteen years, and was a good mother and wife, and was enraged about it. She would have entertained the notion of this little smart-ass pumpkin head, un Lolito. It was hysterical, she was hysterical, it was perfect. But the pumpkin head had not shown his cards.

The next time Mrs. Hollingsworth saw the child he was standing on her front stoop with a new-looking Lawn-Boy mower behind him the color of a katydid. Through the door peephole's fish-eye lens the boy looked obscenely older, his freckles the size of rain splats on concrete.

She opened the door and said, neutrally, "Yes?" and looked from the boy to the mower and back to the boy and then up and down the boy.

"What?" he said. "My shorts?" He looked down at his shorts, which were cutoffs with ridiculously lacerated hems. In fact, she saw then, they had been sliced up from the cut edge about two inches, giving them a kind of surrey-roof frill. His skinny legs hung out of this frilliness like strings themselves.

Mrs. Hollingsworth laughed and said, "No, not your shorts."

"What, then?"

"*What* what?"

"What are you laughing at?"

"I'm not laughing."

"You were too."

Mrs. Hollingsworth laughed again.

"See?"

She laughed some more.

"Goddamn, lady."

"What?"

"*What* what," he said, obviously mocking her.

"Goddamn what?"

"Just *goddamn,* lady."

"Okay. That's better."

The boy drew himself up, as if in summary of certain points he had been making. "Do you want your lawn cut?" When he said this, a hail of profane words and images fell in his brain. Do you want a cherry on it? Do you want nuts on it? Do you want your nuts crushed? Do you want your *tits* blown off? "Do you want your lawn cut?" he said again, strangely almost out of breath.

"No," Mrs. Hollingsworth said. "But you can cut it anyway." She closed the door then and decided that would be the test for this little rogue: if he cut the lawn with no more ado, no price, no terms, no promise, he was to be regarded as a significant little foul ball landing in the happy proper play of her enraging days.

Through the fish-eyed peephole Mrs. Hollingsworth watched him address the Lawn-Boy. He took a deep breath and glanced at the sky before securing the machine with his foot and pulling the cord. It started right up. He took the handle and pressed against it, stood there not moving, and momentarily seemed to wilt over the handle before taking a giant stride. He marched the machine over the lawn faster than she had ever seen a lawn mower go. He was flying over the lawn, blasting sticks and ant beds into flakbursts of airborne detritus that was collecting around his nostrils. He was a cute little thing.

When she let him into the backyard, and he did not talk or even look at her, Mrs. Hollingsworth confirmed her suspicions that the child was on a sexual mission. He was bold and terrified.

"I'll make the lemonade," she said.

He said, "Yes'm."

Not "make us some lemonade," not "Would you like some lemonade or something?" *The* lemonade. She was thrilled by this little stage irony. The boy was not himself unaware of something off. "Yes'm" was as close as he had ever come in his life to saying "ma'am."

When he finished the blitzkrieg of the yard, he sat on the little two-seater rowing swing on the children's gym set and Mrs. Hollingsworth emerged with a tray. On it was a hand-painted pitcher and tumblers and loose lemons as garnish—impractical but irresistible to Mrs. Hollingsworth's sense of kitsch in still life. She noted how unadult the boy looked sitting where her own children sat, even though he was obviously consumed with adult concerns. She wondered for the first time why he was not, as her children were, in school.

She put the tray on one seat of the glider. It was a swinging double-benched arbor, actually, and her plan was to sit them both on one of the benches opposite the lemonade and serve the child properly until the accidental touch, or his blurting whatever he might blurt, set the lunacy of his early need and her late fatigue in motion.

Before any of this was effected they heard the crackle of a police radio and Mrs. Hollingsworth saw, over the gate of the wooden fence through which she had let the boy, the cap and face of a police officer. He said, in a preposterously deep-voiced tone of authority, "What's going on here?"

"We're having *lemonade* in the *shade,* officer," Mrs. Hollingsworth managed, attempting with her emphases—unsuccessfully, she knew—to insult the policeman.

"Who?" he said.

"Whose business—" Mrs. Hollingsworth noticed that the boy was gone. In a decimated patch of earth beside the glider there was a deep sneaker print pointed in the direction of the back fence. She could imagine a blur of surrey frill and skinny leg going over her good six-foot redwood fence. The image made her inexplicably, inordinately fond of her little charge, though suspicious of this rather simple affection for insouciance, or whatever it was that made a boy escape authority and made authority—in this case, herself—like it. She could also not help thinking, as the officer rather brazenly let himself through the

gate, *sex with cops*. He came up—a shiny-shoed, flashing, noisy
navy-blue binding of regulations and procedure.

"Have a look at that lawn mower, ma'am?"

Mrs. Hollingsworth gave him permission, which he did not
wait for, with a wave of her hand. She was observing things she
had no real time to observe. How, of late, she had begun to like
the idea of losing her mind. That was the conventional expression for it, not hers. She was toying with the idea of losing herself. She did not want her mind to depart, like the whole house
of one's Kansas spinning to Oz; she wanted the little craft of
things that were considered *her*, that she considered her, to get
loose and drift and turn just a little off-line, keelless rowboat
about 45 degrees to the current in a gentle, non-threatening high
water. The officer was telling her, standing before her and minc-
ing as if he had to go somewhere or pee, that the lawn mower
had been stolen from the hardware store eight blocks away by a
boy on foot.

"Get your plaster, officer."

"Ma'am?"

"Here's his track."

"The alleged individual who perpetrated was in the apparel
of a shirt of the variety of a T-shirt that had printed on it an
obscene . . . ah, saying. Or remark." This speech endeared the
officer to Mrs. Hollingsworth in a way that surprised her, but
she caught herself. If she was going to have immoral affections
for Lolito, she was not going to accommodate Sergeant Garcia.
She had no idea what the obscene-shirt business was about. The
boy had had on a clean white shirt. That was the only true thing
she told the officer about the boy.

She wondered how disruptive to the courtship this unfortu-
nate incident would prove until an hour later, when she picked
up the phone and heard a voice coming through what sounded
like a pillow say, "Bonnie? This is Clyde. Rain check on that
lemonade," and hang up giggling. She had a card on her hands
and she was going to have to decide if she really was one herself. To do that, you had to look boredom in the eye and forget
all other considerations: your own failures contributing to your
boredom, for example. Does God, you had to ask, want us to be
bored? You answer that to find out if you are a card or not. You

do not entertain highfalutin notions of decadence. Just *boredom*. That is, to some extent, what the kid was operating on, that and hormones, even though he didn't know it (he knew the hormones, but not boredom as such, yet, she figured). He was arguably a little visionary, if you took the long, charitable view of him. If you took the short, niggardly view, he was a young dog with a blue steel. Her husband came home shortly after these thoughts and Mrs. Hollingsworth took the long, charitable view of the boy.

Her husband lugged his business-day you-wouldn't-believe-it opera of sigh and grunts into the house and she gave him the kiss to make it all better. This kiss, on the cheek, had a special feature: she touched the back of his neck with the back of her left hand while holding his arm, at the biceps, with her right hand. The kiss had originated, she supposed, from having wet hands while doing dishes and not wanting to wet her husband. But she had noticed that it was now the only way she would kiss him. It had become a symbol of her dissatisfaction. She thought of kissing the boy: taking his little fine-haired neck with her hand and fingers up into his hair, cradling the little pumpkin properly, and kissing him as tenderly or roughly as he seemed to suggest movies and television had taught him he wanted to be kissed. She realized at dinner—meat loaf with Lipton onion-soup mix in it, they'd have it no other way—that her affair with this rogue lawn boy was as unknowable a thing as anything available to her in her life as it stood, and as it was ever likely to stand. As silly or sad as it was, it was possible to regard entertaining the boy and his desire as an act of survival.

Her husband and her children occupied spaces at the dinner table in dark, undefined silhouettes, as if they were witnesses whose identities were being masked. She was not shocked by this. It was not that these stolid, regular people she held together with daft toughness and maternal Saran Wrap were anonymous; it was that she was really anonymous to them, and had been for a long time. She held no one to account. It was life. She was, again by the perverse charts of life, not anonymous to the frilly-legged, petty-larcenous, pumpkin-headed, overheated lawn boy. Nor would he be anonymous to her.

.   .   .

Suddenly, it seemed, as if her thinking the child's head resembled a pumpkin two weeks before had precipitated it, Halloween was upon her, and with it distractions she found unnerving. Somehow Halloween had come to epitomize the problems in her life. At the least of it there was what she called the "dick costume frenzy," which meant divining the particular misconceptions three children might have about what fairies and pirates and cats were supposed to look like and then purchasing —at a costume store, mind you—the exotic effects that would satisfy these bizarre whims, and then sewing . . . and it did not end, it seemed, for weeks. The ban on treats not factory-wrapped was of course de rigueur, but last year someone had rented a metal detector. When Mrs. Hollingsworth saw a set of parents who did not know how to drive their Volvos very well place a bag of candy on a lawn and run a metal detector over it as if it were a bomb, she herself wanted to explode. She wanted to include Halloween in her catalogue of what constituted the South: ". . . stray pets collected and neutered by alcoholics, unless it rains; automotive mechanical intelligence in inverse proportion to dental health; and *Halloween*."

In this distraction, Mrs. Hollingsworth forgot about the lawn boy until he appeared again on her stoop wearing a suit and a fedora.

"Not another one," she said, referring to costumes.

"No, ma'am," the boy said, removing his hat. "It's me."

"I know it's you," Mrs. Hollingsworth said. "You think I'd have *two* boys stealing lawn mowers for me?"

"I don't know *what* you'd have, lady." He looked her in the eye. This was a fully matured something with a mouth on it, she thought, like a baby snake.

"You *ought* to have me in before they spot me." She swung open the door and swept her arm into the foyer, into which the lawn boy strode, hitching the pants of his too large suit and looking, she thought, for a place to throw the hat. She had a momentary loss of composure as Mickey Rooney as Andy Hardy crossed her mind, and she might have lost her nerve altogether had the child hung the hat on anything. But he did, instead, something rather redeeming: he went directly to the kitchen, opened the sink cabinet, and put the hat, and then the suit, which he removed, revealing the same shirt and surrey-frilled pants as before, into the trash compactor.

"That's the old man's and that's the old brother's," he said, hitting the compactor switch. "They're dumb. All I knew, they'd have the joint staked out."

Mrs. Hollingsworth started laughing, aware that it might sug-gest again to the boy that she was laughing at him. But the boy sat at the kitchen table, apparently not bothered by her laugh-ing, and drummed his fingernails. With a short glass of whiskey and some smoke in the room and a little hair on his face, he'd have looked like a seasoned drinker in a bar.

She got to the table and sat, trying to behave herself, wiping tears from her eyes. "God, I'm sorry."

"For what?"

For what indeed. "Do you steal much?"

"Whenever," he said. He looked around, finally at the calen-dar on which she recorded family doings: lessons, parties, drudge.

"Have you ever been arrested?"

"You talk a lot, lady," he said, and laughed himself. "I'm kid-ding." She looked at him: he was playing a part. He *was* a card.

"It's a strange thing," he said. "You'd never get caught taking a whole lawn mower, for some reason. I got caught once. You know what for?"

"What for?"

"Do you know what a WD-40 straw is?"

"No."

"It's a straw . . . a red plastic straw too skinny to even stir coffee or something. It, it sprays WD-40. It costs about nothing. It comes *with* the WD-40, for free. I got caught stealing one. It's six inches long. It's red."

"What's your name, son?"

He looked at her, rather sharply, she thought, and she also thought, *Not acting now.* She said, before she knew why, but immediately knew why, "I mean, what's your name?"

"Jimmy." His attitude said, *That's better.*

"Jimmy what?"

"Well . . . I thought this would be a, ah, first names only, like a hot line."

"No, it won't."

"Teeth."

"What?"

"My name."

"Your name what?"

"Jimmy Teeth."

"Jimmy Teeth."

"Yes'm." He said this squarely, defiantly.

"Jimmy Teeth," she said, "I'm Janice Halsey," and extended her hand to him. He shook it, firmly.

"You ain't no Mrs. Halsey."

"No, I'm not no *Mrs.* Halsey."

She couldn't tell if he got this, nor could she expect him to know it was not a lie but her maiden name. It seemed time to use her maiden name again with a twelve-year-old suitor, or whatever he was.

"Okay," he said, "Janice Halsey."

"Okay, Jimmy Teeth." She wondered if *he* were lying but didn't think he was. He'd have said Jimmy Diamond if he were lying.

A silence followed that could have been, as Mrs. Hollingsworth's laughing earlier could have been, misinterpreted, caused in this case by the awkwardness of Jimmy Teeth's name or Mrs. Hollingsworth's apparent lying about hers or both, but it seemed finally just a silence, an odd, agreeable calm between two people in a situation that would presumably not make for agreeable calm. A boy who had stolen lawn mowers and clothes to present, apparently, a boundless need, who had to be no matter how savvy on some levels completely innocent on others, who had in disguise matriculated in the kitchen of a woman whose reactions to his proposition he could not possibly predict, who had to be therefore in part terrified, sat before that random, unknown woman twenty-five years his senior as placid as a gangster; the woman who entertained him, entertained his lunatic hope, who had borne children before another woman had borne this one, who had certain fears of the sexual abuse of children, who had once allowed death-do-us-part vows to be read before her as she smiled and cried in an expensive white dress and believed, who had packed lunches and packed the issue of that marriage off to school and that husband off to work, who had had soap-opera days and ironing and long adult afternoons, who had had Sunday brunch and vacations on tropical islands and new station wagons and could read *Bovary* in the French and whose parents were dead, looked calmly at the boy who had stolen a lawn mower and clothes and calmly looked back at her.

She let the moment continue—suspire, as she was wont to put it.

"Well," Jimmy Teeth said, "*do* you like it?"

"Like what?"

"The South."

"Oh. Sure."

"Me too."

He has no idea what he's talking about, she thought. He's making talk. Her job, as superior here, was to rescue him from babbling. He'd shown that under ordinary circumstances he was not prone to babble or to other loose business. But still, the non-awkwardness of the definitively awkward minuet they were in continued to please her.

"The thing about the South," she said, getting up with the sudden perfect idea that she have a drink—a very sweet Manhattan struck her in the cortex, and she got Jimmy Teeth the lemonade the law had earlier cost him—"the thing about the South is that it's a vale of tears that were shed a long time ago. It's a vale of *dry* tears." She looked at Jimmy Teeth.

"Yes'm," he said. "Good 'ade." He thought that this woman was likely too square for him. She had probably not gotten any further in the video age than, say, Pac-Man and Donkey Kong, if that. She had on some kind of sweater without buttons.

"Do you understand?" she was saying. "A vale of dry tears stands in relation to true weeping as dry cleaning stands to true washing and cleaning."

"Yes'm, I got that."

They sipped their drinks, and Jimmy Teeth feared that the thing had gone this far and yet might not work—how could it do that? Where would he begin anew, with whom? Talk about a vale of dry tears—when Mrs. Hollingsworth again extended her hand to him, only this time it was flat on the table, palm up. The only thing he could figure to do was cover it with his, noting his dirty fingernails and thinking his mother was right in her constant fingernail vigilance. Mrs. Hollingsworth covered his hand with her other one and pressed their hands together and Jimmy Teeth felt something he had not yet felt in all the considerable feeling of himself he had done to date. He felt a surge of something like liquid that came up warmly into his shoulders and head and almost made him cry.

Mrs. Hollingsworth looked down at the table between her arms, and Jimmy Teeth thought *she* was going to cry. But she did not. He sat there for what seemed a very long time, knowing he could not move his hand but not knowing what else he could or couldn't do. He thought for the first time, what if someone comes in? He didn't have a lawn mower and his suit was in the garbage. Explain *that*. Jimmy Teeth could explain a few things, but he couldn't explain that. Mrs. Hollingsworth was, like, *praying* still, and he had time to think how he might try to explain his presence. My lawn mower's *impounded* and my suit's *compacted*. It was funny if you said it like that, and he laughed. The laugh was like the other inappropriate moments they had already shared: it wasn't inappropriate. They had a little territory here that was, apparently, unique: nothing was inappropriate. Jimmy Teeth saw that. Mrs. Hollingsworth saw that, too, though in an ironic light.

She was not praying. She was thinking. She was thinking that in this bog of impropriety she was preparing to take Jimmy Teeth and herself into, there was only one truly immoral mire, and that was to act *older* than he was. She could *be* older, she could be more experienced, she could take him in ten minutes where he'd take ten years to get on the streets of sex, and that would be that, but if she pulled rank, if she mothered him or protected him or even counseled him, she would be as wrong as the book on this sort of thing said she was. Jimmy Teeth's presumed maturity, the young manliness that dared him into her life with his speaking pumpkin head on a fence and his trembling string-sized legs pushing stolen internal combustion all over her expensively landscaped, highly mortgaged family estate, would be the terra firma for their slouching into a swamp as potentially messy as this one.

"Jimmy," she said, looking him in the eye and despite herself feeling a tenderness for another human being she had not felt in a long time, "Jimmy, I'm going to show you something."

"Yes!" Jimmy Teeth said, making them both laugh.

"Jimmy, first, if I raise you from five dollars to, say, eight, for the lawn, you won't tell Mr. Hollingsworth, will you?"

"That would be a private matter between you and me," Jimmy Teeth said.

"And Jimmy?"

"Yes'm?"

"Do you go trick-or-treating?"

"No'm, I quit that."

That was the right answer. Mrs. Hollingsworth made herself another drink. Jimmy was free to pour himself another lemonade if he wanted one. From there on, Jimmy Teeth was on his own. Mrs. Hollingsworth was not on her own, but to the extent that she became Janice Halsey again, which was a journey that partook of Orpheus's ascent from the underworld with instructions to not look back, with some comical but not ungratifying sex mixed in, she was on her own, too.

Alice Adams

THE HAUNTED BEACH

The room, in this old, west-coast Mexican resort hotel, is unspeakably shabby: a window broken, the bedside table precariously leaning sideways—and not entirely clean. Led there by the aging, barefoot busboy, Penelope Jaspers, an art dealer, and Ben Bowman, a superior court judge, both from San Francisco, exchange a heavy look. In the bathroom, which is not quite as bad as she feared, Penelope, who had requested this particular room (she has been here before, though not for several years), tries a faucet: no water. And then back in the bedroom she finds no electricity. She can see from Ben's face, and his stance, that he is prepared to tough it out if she is, but Penelope has more at stake in this trip, for her a possibly dangerous return to old haunts (although she has changed a lot since then, she feels) and so she rather quickly decides that discomfort will be less than no help. She tells the busboy, Alfonso, who does not seem to remember her (or is he being tactful?), "Things don't seem to work in this room, Alfonso. Could we see another?"

Alfonso does not recognize Penelope; they look so much alike, these North American women. Pale and too thin, they dress either in pants or in immodest bathing costumes. This particular light-haired woman has a smile more pleasant than the rest, and her voice is soft—he thinks that he may have seen her before, although with a taller husband, who had no beard. North Americans quite frequently exchange their husbands and wives with each other, he has been told. Nevertheless, as pleasantly as he can, he tells the woman, whose Spanish is fairly good, for a gringo, that he will return to the desk for another key, he will show them another room.

Penelope and Ben smile at each other, quickly, tentatively, and she tells him, with a gesture, "This room, with the Farquhars in it, you can't imagine the difference. They always came for a month, you know, and put their things around." Not telling him, And Charles and I were in the room next door. Ben "knows" about Charles, a painter; knows that she came here with him often, and that she felt "terrible" when she and Charles broke up (terrible for a couple of years, in fact; but now she is really okay, she has told him that too). "The room even seemed bigger," she adds.

"Empty rooms look smaller." Ben is given to such stray bits of information.

"Lucky there's another room. We hope."

"Probably. This is off-season," he reminds her.

There is another room, seemingly at the top of the flight of steps they have just come down—and which now, following Alfonso and their luggage, they climb again, in the almost stifling, unaccustomed April sunshine, among the still bravely flowering bougainvillea vines.

Happily, the new room is extremely nice. A new structure has been built over the old existing structures, over the tiers of rooms—over all of them, in fact, except the lower row, where the Farquhars, and next door Penelope and Charles used to stay. This room is large and white, with an alcove for bathing, another space for reading, lounging about, with two sofas and a table. A king-sized bed, and a broad porch out in front, with a table and chairs and hammocks—and a sweeping view of the bay, the brilliant sea and its enclosing hills of jungle trees. The sea and the view for which they have come, essentially, to this place.

And how fortunate, really, that they have this room instead of the old one that Penelope asked for, the Farquhars' room. How lucky that the lights didn't work, Penelope is thinking, and the water. If things had been just slightly better they would have stuck it out, and suffered. Ben wanting to please her, to be a good sport, and Penelope, for her pride, pretending that everything was fine. But this is perfect, she thinks. Here we are in San Bartolomeo, but not in the same room or near those rooms. It is simply a much better version of what I had before, she thinks. How fortunate, all around.

She asks Ben, "Do you want a swim?"

He smiles. "Well, why not?"

"I'm over him, really, finally, I think. If I just don't go back to Mexico I'll be all right, probably." Penelope said this to her closest friend from time to time, with decreasing frequency, in the years that succeeded her disastrous breakup with Charles, with whom she had lived for five or six years (depending on whether you counted the months of quarrelsome separations). She said it a couple of times after entering into a "relationship" with Ben, a more or less respectable, though bearded, judge. And then this spring, now about three years "after Charles," as Penelope still thought of it, she finds herself on a trip with Ben, not only to Mexico but to San Bartolomeo itself, the beautiful scene of too much, the scene of too many scenes.

What happened was an airlines deal, promotional: Go anywhere in Mexico for $199. Penelope and Ben read this, and they both began to say, Why not? we need a vacation, swimming, warm weather. In San Francisco, a long mild dry winter had been succeeded by a cold wet dark spring. And then they began to eliminate places: well, obviously not Cancun, and Cozumel's so far away. Acapulco is horrible, and Vallarta's much too crowded. Until at last Penelope said, more or less to herself, Well, why not San Bartolomeo? It's so much in my mind, I have to go back there sometime, why not now? with Ben? with whom, on the whole, she got along rather well—though not lately; lately she had felt rough edges between them.

San Bartolomeo was where every January, for a week, she and Charles struck a truce, or nearly. No really bad fights. Where everything was beautiful: the flowers; the green, encroaching jungle; the white beach and the sea. And the Farquhars, an elderly, distinguished couple, he an astronomer, she an actress, both long retired, were in the cabin next door—unlikely but close, and valued, crucial friends for wild Charles and frightened Penelope. With Carlotta and Travis Farquhar, Charles tamed down, drank less and shouted not at all; he was, in fact, his best, most imaginative, entertaining, generous and sensitive self. And beautiful, Charles was always more handsome than anyone else around. Penelope, losing fear, was more friendly and talkative than usual (she felt this to be so, with the Farquhars).

For those weeks in San Bartolomeo there had been not only the balm of the Farquhars' company but also that of the place itself, its extreme tropical, flowery, seaside beauty. The long days of nothing to do but swim and walk and eat and take naps. And make love.

The Farquhars had died a couple of years ago—as a dedicated couple will, within weeks of each other. And why, Penelope wondered in the weeks succeeding confirmation of plans for their trip, hers and Ben's, why had she so specifically asked for the Farquhars' room? Did she imagine that she and Ben (they sometimes spoke of marriage) might become, eventually, such a couple? Or did she want to be right next to, but not inside the room that she and Charles had shared so happily? (It *was* true, they had been almost always happy in San Bartolomeo.)

In any case, it did seem fortunate that they were to be in quite another room—although, on the way down to go swimming that first day, and every day after that, they walk right past that well-known row of rooms, the bottom row. Vines and bushes have been allowed to grow up almost to the porches, interfering, Penelope supposes, with the view from those rooms.

On the plane down from San Francisco, Penelope had chatted somewhat nervously to Ben, extolling the virtues and beauties of their destination—indeed, until he patted her arm and told her, "Pen, it's okay, I'm sure it will be all right."

One of the attractions described by Penelope was Rosa's Restaurant, a beach shack, at the foot of the path up to their hotel. "Rosa is wonderful," Penelope told Ben. "Very small and dark, this burnished skin. And such a great cook, the best seafood.

She's so energetic! With this slob of a husband who lolls around
in very clean clothes that probably she ironed."

As they reach the foot of the path, that first day, there indeed
is Rosa's: a concrete floor with a thatched, lean-to roof, some
tables and chairs. And, swinging out into the breeze, several
rickety cages, each housing a drowsy, shabby-looking parrot.

And there is Rosa! recognizing Penelope. "Ah, amiga!" and
rushing toward her, as Ben stands off at some distance, dis-
creetly, on the sand.

They embrace, as Penelope thinks that she had not remembered Rosa as being so small. Rosa's head barely reaches Penelope's breast. And then, still embracing Penelope, Rosa
bursts into tears. "My husband!" she cries out. "Now dead two
years!"

"Oh, how terrible. My husband died too," Penelope lies—a
double lie; she and Charles never married, and he did not die,
but ran off to Turkey, finally, with a pretty boy. She does not
understand this lie that she herself has told.

"Ah, amiga." Rosa presses her closer, and then lets go.

"My friend Ben." Penelope gestures vaguely in his direction,
as Ben, who knows no Spanish (and thus did not hear Penelope's curious untruth) smiles.

"Ah, good," says Rosa, vaguely.

"We'll see you later, we'll come down for dinner," Penelope
promises.

"Good."

But Penelope senses that Rosa has already lost interest in her.
Rosa only wanted to say that her husband had died, wanted the
drama of that moment. Her husband, the slob in his clean
freshly ironed clothes, whom Rosa loved.

Having promised, though, they do go down that night to Rosa's
for dinner, Penelope in her long white flowered dress, bought
years ago, down here, in a funny store recommended by Carlotta Farquhar. "You look really pretty," Ben tells her, as they
settle into rickety chairs, next to the view of the night-black,
half-moonlit sea.

Rosa's has all been repainted, a bright yellowish green, but
still the room seems much darker than before. At one end, the

kitchen end, a large TV set emits a murky light and a lot of noise —a Mexican talk show, dancers in frilly costumes, tambourines, guitars. Rosa and a group of assorted, T-shirted adolescents— her children, now five years older than when Penelope last saw them, all huddled, transfixed. Rosa, who used to be always rushing in and out of the kitchen.

The food is good, good fresh fish browned in garlic, but not as good as Penelope remembered it as being.

Ben asks, "Have you ever been to Hawaii?"

"No, why?" Not asking, Do you wish we were there instead? already?

"I just wondered. I used to go there a lot."

"You liked it?"

"Oh yes. With, uh, Betty."

Betty is Ben's former wife, who behaved very badly; she drank, had affairs, all that. Ben almost never speaks of her, conveniently for Penelope, who does not wish to speak of Charles. She asks him, "Do you think of going back there?"

He hesitates—what Penelope thinks of as a judicial pause. "No, I guess not," he tells her.

The group clustered at the TV set seems indescribably sad, to Penelope. She considers the life of Rosa, a life of such hard work, so many children, but successful, in a way: her own good restaurant, there on the beach. Very popular with tourists; or, she once was. But now seemingly all is ruins, in Rosa's mind, nothing is getting through to her but absence and pain, mourning, and noisome TV talk shows. Rosa is so terribly reduced that possibly she has indeed shrunk in stature, Penelope believes. In no sense is she now the woman she once was. All over Mexico, Penelope imagines, there must be women like Rosa, defeated women, bowing to sadness. The emotions that she herself felt after Charles were sufficiently like this to make her now shudder, and some shame for Rosa, for herself, for all of them makes her wish that Ben had not met Rosa in this state.

Ben and Charles are so totally unalike, as men, that Penelope almost never consciously compares them. Ben is dark, quite presentable but not handsome. He is thrifty, extremely thrifty. Intelligent rather than brilliant, tending to be quiet, almost taciturn.

Judicial. His most annoying expression, to Penelope is, "Well, I'd have to see the evidence on that."

His love for Penelope, a love to which he admits, though reluctantly, seems out of character, odd. At times Penelope can hardly believe in its truth, but then Ben is an exceptionally truthful man. She senses that he would prefer a more conventional woman, perhaps another lawyer?—but in that case what was he doing with crazy Betty?

He must wonder, it occurs to Penelope, if she is in fact thinking of Charles, and if so what in particular she remembers.

Actually, what Penelope most remembered about San Bartolomeo, in those years of not going there, was the flowers—the spills and fountains of bougainvillea, the lush profusion of bloom, in every color: pink, red, purple, yellow, orange. And the bright red trumpet vines, and other nameless flowers, everywhere.

This year, though, she notices on their way to breakfast that everything looks drier; the vines are brittle, the palm fronds yellowing. There are some flowers still, some hardy fuchsia bougainvillea, but far fewer.

Can there have been a drought in Mexico that she had not read about, along with all that country's other, increasing problems? Corruption and garbage, pollution, overpopulation and disease. Extreme, unending poverty.

In the dining room things are more or less the same. A buffet table with lovely fresh fruit, and boxes of American cold cereal. An urn of awful coffee, not quite hot. Pretty young maids, who take orders for Mexican eggs, French toast, whatever. Penelope scours the room for some maid that she knew before, but finds none, not beautiful Aurelia, or small, smart, friendly Guadalupe.

The other guests, on the whole, are younger than the people who used to come here. Younger and less affluent-looking. Many couples with small children. They are all probably taking advantage of the new cheap fares—as we are, Penelope thinks, at that moment badly missing the Farquhars, their elderly grace, their immaculate dignity. "You would have liked the Farquhars," she says to Ben—as she has several times before.

. . .

Down on the beach, the scene is much the same as always, couples or groups lounging in various states of undress around their palapas, with their bright new books or magazines, their transistors, bottles of beer and suntan lotion. Too many people. Most of the palapas are taken, the only one available to Penelope is at the foot of the steps, near Rosa's.

"There's not a lot of surf," Ben comments, as they settle into uncomfortable slatted chairs.

"Sometimes there is." Does he mean that he would rather be in Hawaii, where the surf is higher?

"Those boats look dangerous," he tells her.

Penelope has to agree. Back and forth, perilously close to the swimmers, small motor boats race by, some hauling along water skiers, others attached to a person who is dangling from a parachute, up in the sky. The boats are driven by young boys, sixteen or seventeen, from the look of them, who often turn back to laugh with their admiring girlfriends, on the seat behind them. In fact Penelope has always been extremely afraid of these boats —though Charles reassured her that they would not hit anyone (laughing: "They never have, have you noticed?"). But this year there seem to be more of them, and they seem to come in much closer than before.

A young Mexican woman with a bunch of plastic bottles, strung together, comes up to their palapa and asks if they want to buy some suntan lotion.

No, thank you.

A very small girl with enormous eyes comes by selling Chiclets.

No, thanks.

"It's odd about vendors this year," Penelope tells Ben. "There used to be lots of them, and they had some good stuff. Carlotta got some incredible necklaces. There was one in particular, a tall pretty young woman in a white uniform, sort of like a nurse. She had a briefcase full of lovely silver things. Pretty opal rings, it's where I got mine." And she spreads her fingers, showing him, again, the two opal rings, one pink and one green, with each seeming depths of fire, each surrounded by a sort of silver filigree. "About ten bucks apiece," Penelope laughs. "Augustina, her name was. I wanted to get more rings on this trip, but I don't see her."

"Why more?"

"Oh, they don't last. They dull and come apart. But I suppose I don't really need them." Though thrifty, Ben no doubt disapproves of such cheap rings, or so Penelope imagines—the wives of successful lawyers, and certainly of judges, do not wear ten-dollar rings. And in a discouraged way Penelope wonders why they have come here to Mexico together, she and Ben. Most recently in San Francisco they had not been getting on especially well; there was a string of minor arguments, the more annoying because of utter triviality—where to eat, whom to see, what to do—arguments that had left them somewhat raw, on edge. It comes to Penelope that she must have expected some special Mexican balm, she must have thought that somehow Mexico would make everything come right, would impart its own magic. And she thinks, Alas, poor Mexico, you can hardly heal yourself, much less me.

"Well, how about a swim?" Ben stands up, so trim and neatly made, in his neat khaki trunks, that Penelope sighs and thinks, He's so nice, and generally good, do I only truly like madmen, like Charles? Even as she smiles and says, "Sure, let's go."

As always, the water is mysteriously warm and cool at once, both nurturing and refreshing and green, glittering there for miles out into the sunlight. But perhaps not quite as clear as before? Penelope thinks that, but she is not entirely sure.

Despite a passing motorboat, this one lolling at low speed, its owner smiling an invitation, drumming up trade—Ben strikes out into deep water, swimming hard. For an instant Penelope thinks, Oh Lord, he'll be killed, that's what this ill-advised (probably) trip is all about. But then more sensibly she thinks, No, Ben will be okay. He is not slated to be run over by a Mexican motor-boat (or is he?). She herself, more and more fearful as another boat zips by, this one trailing a large yellow inflated balloon, astride which six young women shriek and giggle— Penelope moves closer to a large, wave-jumping group of Americans for protection.

.   .   .

She persuades Ben to go back to Rosa's for lunch, but the day scene there is even more depressing than what goes on at night: the same blaring TV, same group clustered in front of it—in broad daylight, the sun streaming outside on the beach, the lovely sea not twenty yards away. Rosa hardly looks up as they come in. And the food is indifferent.

Walking up the path to their room, Penelope observes, again, the row of empty rooms. And she remembers an elderly couple, the Connors, friends of the Farquhars, who always took the room on this end, that nearest to the path, and they sat there, calling out to their friends who passed. The lonely old Connors, now very likely dead. But how easy to imagine them sitting there still, he with his binoculars, she with her solitaire cards. And, in the room after next, Penelope and Charles, and in the next room the Farquhars. It seems impossible, quite out of the question, for all those people to have vanished. To have left no trace, in this air.

Instead of saying any of that to Ben (of course she would not) Penelope says, "I do wonder how come Augustina's not around anymore. Her things were great, and she was so nice."

During their siesta Penelope has a most curious dream—in which she and Charles and Steven, Charles's beautiful boy, are all good friends, or perhaps she and Charles are the happy parents of Steven. The dream is vague, but there they are, the three of them—cornily enough, in a meadow of flowers. And, as Penelope awakes, the even cornier phrase, "Forgiveness flowers," appears somewhere at the edges of her mind.

Nevertheless, it seems a cheering, on the whole restorative dream, and she awakens refreshed, and cheered.

That night she and Ben walk into the town for dinner, a thing that she and Charles almost never did, and they find the town very much as it was: dingy, rutted, poorly lit streets leading toward the center, along which wary old men loiter, sometimes stopping to rest on the stoop of a darkened house, to smoke a cigarette, to stare at the night. Then stores, small and shabby at first, little groceries, ill-equipped drugstores, with timid souvenirs, faded postcards, cheap cosmetics. And then more light, larger and gaudier stores. More people. The same old mix of tourists, always instantly identifiable as non-Mexican. And Mexicans, mostly poor, some very poor, beggars, pitiful dark thin women, holding babies.

At their chosen, recommended restaurant, no table will be available for half an hour. And so Ben and Penelope go into the small, white, rather austere church that they have just passed. A mass of some sort is going on, a white-robed priest is at the altar, everywhere there are white flowers. Penelope and Ben take back-row seats, and she watches as three little girls clamber all over their mother, who prays, paying them no heed. The girls and their mother wear church-going finery, black skirts and embroidered white shirts, and all the family black hair is braided, beautifully. Whereas, the more Anglo-looking (less Indian) families in the church are dressed more or less as tourists are, in cotton skirts or pants, camp shirts, sandals.

Their dinner, in an attractive open court, is mildly pleasant. A subdued guitarist plays softly in one corner; there is everywhere a scent of flowers.

"Do you really think we should marry?" Ben asks, at some point.

At which Penelope more or less bridles. "Well no, I'm not at all sure, did I say that I did—?"

He pauses, just slightly confused. "I didn't mean you had, but —well, I don't know."

She laughs, "You mean, not in Mexico."

He looks less nervous. "Oh, right." He laughs.

The next morning, very early, Ben says that he wants to swim. "Before those damn boats are around," he quite reasonably says. "You too?"

"I don't think so." What she wants is just to lie there for a while, savoring the Mexican dawn, just now visible between the drawn window draperies. "I'll come down in a little while."

"Leave the key in the blue sack, okay?"

Penelope lies there, deliciously, for ten or fifteen minutes. Ben will want to swim for close to an hour, she knows. She lies there, thinking of nothing—and then she puts on her bathing suit, a red bikini, puts the room key in the small blue airline bag, and starts down the path—down past the empty row of rooms where they all used to stay (it now seems very long ago), past Rosa's restaurant, and out onto the beach, where she leaves the bag with the key on a table, beneath one of the palapas. And she steps out into the water, the marvel of cool, of freshness. She thinks she sees Ben's dark head, far out to sea, but what she sees could as easily be a buoy.

She swims for a while, fairly sure that dark head is indeed Ben's. She waves, and whoever it is waves back. Looking to shore, for the first time she notices a sign, Tourist Market, and she wonders what that is. She heads back in, stands up and starts walking out of the water, up onto the beach.

She is trying to remember which palapa table she put the bag on, and does not remember. She does not see the bright blue bag on any table.

And slowly it registers on Penelope's frightened consciousness that the bag is not there. Gone. No key to the room. At the same moment, the moment of realizing her loss, she sees an old man, a sort of beach bum, wrapped in something orange, rags, hobbling down the beach. And Penelope, wildly out of character, for her, now thinks: I have to run after him, I have to chase that old man, who must have my key. Whether I get it back or not I have to run after him.

And so she does. She starts off down the beach, running as best she can, but clumsily, in the deep dry sand.

She is unused to running, but the man ahead of her is very old. She is gaining on him, as suddenly he veers off the beach, to the left, and into the Tourist Market. Where Penelope follows, not far behind.

Getting closer, she begins to shout: Stop! stop!

The market is a row of booths, now mostly empty, so early in the morning, but here and there a solitary figure pauses, putting aside a broom or a dusting cloth, a crate—to observe this chase. Penelope imagines herself, as she must look: a tall blonde skinny American woman in a red bikini, chasing after a poor old man, a derelict, hysterically shouting. Why should anyone help her?

But there, ahead of her, at the end of the row of rickety booths, to her surprise she sees the old man wheel and turn. He is standing there on one leg, a tattered old bird, maybe too tired to keep on running.

His dark, grizzled face is all twisted, one eye is gone, the skin closed over, and most of his teeth are gone. His mouth contorts, and the bright remaining black eye stares out at Penelope. A dying Aztec, she thinks. She thinks, *Mexico,* I should not have come back here.

Over one of the old man's shoulders a large old brown leather sack is slung, zipped up. In which there must be her blue bag. Her room key.

But what she (ridiculously) says is, "Did you happen to see my bag? on the table?"

"No—" His voice is tentative, querulous, but his eye is challenging, accusing, even. Perhaps it was not he who took her bag, but someone else, earlier, while she was swimming.

Penelope finds no way to say: Open your sack up, let me see what you have inside. How could she?

She says again, "My blue bag, are you sure you didn't see it?"

"No." He turns from her.

Defeated, Penelope begins to walk back through the market booths, past a sort of workers' restaurant, just opening up, past more booths, with jewelry, scarves, leather—to the beach.

Where bearded Ben is getting out of the water. Shaking himself, like a dog.

He frowns a little at what Penelope tells him, but then he says, "Well, it's not too bad. We'll go up to the room, and you wait there while I go up to the desk for another key. They should have given us two. As I said."

However, after the fifteen or twenty minutes that Penelope has been standing there in the hallway, outside their room, in the gathering heat of the day, Ben comes back to inform her that it is not so simple, after all. They don't *have* another key. "Honestly, Mexico. Someone has gone to find the housekeeper. God knows how long that will take. It's Sunday, remember?"

Since there is no existing key to their room—many keys have been lost, they are told, or simply not turned in—the only solution to a keyless room is for Penelope and Ben to move into another room. Which, once the housekeeper has been found (an hour or so) and their old room wrenched open, they finally do: with the help of several maids they repack and move all their clothes.

The new room is lower down, and smaller, with less of a view. Not as nice.

However, they are only here for two more days. Ben and Penelope, over their much-delayed breakfast, remind each other of this fact.

That old man with his rags, his toothless twisted mouth and his one defiant eye is in Penelope's mind all that day, however. How angry he must have been, she thinks, if he opened the blue bag, expecting money, to find nothing but an old key.

And was it, after all, that old man who took the bag, or someone else, some other stroller on the beach who had vanished in another direction before Penelope got out of the water?

That night in the bar a young woman, another American whom they have seen around, with her fat young husband and two very fat small children, comes up to them to say, "Are you the guys who lost a blue flight bag, with your room key? My husband found it, in back of that tourist market, and he couldn't find anyone to claim it, so he turned it in at the restaurant there. Just go and tell them it's yours."

The next morning Penelope, dressed, sets out for the Tourist Market. She approaches it from a back road she knows that passes Rosa's, and leads to the corner where she and the ragged old man confronted each other. Where now for a moment she pauses, imagining him, and she looks around, as though he might have come back, and be lurking around. But of course he is not, there is only the road, and back of the road the yellowing jungle brush, in the beating Mexican sun. Penelope continues to the restaurant.

A pleasant-faced, plump young woman tells her, "Oh yes, your bag. Right here."

Penelope thanks her very much, gives her some pesos, and walks on with her bag, in which she can feel the room key, still there. And she thinks again of the old man, how angry he must have been to find only a key. Crazily, for a moment this seems to Penelope unfair; she even thinks of trying to find that old man, to give him some money—and she smiles to think of what Ben would make of that gesture, combining as it would two of her (to him) worst qualities: thriftlessness and "irrationality."

She continues through the booths, until she is stopped by a display of rings. She bends over, as always hoping for opals—

and sees that there are several: opal rings of just the sort that she likes, the lovely stones with their fiery interiors.

A pretty Mexican woman in a yellow sweater, dark skirt asks if she can help. These rings are about twenty-five dollars for two, but still so cheap! and so pretty. Penelope feels a great surge of happiness at having found them. The rings seem a good omen, somehow, though she is not sure of what: of this trip? she was right, after all, to come back to Mexico, and to this particular place?

Negotiations with the young woman concluded, rings chosen and pesos paid, Penelope then asks her, on some whim, "Did you ever know a very nice woman who used to sell jewelry along the beach, named Augustina?"

"But I am Augustina!!" *Yo soy Augustina.* The woman laughs, and the two of them embrace.

"Ah, amiga," says Augustina.

"I didn't recognize you, you always wore that white uniform," Penelope tells her. "I bought these rings from you!" and she shows Augustina her hand.

"Amiga, this time you come back very soon," Augustina says.

"Oh, I will. Very soon. Augustina, thank you." And with her rings, and the bag with its key, Penelope walks back to the hotel.

Their new room, she realizes as she goes out onto the balcony for a dry bathing suit, directly overlooks the old tier of rooms, where once she stayed with Charles, next door to the Farquhars.

On their last night in San Bartolomeo, Ben and Penelope have dinner in the hotel dining room, where, as always, the food is very bad—and the view magnificent: glittering black water, down through palm fronds. Stars, and a partial moon.

"Well, it's not the worst place I've ever been," is how Ben sums up their trip. Judiciously.

"It was really okay," Penelope tells her closest friend, a couple of days later, on the phone. "I'm glad we went. As a matter of fact I hardly thought about Charles. He wasn't there." Then she laughs. "Actually I didn't think much about Ben either. I don't think he liked it very much there. But I thought a lot about

Mexico." And then she adds, "But not thinking about Charles is the same as thinking about him all the time. If you see what I mean."

The friend does see.

"Anyway, the trip made me feel a lot better," Penelope continues. "About everything. More free." She adds, with a laugh, "I can't think why."

Elliot Krieger

CANTOR PEPPER

No one wanted to admit this, but everyone was happy when the old cantor announced that he was going to retire. And the rabbi was happiest of all. Rabbi Alan Salt liked to think of himself as a progressive, part of the flying wedge of Reform Judaism, a man destined to turn things around at Temple B'nai Israel, to leave a mark, and Cantor Lemon—that was the rabbi's nickname for the old cantor, his own little joke about the cantor's dreadful voice —didn't fit in with his plans. Rabbi Salt had been at the temple for only two years, but he had already begun to make the place over in his image. The art in the offices, for example, was more dashing—abstract and postmodern and no longer the heavy, al- legorical, pseudo-Chagallian primitives that made the place feel so gloomy and thick with Eastern European pessimism. And it wasn't just the look of things. The whole mood of the temple was changing, the rabbi could feel it. The board of trustees seemed ready to hear his proposal to sponsor an annual inter- faith pastoral retreat at the Jewish Y camp in the Poconos, and the board liked his idea of pushing hard to put all the young girls in the congregation on the track toward a bat mitzvah. Good for the catering business, anyway, said one of the senior board members, a restaurateur.

But Temple B'nai Israel still had a long way to go. Despite

Rabbi Salt's best efforts, his witty sermons filled with references to the Mets and the Beatles, his movie-star good looks, his occasional appearances on the Sunday morning TV show *Ethical Forum*, Temple B'nai Israel was slipping in the ratings. Membership had leveled off, and some of the younger families, while remaining on the books, had begun to drift away. Men's club and Hadassah meetings were becoming more geriatric, and the building fund never recovered from the decision made five years ago—foolish, most now agree—to build a new Hebrew school adjacent to the old temple. Now, as Rabbi Salt well knew, the temple was wedded to its present site, on an old street of long-ago elegance in the deteriorated city of East Orange, where the doorman apartments had been turned into public housing, the department stores had gone discount, the movie theaters had turned to skin houses or Baptist churches, and the Jews had fled in a mass exodus to the hills, to the new temples that had sprung up (ugly, to his mind, like great engineered gashes of glass and steel) among the swank suburbs on Orange Mountain.

Frankly, in his lower moments, Rabbi Salt couldn't blame them for switching allegiances to the brand new Beth El, with its indoor/outdoor health spa and drive-thru Kosher Kafeteria, or the migratory Temple Shalom, which had sold its landmark Newark synagogue building to the New Jersey Dental College for conversion to labs and now sat at the very top of the mountain in a massive structure modeled on the TWA terminal at Kennedy. He'd heard the grumblings. People no longer felt safe coming in for services in East Orange. The mothers didn't want to schlep their kids all the way down there for Hebrew lessons. On the holidays, you had to park on the street, at a meter. And so on. He'd heard it all, but to Rabbi Salt these were just words, excuses, air. He knew that he could bring the temple around, make it, if not the place to be on Friday nights, at least the most talked-about reform synagogue in Essex County.

But not so long as Cantor Lemon shared the billing. The old fellow was exactly the kind of dead weight that had been dragging Temple B'nai Israel down. A stuffy Polish refugee with no command of English, the old cantor never participated in any of the temple social functions. He was shy with children and scared of teenagers. He sang everything in a kind of mournful bellow—the closest, Rabbi Salt thought to himself, that the human voice could come to the sound of the ram's horn—and he generally preferred to sing solo. "Tell me, why do we even bother hiring a choir?" Rabbi Salt used to ask in frustration Friday mornings while going over the musical arrangements for the weekend services. Calling them arrangements was an exaggeration, for the plans merely called for the old cantor to plod through one boring, predictable prayer after another, while the choir—a group of elderly Protestants from a nearby church hired by the week, who learned the Hebrew prayers phonetically, they might as well have been singing opera in Urdu for all they cared—joined in on maybe the Shema or offered some meditative humming during the silent prayer.

Yet it was clear that there was nowhere else Cantor Lemon could ever work, and that the temple had to keep him on forever, a sinecure, a charity case. Rabbi Salt had resigned himself to the situation long before the old cantor made his surprise announcement. He told Rabbi Salt guardedly, as always, that his wife had accrued unexpected tax benefits through her pension plan at the county hospital, and they were hoping to retire to the Arizona desert. His leaving seemed at first like a golden opportunity, a godsend Rabbi Salt might have called it if he'd believed in answered prayers, a chance at last to bring in the kind of musical direction that the temple needed to enter the modern age. Rabbi Salt's smoldering dream of becoming a great modern rabbi, of leading a benighted congregation of Philistines into the light of modern culture, was rekindled. Maybe a new cantor would use Hebrew folk melodies as part of the services, maybe they could bring in the Newark Symphony and Chorale to stage a performance of Mendelssohn's *Elijah*. Yes, that could be the entire service some Friday night, completely defiant of tradition, maybe the *Star-Ledger* would cover it on the religion page.

But hiring a cantor proved to be no simple matter. It seemed that Rabbi Salt had no idea how the job market for cantors had turned around. When he was in school, cantors used to go begging for jobs—any temple, anywhere. There were unemployed cantors driving cabs and tending bar, right along with the out-of-work actors and eternal graduate students on the Upper West Side. Rabbi Salt learned how the world had changed, though, when he called his old friend, associate dean now at the Institute, and he got the word: impossible.

"Alan," the dean told him. "Don't even think about it. Do you know how many cantors I graduated this year?" Rabbi Salt didn't know. "Just two. Think of it. When you were here—what was it? Not so long ago, right?—how many cantors would you say graduated with you?" Rabbi Salt recalled them, a group of sour-smelling fellows, many of them stoop-shouldered or pockmarked, who huddled at the bottom of the grade curve in the Hebrew and religion courses. Four dropped out after the first year and achieved some fame, or perhaps notoriety, by forming Manhattan's best Jewish barbershop quartet, the Peyas. He guessed about two dozen cantors finally graduated.

"Now," the dean said, "the word is, if you're in it for the long haul, go for broke. Become a rabbi. No one wants anymore just to sing. They want to run the whole schmear—youth groups, bond drives, the works. Can you blame them? Of course not. So my two cantors, they get to choose. Picky picky. One's going to Los Angeles, cantor to the stars. The other fellow, very good-looking, a bachelor, he's running services on a cruise ship. A Jewish love boat. Alan, I'd help you if I could, but East Orange, I can't even think who might want that kind of job."

The board of trustees wasn't happy to hear the news from Rabbi Salt. What's the matter with this temple, a lovely building, a strong congregation with a long tradition, and so on. They couldn't see it, and, for that matter, neither could Rabbi Salt. All those cantors he graduated with were working now, probably, or off on other careers, junk bonds or leveraged buyouts or something, not driving a cab or waiting tables at the West End Grille. But maybe the temple could become a sort of West End Grille or Checker Fleet, a place of succor for a young musician looking for work. Maybe they could hire someone not yet certified, and help a needy student on his way. Come to think of it, Rabbi Salt thought, the more they know, the more of a nuisance they'll be, always wanting to do things their own way. And why, he began to wonder, would any seminary kid with gumption, career Jews they used to call themselves, even train to be a cantor today? Why bring someone in here to work whose highest aspiration had been to play second fiddle? He decided to hire not a cantor but a musician, the best young Jewish talent that he could find.

That afternoon Rabbi Salt hopped into his Toyota and drove to the city to hand-deliver the job notice to the placement office at the Juilliard School of Music:

VOCALIST WANTED
TO LEAD SERVICES AT A PROGRESSIVE NEW JERSEY SYNAGOGUE.
Familiarity with Jewish musical tradition a plus.

Rabbi Salt looked at his notice and found it good. He signed it, left it with the receptionist, and, moved by a phrase he heard emanating from one of the practice rooms, ambled back to his car whistling a Mozart aria. He was so pleased with himself that he almost forgot that it was Friday.

For the next two weeks, Rabbi Salt waited for replies to his notice. Two students called him. The first lived far off in the Bronx, too far to commute. He had no car and was reluctant to navigate the Garden State by train and bus. The second student sounded promising—a rabbinical-school dropout trying to forge a career as a conductor. But he'd be going to Germany on a spring-semester fellowship, and Rabbi Salt decided to hold out for someone who could give the temple at least a few years and, who knows?, if it works out might decide to stay with the profession.

Exactly two weeks almost to the hour—it was mid afternoon on a crisp fall Friday and Rabbi Salt was reading the *New Republic* in his study, polishing his sermon on aid to Israel—a rap on the inner door, surprising because that door led directly to the pulpit, startled Rabbi Salt in mid-sentence. At the door stood a nearsighted, gangly fellow, nicely dressed—Oxford shirt and tie, corduroy jacket a little threadbare at the elbows, pressed jeans, penny loafers—carrying some books and sheet music. "I saw your ad," the young man said. "About the singer? I think I'd like to try for the job. I'm, you see, I'm at Juilliard?" Rabbi Salt stared at the fellow, first amazed, then perplexed. Sure, he thought, I really need someone for this cantor's job, and if this guy were right I'd hire him on the spot. But there was one very obvious problem. The man was black.

"Okay. Fine. Step in," Rabbi Salt said, flustered, but doing his best to cover up his reaction. "So you think you'd like to work as a cantor?"

"Well, what I like to do, what I'm, I mean, trying to do, is sing," he said.

"Yes, well, that's what I mean. The cantor leads the singing in our Jewish services, which we have here. He's the lead singer, you might say." The young man smiled a little.

"What I'm studying," he said, "is opera. But any music is something I can do."

The fellow—his name was Wilson Wyatt—spotted the job notice on the placement-office bulletin board and copied it down because of the East Orange address. Wyatt was an East Orange kid, living with his parents in an apartment in the Brick Church neighborhood. He told Rabbi Salt that he'd gone to Clifford Scott High, then done a year at Uppsala College, before transferring to Juilliard. He needed the money, and few jobs of any sort, much less jobs in the music field, ever opened up in East Orange. He knew, of course, no Hebrew and next to nothing about Judaism, but he said he was, and he surely looked to be, a quick study. Rabbi Salt rummaged in his files and found one of the crib sheets that the old cantor had prepared for the all-Gentile choir, a simple, sonorous arrangement of the Shema, with the Hebrew written phonetically, and Wyatt sang through it almost perfectly—he didn't come close on *echod,* but what do you expect?—on sight. Rabbi Salt was facing a tough decision.

He'd been almost two months now without a cantor. Bad as old Lemon was, a cantor brought a necessary dignity to the services. Rabbi Salt felt awkward and somewhat diminished trying to perform both roles, as if leading the congregation in song detracted from his capacity to lead it in prayer. He wanted badly to hire a cantor, and he had no further leads, no new nibbles. But a black man—it was risky enough even to think of hiring a Gentile, although that line had already been crossed, so to speak, with the choir. A Gentile cantor, Rabbi Salt had figured, would be a change in degree rather than in kind. A black cantor, though, was another matter. He would always be before the congregation, a reminder of their diminished stature, a symbol of the precarious condition of contemporary Judaism. But wait, Rabbi Salt thought. That might be exactly what this congregation needs to shake it from its lethargy. Here we sit, in the midst of a black city, and we've done nothing but turn inward, creating our own ghetto within a ghetto. Maybe it's time we reach out, Rabbi Salt thought, to our neighbors. A black cantor, a Cantor Wilson Wyatt, was the perfect way to announce to the community of East Orange that Temple B'nai Israel would not be following the Jewish migration to the hills. This temple was here to stay.

Rabbi Salt quickly found phonetic prayers and set off on Wilson Wyatt's crash course in the Jewish liturgical tradition, and by sundown he'd coached Wyatt on the basic movements of the services, the key prayers and songs and the devilishly tricky "ch" sound, like trying to scratch an itch on your soft palate, Rabbi Salt explained.

Cantor Wilson Wyatt's first Friday-night service at Temple B'nai Israel would have to be called a success. At least, none of Rabbi Salt's worst fears materialized. As the two men stepped out of the rabbi's study onto the pulpit, Wyatt in the cantor's white robes, too short for his gangly frame, almost above the knee line like a loose chemise, Rabbi Salt felt a sudden qualm. He could imagine the congregation gasping in unison, filing out in protest. Nothing like this came to pass. Rabbi Salt had forgotten that except on bat mitzvah nights hardly anyone attended services, just the old men, so lost in their own atonal bobbing and weaving that they barely noticed who was on the altar. They didn't notice when Wyatt flipped frantically through his prayer book trying to find and to keep his place—he was reading and turning the pages from left to right—and they didn't notice Rabbi Salt flashing him cues and signs during even the simplest of Hebrew passages and they didn't notice when he sang the Shema in English. Considering how horribly everything might have gone, Rabbi Salt had to admit that things went well, although he did spot, as he was lifting his gaze and settling into the lovely recitative—"Let us adore the ever-living God . . ."—that brings the congregation gently out of the silent prayer, that one of the bleary old men who'd been praying away from a side bench was staring bug-eyed at the altar, with a look on him as if his senses had suddenly taken a turn toward the south, as he said too loud, like the Indian in the old Mel Brooks movie, "A schvartze!"

The next morning, the rabbi learned a lesson that he was not soon to forget: word travels fast. It was a routine November Saturday, no holiday, no bar mitzvahs, no world crisis or day of national mourning, but as Rabbi Salt pulled his Toyota up to Temple B'nai Israel he saw that he was going to have to park at a meter. And inside, the temple was abuzz, the congregants all gathered into little lumpy groups, tittering, tilting their heads back in laughter, turning and covering their mouths furtively as the rabbi whisked past them. At the door to the rabbi's study, Hiram Gold, president of the men's club, was shifting his weight from side to side, like an agitated boxer before the bell. He threw his meaty hands aside in an exaggerated shrug of exasperation when he caught sight of Rabbi Salt coming toward him.

"This can't be the truth, what I hear, Rabbi," Gold said. For a second, Rabbi Salt thought that Gold might cry.

"Hy, he'll be a great cantor for us. You'll hear him sing today. He's like a gift."

"But Rabbi." Hy was not convinced, and Rabbi Salt saw, knew, that nothing would convince him. "I mean a cantor who's not a Jew, this would not be so bad. Who would know, a Jew or not? But you've brought in a black man, a kid, to be our cantor."

"I've been looking for two months now, Hy, and Mr. Wyatt" —the phrase Cantor Wyatt all of a sudden felt provocative for Rabbi Salt—"he's the best."

"So we have, what do you call it, an affirmative-action policy here now, Rabbi?"

"Hy," Rabbi Salt cut him short. "I have to get ready for services."

Gold stepped back to let Rabbi Salt pass into his study. "I'm just warning you, Rabbi," he said. "Speaking for myself, in our swim club, the black boys work only in the kitchen. Never in the cabanas. And I agree with this, Rabbi. And to me, the Shabbat service, it's a little like being in a cabana with God, just me and God, and I don't want a black boy in there with us."

Saturday services always included a few moments for announcements from the pulpit—times and dates of upcoming events, progress reports on bond drives, in short, a moment when the rabbi throws off his religious mantle and speaks to the congregation as a combination social director and bulletin board. Today it was obvious what Rabbi Salt had to do: introduce Wilson Wyatt to the congregation and try as best he could to deflect criticism, to isolate the Hiram Golds and to help the rest of the members see Wyatt not just as the best that the temple could come up with, which he was, but as a great and noble beginning, a step toward forming a spiritual bond between the black and Jewish communities of East Orange. Jews centuries ago lived in peace among the blacks of Abyssinia—many believe that King Solomon himself was a black man—these were the phrases circling at a dizzying clip through Rabbi Salt's mind as he began the services. As it turned out, he didn't have to say anything.

Rabbi Salt expected to hear the elevating notes of the holiest of Jewish prayers, the Shema—he had just set the stage for Wyatt's Saturday debut with the traditional words to the congregation—"Cantor Wyatt will now lead us in singing the watchwords of our faith"—when the rabbi noticed that Wyatt wasn't singing. He was standing in front of the congregation smiling, letting them stare at him, get their fill, as he swept his gaze across the room, soaking amiably in the welling amazement, transforming the whole episode into some sort of fun, a game. And when he had basked in the sudden good will and natural curiosity as long as the moment would hold, Wyatt stood straight up, tossed back his head, and sang the proud, heroic first notes of the Shema in a voice so true and clear and full of feeling that the congregation responded with a gasp of joy. Suddenly the air in the temple seemed pure and fresh, alive with beauty and pleasure. The temple's music had been off for so long that the people had accommodated their senses, the way you come to accept a radio's static on a long night drive. But when the congregation heard its most sacred prayer sung with operatic beauty, the members felt opened and renewed, as if transported from darkness to light, delivered from bondage to gaze on a promised land of freedom and joy. When Cantor Wyatt finished singing the prayer—he even managed a credible pronunciation of *echod*—there was a momentary silence, and then something happened that the rabbi had never seen before. First from a few far corners of the room, then in scatterings here and there and quickly building to the full house, the congregation began to clap, welcoming the new cantor with the spontaneous enthusiasm of applause. Rabbi Salt was proud of his decision to hire Wyatt. He was pleased that his congregation could welcome him so heartily, could set aside suspicion, discomfort, and a history of centuries of mutual antagonism and accept this man with good manners and good humor. Rabbi Salt wouldn't have to do a thing to ease Wyatt into Temple B'nai Israel. Wyatt would do it himself.

At least that's the way it appeared from the early reviews. The more musical members of the congregation were delighted with Cantor Wyatt's singing, such an improvement over poor old Lemon's bellows. One elderly lady, Mrs. Murdoch, a Met subscriber, told Rabbi Salt that the new cantor was a young Jussi Bjoerling, a star tenor someday sure thing. She said that she would be coming to Friday evening services from now on, Cantor Wyatt's singing was better than WQXR. Mrs. Murdoch wasn't the only one. Attendance was picking up at all the services, and the spirit of the congregation was, too. Cantor Wyatt brought a liveliness to prayer, a commitment you might say, that Rabbi Salt had never seen before. He had the congregation members up on their feet, singing the Shema every bit as loud as they'd belt out a drunken Dayenu at the end of a Seder, and he brought the congregation to a hushed stillness when he'd softly toll the sorrowful drumbeat notes of the Kol Nidre.

Cantor Wyatt began showing up at temple youth-group meetings Wednesday nights—attendance was picking up there, too— and the reports that Rabbi Salt was hearing were great. The new cantor, they said, was a natural with kids, a leader, full of enthusiasm and ideas. He was arranging a field trip to bring some temple teens to a Saturday matinee at the Met. Rabbi Salt turned the other cheek and let the trip pass, even though it was on Shabbas. The more culturally attuned temple kids began teaching Wyatt some Jewish folk melodies and Israeli dances. He said that he'd try to incorporate the folk melodies into the Friday-night services. By the end of November, he'd composed an entire Sabbath service based on traditional Jewish folk tunes, and he'd drawn the whole youth group—some twenty-three teenagers—into regular attendance at services. He brought four kids up to the pulpit with him one evening, before the blessing of the Torah. They joined hands and did a kicking, whirling sort of dance, to the delight of the whole congregation, which by now included many of the parents. Word of the revitalized, imaginative services reached the Essex County Jewish weekly, the *Jewish News,* and a reporter came out one Friday and wrote a feature that the *News* ran on its cover beneath a banner head: "Hallelujah! They sing and dance at Temple B'nai Israel, but the walls don't come tumbling down." The reporter tactfully played down the fact that Cantor Wyatt was black, but the *New York Times* stringer who picked up the story and turned it into an "Our Towns" feature on the Metro front played the race angle big: "Temple dances as black man calls the tune. And why not? He's the cantor."

Rabbi Salt had been trying for two years to get a story about Temple B'nai Israel into the *Jewish News*—the *Times* was beyond his dreams—and he was, he had to admit, a little out of joint that neither story had much to say about him. So he was already a little grumpy, and a little guilty for feeling so, when he was disturbed by a gentle tapping at his study door. It was Mr. Hall, a tall, pale man with red-rimmed eyes and thinning hair, the leader of the all-Gentile choir. Rabbi Salt waved him into the small office—it seemed to him that none of the choir members had been in the study before—and offered him a seat. Mr. Hall declined.

"Thank you, but if it's all right with you, Rabbi Salt, I'd prefer to stand." Mr. Hall, Rabbi Salt noticed, spoke in a thin sort of voice, as if he had to reserve all of his energy for singing. Rabbi Salt found Mr. Hall's exaggerated, deferential formality to be irritating.

"That's all right then, Mr. Hall, suit yourself." Mr. Hall just then brushed some lint from his lapel. "What can I do for you?"

"Rabbi Salt." Mr. Hall began as if he had prepared a speech. That was usually a bad sign, Rabbi Salt had learned. "The other choir members and I have come to feel, have come to the position that we cannot work with your cantor any longer."

"Is there something wrong with Cantor Wyatt's music?" Rabbi Salt asked, somewhat ingenuously.

"Well, no, not exactly wrong," Mr. Hall reedily replied, his voice edging toward a wheeze. Perhaps he smoked. "But we can't keep up with his demands, Rabbi Salt. He has new scores every Friday night. He has us singing prayers we never knew existed. Now he wants us to begin rehearsals for a Friday night performance of Mendelssohn's *Messiah*."

"*Elijah*."

"Certainly. But Rabbi Salt, it's more than we bargained for and it's more than we're capable of, we think. We all have been very comfortable working here, Rabbi Salt. But not anymore. I'm sorry, but we won't be coming back here after this Saturday's services." Mr. Hall was kneading his fingers, as if he were crumpling papers or twisting a hat. He seemed to be waiting for Rabbi Salt to countermand him.

Suddenly, Rabbi Salt found himself pushed into Cantor Wyatt's corner. He'd never much liked Mr. Hall and his blue-stockinged, nasal, old-lady choir anyway, the perfect patsies for old Cantor Lemon. Naturally they felt unequal to the demands— real musical demands—imposed on them by Wyatt.

"I'm sorry, Mr. Hall," Rabbi Salt said. "You have given us so many beautiful evenings over the years, and you and the others were such a blessing to Cantor Lem"—he caught himself—"to the old cantor, that I will be sorry to see you go. But if you feel that way . . ."

". . . unless something can be worked out, Rabbi Salt . . . ?"

". . . then I'll just wish you the best of luck." Rabbi Salt stood and ceremoniously shook Mr. Hall's damp hand. Mr. Hall, nodding slightly, backed his way out the door to the corridor. Rabbi Salt was holding a copy of the *Times*. During the conversation, he'd rolled it tight, like a club. But now he felt lightheaded, giddy, as if he'd just shed some care or responsibility. He wished that he could just hop in his Toyota and drive somewhere, maybe the shore, not exactly to get away, but to exalt in solitude, to pray, for once, silent and alone.

Oddly, Cantor Wyatt seemed put out by the defection of the all-Gentile choir. "Why would they do that? Everything was going fine. They never said a word about it to me." He covered the ground again and again, with Rabbi Salt, with anyone who'd listen to him. Rabbi Salt feared that for Wyatt the departure felt like a strike at his tenure, as if the Gentiles detected an emptiness in him, a hollow core beneath the surface of his mellifluous phonetic Hebrew. To cheer him up and to show him that the temple didn't blame him for the loss, in fact could turn the loss to advantage, Rabbi Salt gave Cantor Wyatt his first administrative responsibility. He asked Cantor Wyatt to hire a new choir.

The next Friday night, the faithful members of Temple B'nai Israel were surprised to see, lined up alongside the ark, the All Souls Baptist Church Gospel Chorus, four men in dashikis and four women in floor-length purple robes. The all-Gentile choir had been confined to an upper loft beside the pipe organ, hidden behind a silky scrim, so their voices had wafted, disembodied and ethereal, through the temple. There was nothing disembodied about the eight black gospel singers swaying shoulder to shoulder on the crowded altar. The glow from the everlasting light pooled around the choir like a halo. This choir, Cantor Wyatt told Rabbi Salt, had a strong following in the black community and was in great demand for Sunday services, but, never having been asked to perform in a Jewish temple before, they had a wide open schedule for Fridays and Saturdays. During the week, Wyatt had run them through some simple Jewish prayers and, if Rabbi Salt liked the performance, the All Souls Baptist would double up as the Temple B'nai Israel Hebrew gospel choir.

From the first *Baruch atah adonoi* of the evening, everyone in the synagogue knew that Jewish ritual that night was being taken to new heights. The plaintive gospel notes, the exultant melodies, the holy mixture of sorrow and rapture seemed to bring out in the prayers an Old Testament richness, an exotic and fervent quality in the text that none in the congregation, numbed to their own rituals, had ever felt. "They sing our prayers," Mrs. Murdoch told Rabbi Salt, "the way David must have sung the Psalms." The members of the congregation were enthralled. They didn't know what to do, how to behave, after services. Should they weep? Applaud? Embrace one another? The choir was hired, or booked, as Rabbi Salt put it, and word spread fast, even reaching out to the H20 Jews (holidays, two only): come to the temple Saturdays, it's better than the Met.

It was getting so that every Saturday was like the high holidays: off-street parking only, and you practically had to reserve a seat. Collections were up; Rabbi Salt was considering asking the board about hiring a detail patrolman to help the traffic flow. He loved all this, the bustle and frenzy, the sense that the once-dispirited temple was being reborn, or at least rejuvenated. But Rabbi Salt also was noticing a strange, somewhat disturbing current within this great tide. At first he thought that it was an illusion; then, for a week or two, he thought that his eyes were bothering him, his vision failing, he needed a rest. But now, in this, the fifth week with the Temple B'nai Israel gospel choir, he was sure: the sea of faces before him each Friday and Saturday was becoming darker and darker in hue. He realized now the source of his confusion. He'd been looking at the crowd—like all contemporary rabbis, he was unused to crowds except at funerals and on the holidays—as if it were one big mass. When he scanned the crowd, looked at the individuals, he saw that in fact there were more blacks attending services each week. From a handful at first, people he'd assumed were related to Wyatt or to the choir members, the numbers of blacks at services had grown steadily, week by week, to the point where, hell, maybe half the crowd was black, the men without yarmulkes, the women humming along dreamily, accompanying all of Cantor Wyatt's *baruchs*. At times, the crowds got to be too much for the volunteer ushers from the men's club, wheezy old duffers in their double-knit jackets with white carnations in their lapels and lox on their breath. These men were not commanding figures, and they had difficulty conveying to some of the visitors that they were in a Jewish house of worship. In fact, Rabbi Salt noticed, the temple was looking less and less like a synagogue. During services, kids would squirm into the aisle. Teenagers would sneak out during Torah readings to smoke and to elbow one another and sing a cappella in the parking lot. Crowds began to hang around on the temple steps, at first just before and after services, but soon all through the week, joking and jiving, the kids listening to portable radios and the older boys whistling and flirting with the pretty girls on their way to and from confirmation classes.

In short, Temple B'nai Israel was no longer a place where Jews felt comfortable.

"That's what we've been trying to tell you," Mr. Rosenstein, jeweler and president of the temple board, said to Rabbi Salt at the January board meeting. "But you wouldn't listen."

"The man wouldn't hire a regular cantor, a Jewish cantor, and now look what we've got." Mr. Green looked around the room for effect, but there was nothing very alarming to see in this room, just five middle-aged Jewish men in leisure suits and Rabbi Salt, his face passive, ready to face the firing line. "We've got a temple I'm ashamed to bring my kids to is what."

"My wife won't even come to temple with me, she's afraid."

"Gentlemen, look," Rabbi Salt intervened. "I felt at the time, and I still do now, that hiring Mr. Wyatt was a gesture we could be proud of, a way of reaching out to the community, showing that Jews and blacks, people of whatever race . . ."—he was in his sermon mode now—". . . share more than their differences and . . ."

"Okay, Rabbi, differences," said the gravelly Mr. Bookbinder, known throughout Essex County as the world's oldest and most successful Fuller Brush salesman. "Differences, yes. I know these people, Rabbi, that have been coming to our services, and they're different from you and me."

"Yes, they're black and we're white, but other than . . ."

"Oh come on, Rabbi." The voice was that of Zarin, former starting linebacker at Rutgers, a charter member of the New Jersey Jewish Athletes Hall of Fame. "Wake up. It's bad enough that our temple is in the middle of East Orange and we decided, God knows why, I wasn't on the board then thank God, to build the new Hebrew school and stay here. But the temple used to be, for some of us anyway, an island in this ghetto, and look at it now. There's black kids hanging out in our lot all day and night, smoking God knows what out behind the dumpster, maybe waiting to grab the radio from your Honda."

"Toyota."

"Whatever. Or worse."

"You mean grab someone's daughter, some nice Jewish girl, a Rebecca carried off by an Ishmael, is that what you mean?"

"Rabbi Salt," Green said. "Our youth group will be having dances this spring. Do we keep black kids out? Tell them, like we're in Johannesburg, sorry, whites only?"

"And what about the basketball team," Zarin asked. "Can our black brothers play?" The team, the Stars of David, formerly a comical doormat in the Greater Orange Church League, was this year beginning to show some spirit and threatened a few of the powerhouse Baptist churches with the possibility of upset. "Try putting blacks on our team and you'll find you've started a recruiting war and Temple Beth El will sign up a team of ringers . . ."

"Niggers?"

". . . ringers, I said, out of Newark."

"Rabbi," Rosenstein said. "We'll put it to you plain. This thing has gone far enough. He goes, or you do."

Rabbi Salt knew that they were, from their point of view, correct. One of us must go, he thought to himself, as he drove to Wyatt's home. He planned to talk with Wyatt on, if not neutral ground, at least a playing field not so tilted as the tabernacle floor. One of us must go, but, as he drove along the bumpy, cobbled side streets of East Orange looking for the Wyatt family's tenement on Nutley Avenue, Rabbi Salt realized that, even this late, he didn't know who would stay.

In some parts of East Orange, the buildings that had once been gracious apartment houses with marble lobbies, doormen, canopied walkways, private garages, had degenerated into dangerous low-income projects, welfare hotels, and mental-health warehouses. But the Brick Church district, where the Wyatts lived, had not changed in twenty years. It had always been a blue-collar neighborhood of run-down tenements with rust-stained asbestos siding, dusty front yards staked out by cyclone fences, and a rubble-strewn patchwork of vacant lots criss-crossed by drooping clotheslines and telephone wires.

Mrs. Wyatt let Rabbi Salt into the apartment. He began to introduce himself, but she cut him off—"Oh no, I know who you are, Rabbi"—with an unwelcoming tone of impatience, as if she'd been expecting him to stop by for some time and were perhaps miffed that he never had.

Mr. Wyatt, wearing a porter's uniform, sat glumly in front of a TV (afternoon soaps), tapping a smoldering cigarette on the rim of a metal ashtray with a beanbag bottom. Perhaps filched, Rabbi Salt wondered. He'd never seen one for sale. He noticed that Mr. Wyatt was a thickened version of his son Wilson, the same long neck and bean-shaped head, but the whole figure distended, as if seen through a warp in glass. Rabbi Salt was about to introduce himself, but Mr. Wyatt didn't budge from his chair; he just stared at Rabbi Salt with a look of weary resignation. "My son"—baritone, Rabbi Salt noted—"is in his bedroom," Mr. Wyatt said. And just then Wilson Wyatt stepped into the room. He was wearing a robe and slippers. Rabbi Salt realized that he should have called before stopping over; he would have, if he were visiting a temple member.

"I, I'm surprised to see you here, Rabbi," Wyatt said. He waved his hands, a sweeping gesture, then shrugged, as if to apologize for the inhospitality of the setting, or of his family. "Shall I get dressed? Would you like to talk?"

Rabbi Salt was tempted to say, yes, get dressed, but he also didn't want Wyatt to feel reprimanded. "No, no, that's fine, Wilson," Rabbi Salt said. "I'm sorry I barged in like this. I won't take but a few moments."

Wyatt led the rabbi into the kitchen, and they sat in unmatched bridge chairs at the small Formica table. Mrs. Wyatt banged a few cannisters around on the counters and then huffed out to the living room. "I'm sorry, Rabbi," Wyatt said. He was sliding a glass salt shaker back and forth across the table like a hockey puck. "It's hard for my mother to see you here."

"Yes, I should have introduced myself at least," Rabbi Salt said. "Have you brought her to the temple, Wilson? I think I've seen her there, haven't I?"

"No, Rabbi. She won't go to the temple." He watched his hands as he spoke. "It's not that it's your fault or anything. She just doesn't feel she belongs there."

"I know how she feels." Rabbi Salt checked the note of bitterness in his voice. "I mean I feel," he added, "as if everyone's most at home in his own house of worship."

"I do too, Rabbi, and that's my problem, you see."

"Not exactly." He did, but he hadn't expected this turn in the conversation, and he wanted to draw Wyatt out.

"Well, when I came to you in the fall, I came like I was applying for a job. All I knew was, you needed a singer. I didn't know then what you called it, a cantor."

"Right, Wilson. You were the best man, person, to apply for the job. That's why I hired you. Irregardless of race."

"That shouldn't matter."

"But I guess I've learned, Wilson, that it does matter. Not that you couldn't do the job, so far as it is a job. But a cantor is more than a job."

Wyatt knew why the rabbi had come to call. "Rabbi, you can't complain about the way I've done the job. I've done everything you've asked of me, and more, and you know that. I don't think a Jewish cantor could have done better."

"Okay, Wilson, that's true. But there are some things I just can't ask of you. You know, being a cantor isn't just doing a job. It's an image, a role. The rabbi speaks for the temple, and the cantor tunes its soul, you might say"—sermon mode again—"and you did so, very well. So much that I don't think it was my temple anymore. What I'm trying to say, Wilson, is that if you stay there any longer, with the terrific job you're doing and all, Temple B'nai Israel won't be Jewish much longer."

"Well, Rabbi, you know," Wyatt flashed his animated smile, "you don't have to be Jewish."

"I'm afraid in my line of work you do."

"So you want me out?"

"Well, the board, the board of trustees, they just don't seem to . . . oh, hell, Wilson. Yes, I have to fire you."

Wyatt leaned back in his seat and sighed. "You know of course I saw this coming, Rabbi. It was such a, a ridiculous job for me. I was terrified when I applied. But I needed the work and, well, you know there aren't many jobs that come up in East Orange, at least not in the musical field."

"Your singing was always beautiful, Wilson."

"The music was the easy part. Of course what surprised me, Rabbi, was that I was beginning to like the Jewish part."

"Yes, that's the part I like, too."

"I think if I could get this across to my people, maybe you wouldn't lose your temple. I know you think I was leading the temple away from you, but maybe all the time I was just saving it for you, holding it in my hands, like a gift. We have so many wrong ideas about each other, you see."

Rabbi Salt was genuinely touched by this. He felt like reaching out toward Wyatt, but he knew that it would, in the circumstances, be a gesture made in bad faith. "I hope you can still do that, Wilson. But you see my position. I'm afraid you might, so to speak, destroy my temple by trying to save it."

"Rabbi, I don't think your temple was in danger of destruction so long as I was working there."

"What you think you offered us was some kind of protection?"

"No, but I mean the only party in danger," Wyatt said, "was me. I've been getting letters, unsigned letters, and some phone calls, too. They're pretty nasty, threatening, if I took them seriously, which I don't really. But still . . ."

"You should have told me, Wilson. I'd have addressed the congregation. These are problems we should have faced as a community."

"But the thing is, Rabbi, I don't know that all the letters came from the Jews. Excuse me, I mean . . ."

". . . you think it's black people who have been threatening you?"

"Maybe. Not everyone liked seeing gospel brought into the temple. Not everyone liked seeing the temple become so popular. A couple of ministers around here, I've heard, have their sights set on that building, come the day that you move off to Orange Mountain. I've heard, anyway."

"Oh, God, Wilson. We should have talked more."

"Maybe that will be possible, some time," Wyatt said.

At that point, their conversation, which had seemed to both of them so lofty, so elevated, began to float away from them, like a balloon lost against a vast white sky, and they felt, here in the tiny kitchen—harshly lit, the air thick with the pungent smell of vinegar and barbecue, cramped and uncomfortable—as if their words had risen, like prayers, leaving them moored to the earth by something as strong and immutable as gravity. Like two windup toys, they stood and shook hands, and no one watching them could have known, from their cautious and somewhat perfunctory leave-taking, all that they had been through, all that they had said. It was as though, during their talk, they had approached each other too rapidly, recklessly. And now, having reached the edge of a chasm, they stopped, for it was safer to talk to each other in these broad, vague terms, in generalities and social platitudes, from their opposite sides of the abyss.

Rabbi Salt felt uneasy about this later, as if his whole visit, the whole episode of Wyatt's cantorship, had somehow been a judgment—of the two of them, but more so of him—and he wasn't sure that he had passed. He had listened to the board members, had done their bidding, made the sacrifice that they had demanded of him, but in doing so he had shown himself to be not weaker than them but stronger, strong enough to loosen his grip on the congregation and to let it float away from him gently, like dust in the wind or like a prayer. Rabbi Salt knew that Wyatt's prophecy, if he could call it that, was correct, that the congregation could no longer hold fast against the tide of westward migration. Someday soon the board would announce that B'nai Israel would be joining its more prescient brethren in the flight to the hills. They would leave the old temple behind, perhaps, as Wyatt had said, to be reborn as a church.

Rabbi Salt drove back to the temple. It was twilight already. The streets, even the main streets, Central and Harrison, were gloomy. Men gathered in gated storefronts, passing bottles half-concealed in paper bags. The temple itself looked shabby, too, as if the urban decay all around were being sucked right into the building by osmosis. One outside wall was stained a mossy brown by rain that leaked from the gutters. The rabbi had never looked at the temple this way before, as so much like its surroundings, decrepit, yet lovely because of its vulnerability, its need. The side door was padlocked shut, protected by a heavy iron gate. Before he reached for his key, Rabbi Salt looked up and made a promise: he would remember his kin in the valley, even as he led his people up the mountain, to the promised land. And then, with a sudden flash of joy, he thought of a perfect nickname for Cantor Wilson Wyatt.

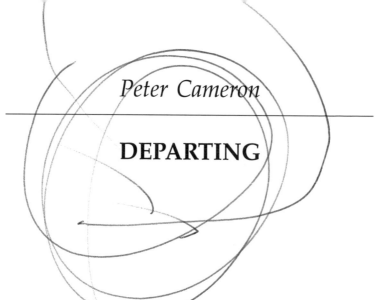

Peter Cameron

DEPARTING

Marian was far enough away from the two men to suggest, rather than guarantee, their privacy. Robert lay in the sun on the lawn; Lyle sat nearby in an Adirondack chair in the shade. Marian—their hostess—sat nearer the river, painting with a child's watercolor set. She dunked the tiny brush into a goblet of water that stood on the grass beside her.

It was a lovely yard to sit in, and to paint, although Marian's painting was not a success: the colors in the tiny compact were all wrong. They were intense and synthetic, and her attempts to mix them on the paper to suggest the sun-stunned colors around her had only muddied them. But the scene itself was lovely: the old stone house and the long lawn, studded with trees, that sloped down between high unkempt hedges toward the river.

"Take you, for instance," Marian heard Robert say to Lyle. "You look better now than you did at thirty."

"Am better looking," corrected—and conceded—Lyle. "But how do you know? You didn't know me when I was thirty."

"Marian showed me a picture," said Robert. "Of you and Tony in Egypt."

"Oh," said Lyle, "did she?"

Marian glanced up from her painting and found that Lyle was

looking over at her. He made a face. "How's the painting?" he called. Robert turned his head.

"It's a mess," she said. And then, as if such a judgment precluded its continuation, she ripped the thick, damp page from the pad and crumpled it up.

Lyle had brought the paints for Roland, his godson, the child of Marian and John. John was working in the garden beyond the hedge. Every so often they could hear him whistling, talking, or singing to himself. John enjoyed being alone on the other side of the hedge. He spent most of the summer there. Lyle was an old friend of John and Marian's and had spent countless weekends at their house with Tony, his lover. Last summer Tony had died. Lyle had been solitary and despondent all winter and spring, and everyone had urged him to get out and meet people, but no one had expected him to meet someone so quickly—especially someone as young and as unlike Tony as was Robert.

"I wanted to see it," said Lyle. He meant her painting.

"I'll do another," Marian said. "I'll do one of you two." She moved her chair and in doing so overturned the goblet. "That was careless," she said.

"I'll fill it up," said Robert. He stood and crossed the lawn.

She handed him the glass. "Thank you," she said. She expected him to walk up to the spigot beside the back stoop, but instead he walked toward the river. Of course, she thought, Robert's a stranger here: he doesn't know where the spigot is. She knew this did not make him inferior in any way but she had an urge to think so. Stop it, she told herself. She watched him squat on a rock at the river's edge, dip the glass, and return. The water was much clearer than she had imagined. It was clear, seen a glass at a time; only all together was it opaque.

"Now go lie down," she said, "and pretend I'm not here."

Robert resumed his position, but Lyle had stood up.

"Sit down," said Marian. "I'm going to paint you."

Lyle frowned at her, and she understood that he did not wish to be painted with Robert. She wondered if she had once painted Lyle and Tony. She must have, although she did not remember.

"I feel in desperate need of a nap," Lyle said. Marian and Robert watched him walk toward, and into, the house.

"I don't know how he can be tired," said Robert. "We've just lay about all day."

Lain about, Marian wanted to say, but then she remembered that Robert was young and not properly educated, so she said, "Sometimes indolence can be exhausting." She sat down in Lyle's vacant chair. She felt she should offer to paint Robert but she didn't really want to. His back, which had appeared smooth and brown from a distance, was actually, she now realized, mottled by acne scars.

"I thought Lyle brought those for Roland," Robert said, nodding at the paints.

"He did," said Marian, "but Roland is a baby. Lyle is a loving, but inattentive, godfather."

"I didn't know Lyle was Roland's godfather."

"Yes," said Marian. Tony as well, she thought.

"Lyle said he wanted Roland to be an artist. That's why he bought the paints."

"If only it were that easy," said Marian. "Or rather, thank God it's not."

"What do you want him to be?"

Roland was eleven months old and sickly. Marian wanted him to be alive the next morning. She avoided the question by asking, "Do you like children?"

Robert flipped a few pages of the magazine. "I like their hands," he said. "And feet."

Marian found this answer unnerving. It was as if she had asked him what part of the chicken he preferred. She looked away for a moment, trying to think of an appropriate response. None came to mind. "How old are you?" she asked.

"Twenty-four," said Robert. He looked at her. "I was twenty-four in June. How old are you?"

"Thirty-eight," said Marian.

"Ages are fascinating," said Robert.

He wants me to ask why, thought Marian, but I don't want to hear him tell me. It is something he has read in a book. "Where did you and Lyle meet?" she asked. She, at least, would be direct.

"At an ACT UP meeting," said Robert.

"I didn't know Lyle was going to ACT UP meetings."

"He just went to one," said Robert.

"And are you very involved? Do you go to those demonstrations?"

"Yes," said Robert. "Sometimes."

"I think it's all so terribly important, what ACT UP is doing," Marian said.

This comment was followed by an awkward silence, which Marian interrupted by saying, "I'd better check on Roland."

"Of course," said Robert, but in a way that let Marian know he knew she wanted to be away from him.

"We're so happy you're here," she said.

"So am I," said Robert.

"And we're happy to see you with Lyle," said Marian. "We're happy about that."

Robert did not respond to this comment.

"What are you doing this summer?" Marian asked. "Lyle told me you were an actor."

"Actually, I'm a painter. But I have a job."

"Really? Where?"

"As a waiter. In an Indian restaurant."

"Are you Indian?"

"Half," said Robert. "My father was Indian."

"Was?"

"Is. He lives in India."

"Do you see him?"

Robert thought for a moment, as if this question required contemplation. "No," he said. "I haven't in a while. I don't think he likes how I've turned out."

"Oh," said Marian, "that you're an actor?"

"I'm really a waiter," said Robert. "I meant he doesn't like that I'm gay."

"What a shame," said Marian.

"Would you be happy if Roland was gay?"

"Happy? Well, yes, I suppose. If he were happy."

"But you wouldn't be happy first. You'd wait for him to be happy and then be happy?"

"Actually, to tell you the truth," said Marian, "this isn't something I've given any thought to. Roland isn't even a year old. It seems a bit premature."

"Of course," said Robert. And then, after a moment, he added, "I'm sorry."

"There's no need to apologize," said Marian.

They were silent a moment. A bee alit on the lip of Marian's glass of river water, and they both observed it. She waved it away. "I'd better go check on him," she said. "We'll be eating about eight, so if you get hungry before then please help yourself to anything you can find. There's lots of fruit in the kitchen."

"Thank you," said Robert.

Robert fell asleep on the lawn, his face pressed against the magazine he had been reading, so that when he awoke, he found the page blurred. Some of the ink had rubbed off, forming a smudged, moist tattoo on his cheek. He walked up to the house. There was a large bowl of fruit on the kitchen table. He ate a peach, sucked the juice from his fingers, and went upstairs.

He passed a room where Marian sat in a rocking chair before an open window nursing Roland. They both seemed to be asleep. Roland had slipped off Marian's nipple but he worked his mouth nevertheless. Robert continued walking down the hall, thinking that every room he passed might reveal a similarly transporting sight, like a museum in a dream. At the end of the hall and down a few steps was the room he and Lyle were sharing. Robert pushed open the door, bowed his head beneath the low door frame, and entered.

Lyle was sleeping naked on the bed. The strong afternoon light infused itself through the peony-patterned curtains drawn across the windows. Robert sat on the bed. Lyle's back was sweating; Robert resisted the urge to bend over and lick it. Most of his urges concerning Lyle were resisted. He traced the indentation of Lyle's spine down into the tight valley of his buttocks. This motion, though intended to, did not rouse Lyle. And then Robert realized that Lyle was awake, and pretending to sleep: a telltale skein of tension appeared across his shoulders. Robert removed his hand. He stood beside the bed for a moment, looking down at Lyle, who continued to feign sleep. An insect could be heard but not seen in the room. Robert left the room. He went outside and stood in the front yard for a moment, and then walked up the long dirt driveway. It was a communal driveway, with tributaries leading to other houses, which, Robert supposed, made it technically a road. But it had the feel of a driveway. The paved road it adjoined was surprisingly heavily traveled. The cars went by quickly and noisily, blowing up hot storms of wind and dust as they passed. Robert turned around, but instead of walking back along the driveway he veered into the woods.

Lyle was lying on the bed, thinking of Tony, when he heard Robert come into the room. He closed his eyes. I just need a moment to compose myself, he thought. A moment. He felt Robert sit beside him, felt Robert's fingers touch and descend his back. Robert is amorous, he thought. It is both a delight and a burden. Tony would have come into the hot, still room and lay down without a word. On the other bed. But Tony is dead, Lyle told himself. It was something he told himself repeatedly and yet it never ceased to have an effect, an incessant paparazzi flash that followed him everywhere. Tony is dead and so now I am in this room with Robert. With Robert who is standing up. Who's leaving.

Lyle lay on the bed for a while, trying to think something clear and definite, but everything his mind touched seemed to lack a necessary, focusing dimension. Except for *Tony is dead*. He put on his bathing suit and a T-shirt and a pair of sandals and went downstairs. He walked out the back door and down the lawn, through a chink in the hedge, and into the garden. John was doing something fierce with a hoe: thrusting it into the ground, wriggling it, and removing it. Lyle stood outside the gate for a moment, watching John, and then he said, "You're such a hard worker. You put the rest of us to shame."

John poked the hoe into the ground and turned around. He wiped his brow with the back of his hand. "You don't really mean that," he said.

"I think you're a hard worker."

"I meant the shame part," said John. "You were never one to be intimidated by physical labor."

"I suppose not," said Lyle. "Yet one feels one should. It is so much more evident than mental labor."

John sensed a complicated conversation he had no energy for. "I'm ready for a swim," he said.

"Good," said Lyle. "So am I."

They began to walk down toward the river. "I like Robert," John said. "He seems nice."

"Yes," said Lyle. "He is nothing if not nice."

"What does that mean?" asked John, irritably, for he wanted to talk directly, and that was something Lyle sometimes had to be coaxed into doing.

Lyle sensed his impatience. "I'm doing a terrible thing."

"What?" asked John.

"I am . . . I have no business being with Robert. I'm not ready."

"How do you know?"

"I know," said Lyle. "Being here makes it awfully clear. It was very sweet of Marian to give us another room, but still. Being here with you and Marian, in summer, it's just . . . I feel as if I'm betraying Tony."

"That's to be expected," said John. They had reached the bank of the river. A slender wooden pier extended itself into the water. They walked to the end of it, carefully avoiding the planks that had lost their grips.

"I should stop seeing him," said Lyle.

"Why?"

"It isn't right. It isn't fair."

"Do you like being with him?"

"Yes," said Lyle. "I do."

"And it's obvious he enjoys being with you."

Lyle shrugged. John unlaced his sneakers and took off his shorts and underwear. He stood for a moment, naked, his toes curled around the edge of the final plank. John liked people but did not enjoy talking to them about their personal lives. It had always seemed to him an odd thing to talk about. Besides, he was no good at it. So he reached out and touched Lyle's shoulder. "Relax," he said. "That's why you're here." He dove into the river. He didn't resurface until the stain of his entrance had been absorbed. He had swum out very far. Lyle considered for a moment shedding his bathing suit, but did not. His dive was less exact.

. . .

Robert came out of the woods onto the bank of the river. Lyle and John were swimming out in the middle. Or not swimming —treading water, being slowly carried downstream with the current. Robert stood for a moment, watching them, wondering what to do. Should he call out? Should he join them? Or should he disappear back into the woods? That would be the easiest thing, he thought, the weakest, the most characteristic of me. But once he realized that, he could not do it without shaming himself, so he took off his clothes and waded out into the river. He held his arms up in the air and felt the chill ascend his body. The mud was slimy and unpleasant beneath his feet. He dove into the water with enough noise and force so that when he surfaced both John and Lyle were looking toward him. He tried to wave at them while he swam but the movement was awkward. He was a mediocre swimmer and the distance to them was greater than he had thought. He arrived at their side breathless.

"There you are," said Lyle, as if John and he had been searching the river for him.

"I went for a walk," Robert said, between gasps, "and then saw you swimming. So I joined you."

"Good idea," said John.

"It's beautiful," said Robert.

They were all three silent for a moment. Robert had the feeling he had interrupted something. "I think I'll swim to the other side," he said.

"You'd better get your breath back first," said John.

"I'm fine," said Robert. "It's just the cold that makes me pant." He began swimming to the opposite shore. When he turned around, John and Lyle were swimming toward the house. Robert floated on his back and watched them get out of the water and stand on the dock. They waved at him to return, but he purposely misinterpreted their gesture and waved back. He waited until they were walking up the lawn before he began swimming to where he had left his clothes. The sun had sunk behind the trees, and the water, luminous moments ago, was now dark.

. . .

Lyle was waiting for him, sitting in a lawn chair carefully placed on the one small ragged patch of sun that remained. "How was your swim?" he asked.

"Good," said Robert.

"I didn't know you were such a swimmer."

Robert didn't know what to say. He was not a swimmer. It had been a miserable swim. He felt for a moment like crying. Lyle reached up and touched one of Robert's nipples, which was shriveled with cold. "How about a hot shower?" he asked. "It's time to get ready for dinner."

Upstairs, in the bedroom, Robert shut the door. Lyle sat on the bed. Robert came over and knelt on the floor, placing his face on Lyle's lap, on his damp bathing suit. It smelled of the river, and, more faintly, of Lyle. He could see Lyle's hand poised on the peony-patterned bedspread. He picked it up and placed it on top of his own head. Lyle held it still for a moment, and then began to sift his fingers through Robert's hair.

Birds had inhabited the garden John had deserted, pecking at the moist, upset earth.

Robert, showered and dressed for dinner, opened the door to the back staircase, which descended from the upstairs hall to the kitchen, and heard Marian's voice.

"What do you think of him?" she was saying.

"He seems nice," said John. "Young."

"I don't like him," said Marian.

"Why not?"

"He's . . . there's something prickly about him."

"Well, it must be awkward for him. Coming here, and us being so close to Lyle. And having been so close to Tony."

"I understand that. I mean apart from that. There's just something about—I hate young people who are judgmental. Who observe you and judge you and think they know better. He's like that, I can tell."

"But you're judging him."

"Well, of course. I mean, everyone judges everybody. You can't help but form impressions. But you can be—well, tactful. I don't think he's very tactful."

"He seems tactful enough to me."

"It's not tact, then. It's something more contrary. I don't know what it is. I just sense it."

"Well, it's nice to see Lyle with someone again."

"He's all wrong for Lyle. It won't last."

"Of course it won't last. That's why you should be nice to him. It's just something Lyle's going through, part of his healing."

"It just makes me miss Tony so dreadfully."

"We all miss Tony. Do you mean for this to boil?"

"Oh no, darling. Turn it down."

Robert closed the door. He waited there for Lyle, and they went downstairs together.

There was a guest for dinner—an older, glamorous woman named Rosa Ponti. She drove up the driveway in her little red sports car and pulled onto the lawn, parking in front of the house, as if she were in a commercial for automobiles.

They ate outside beneath a big tree. Roland slept in a basket. Terra-cotta pots held sweating bottles of white wine. Their talk was general and convivial. When the meal was finished, Marian stood up and began stacking plates. "Let me help you," said Robert, standing up as well.

"No, no," said Marian. "Sit down."

John and Lyle and Rosa Ponti were seated. Rosa was smoking a thin brown cigarette, exhaling drifts of smoke over her shoulder into the darkness. "No," said Robert. "I'll help." He wanted to hurt Marian in some way, and helping her when she did not want help was the best way he knew how. They carried the dishes up the terraced steps to the house. Lanterns glowed in the tumbled pachysandra. They paused at the kitchen door, both with their hands full. "Here," said Robert, shifting his load, reaching out for the door. He dropped a plate on the bricks. The sound of it smashing seemed very loud.

"Oh no," he said. "I'm sorry."

"Just get the door," said Marian. "It's nothing. No—don't try to pick it up. I'll get the broom."

John appeared behind them. He opened the door and took some dishes from them. Robert heard Rosa laughing at something Lyle had said down in the garden.

They piled the dishes in the sink. The light in the kitchen seemed unusually bright and artificial after the candlelit gloom of the backyard. Robert began to rinse the plates under the tap but Marian said, "Leave them, please. Join the others."

"Are you sure I can't help?"

"I'll give you a shout when I'm ready with the dessert," said Marian. She actually pushed him a little.

Back at the table Rosa Ponti was drawing the floor plan of the apartment she had just bought in Lucca on a blank page of her Filofax. Then she drew another of how the apartment would be when the renovation was complete. The floor, she announced, would be sheathed in anodized aluminum.

Marian came down the steps sideways, balancing a large platter to one side of her. Everyone stopped talking and watched her descent, as if she were a Ziegfeld girl. She waited for Rosa to remove her sketch, and then lay the platter on the middle of the table. A pyramid of lacy, nearly transparent cookies was surrounded by grapes. The grapes were red, their underbellies flushed lime green.

Robert could feel Lyle's bare foot caressing the muscle of his calf beneath the table, but Lyle was not looking at him. He was smoking one of Rosa Ponti's cigarettes, and in the way he held and inhaled the cigarette Robert could tell he had once been a smoker. Robert watched Lyle smoke, his arm extended along the back of Rosa Ponti's chair, inches from her bare neck. He was not flirting, Robert knew, but simply being charming.

Robert reached out and tugged at a bunch of grapes, plucking one from its thin stem, so that just a touch of its moist insides remained behind on the stalk.

"Oh, darling, here," said Marian. She picked up a pair of tiny scissors and held them toward Robert. They glowed in the candlelight.

Robert put a grape into his mouth, and held it there, intact. He was confused.

Lyle removed his hand from the back of Rosa Ponti's chair and took the scissors from Marian. "You use these to cut a small bunch of grapes," he said to Robert, "instead of yanking them off one by one." He demonstrated this phenomenon, and then held the scissors toward Robert.

Robert did not take the scissors.

"Oh, don't tame him!" cried Rosa Ponti. "Let him be free! Let us all be free of these stupid affectations!" She grabbed the scissors from Lyle and flung them over her shoulder.

Everyone was silent for a moment, and the drone of the insects and the chafe of the leaves in the trees, which hovered above them in great dark clouds, were suddenly evident. Rosa Ponti laughed a little, but to herself. She pushed back her chair, got up, and retrieved the scissors from where they had fallen on the lawn. She placed them on the table. Everyone looked at them. They were lovely: gold, their loops a trellis engraved with vines.

Marian picked them up. "They were my grandmother's," she said.

Soon thereafter the party dispersed. Marian and Roland disappeared upstairs, John and Rosa Ponti did the washing up, and Lyle and Robert went for a walk along the river.

When the lights of the house had disappeared behind them, Robert said, "John and Marian think I'm all wrong for you."

"No, they don't," said Lyle, who was walking a few steps behind Robert. He held his hand out a ways in front of him, for he was having trouble seeing in the darkness. Robert, judging by how fast he was walking, was not.

"Yes, they do," said Robert.

"Do you mean about the scissors? That was just Marian being Marian."

"I don't mean about the scissors. I heard them talking and saying they didn't like me and they don't think I'm right for you and that we won't last."

Lyle took this opportunity to stop walking and said, rather stupidly, "What? Were you eavesdropping?"

"Yes," said Robert.

"Where? When?"

"At the top of the stairs. Before dinner."

"You shouldn't have been."

"Why?"

"Because it's wrong. It's impolite."

"Like eating grapes without scissors?"

"No," said Lyle. "That's different."

"How is it different?"

"That's culturally impolite, while eavesdropping is—well, the impoliteness is more intrinsic."

"How can something be intrinsically impolite?"

"Some things can. Like murder."

"But I didn't murder anyone. I just opened a door and overheard a conversation."

"I wish you hadn't listened."

"I'm sure you do. But I did."

"Well, you shouldn't take to heart what you weren't meant to hear. That's a good rule."

"I think just the opposite. I think things you weren't meant to hear are often the most important. Nobody tells you things directly."

"So you're going to make a big deal out of this?"

"Mentioning it is making a big deal?"

Lyle considered for a moment. "No, I suppose not. But can't we just forget it?"

"We? You can."

"And you?"

"Why should I?"

"Because what's the point of dwelling on it? What good does that achieve?"

"I hate when you do this," said Robert.

"Do what?" said Lyle.

"Make things into a debate."

"We're just talking," said Lyle. "It isn't a debate."

"Then talk to me," said Robert. "What do you think?"

"About what?"

"About what Marian said. Do you think I'm right for you? Do you think we'll last?"

"I think it's a bit premature to think in those terms." Lyle wished there were a place to sit down. Mostly he wished to be back at the house and helping with the cleaning up. He could picture the bright kitchen, the plates stacked in the sink, and Rosa Ponti and John laughing. "I think," he said, carefully picking his way among words, like a cat walking through wet grass, "I think that at this point in my life, no one is right for me. In fact I doubt that I'll ever find anyone who is right for me again."

"Was Tony right for you?"

Lyle looked out at the river. This is what I deserve, he thought, for getting involved with a twenty-four-year-old: discussions about Mr. Right.

"Was he?" Robert insisted.

Right? thought Lyle. At moments Tony had been right, but then he had been wrong, too. But at moments it had hurt, and it hurt more now, when he was dead, how right Tony had been, for it had been a rightness that seemed to preclude all others; a rightness that had staked its territories in Lyle's heart, had followed his rivers to their sources, and left flags there, high in the uncharted parts of him. "Yes," he said. "In some ways, Tony was right."

"And I'm not."

"I didn't say that. I don't know yet. I've only known you a short time. I think this whole conversation is foolish."

"But if you had to guess."

"I would never want to guess about something as important as that."

"But if you had to. If I made you."

Lyle was still looking at the river. "I would guess no," he said.

"And what?" said Robert. "I'm supposed to just stay here and . . . bleed?"

"You are not bleeding."

"I feel like I'm bleeding. Like what's me, the inside liquid part of me, is oozing out. Like I'm losing myself."

"You're just being melodramatic," said Lyle. "You're not losing yourself. In fact, I doubt very much that you've even found yourself yet."

"I hate that worst of all," said Robert. "I hate when someone else tells you what's happening inside yourself."

"Then you should be careful what you tell people. Especially when you articulate your hurts."

They stood there for a moment.

"I'm going," said Robert.

"Wait," said Lyle. "I'll come back with you."

"No," said Robert. "I'm not going back to the house."

"Where are you going?"

"I'm going home," said Robert.

"And how are you getting there?"

"I'll walk. I'll walk to the train station and take a train."

"The train station is ten miles from here. And I doubt very much the trains run this late."

"I have no problem walking ten miles. And I have no problem waiting for a train."

"Come back to the house," said Lyle. "And we'll leave first thing in the morning."

"No," said Robert. "I'm leaving now." He began to walk into the dark woods purposefully, as if a trail were clearly marked to the railroad station.

Lyle tried to make himself call out, or follow, but did neither. It had been wrong to bring Robert here. He had done it because he thought it might have worked. There was a way, he felt, that things between them could succeed, but it was not a way that included weekends at John and Marian's. It was a strange way more difficult than that. And standing alone in the woods, Lyle felt old and tired and not inclined toward difficulty. In fact, he realized, at the very moment, he felt inclined toward nothing at all.

Sunday evening Marian drove Lyle to the station. The light had gone stark, and was attacking the trees with a clarity that suggested autumn. Yet it was midsummer.

In the parking lot Lyle went to get out of the car but Marian touched his arm and said, "No. Stay a minute."

Lyle closed the door. Marian dusted the steering wheel with her middle finger, round and round, and then looked at it: clean. "I feel so . . . awful," she said.

"Why?" asked Lyle.

"I feel it was my fault," said Marian.

"It wasn't," said Lyle. "I told you. It was something between us. It had nothing to do with you."

"But when you arrived you were both so happy."

"Yes," said Lyle. "But it wasn't you."

"I wasn't nice to him," said Marian.

Lyle said nothing. He looked down the empty curve of track, but there was no train.

"I don't know if I like him or not," said Marian. She was talking to the steering wheel. "I mean, to be honest, I don't think

I do. But it wasn't about him, how I was behaving. How awful I was."

"What was it about?" asked Lyle.

Marian looked at him as if he were simple. "It was about Tony," she said. "It was about you and Tony."

"Oh," said Lyle. "Yes."

"I couldn't allow myself to be nice to him, I was awful to him, I drove him away, I did it, I know I did, and it's unforgivable. It is."

"I think the train is coming," said Lyle.

"Will you invite him back?" Marian asked. "Make him come. And we'll have a really lovely weekend, I promise, it will just be very relaxed and . . . lovely."

"He won't come," said Lyle. He opened the door, and stepped out of the car.

"But ask him," said Marian. "Promise you will. Or should I call him? Why don't you give me his number and I'll call him?"

"Let me talk to him first," said Lyle. He closed the door.

"Call me," said Marian. "As soon as you have."

"I will," said Lyle.

"Promise," said Marian.

The train was just pulling in. Lyle hurried up the stairs to the platform. There was an overpass above the tracks, and Marian watched him run across it, and descend the stairs on the other side, where she lost sight of him behind the arriving, and then departing, train.

Allegra Goodman

SARAH

Sarah Markowitz parks at the Jewish Community Center of Greater Washington, her large purse on the seat next to her, along with a bunch of marked assignments. She has written copiously on each one, making her comments in green because the students find red threatening. Sarah took a series of pedagogy workshops years ago, and she scrupulously applies the techniques she learned. Her students, all adults, always comment on her warmth and motherliness. They don't realize that these are aspects of Sarah's professionalism. They do not see the teacher within, by turns despairing and chortling.

She takes out her compact and applies fresh lipstick, gathers all the papers and her purse, and strides into the building. She walks quickly, with a firm step; she has short gray hair, and eyes that had been blue when she was younger but are now hazel flecked with gold. The class is called "Creative Midrash," and it combines creative writing with Bible study. Like the commentators in the compendium the Midrash, the students write their own interpretations, variations, and fantasies on Biblical themes. Sarah developed the concept herself, and she is happy with it because it solves so many problems at once. It forces the students to allude to subjects other than themselves, while at the same time they find it serves their need for therapy—because they quickly see in scripture archetypes of their own problems. Above all, Creative Midrash forces the students to read, so they realize they aren't the first to feel, think, or write anything down, for God's sake. She always begins on the first day by playing a tape of Thomas Tallis and then Vaughan Williams' variations on the theme.

It is five-thirty in the afternoon, and they are waiting for her, all ready to go, their notebooks out and turned to a fresh page, their pens poised. They love pens: fountain pens and three-color ballpoints, even elaborate, hollow pens that store twelve different ink cartridges inside. "Fifteen minutes of free writing," Sarah says, and they begin, covering their white notebook pages. She watches them. They range in age from thirty to somewhere near sixty, three women and one man. They are, in their own words, a mom, a retired homemaker, an actress, and a landscape-maintenance specialist. Sarah watches them all and thinks about dinner. She has a chicken thawed and the leftover sweet potatoes, but they need a vegetable. She'll have to stop and pick something up on the way home. She has to get something else, too. They are out of something, but she can't remember what. Something small, perishable. "All right," she says. "Why don't you finish up your thought." She waits. "Then let's begin. Debbie." She turns to the actress. Debbie has long hair and pale blue eyes. You could call her nose large. It is a strong nose, beautifully straight. Everyone, including Sarah, takes out a copy of the poem Debbie wrote last week, and she shakes back her hair and intones:

EVE
flesh of your flesh
bone of your bone
wo   man
womb an
I am Eve
you are my day and night
I am Eve the twilight
in between
sweet soft neither dark nor bright
and how did I feel when

I was born from your dream?
no one was interested

Tomatoes! The thought comes to Sarah unbidden. That's what she has to pick up, because the ones in the fridge spoiled.

from my birth I belonged to you
you had named the beasts
already you had named me
you are the sun and I the moon
you burn
but I pull the waters after me
I slip from your garden to consort
with the enemy
because I would rather be wild
than beget your patriarchy
I would rather cover you with shame
you can have the cattle the foul of the air
and all the beasts of the field
the night will glow with the eyes of my cats

"Comments?" Sarah asks. No one says a word, so she begins. "Debbie, that was very strong. I like the way it flows and builds momentum. There was almost a rhythmic expression in your tide image. Were you playing with the word 'foul' intentionally?"

"Where?" asks Debbie.

"Where you wrote 'foul of the air.' "

"Oh, that wasn't on purpose," Debbie says.

"You might want to change it, then," Sarah suggests. "Other comments?"

Michelle, who is the mom, says, "I noticed you didn't use any capital letters, except for 'I' and 'Eve.' "

"Yeah, I did that because I feel that capital letters and punctuation interrupt the flow of the poem and I associate them with male discourse and hierarchy, sort of dichotomous and either-or oriented, night-day, yes-no, and I see Eve as more of a mediator figure. But I didn't want to use a lower-case 'i' or write 'eve' without a capital because I feel that in a way E. E. Cummings appropriated that idea, and what I was trying to do was take back the 'I' for the female voice."

"It's about subversion," says Brian, the landscaper, once a graduate student, then sidelined for ten years by drugs, but now making up for lost time. He is an unnaturally thin man, sun-burned, with a scant beard.

"Yeah, and it's very close to what I'm going through right now," Debbie says. "I'm having a conflict with my boyfriend about my cats right now."

Then Brian begins to read his "Dialogue Between Jacob and the Angels on the Ladder."

Scene: Desert at midnight, countless stars shining. On the rungs of Jacob's ladder, the spirits of THOREAU *and* WALT WHITMAN, *sitting with* JACOB.

WHITMAN *(to Jacob, with a look of ecstasy):*
You shall be as many as the stars in the sky
You will multiply into millions
and every last one of your children will be
    million heirs because this is the night of
    your
birth
this is your birth-night
and every grass blade, every insect and
    tiniest being in the world knows it
every animal, bird, fish, and locomotive
    knows it
THOREAU: Given a choice, I think any
    man would rather sit by a warm fire than
    become a nation.

"Wait, wait," Debbie says. "You're talking about grass blades? I thought this was supposed to be a desert."

"Maybe you should say grains of sand," Michelle suggests.

"Well, I think that's already in the Bible." Ida, the retired homemaker, is wearing her reading glasses and flipping through Genesis.

"There's nothing wrong with using images that are already in the Bible," Sarah says.

Ida pulls off her reading glasses and looks over at her. She has snowy white hair. "Then I want to change mine," she says. "Can I change mine?"

"All right," Sarah says. "Brian, what do you think about using grains of sand?"

"But I was trying to sort of allude to 'Leaves of Grass.'"

"I don't know, this is really heavy. Really—abstract," Debbie is staring at the play. "Have you thought about getting some more action into it? I mean, I don't think you want to end up with just all these talking heads!"

Brian looks dismayed.

"I see it more as a Platonic dialogue," Sarah says.

This seems to cheer Brian. "I want it to be like *Under Milk Wood*," he confides to the class. "That's my dream."

Sarah picks up the groceries and then the dry cleaning on her way home. "Four shirt, two dress, one skirt, pleated, one blouse. This could not come out," the cashier tells her. She looks around wearily as the cashier rings everything up. As always, hanging in the window is a wedding dress, freshly cleaned, in clear plastic, the dry cleaner's tour de force.

When Sarah gets home, Ed comes out of the house to help her carry everything, so they are both outside when the phone rings, and Ed runs up the steps in front of her with his keys jingling in his pocket and his shirt coming untucked. "Who is it? Your mother?" Sarah calls out as she comes in.

He waves his hand at her impatiently. "Ma? What is it? What? You're in the hospital? What happened?"

Sarah picks up the phone in the kitchen and hears her eighty-three-year-old mother-in-law crying. "Yes, yes, I'm in the hospital," Rose sobs from California. "They took me here. I didn't even know what was happening to me. I was unconscious. I could have been dead."

"Mother, wait, slow down. Start from the beginning. What happened?"

"What hospital are you in?" Sarah breaks in.

"St. Elysius? Or Egregious?"

"No, no, that can't be it. That's a TV show. Try to think, Ma."

"Maybe St. Elizabeth's," Rose says. "How should I know? I was unconscious."

"Ed, I think we should talk to Dr. Klein," Sarah says.

"Sarah, I'm trying to hear what happened. Start from the beginning, Ma."

"I told Klein I needed a new prescription. My refills ran out. I went to three different pharmacies, and they wouldn't fill the prescription for my pills. I went to Longs, Rexall, and Pay Less, and they all said I needed a new prescription from my doctor. But when I told Klein I needed him to write a new one he wouldn't do it, and so I told him that if he didn't write me one I would tell the state medical board he drugged Gladys and Eileen when they passed away, and he just said he didn't know what I was talking about. I said, 'You damn well know what I'm talking about. You killed them with morphine.' Then he just walked out and left me alone in his office. So I had to go all the way home, on the bus, by myself. I was exhausted, I was ill. I went straight to bed. I put on my videotape of *Pride and Prejudice* and I took some of the pills I had saved, because I felt so ill. Then, when I woke up, I was in a hospital bed in a hospital gown."

"Oh, Christ," Ed groans. "Ma, now I want you to give me the telephone number by your bed. I'm going to call the doctor."

This is not the first time Rose has overdosed and collapsed, but that doesn't make it any easier. Sarah remembers Rose's second husband, Maury, who passed away in 1972. He was a cheerful man ten years older than Rose, and as the years went by he only seemed to become more jovial. He whistled happily, walking with his cane through the increasingly grim streets of Washington Heights. He became ever smaller and more spry, his clothes hung on him, and his face was shrunken behind his black-framed glasses; he had almost turned into Jiminy Cricket, but every day he and Rose went out to lunch at the deli, and every week he brought home stacks of large-print books from the library. The two of them travelled, and he used to collapse in dramatic places. On the observation deck of the World Trade Center. In the botanical gardens in Montreal. In Hollywood, on Hollywood Boulevard. He would sit in the hospital and talk about the service in different cities. Sarah had always marvelled at him because he was such an extraordinarily cheerful man. When he died, she found out that he had been taking Percodan, among other things. It wasn't just good nature. He'd got Rose started on pills. After the funeral, they also found out that he hadn't paid taxes for years, and that he had squirrelled away his money in small sums in over a hundred different bank accounts around the country. It was then that Rose sent her amazing handwritten letter "To I.R.S. Please excuse the lapse in taxes. My dear husband was a Maoist." Ed was the one who took care of all Maury's deferred aggravations. He closed up the Washington Heights apartment, collected the money from all the accounts, and moved Rose to Venice, California, where she could be near her other son, Henry, who was managing a gallery there. But Henry left for England—years ago—to start one of his new lives, and taking care of Rose is again Ed's responsibility.

Ed is pacing in the living room with the phone, talking to Dr. Klein, and Sarah picks up her extension in time to hear Klein say, "Well, it seems that she was stashing the pills away. She wasn't taking the prescribed dose. Unfortunately, she took them for her moods."

"Well, why didn't you check on her before?" Ed says.

"Well, Ed, I cannot control everything that she does in the privacy of her own apartment. I cannot take total responsibility for her actions. Of course, I asked her whether she was complying with the prescription, but I'm afraid she didn't tell me the truth."

"No, no, I'm sorry, my mother is not a liar."

"She has a severe dependency on her medication and—"

"Well, that's the point. I thought that was what we were trying to work on, to wean her away with the limited doses."

"Yes, that is what we were trying to do, Ed," Klein says. "But it wasn't working. I think we've had this discussion before. It's really a question of patient management. Now, Rose has decided to enter a residential treatment program at Santa Rosa."

"Why weren't we consulted about this?"

"It was her decision."

"No, I think it was *your* decision," Ed snaps. "You told her she had to do this."

"I advised her to do it, because she has got to start understanding her dependency. She has to find other ways to deal with her boredom and loneliness."

"Oh, so this is really all my fault," Ed says. "Because I'm trying to take care of her long distance. It all comes down to me. I should be there twenty-four hours a day. It's not your fault and it's not her fault, so it's got to be my fault."

Sarah is up half the night because Ed is so upset. He lies on his left side and then rolls over, punching his pillow with his fist. He kicks at the blankets, then flops onto his back. Sarah lies on her stomach and thinks about Rose. Boredom and loneliness. It's a real question: Can an elderly woman subsist on "Masterpiece Theatre" alone? Rose is, as Sarah's student Ida calls it, a "retired homemaker"—except that she was never so professional about being a homemaker, or about being retired. What she really wants, Sarah thinks, is to return to the houses of her childhood. She is nostalgic for them; they are still the backdrops of the romance she has developed about her life. Her parents' house in Bukovina, her foster parents' grand house in England, where she was sent during the First World War—a place with servants and vast drawing rooms. Rose did not suffer in the wars directly, but she imagines she did, and in her mind's eye sees them sweeping away the world she loved. She has often told Sarah that *Gone With the Wind* is the most beautiful novel ever written, and urged her to try to write one like it, threatened to write it herself, although she says she has never had the strength. But it is hard to sustain a life with memories, especially when the best memories come from novels.

"I call these 'Identity Haiku,'" Michelle tells the Creative Midrash class the following week. She pauses, then adds, "I was going to do traditional haiku, but it was really cramping what I wanted to say, so I didn't do the syllable thing."

1.
generations
stars in sky
yellow stars

holocaust
2.
sun rise
moon rise
tower
sun down
moon down
babel
3.
cut
cry
covenant

"These are really beautiful," Debbie says.

"Why didn't you use titles?" asks Ida.

"Um, I just thought it would be overkill. I felt like it would be almost stating the obvious if, say, I titled No. 3 'Circumcision.' "

"I love the way you stripped down your images to the essentials," Sarah says. "Tell us more about why you called them 'Identity Haiku.' " As she learned in her pedagogy class, Sarah shows with her body language that she is listening to Michelle. She leans forward and nods her head, but she is thinking about Rose, who has been calling each night. The residential treatment center is a prison! It's Sing Sing. Auschwitz. No one can leave. What do they do there? They sit in a circle; they have to talk about their past with a facilitator. She can't bear it. To listen to them talk. This one was raped when she was seven years old! That one was assaulted by her own father and brother. This one was a prostitute! "Such horrible things! Things we would *never* talk about. Now they put all of it on TV, but I would never watch!" Sarah can only imagine Rose sitting in that circle of chairs with these other patients, some the age of Rose's children, some the age of her grandchildren. And then Rose herself, half dead from shock, asked to tell about her own abuse. And even to begin, to talk about her childhood after what she has heard! To speak of her own treasured past, the elegant life that she has always treated as something to fold and fold again in tissue paper. No one listening to her, no one interested except the facilitator, probing with long needles, trying to draw blood. Naturally, she wants to go home, but she cannot just check out. "This is a clinic," the doctor told her, "not a hotel." Ed took a flight out to L.A. last night to talk to the doctors or straighten out the Medicare insurance claims or save Rose, depending on how you want to look at it.

It is Ida's turn to read. She is a beautiful woman. A woman who goes to the hairdresser every week and comes to class with her white hair curled and shaped. And she dresses up for the class. She comes in suits and gold jewelry—quite a contrast to Debbie in her rumpled shirts or Brian, who sometimes forgets to take off his bike helmet. She is the oldest in the group, just as Rose is. Her voice is tense as she reads; it chokes up on her and she is embarrassed.

NAOMI AND RUTH

My daughter and I are like Ruth and Naomi, but with a twist. When my husband passed away, may he rest in peace, and we went on the way, as it says in the Bible, I said to Ellen, "Don't stay with me, go on and live your life."

"I want to stay with you and take care of you," she said.

"No, you need to live your own life," I said.

"O.K.," she said. So she went back to New York where she was attending N.Y.U. film school.

I stayed here alone in the house. She wants to make films, and if that is what she wants, so be it, but I tell her, "Ellen, I wish you would meet someone. You are almost thirty."

She tells me, "Mother, I have met someone, and we have been living together for five years." But this is something that is breaking my heart. This man, a broker, is eleven years older than Ellen and not Jewish.

This is what I want to ask her—"How do you think you can live in New York like a Ruth gleaning in the alien corn? How do you think you can come to him and lie at his feet in the night so that one morning he will marry you? How can you go on like this living in his apartment for five years? If I had known this would happen when we went on the way, I would not have told you to go. I would have said, 'Stay.' "

Something about this pricks at Sarah. Tears start in her eyes. Debbie rakes back her long hair and says to Ida, "Well, she's got to make her own choices."

"I have a question about the genre of this," Michelle says. "Is this like an essay or a short story?"

"Ida," Sarah says, "this is—" She wants to say that it moved her, but she cannot. The words would sound cheap in the context of the class with its formalized intimacy. "It's very simple and beautiful," she says.

Debbie is looking over her copy, pondering Ida's work. "I guess it's an age thing," she says.

Sarah's desk stands at the window of her bedroom. She has always wanted a study, and she and Ed are hoping to redo one of the other bedrooms in the next few years. The kids are away at college—one at medical school—so they don't have the money to do anything with the house. Sarah and Ed went to a local one-woman performance of *A Room of One's Own,* and it occurred to Sarah as she left the theatre that Virginia Woolf never had any children. Her own desk is piled with papers, some hers, some Ed's, also bank statements she has not yet filed, bills marked paid, issues of *Writer's Digest* and *Poets & Writers Magazine,* and copy for the Sha'arei Tzedek newsletter, which she edits. Sarah is the Washington stringer for several national Jewish periodicals, and she writes frequent book reviews. She sits at her desk and thinks about what insufficient time she has for her own work. She has written one novel, published in 1979 by Three Penny Opera, a book about a woman—a painter—growing up in Brooklyn and Long Island, but she didn't move fast enough after that publication, didn't follow it quickly enough with a second novel, and she regrets this, the loss of momentum. She writes poetry as well, poetry that is perhaps too old-fashioned for a contemporary audience. With its wordplay and complicated rhymes it is closer to the seventeenth century than to John Ashbery. It has been difficult for her as a poet, to be influenced by Donne, Marvell, and Herbert, but to write about giving birth, a son's bar mitzvah, Yom Kippur. Several years ago she sent a collection of her poems to her brother-in-law, Henry, who runs a small press of his own in Oxford. But Henry felt that Sarah's work, while "extraordinary," was not moving in quite the direction that Equinox was trying to move in with its current series. She still finds it strange that even Henry, who loves Victorian furniture, eighteenth-century books and bindings, antique china, and plush novels—he who, as a person, is almost baroque —nevertheless admires poems that are sleek, smooth, minimalist, functioning like state-of-the-art appliances. As she boots up her computer, the phone rings.

"Sarah?" Ed says. "Hi. Listen, we've got a mess here. She's already racked up twenty thousand dollars for hospitalization. That and the treatment program are covered, but there is another sixteen hundred for consultations with Klein, which they aren't covering."

"What do you mean?"

"They say they aren't covering it. We're disputing the bill, so—"

"How is she?" Sarah asks.

"Not so hot. Disoriented, exhausted. She's lost weight." He sighs. "Sarah, I got here and I realized this is it. We can't kid ourselves about this any longer—she can't stay out here alone. We've got to bring her home."

"You mean bring her here?"

"Yeah, we've got to bring her back to Washington."

She thinks for a moment. "I can cancel my Thursday class," she says. "I'll try to get a flight out tomorrow."

Sarah and Ed sit in a pair of chairs in Dr. Stephen Klein's office. For Sarah, the scene is vaguely reminiscent of certain meetings with the assistant principal of Woodrow Wilson Junior High School concerning their son, Ben, and his academic progress.

"Well, I have spent at least an hour with her in private consultations each day of her stay here," Klein is telling them.

"And these were the sessions where you . . . ? What did you do exactly?"

"I listened to her. I talked to her about dependency, addictive behavior—"

Ed interrupts. "All I know is that my mother looks terrible, she's lost weight, you've run her ragged."

Dr. Klein shakes his head. "Remember, you haven't seen her for at least six months. And she is recovering from a massive overdose."

"Massive overdose!" Ed's face reddens. "Is that the way you like to dramatize it to your patients? Look, my mother is eighty-three years old. Spare her the shock therapy. You've got her out at Santa Rosa in a program with a bunch of teen-age junkies. I thought this was the age of multiculturalism, mutual respect, universal access, emancipation of the elderly. You're sitting here rubber-stamping an elderly woman, putting her onto the therapeutic conveyor belt with no regard to her age, her cultural background—"

"Can I show you something?" Klein asks. He puts a video-tape in the VCR and turns on the television. "Rose?" a woman's voice asks. "May we have your permission to videotape this conversation for you and/or your family to look at later?"

"All right," Rose replies. She is sitting up in a hospital bed looking small and gray, an I.V. in her arm.

"Now, Rose, tell me, how are you feeling—on a scale of one to ten, with one being the worst and ten the best."

"I feel lousy," Rose says.

"But on a scale of ten, how do you feel?"

"One is the best?"

"One is the worst, ten is the best."

"Ten is the best?"

"That's right."

"And what's the worst?"

"One. Rose?"

"I have a one."

Sarah smiles in spite of herself, but Ed bursts out, "Can—can you turn that off?"

"Why?" Klein asks.

"Because we are having a conversation here!"

"I understand that, Ed, but I thought the tape was relevant."

"It may be relevant. However, I am not going to watch my mother being interrogated, O.K.? It's ugly."

"Addiction is ugly. It's also complicated, and really I think this is something you should consider—not now, when you're upset, but later on. I think counselling as a family would be very valuable for Rose—and for you."

"Oh, my God," Ed snaps.

"I see a lot of anger here," Klein points out gently.

"Damn right."

"No, I don't mean the anger at me. The conflict is between you and your mother. This isn't about me at all."

"Oh, yes it is," Ed fires back. "This is all about you and your indiscriminate diagnoses, your mismanagement of an elderly patient's prescriptions, and the fact that you railroaded her into entering a totally inappropriate treatment program."

"That's—that's a serious charge," Klein says. "I repeat that it was her decision to enter the program. I have her signature on all the paperwork."

"You can give me the paperwork, because you are no longer her doctor," Ed snaps.

"I'll be happy to release the records to you as soon as her account is clear. I know that you're worried, I see that you're upset, but I can assure you I have given Rose the best treatment I knew how to give, and I have been generous with my time. I'm not even charging you for our session here today."

At this, Ed stands up, turns on his heel, and strides out of Klein's office through the reception area and out the door.

Sarah turns and walks out after him, but she stops at the desk of Klein's receptionist. "Do you take Visa?" she asks.

For the next three days, Ed and Sarah pack up Rose's apartment in Venice. They phone Goodwill and several of the Jewish agencies to try to give away the washer, the dryer, and some of the big furniture. "You know, it's telling," Ed says to Sarah. "Now you have to pay a collection fee to give things away."

"Well, sure," Sarah says. "They have to come with a truck. They have to sort the stuff." She imagines the warehouses with piles for everything that comes in: REHABILITATE, SCRAP, SMITHSONIAN. A triage system, something like the Santa Rosa treatment center? Now that Rose is home, she looks much better. She is frail, of course—thin—but her color is back, her eyes bright. The apartment is bustling. She is going home with her dear son and

daughter-in-law, and she will not be alone anymore. She is su-
pervising the movers as they pack up her china and her little
cut-crystal liqueur glasses. She is being swept away to a new
place, beginning a new chapter, and this is something she enjoys. But Ed and Sarah look terrible. Dishevelled, exhausted
from packing, paperwork, and schlepping. Each night they drag
themselves back to the Sea Breeze Motel and collapse with muscles aching. The motel has bars on the windows and, in the bathroom, tiny white towels that seem to have been put there mostly
for symbolic value. They picked the place because of its location
near Rose, and it turned out to have one other advantage. For
fifty cents they can get the bed to vibrate, and this soothes their
aching backs. At the end of the day they try to unwind, lying on
their backs, feeding quarters to the bed and watching C-SPAN
on television.

On the third night, they are lying there on their backs watching the Prime Minister's Question Time, the bed vibrating beneath them, and Ed is talking on the phone to his brother Henry.
"Well, of course we're giving away the secretary," Ed says.
"We're giving all the big furniture to Hadassah. That's what Ma
wants. What? What?" He turns toward Sarah. "He says he
wants the secretary."

"So let him ship it to England," Sarah says.

"It's a very fine piece? No, O.K. No, I would call it a—nice
piece, not a very fine piece . . . You want to ship it to England,
you go ahead . . . What—are you crazy? Where are we going
to put it in D.C.?" He looks over at Sarah.

"If he really wants it, he can ship it to England," Sarah says.

"What? I can't hear you," Ed talks over her into the phone.
He turns to Sarah again. "Henry says Ma will want the secretary
in Washington. She may not want it now, but she will later. And
she'll want the lamps with the silk—shantung lampshades."

"He may be right," Sarah says. "She'll want them later."

"Henry, have you *seen* those lampshades in the last five
years?"

"Ed, maybe we should get a container and ship everything to
D.C."

"What did you say?" Ed asks her. She repeats what she said.
"All right, fine." He hands her the telephone. "You and Henry

work it out, I'm getting an Excedrin." He takes another couple of quarters off the Formica nightstand and feeds them expertly into the meter on the headboard.

Henry is still talking, unaware that the phone has changed hands. "Now, the carpets are simply not worth shipping. They aren't really Chinese carpets, you know. We could very well give those away, but the lamps could be considered antiques in a few years, and silk-shantung lampshades are almost impossible to find anymore. They just don't make—"

Sarah teaches the first class after her return home in a haze of jet lag. She had given the students an assignment to do while she was gone: "Write a midrash about the crossing of the Red Sea in a genre you have not yet used in this course." Now, as she listens to the students, she finds that the results are mixed. Michelle has written a short story about a young Jewish girl who is in love with an Egyptian and has to watch her lover fall with his horse and chariot into the sea. Naturally, she refuses to join Miriam and the other women as they sing and dance in triumph after they have crossed to safety. Instead, she writes her own song to sing by herself to the desert air. Brian has written an essay of questions, hypotheses, and test cases in true Midrashic fashion. It begins: "It is a mystery why it says in the Torah that after all Moses' pleas, God hardened Pharaoh's heart. Why would God want to make it harder for the Israelites if he was on their side? Was it a test? Or is this some kind of mystical metaphor? I, being of philosophical inclination, take it as such. I think these phrases in the ancient scriptures are invitations to us to ask questions about the nature of human agency and its interactions (reactions?) to God as a historical agent in the world."

After hearing only seven pages of this, Debbie looks at Sarah and asks, in her blunt way, "Is this creative writing?"

Sarah is annoyed. "Let's let Brian finish," she says.

"Sorry," Debbie mutters.

When it's Ida's turn, she shakes her head. "I apologize," she says. "I wasn't able to complete the assignment. I'm still waiting for an idea."

"Don't censor yourself," Michelle advises her.

"Yeah, I used to be really bad about that," Debbie says. "Do you ever try brainstorming?'' For her part, Debbie has written an autobiography of Pharaoh's sacred cat: "I with my green eyes have seen three hundred generations. My dam was the Upper Nile and my father the Lower Nile; my older sister the Great Sphinx, who taught me the riddles of man.''

When Debbie finishes, Sarah nods her head. "That's very— strange and compelling,'' she says. She hates it. Rose is staying in their daughter Miriam's old room. Sarah has been taking her to look at residences. Every day she drives her out to see them, and every day Rose insists she could not possibly live in one, and that the only times she was ever happy were when she was in the midst of the family.

"I was wondering,'' Michelle says, "would it be possible for us to do an assignment that isn't a midrash? Because, for me, it's hard to connect my feelings to the Bible all the time.''

"It's *really* hard,'' Debbie agrees.

"Could we just try to write a story set in modern times?'' Michelle asks.

Ida adds to this, "I'd like it if you would bring in a midrash of your own that we could look at.''

"Have you ever written one?'' Brian asks.

"Yes, I think I did one years ago,'' Sarah says. "I could look for it. But I want to remind all of you that creating art is hard work, and that the artist sees restrictions as opportunities. Now, for your next project, your first restriction is that you cannot use the word 'I.' ''

"Oh, jeez,'' Debbie groans.

"What about using 'me'?'' Michelle asks. Nope.

"But we can use all the other pronouns?'' Brian asks.

Sarah makes hamburgers that night, and the three of them sit down for dinner—Sarah, Ed, and Rose, who eats her burger plain on her plate with a knife and fork. "I heard you didn't like the Helena,'' Ed says to his mother.

"The facilities were gorgeous,'' Sarah says.

"Were they gorgeous, Ma?'' Ed asks.

"Cold,'' Rose says.

"What? You said the air-conditioning was wonderful!'' Sarah says.

"I mean the atmosphere was cold. It was institutional."

"Well, it's an institution," Ed says.

"Yes, it was no home for me."

"They had a lovely swimming pool."

"I don't swim," Rose points out.

"And they have buses to the Kennedy Center for all the performances."

"You could go to the symphony and the ballet, Ma. And the theatre!"

"I didn't like it," Rose says.

"What's not to like?" Ed demands.

"The people." Rose taps her head. "Not all there."

Sarah shakes her head, "They were lovely people. Cultured people!"

"You see what you want to see," Rose tells her.

Ed takes another burger under Sarah's disapproving glare. "Your furniture is coming, Ma. We have to settle you in."

"You know, they have chamber music there every week," Sarah tells Ed.

"Look, I'll tell you what, Ma," he says. "Sarah and I are going to move to the Helena, and you can stay here. How would that be?"

Sarah sits down at her desk after dinner. She tries to work on one of her overdue book reviews, but her heart isn't in it. She is too tired, her mind full of too many other things: the knowledge that in order to get any work done, she and Ed need to settle Rose in a residence. They hate pushing her into it, but Rose is not going to leave their house happily. They are going to have a fight about it. Ed will be miserable. The knowledge that her class is not going well. These particular students do not work well together as a group. Discussion is fractured. All sniping and defensiveness. The chemistry is all wrong. She told them today she once wrote a midrash of her own, but she does not know where it is. It was a little piece about the Biblical Sarah and about her own feelings about becoming a mother. She picks up the King James Bible that she had assigned as a class text along with Robert Alter's *The Art of Biblical Poetry*, and Peter Elbow's *Writing Without Teachers*, and she turns to Genesis 21.

She reads: "And the Lord visited Sarah as he had said, and the Lord did unto Sarah as he had spoken. For Sarah conceived, and bare Abraham a son in his old age." And her eye skips down to where it says that Sarah said the child's name is Isaac because "God hath made me to laugh, so that all that hear will laugh with me." As she looks at these verses, she sees them differently now from the way she saw them in the past. She is fifty years old, and she has four grown children, and it occurs to her that she is not much like the Biblical Sarah in that respect. She did not have a child in her old age. She has certainly never had any problems with fertility. She has pined, but not for children. She has pined to have a literary career, to have her work discovered by the world. This has been her dream since her school days, when she discovered John Donne and felt suddenly and secretly clever, as if, like a safecracker, she could find the puns and hidden springs in his poetry. And when she wrote her essays in college about this image and that metaphor, what she was really wondering was how to become like Shakespeare—without seeming to imitate him, of course. When would she be called into that shining multitude of poets and playwrights, mainly Elizabethan, who rose in shimmering waves before her at Queens College? She wrote her M.A. thesis in English Literature about Emma Lazarus—not about the poem on the Statue of Liberty but about her major and forgotten works, the verse plays and poems.

But she did not have enough time to be poetic. She had her small children, and she had Ed's career to think about. Her professors warned her of the time and the sacrifices she would have to make if she pursued a Ph.D. One old codger had even suggested that if she got a Ph.D. and an academic position she would be blocking the career of some talented man with a family to support. Of course, that idea never went far with her. But she did have the idea that a Ph.D. would be hard to get. And a job harder. She decided against it. The truth is it was easier for her to worry about Ed's career. She did not have to face the possibility of failure.

She had wanted fame, not classes at the Jewish Community Center; she had wanted to write dazzling poems, not just for her friends and relatives, but for the world. She was thirteen when she lay in bed in her parents' house, read *Hamlet,* and wanted to be as good as Shakespeare. And now that she is fifty, if the Lord came to her in a dream and said, "You will achieve what you desired," she would laugh, certainly. If an angel or an agent came down from New York and said, "You, Sarah, will write a great novel, a bestseller. Not a pulp romance, but a good book, wise and luminous, with a future movie bursting from its pages," then she would laugh for all to hear—although she would take down the phone number of the agent just in case. In the meantime, she has her book reviews, her class, her children, her mother-in-law. She gets up from her desk. She has written none of this down, and so she will have no model for her students when she comes in to the next class. She can tell them that she looked in her files and couldn't find the midrash she wrote. Or she could tell them she thinks it is important for them to find their own voice, and that she doesn't want them to look at her work because it might cramp their style.

"Knock, knock," Rose says at the door.

"Yes. Come in," Sarah calls back.

Rose opens the door. She is wearing a pink quilted robe and matching slippers. "Sarah, dear, do you have any books? They packed all my books, and I can't find any."

"Oh. Of course we have books. Downstairs." Sarah adds absent-mindedly, "What kind of book do you want?"

Rose considers the question. "I like trilogies," she says.

"You know, I think the only trilogy in the house is Ed's *Gulag Archipelago.*"

"Nonfiction?"

"I'm afraid so."

"Ed never read fiction. Do you have a novel? I like any kind of novel, not too sad. About a family—with some romance. But well written. It must be well written."

On a whim, Sarah opens the closet and hunts around on the floor for the box where she keeps copies of her own novel. "Here, Rose, why don't you read this?"

"*Irises, Irises.*" Rose ponders. "Oh, that's your book. Sarah Markowitz. I've read that already. Of course. Years ago. Do you have a sequel?"

"No, I don't."

"You must write a sequel."

"Well, I have to come up with an idea."

"The next generation," Rose says immediately.

"Well, maybe you could reread it and give me some advice."

Rose takes the book, and the two of them walk down the hall to Miriam's old room. Sarah mentions that there is a literary discussion group at the Helena.

Rose shakes her head. "I could never live there."

"But all your things are going to arrive, you know. We couldn't fit the secretary in here."

Rose looks around the little bedroom. "It could fit," she says. "But it wouldn't look very elegant, one thing on top of another."

Sarah hardly expected this. She feels a rush of pragmatic joy. Her house to herself, and Rose at the Helena. Of course, she doesn't know that in the next three weeks she will be looking for new silk-shantung lampshades and spending hours at House of Foam, out near the airport, as workmen pump new, high-density stuffing into Rose's sofa. For now, she sees free evenings unfolding before her, the empty rooms expanding. What are wistful literary dreams compared to that?

Ellen Gilchrist

THE STUCCO HOUSE

Teddy was asleep in his second-floor bedroom. It was a square, high-ceilinged room with cobalt-blue walls and a bright yellow rug. The closet doors were painted red. The private bath had striped wallpaper and a ceiling fan from which hung mobiles from the Museum of Modern Art. In the shuttered window hung a mobile of small silver airplanes. A poet had given it to Teddy when he came to visit. Then the poet had gone home and killed himself. Teddy was not supposed to know about that, but of course he did. Teddy could read really well. Teddy could read like a house afire. The reason he could read so well was that when his mother had married Eric and moved to New Orleans from across the lake in Mandeville, he had been behind and had had to be tutored. He was tutored every afternoon for a whole summer, and when second grade started, he could read really well. He was still the youngest child in the second grade at Newman School, but at least he could read.

He was sleeping with four stuffed toys lined up between him and the wall and four more on the other side. They were there to keep his big brothers from beating him up. They were there to keep ghosts from getting him. They were there to keep vampires out. This night they were working. If Teddy dreamed at all that night, the dreams were like Technicolor clouds. On the floor beside the bed were Coke bottles and potato-chip containers and a half-eaten pizza from the evening before. Teddy's mother had gone off at suppertime and not come back, so Eric had let him do anything he liked before he went to bed. He had played around in Eric's darkroom for a while. Then he had let the springer spaniels in the house, and then he had ordered a pizza and Eric had paid for it. Eric was reading a book about a man who climbed a mountain in the snow. He couldn't put it down. He didn't care what Teddy did as long as he was quiet.

Eric was really nice to Teddy. Teddy was always glad when he and Eric were alone in the house. If his big brothers were gone and his mother was off with her friends, the stucco house was nice. This month was the best month of all. Both his brothers were away at Camp Carolina. They wouldn't be back until August.

Teddy slept happily in his bed, his stuffed animals all around him, his brothers gone, his dreams as soft as dawn.

Outside his house the heat of July pressed down upon New Orleans. It pressed people's souls together until they grated like chalk on brick. It pressed people's brains against their skulls. Only sugar and whiskey made people feel better. Sugar and coffee and whiskey. Beignets and café au lait and taffy and Cokes and snowballs made with shaved ice and sugar and colored flavors. Gin and wine and vodka, whiskey and beer. It was too hot, too humid. The blood wouldn't move without some sugar.

Teddy had been asleep since eleven-thirty the night before. Eric came into his room just before dawn and woke him up. "I need you to help me," he said. "We have to find your mother." Teddy got sleepily out of bed, and Eric helped him put on his shorts and shirt and sandals. Then Eric led him down the hall and out the front door and down the concrete steps, and opened the car door and helped him into the car. "I want a Coke," Teddy said. "I'm thirsty."

"Okay," Eric answered. "I'll get you one." Eric went back into the house and reappeared carrying a frosty bottle of Coke with the top off. The Coke was so cool it was smoking in the soft, humid air.

Light was showing from the direction of the lake. In New Orleans in summer the sun rises from the lake and sets behind the river. It was rising now. Faint pink shadows were beginning to penetrate the mist.

Eric drove down Nashville Avenue to Chestnut Street and turned and went two blocks and came to a stop before a duplex shrouded by tall green shrubs. "Come on," he said. "I think she's here." He led Teddy by the hand around the side of the house to a set of wooden stairs leading to an apartment. Halfway up the stairs Teddy's mother was lying on a landing. She had on a pair of pantyhose and that was all. Over her naked body someone had thrown a seersucker jacket. It was completely still on the stairs, in the yard.

"Come on," Eric said. "Help me wake her up. She fell down and we have to get her home. Come on, Teddy, help me as much as you can."

"Why doesn't she have any clothes on? What happened to her clothes?"

"I don't know. She called and told me to come and get her. That's all I know." Eric was half carrying and half dragging Teddy's mother down the stairs. Teddy watched while Eric managed to get her down the stairs and across the yard. "Open the car door," he said. "Hold it open."

Together they got his mother into the car. Then Teddy got in the back seat and they drove to the stucco house and got her out and dragged her around to the side door and took her into the downstairs hall and into Malcolm's room and laid her down on Malcolm's waterbed. "You watch her," Eric said. "I'm going to call the doctor."

Teddy sat down on the floor beside the waterbed and began to look at Malcolm's books. *Playing to Win, The Hobbit, The Big Green Book.* Teddy took down *The Big Green Book* and started reading it. It was about a little boy whose parents died and he had to go and live with his aunt and uncle. They weren't very nice to him, but he liked it there. One day he went up to the attic and found a big green book of magic spells. He learned all the spells. Then he could change himself into animals. He could make himself invisible. He could do anything he wanted to do.

Teddy leaned back against the edge of the waterbed. His mother had not moved. Her legs were lying side by side. Her mouth was open. Her breasts fell away to either side of her chest. Her pearl necklace was falling on one breast. Teddy got up and looked down at her. She isn't dead, he decided. She's just sick or something. I guess she fell down those stairs. She shouldn't have been outside at night with no clothes on. She'd kill me if I did that.

He went around to the other side of the waterbed and climbed up on it. Malcolm never let him get on the waterbed. He never even let Teddy come into the room. Well, he was in here now. He opened *The Big Green Book* and found his place and went on reading. Outside in the hall Eric was talking to people on the phone. Eric was nice. He was so good to them. He had already taken Teddy snorkeling and skiing, and next year he was going to take him to New York to see the dinosaurs in the museum. He was a swell guy. He was the best person his mother had ever married. Living with Eric was great. It was better than anyplace Teddy had ever been. Better than living with his real daddy, who wasn't any fun, and lots better than being at his grandfather's house. His grandfather yelled at them and made them make their beds and ride the stupid horses and hitch up the pony cart, and if they didn't do what he said, he hit them with a belt. Teddy hated being there, even if he did have ten cousins near him in Mandeville and they came over all the time. They liked to be there even if their grandfather did make them mind. There was a fort in the woods and secret paths for riding the ponies, and the help cooked for them morning, noon, and night.

Teddy laid *The Big Green Book* down on his lap and reached over and patted his mother's shoulder. "You'll be okay," he said out loud. "Maybe you're just hung over."

Eric came in and sat beside him on the waterbed. "The doctor's coming. He'll see about her. You know, Doctor Paine, who comes to dinner. She'll be all right. She just fell down."

"Maybe she's hung over." Teddy leaned over his mother and touched her face. She moaned. "See, she isn't dead."

"Teddy, maybe you better go up to your room and play until the doctor leaves. Geneva will be here in a minute. Get her to make you some pancakes or something."

"Then what will we do?"

"Like what?"

"I mean all day. You want to go to the lake or something?"

"I don't know, Ted. We'll have to wait and see." Eric took his mother's hand and held it. He looked so worried. He looked terrible. She was always driving him crazy, but he never got mad at her. He just thought up some more things to do.

"I'll go see if Geneva's here. Can I have a Coke?"

"May I have a Coke." Eric smiled and reached over and patted his arm. "Say it."

"May I have a Coke, please?"

"Yes, you may." They smiled. Teddy got up and left the room.

The worst thing of all happened the next day. Eric decided to send him across the lake for a few days. To his grandmother and grandfather's house. "They boss me around all the time," Teddy said. "I won't be in the way. I'll be good. All I'm going to do is stay here and read books and work on my stamp collection." He looked pleadingly up at his stepfather. Usually reading a book could get him anything he wanted with Eric, but today it wasn't working.

"We have to keep your mother quiet. She'll worry about you if you're here. It won't be for long. Just a day or so. Until Monday. I'll come get you Monday afternoon."

"How will I get over there?"

"I'll get Big George to take you." Big George was the gardener. He had a blue pickup truck. Teddy had ridden with him before. Getting to go with Big George was a plus, even if his grandfather might hit him with a belt if he didn't make his bed.

"Can I see Momma now?"

"May."

"May I see Momma now?"

"Yeah. Go on in, but she's pretty dopey. They gave her some pills."

His mother was in her own bed now, lying flat down without any pillows. She was barely awake. "Teddy," she said. "Oh, baby, oh, my precious baby. Eric tried to kill me. He pushed me down the stairs."

"No, he didn't." Teddy withdrew from her side. She was going to start acting crazy. He didn't put up with that. "He didn't do anything to you. I went with him. Why didn't you have any clothes on?"

"Because I was asleep when he came and made me leave. He pushed me and I fell down the stairs."

"You probably had a hangover. I'm going to Mandeville. Well, I'll see you later." He started backing away from the bed. Backing toward the door. He was good at backing. Sometimes he backed home from school as soon as he was out of sight of the other kids.

"Teddy, come here to me. You have to do something for me. Tell Granddaddy and Uncle Ingersol that Eric is trying to kill me. Tell them, will you, my darling? Tell them for me." She was getting sleepy again. Her voice was sounding funny. She reached out a hand to him and he went back to the bed and held out his arm and she stroked it. "Be sure and tell them. Tell them to call the President." She stopped touching him. Her eyes were closed. Her mouth fell open. She still looked pretty. Even when she was drunk, she looked really pretty. Now that she was asleep, he moved nearer and looked at her. She looked okay. She sure wasn't bleeding. She had a cover on the bed that was decorated all over with little Austrian flowers. They were sewn on like little real flowers. You could hardly tell they were made of thread. He looked at one for a minute. Then he picked up her purse and took a twenty-dollar bill out of her billfold and put it in his pocket. He needed to buy some film. She didn't care. She gave him anything he asked for.

"What are you doing?" It was Eric at the door. "You better be getting ready, Teddy. Big George will be here in a minute."

"I got some money out of her purse. I need to get some film to take with me."

"What camera are you going to take? I've got some film for the Olympus in the darkroom. You want a roll of black-and-white? Go get the camera and I'll fill it for you."

"She said you tried to kill her." Teddy took Eric's hand and they started down the hall to the darkroom. "Why does she say stuff like that, Eric? I wish she wouldn't say stuff like that when she gets mad."

"It's a fantasy, Teddy. She never had anyone do anything bad to her in her life, and when she wants some excitement, she just makes it up. It's okay. I'm sorry she fell down the stairs. I was trying to help her. You know that, don't you?"

"Yes. Listen, can I buy Big George some lunch before we cross the Causeway? I took twenty dollars. Will that be enough to get us lunch?"

"Sure. That would be great, Teddy. I bet he'd like that. He likes you so much. Everybody likes you. You're such a swell little boy. Come on, let's arm that camera. Where is it?"

Teddy ran back to his room and got the camera. He was a scrawny, towheaded little boy who would grow up to be a magnificent man. But for now he was seven and a half years old and liked to take photographs of people in the park and of dogs. He liked to read books and pretend he lived in Narnia. He liked to get down on his knees at the Episcopal church and ask God not to let his momma divorce Eric. If God didn't answer, then he would pretend he was his grandfather and threaten God. Okay, you son of a bitch, he would say, his little head down on his chest, kneeling like a saint at the prayer rail. If she divorces Eric, I won't leave anyway. I'll stay here with him and we can be bachelors. She can just go anywhere she likes. I'm not leaving. I'm going right on living here by the park in my room. I'm not going back to Mandeville and ride those damned old horses.

Big George came in the front door and stood, filling up the hall. He was six feet five inches tall and wide and strong. His family had worked for Eric's family for fifty years. He had six sons and one daughter who was a singer. He liked Eric, and he liked the scrawny little kid that Eric's wife had brought along with the big mean other ones. "Hey, Teddy," Big George said, "where's your bag?"

"You want to go to lunch?" Teddy said. "I got twenty dollars. We can stop at the Camellia Grill before we cross the bridge. You want to do that?"

"Sure thing. Twenty dollars. What you do to get twenty dollars, Teddy?"

"Nothing. I was going to buy some film, but Eric gave me some so I don't have to. Come on, let's go." He hauled his small leather suitcase across the parquet floor and Big George leaned down and took it from him. Eric came into the hall and talked to Big George a minute, and they both looked real serious and Big George shook his head, and then Eric kissed Teddy on the cheek and Big George and Teddy went on out and got into the truck and drove off.

Eric stood watching them until the truck turned onto Saint Charles Avenue. Then he went back into the house and into his wife's workroom and looked around at the half-finished watercolors, which were her latest obsession, and the mess and the clothes on the floor and the unemptied wastebaskets, and he sat down at her desk and opened the daybook she left out for him, to see if there were any new men since the last time she made a scene.

June 29, Willis will be here from Colorado. Show him the new poems. HERE IS WHAT WE MUST ADMIT. Here is what we know. What happened then is what happens now. Over and over again. How to break the pattern. Perhaps all I can do is avoid or understand the pattern. The pattern holds for all we do. I discovered in a dream that I am not in love with R. Only with what he can do for my career. How sad that is. The importance of dreams is that they may contain feelings we are not aware of. FEELINGS WE ARE NOT AWARE OF. The idea of counterphobia fascinates me. That you could climb mountains because you are afraid of heights. Seek out dangers because the danger holds such fear for you. What if I seek out men because I want to fight with them. Hate and fear them and want to have a fight. To replay my life with my brothers. Love to fight. My masculine persona.

Well, I'll see Willis tonight and show him the watercolors too, maybe. I'll never be a painter. Who am I fooling? All I am is a mother and a wife. That's that. Two unruly teenagers and a little morbid kid who likes Eric better than he likes me. I think it's stunting his growth to stay in that darkroom all the time . . .

Eric sighed and closed the daybook. He picked up a watercolor of a spray of lilies. She was good. She was talented. He hadn't been wrong about that. He laid it carefully down on the portfolio and went into her bedroom and watched her sleep. He could think of nothing to do. He could not be either in or out; he could not make either good or bad decisions. He was locked into this terrible marriage and into its terrible rage and fear and sadness. No one was mean to me, he decided. Why am I here? Why am I living here? For Teddy, he decided, seeing the little boy's skinny arms splashing photographs in and out of trays, grooming the dogs, swimming in the river, paddling a canoe. I love that little boy, Eric decided. He's just like I was at that age. I have to keep the marriage together if I can. I can't stand for him to be taken from me.

Eric began to cry, deep within his heart at first, then right there in the sunlight, at twelve o'clock on a Saturday morning, into his own hands, his own deep, salty, endless, heartfelt tears.

Big George had stopped at the Camellia Grill, and he and Teddy were seated on stools at the counter eating sliced-turkey sandwiches and drinking chocolate freezes. "So, what's wrong with your momma?" Big George asked.

"She fell down some stairs. We had to go and get her and bring her home. She got drunk, I guess."

"Don't worry about it. Grown folks do stuff like that. You got to overlook it."

"I just don't want to go to Mandeville. Granddaddy will make me ride the damned old horses. I hate horses."

"Horses are nice."

"I hate them. I have better things to do. He thinks I want to show them, but I don't. Malcolm and Jimmy like to do it. I wish they were home from camp. Then he'd have them."

"Don't worry about it. Eat your sandwich." Big George bit into his. The boy imitated him, opened his mouth as wide as Big George's, heartily ate his food, smilingly let the world go by. It took an hour to get to Mandeville. He wasn't there yet. He looked up above the cash register to where the Camellia Grill sweatshirts were displayed—white, with a huge pink camellia in the center. He might get one for Big George for Christmas or he might not wait that long. He had sixty-five dollars in the bank account Eric made for him. He could take some of it out and buy the sweatshirt now. "I like that sweatshirt," he said out loud. "I think it looks real good, don't you?"

"Looks hot," Big George said, "but I guess you'd like it in the winter."

.   .   .

Teddy slept all the way across the Causeway, soothed by the motion of the truck and Big George beside him, driving and humming some song he was making up as he drove. Eric's a fool for that woman, George was thinking. Well, he's never had a woman before, just his momma and his sisters. Guess he's got to put up with it 'cause he likes the little boy so much. He's the sweetest little kid I ever did see. I like him too. Paying for my lunch with a twenty-dollar bill. Did anybody ever see the like? He won't be scrawny long. Not with them big mean brothers he's got. The daddy was a big man too, I heard them say. No, he won't stay little. They never do, do they?

Teddy slept and snored. His allergies had started acting up, but he didn't pay any attention to them. If he was caught blowing his nose, he'd be taken to the doctor, so he only blew it when he was in the bathroom. The rest of the time he ignored it. Now he snored away on the seat beside Big George, and the big blue truck moved along at a steady sixty miles an hour, cruising along across the lake.

At his grandparents' house in Mandeville his grandmother and grandfather were getting ready for Teddy. His grandmother was making a caramel cake and pimento cheese and carrot sticks and Jell-O. His grandfather was in the barn dusting off the saddles and straightening the tackle. Maybe Teddy would want to ride down along the bayou with him. Maybe they'd just go fishing. Sweet little old boy. They had thought Rhoda was finished having children and then she gave them one last little boy. Well, he was a tender little chicken, but he'd toughen. He'd make a man. Couldn't help it. Had a man for a father even if he was a chickenshit. He'd turn into a man even if he did live in New Orleans and spend his life riding on the streetcar.

Teddy's grandfather finished up in the barn and walked back to the house to get a glass of tea and sit out on the porch and wait for the boy. "I might set him up an archery target in the pasture," he told his wife. "Where'd you put the bows the big boys used to use?"

"They're in the storage bin. Don't go getting that stuff out, Dudley. He doesn't need to be out in the pasture in this heat."

"You feed him. I'll find him things to do."

"Leave him alone. You don't have to make them learn things
every minute. It's summer. Let him be a child."
"What's wrong with her? Why's she sick again?"
"She fell down. I don't want to talk about it. Get some tea and
sit down and cool off, Dudley. Don't go getting out archery
things until you ask him if he wants to. I mean that. You leave
that child alone. You just plague him following him around. He
doesn't even like to come over here anymore. You drive people
crazy, Dudley. You really do." She poured tea into a glass and
handed it to him. They looked each other in the eye. They had
been married thirty-eight years. Everything in the world had
happened to them and kept on happening. They didn't care.
They liked it that way.

Teddy's uncle Ingersol was five years younger than Teddy's
mother. He was a lighthearted man, tall and rangy and spoiled.
Teddy's grandmother had spoiled him because he looked like
her side of the family. Her daddy had died one year and Ingersol had been born the next. Reincarnation. Ingersol looked like a
Texan and dressed like an English lord. He was a cross between
a Texan and an English lord. His full name was Alfred Theodore
Ingersol Manning. Teddy was named for him but his real father
had forbidden his mother to call him Ingersol. "I want him to be
a man," his father had said, "not a spoiled-rotten socialite like
your brothers."
"My brothers are not socialites," Teddy's mother had answered, "just because they like to dance and have some fun occasionally, which is more than I can say for you." Teddy always
believed he had heard that conversation. He had heard his
mother tell it so many times that he thought he could remember
it. In this naming story he saw himself sitting on the stairs
watching them as they argued over him. "He's my son," his
mother was saying. "I'm the one who risked my life having him.
I'll call him anything I damn well please."
Teddy's vision of grown people was very astute. He envi-
sioned them as large, very high-strung children who never sat
still or finished what they started. Let me finish this first, they
were always saying. I'll be done in a minute. Except for Eric.
Many times Eric just smiled when he came in and put down

whatever he was doing and took Teddy to get a snowball or to walk the springer spaniels or just sit and play cards or Global Pursuit or talk about things. Eric was the best grown person Teddy had ever known, although he also liked his uncle Ingersol and was always glad when he showed up.

All his mother's brothers were full of surprises when they showed up, but only Uncle Ingersol liked to go out to the amusement park and ride the Big Zephyr.

Ingersol showed up this day almost as soon as Big George and Teddy arrived in the truck. Big George was still sitting on the porch drinking iced tea and talking to Teddy's grandfather about fishing when Ingersol came driving up in his Porsche and got out and joined them. "I heard you were coming over, namesake. How you been? What's been going on?"

"Momma fell down some stairs and me and Eric had to bring her home."

"Eric and I."

"I forgot."

"How'd she do that?"

"She said Eric tried to kill her. She always says things like that when she's hung over. She said to tell you Eric tried to kill her." There, he had done it. He had done what she told him to do. "If she divorces Eric, I'm going to live with him. I'm staying right there. Eric said I could."

His grandfather pulled his lips in. It looked like his grandfather was hardly breathing. Big George looked down at the ground. Ingersol sat in his porch chair and began to rub his chin with his hand. "You better go see about her, Son," his grandfather said. "Go on over there. I'll go with you."

"No, I'll go alone. Where is she now, Teddy?"

"She's in bed. The doctor came to see her. He gave her some pills. She's asleep."

"Okay. Big George, you know about this?"

"Just said to bring the boy over here to his granddaddy. That's all they told me. Eric wouldn't hurt a flea. I've known him since he was born. He'll cry if his dog dies."

"Go on, Son. Call when you get there." His grandfather had unpursed his mouth. His uncle Ingersol bent down and patted

Teddy's head. Then he got back into his Porsche and drove away.

"I'm going to stay with Eric," Teddy said. "I don't care what she does. He said I could stay with him forever."

Ingersol drove across the Causeway toward New Orleans thinking about his sister. She could mess up anything. Anytime they got her settled down, she started messing up again. Well, she was theirs and they had to take care of her. I wish he *had* thrown her down the stairs, Ingersol decided. It's about time somebody did something with her.

Teddy's mother was crying. She was lying in her bed and crying bitterly because her head hurt and her poems had not been accepted by *White Buffalo* and she would never be anything but a wife and a mother. And all she was mother to was three wild children who barely passed at school and weren't motivated and didn't even love her. She had failed on every front.

She got out of bed and went into the bathroom and looked at how horrible she looked. She combed her hair and put on makeup and changed into a different negligee and went to look for Eric. He was in the den reading a book. "I'm sorry," she said. "I got drunk and fell asleep. I didn't mean to. It just happened. *White Buffalo* turned my poems down again. The bastards. Why do I let that egomaniac judge my work? Tell me that."

"Are you feeling better?"

"I feel fine. I think I'll get dressed. You want to go out to dinner?"

"In a while. You ought to read this book. It's awfully good." He held it out. It was *The Snow Leopard*, by Peter Matthiessen.

"Has the mail come?"

"It's on the table. There are some cards from the boys. Malcolm won a swimming match."

"I wasn't sleeping with him, Eric. I went over there to meet a poet from Lafayette. It got out of hand."

Eric closed the book and laid it on the table by the chair. "I'm immobilized," he said at last. "All this is beyond me. I took Teddy with me to bring you home. For an alibi if you said I pushed you down the stairs. I can't think about anything else. I took that seven-year-old boy to see his mother passed out on the stairs in her pantyhose. I don't care what you did, Rhoda. It doesn't matter to me. All I care about is what I did. What I was driven to. I feel like I'm in quicksand. This is pulling me in. Then I sent him to Mandeville to your parents. He didn't want to go. You don't know how scared he is—of us, of you, of everything. I think I'll go get him now." Eric got up and walked out of the room. He got his car keys off the dining-room table and walked out into the lovely hot afternoon and left her there. He got into his car and drove off to get his stepson. I'll take him somewhere, he decided. Maybe I'll take him to Disney World.

Teddy was sitting on an unused tractor watching his grandfather cut the grass along the edge of the pond. His grandfather was astride a small red tractor pulling a bush hog back and forth across a dirt embankment on the low side. His grandfather nearly always ran the bush hog into the water. Then the men had to come haul it out and his grandfather would joke about it and be in a good mood for hours trying to make up for being stupid.

Teddy put his feet up on the steering wheel and watched intently as his grandfather ran the bush hog nearer and nearer to the water's edge. If his grandfather managed to get it in the water, they wouldn't have time to ride the horses before supper. That's what Teddy was counting on. Just a little closer, just a little bit more. One time his grandfather had turned the tractor over in the water and had to swim out. It would be nice if that could happen again, but getting it stuck in the mud would do. The day was turning out all right. His uncle Ingersol had gone over to New Orleans to get drunk with his mother, and his cousins would be coming over later, and maybe Eric and his mother wouldn't get a divorce, and if they did, it might not be too bad. He and Eric could go to Disney World like they'd been wanting to without his mother saying it was tacky.

His grandfather took the tractor back across the dam on a seventy-degree angle. It was about to happen. At any minute the tractor would be upside down in the water and the day would be saved.

. . .

That was how things happened, Teddy decided. That was how
God ran his game. He sat up there and thought of mean things
to do and then changed his mind. You had to wait. You had to
go on and do what they told you, and pretty soon life got better.

Teddy turned toward the road that led to the highway. The
Kentucky Gate swung open, and Eric's car came driving
through. He came to get me, Teddy thought, and his heart
swung open too. Swung as wide as the gate. He got down off
the tractor and went running to meet the car. Eric got out of the
car and walked to meet him. Crazy little boy, he was thinking.
Little friend of mine.

Joyce Carol Oates

YOU PETTED ME, AND I FOLLOWED YOU HOME

This thing that happened to them, the little lost dog, it was like nothing that'd ever happened to them before.

They'd been at their friends' place, drinking. Got there at nine and left at maybe one-thirty in the morning. Which was early, for Vic, for a weekend night, but now that they were married, and Dawn still recovering from her four days in the hospital, they kept different hours.

And just their luck it was the first snow of the season, a gritty wind-blown snow, and only October. And Dawn lightly dressed. And no car. And it was too far to walk home. Vic was out in the street looking for a taxi, stiff head and back, angry eyes, they were between cars now that the five-year-old Mercury had broken down, a piece of shit as Vic called it, he was a man not used to not having his own car so maybe it wasn't the right thing for Dawn to ask, touching his arm, the only way you could talk to Vic sometimes, by touching him first, "Honey, why don't we go back upstairs, maybe somebody can drive us home? Frank, maybe?" But Vic didn't hear. Ignored her. She guessed he hadn't told his friends about the Mercury, he'd only be able to tell them when it had become a joke, something he could laugh at, but that wasn't yet. Dawn said, pushing it, "Do you have enough for a cab?—I mean, a tip, too? I didn't bring along my wallet."

Vic turned, and pushed her a little, not hard but so she'd know she'd been pushed, toward the curb. "Wait up there," he said. "Those shoes—!" Meaning Dawn's spike heels, soft black leather with spaghetti-thin straps through which her textured black stockings shone like her own skin, translucent. Shoes impractical for walking a block let alone miles but Vic liked them, didn't he? Liked Dawn's sexy shoes, clothes?

Sure he did.

Dawn went to stand, not very steadily, in the arched brownstone doorway of the building they'd just left. Shivering in the damp wind that smelled of the river, a metallic-rot taste. That smell that, when it washes over you, reminds you of all the other times—winter, the wind, swirling-drunken snow, your eyes tearing so you're half-blind—you've endured it, and getting older doesn't make it any easier. Dawn was hoping that none of their friends would leave the party just now, and see them. For sure, then, they'd be driven home, but Vic wouldn't like it, and she'd had to deal with his mood, at home. It wasn't Dawn but Vic who felt it: not having their own car, even if it was temporary. (The Mercury was so shot, Vic couldn't get a decent trade-in. So he'd have to borrow from—who? His brother maybe. His father. Dawn didn't inquire, and Vic didn't say.) And not only not having a car, but the prospect of other people knowing. It was humiliating. For him, not her. But, if for him, for her too. If for the man, for the woman too. They were married now.

It was Dawn's mother who'd said that. *If for the man, for the woman too.* What the hell it meant, why she'd said it, and when, Dawn didn't know.

And there it was, as if it'd been waiting for them: a little lost dog.

A little lost dog, out of nowhere suddenly, on the sidewalk. Shivering in the wind, peering up anxiously at Dawn. Panting—its breath steaming. Its brown fur was curly, matted, wet. Dawn saw how it was blinking, rapidly, snowflakes melting against its eyes.

"Aren't you—darling! Darling little doggie," Dawn cooed. It

was her party manner, meant to be overheard. Girlish, good-hearted. Flirty. Dawn wouldn't know she'd been drinking until she exclaimed like this, over some small or silly or sentimental thing. "Oh—are you *lost?*"

The dog was a mongrel, Dawn guessed, small, wiry, ribs prominent through its fur. Part cocker spaniel, with a spaniel's long loose ears, a stubby battered tail, mournful eyes—eyes that stared right into her own. Dawn murmured, baby-cooing sounds, stooped to pet the poor thing and it licked her gloved hands eagerly, and its malnourished body quivered with excitement. "Oh, oh! Not so fast! Oh, you're getting me all wet—" She was laughing, she wasn't scolding, but the dog cringed a little, then continued licking her hands, then Vic came over, and petted the dog too, more roughly, scratching it behind the ears like they were old buddies so the dog whimpered and squirmed with a pleasure almost too intense, like sex almost, Dawn laughed to see. It licked Vic's bare hands urgently, hungrily, its bony hindquarters thrashing from side to side. Vic laughed, Vic liked dogs, he'd had dogs as a kid, growing up. His banter was rapid-fire, good-natured, "Hey boy, hiya boy, poor little bastard you lost?—no collar?" To Dawn he said, in disgust, "Somebody must've dumped him. See, the fur's worn on his neck, from a collar. They took the collar *off.* Sonuvabitch."

Dawn said uncertainly, "Oh, let's take it home!"

"Yeah, that's all we need," Vic said. He was rubbing the dog's head with his knuckles and the dog was making flurried, flailing gestures with its front paws, as if about to leap up against Vic's legs, simultaneously restraining itself, a dog that has been kicked often, and has grown wise.

A cab came by, and Vic ran out into the street to stop it, and he and Dawn climbed inside, and the dog followed them as far as the gutter, the last glimpse Dawn had was of its sad searching eyes. A dog's eyes, but wise.

A ten-minute drive to their apartment on the west side. The young Hispanic driver kept missing lights, braking on the wet pavement for the yellow, you couldn't have said he did it deliberately but Vic was tense watching the meter, Dawn tried not to notice.

He surprised her then by gripping her hand. As, before they

were married, when the emotions between them were quick-shifting and unpredictable as a wind-tattered cloudy sky, he'd often surprised her, scaring her a little, teasing. A man like Vic, you never knew. You prepared yourself for being hurt, thrown off-balance, but he'd smile, he'd gaze at her sidelong, his eyes hooded, suggestive, like now. Like he knew something about her she didn't know, herself. Saying, "You were having a good time tonight, eh?—like I haven't seen you in a while."

Dawn felt a stirring, a quick stab in the pit of her belly. That quick sexual ache. Not knowing if this man was serious, or maybe was he testing her, hoping to get a rise out of her. She said, "I still don't feel they *like* me, those friends of yours, it's like they're always judging me, you know?" Vic said, "Shit, no. They think you're terrific." Dawn said, leaning against Vic, kissing his cheek that was damp from the snow, "I don't care what they think, just what you think." A thought crossed her mind, quick and fleeting as a shadow. "That poor darling little dog— we should've brought it home with us."

Vic laughed, in irony. "Yeah. Sure."

This was when they were living in the cramped, ground-floor apartment in the rust-colored brownstone building on Water Street. It was a neighborhood of aging apartment buildings and auto-parts stores and, a short block away, van line warehouses. Two blocks farther, though not visible from any of their windows, was the broad choppy river the color, most days, of steel filings. The apartment was *just temporary*, and furnished with things Dawn hadn't exactly chosen, most given to them by relatives.

When the taxi pulled up in front of the building, Dawn got out and carefully, weaving on her high heels, walked away. She'd heard Vic with taxi drivers in the past, heard exchanges she'd wished she hadn't heard. She never looked at the meter.

Sometimes Vic tipped, and sometimes he didn't. When he worked, he worked damned hard; he had a union job, and it hadn't been easy to come by. It was his reasoning that not everybody, not just everybody doing their fucking job, deserved a tip.

Dawn, who'd waitressed off and on since the age of seventeen, did not agree with that philosophy, but didn't care to argue.

However it worked out tonight, Dawn wouldn't know. When Vic joined her, his face was tight but neutral. He was just putting his wallet back into his pocket.

Dawn cried, incredulous, "Oh, Vic! Look!"

She was pointing at the little lost dog, trotting breathless in the street. All those blocks, two miles at least—was it possible?

Vic whistled through his teeth. "Christ!"

Dawn said uncertainly, "It *is* the same dog isn't it?"

The little mongrel spaniel with the ragged ears, panting from its ordeal. The stubby tail wagging hesitantly. Those eyes. As they stared in amazement, the little dog sidled up to them at an angle, wary of being kicked. It seemed to be favoring its left back leg.

Dawn murmured guiltily, "Oh, poor thing!—you're all wet, all cold. What if your fur freezes?" Swaying in her ridiculous shoes she stooped awkwardly to pet the dog, guessing it was probably a mistake, and the dog threw itself desperately against her legs and nearly knocked her down. "No, no! No—*stop*." Dawn was laughing, a little agitated. When she had too much to drink, she was susceptible to sudden laughing jags that could sound like sobs. "Vic, should we feed it something?—we can't just let it go, it's starving."

Vic said quickly, "Hell, no."

"It's so skinny, poor thing just be starving. Look at those eyes!"

"No."

"Oh, please!"

"He'll get the wrong goddam idea."

"But it—he—he's starving."

Vic turned impatiently away, reaching for his keys. Dawn stared stricken at the little dog, its cold damp nose nudging against her knees. Flesh, living flesh, touching flesh. And those eyes. Dawn felt snowflakes melting against her warm skin, into her glossy black hair that had grown back to almost its original lushness, fanned out on her shoulders like a young girl's. A sound escaped her that was just raw noise—a sob, a moan of protest.

Vic was up the steps, keys in hand. He said, grudging, "He can't stay, though. Just feed him, and that's that, you got it?" Dawn said, biting her lip, "Of course."

So at one-thirty in the morning, in her spike-heeled shoes and a headache coming on, there was Dawn feeding a little lost dog outside, on the pavement. She'd wanted to feed it inside the vestibule at least, but Vic said no, absolutely not. So she was feeding it in a part-sheltered space beside the front stoop, on sheets of newspaper, lardy stew-scraps from the refrigerator, and some pieces of stale bread, and a bowl of water. God, how the dog gobbled its food! It even growled, tremulously, deep in its throat; its stubby tail went stiff. There was something absurd about the dog, yet so sad, Dawn couldn't help her eyes filling with tears. How old was it, she wondered. The muzzle wasn't gray, which meant it wasn't an old dog, but it didn't look like a puppy, either. And was it male, or female?

Within a minute, the food Dawn had given the dog was gone. And part of the newspaper devoured. And the dog was looking up anxiously at Dawn, and whimpering. Vic, of course, was nowhere in sight. He'd gone inside, leaving her to her folly.

You want to do it, do it. But don't come bellyaching to me afterward.

She wasn't sure which one of them had said that, or even when. Might've been years ago when she'd first met Vic, and so crazy for him.

The dog was begging for more, and Dawn didn't know what to do. Her temples began to ache as if something was tightening them from the inside. Her eyes and her skin felt seared, parched. She'd wanted to leave the party by midnight but Vic hadn't responded to her cues, he was having too good a time with his friends and she hadn't wanted to push it. So she'd let herself be talked into drinking too much, you'd think she would know better by now, not seventeen but thirty-one years old drinking beer on top of red wine, that bitter mouth-aching red wine the guys liked, then, later, two "Jell-O shots"—new to her, vodka sweetened with grape-flavored gelatin. A woman's drink they called it, and Jesus it *was*, delicious and deadly. She might've expected her own husband to warn her but he hadn't.

The little lost dog was nuzzling its nose up beneath her skirt, tickling her. Christ, those eyes!

"O.K., sweetie. A little more, then that's it."

In the apartment, Dawn heard Vic running water in the bathroom, good he was out of the way, wouldn't know what she was doing. She found a few more scraps in the refrigerator, greasy pan-fried potatoes with bits of bacon, and some slices of cheese, fairly fresh slices she shouldn't be giving to a dog but there wasn't much else unless she opened a can of soup or something, Campbell's beef barley was Vic's favorite, but she hadn't better. When she went out into the vestibule, there was a surprise—the dog had gotten in somehow, inside the front door, though she'd have sworn she'd shut the door, carefully. "Sweetie, what? What are you doing in here? Bad dog—" She had to lead it back outside, back into the cold, the damned wind, awkwardly luring it out with the promise of the food, giving it a gentle nudge with her foot. It had begun to whine anxiously. "No, baby!—quiet! You'll wake the building."

Their upstairs neighbors were hostile to Vic and her. An older couple, the man a retired teacher. Complaining to the landlord of "noise and commotion"—when Vic got a little loud, raising his voice sometimes. Dawn kept out of it, as best as she could.

She was having trouble maneuvering the dog out of the vestibule, it wanted so desperately to come inside. *It knows the difference between outside and in,* Dawn thought. *The difference between living and—the other.* She'd taken off her gloves, and the dog's tongue on her hands was unnerving, thrilling—oddly cool, soft as chamois cloth—made her shiver. "That's enough. Enough!" she cried. Finally she was able to divert the dog's attention to the potatoes and cheese slices scraped onto what remained of the newspaper, and it began eating frantically again, its body quivering as if with electric current. So hungry! So—physical!— without a mind. You thought you could never be like that, just a body, just appetite, so raw, so not-human, but it happens.

Dawn stared down at the dog, feeling a sense of loss, terrible and final and irrevocable loss, not to be named.

Oh God. The pain glimmering in her head.

Saying lightly, as if the dog was one of those who had to be shielded from her truest deepest thoughts, "Now that's *all*. It really *is*. You'll have to go away, now."

She climbed back up the steps quickly, hoping the dog wouldn't follow. It paused in its eating to peer up at her, eyes stricken, quizzical. Muzzle damp with saliva and grease. Dawn shuddered, hardened her heart and went inside.

Making sure this time that the outer door, and the vestibule door, were both shut tight, and locked.

Instead of being in the bedroom, or in bed, as Dawn hoped he'd be, there was Vic in the kitchen, drinking from a can of Coor's. Not a good time for drinking but Dawn wasn't going to say anything, nor even suggest by a frown what she was thinking. Vic asked her about the dog, irritated, bemused, her concern for the poor damned thing, wasn't that just like her, just like a woman, and at such a time. Wiry dark hairs bristled on Vic's chest, which was a compact, muscular chest, pushing through the thin cotton fabric of his undershirt, thick under his arms and on his forearms. In the early months of them being lovers, just the look of Vic's arms, like that, made Dawn's mouth go dry. She was saying, "God, I'm glad to be home." But in a way signaling there was something unsaid.

Vic shrugged. Acknowledging he'd heard her, but whatever she'd said, or hinted at saying, didn't call for a reply.

Dawn was feeling reckless, risky. Her cheeks flushed from the cold. She kicked off the damned spike heels, her ankles aching, now standing in her stocking feet on the cold linoleum floor. Vic was looking at her, steady, level—that look of his, in this mood like they'd been quarreling, almost, and tense, excited with their awareness of each other; that look that cut through her like a razor. When they'd first started going together and she'd see him look at her like that, his eyes narrowed, she'd felt the shock of it, of him, his wanting her, in the pit of her belly, leaving her weak, faint. Like she could not have said even her name, who she was. Now, since the pregnancy, that's to say the miscarriage, Dawn saw that look in Vic's eyes less frequently, and then only when he was drunk. And she was drunk. And the anger, the bafflement, beneath.

"Nightcap?" Vic asked, and Dawn said, "No thanks!" but

when he held out the Coor's, smiling at her, she couldn't resist, steadying his hand and tilting the can so she could take a sip. Cold, sour-malt taste, a trickle down her chin. She saw him watching her closely. His forearm grazing her breast.

In her stocking-feet Dawn felt unprotected, vulnerable. And heavier: her jersey dress tight across her hips. She'd gained maybe fifteen pounds these past few months, eating alone, odd hours of the afternoon, so hungry her hands trembled. Other times, sitting with Vic, she hadn't any appetite at all.

At the time of the miscarriage she'd been six months pregnant, and big. All the women in our family get big, Dawn's mother had said. Then she'd lost it, and lost weight, steadily, for weeks. How sick she'd been exactly she didn't want to know and no one, especially not Vic, was going to tell her. Don't look back, she instructed herself, don't dwell on what's lost, gone. *Here-and-now* is all there is. Right? It's useless to make yourself sick, crying, grieving when your truest personality isn't like that at all—it's a *happy personality*. Basically. Dawn's own mother had lost patience with her, finally. When Dawn was calling her two, three times a day crying over the phone. You can't let yourself go like that, Dawn's mother had said. Once you start, you can't stop. So *stop*. Dawn's mother had sounded actually scared of her, she'd started hanging up the phone when Dawn bawled. Hanging up! On her own daughter! Thank God, Vic hadn't known. Hadn't known any of it, and never would.

Now she'd gained back weight but it was just *fatty flesh*, nothing growing inside, pushing her belly out. It was just—*her*. Soft flesh at her waist she'd knead unconsciously, wanting to pinch it off. And her belly that had been so swollen from the inside, the skin so incredibly tight, and so luminous-white: Vic was touching her there now, teasing, but a little rough, squeezing. He liked her, he'd said, with a little more weight than she'd had, when they'd first met; getting a grip on her hips, her buttocks; though never, when they made love, did he speak of such things, or speak much at all. How great she was, he might say. How beautiful. *Oh baby!—beautiful.*

All that passed between them, or had passed, how many times uncounted, too profound to be recalled—there were no words, no adequate words.

Dawn laughed and pushed Vic's hand away. He'd been backing her half-consciously against the kitchen table and, damn it, it *hurt*.

They were headed for bed, Vic's arm around Dawn's shoulders, and heavy, when suddenly there was a sharp scratching noise, close by. A dog's claws against the apartment door?—a dog's forlorn, high-pitched whining? Vic turned, his smile fading. How was it possible, the dog had gotten back inside the building?

Vic cursed, and went to the door and opened it—and there was the little lost dog, barking in quick begging yelps, pawing at his legs. In the half-light its fur looked coarse and whorled, the drab dun camouflage-color of deer in winter. It tried to scramble inside but Vic blocked its way with his foot. Vic said, furious, to Dawn, "How the hell did he get in here?—you must've left the front door open."

Dawn said, weakly, "But I didn't."

"You must've. How else?"

"Vic, I *didn't*."

"Fuck it, I told you—it's a mistake to feed a stray dog."

"It isn't a stray, it's *lost*."

Vic pushed the dog back out into the hall, with his foot. The vestibule door was wide open: the hall was freezing: someone must have come inside just now and forgotten to close it. Dawn said, "*I* didn't do it." Tears were smarting her eyes, she pulled at Vic's arm saying, "Why's it so important?—whether the dog is inside, or what?"

Vic said, "Look, you're drunk. Go to bed."

"I mean, my God, it could sleep in our place, couldn't it? Our kitchen where it's warm? Why not?"

"Are you crazy?"

"It's freezing out—"

"Dawn, for Christ's sake. Go on inside. I'll take care of the poor bastard."

Vic pushed Dawn, not really hard but Dawn's head struck the doorframe, it was like her headache exploded and she ran clumsily back inside, ran into the darkened bedroom, hands pressed against her ears. She heard Vic cursing the dog, and the dog's squeals. Thumping, thudding sounds. The front door slamming shut.

Dawn felt sick, faint. *It knows us*, she thought.

Out of nowhere such a weird, wild thought, of course she was drunk as Vic said, not in control, yet, still, bending now like an old woman, gripping her stomach in sudden cramping pains, it came to her again, unmistakable.

It knows us, that's why.

Dawn undressed with numbed vague fingers, slipped her nylon nightgown over her head and stood at the bedroom window, staring out, not knowing what she was looking for at first—she couldn't see much of Water Street, mainly the narrow alley, garbage cans, the brownstone building next door. Even by day the bedroom had a dim undersea look.

Snow was falling thicker now, not melting on the pavement.

Dawn said, not accusingly so much as wonderingly, "How could you do it! Put that poor little dog out in this cold."

Bedsprings creaked like derisive laughter as Vic settled into bed. She knew without looking at him that he was lying with his hands behind his head, watching her, his eyes narrowed. She'd seen Vic look at other men like that, calculating how to hurt them. If it was worth it, for him. But she wasn't going to turn.

Vic said, "C'mon to bed, honey. Forget it."

Dawn pressed her forehead against the window pane. She wondered if she had a temperature, her skin was so dry, parched. Her eyeballs ached in their sockets.

"Hey," said Vic. "I love you."

"Well," said Dawn, not turning, "I don't love you."

"Yeah? You don't?"

"Because you're cruel."

"Yeah?"

"Cruel, and selfish. You don't give a damn."

"Sweetheart, I told you not to feed that dog. What'd you expect, he'd eat what you gave him, then go away?"

"What was I supposed to do, let him starve?"

"What's it to you? There are a million strays in the city."

"He wasn't a stray, he was *lost*."

Dawn now pressed the back of her hands, which were cool, against her forehead and cheeks. Christ, she *was* hot: a hot-skinned woman: especially when she'd had a few drinks, and people looked at her, men looked at her, that kind of attention she'd first drawn as a girl of maybe twelve, basking in it, but scared, too. Because you can't turn it off when you want to. Because it isn't yours to control.

Thinking of the little dog now as *he*. But why?

For sure, it could be *she*.

Dawn saw nothing, no one on the street, a blur of passing headlights. She turned on her way to the bathroom and Vic grabbed her around the hips and pulled her down onto the bed. Meant maybe to be playful, just kidding around but Dawn gave a little scream and began fighting him, elbows, knees, fingernails, and Vic cursed her, and forced his weight on her, pinioning her against the quavering bed with his fingers closed hard around her wrists, her arms flung up beside her head. They struggled, panting. Dawn strained to bring her knee up against him but he blocked her, grinning angrily down at her, the color up in his face, cursing, as she cursed him, sobbing, "Damn you! God damn you to hell! You—" Vic yanked her nightgown up past her waist. Uncovering her breasts. His face was dark with blood, his skin burning. Jaws clenched tight. A man she didn't know, didn't love, a man she'd never seen before, veins livid on his forehead, in his throat. He wanted to hurt her, he knew how to hurt her. He nudged her knees apart, wrestled her down where she'd almost slipped from the bed, kept her thrashing hips in place on the violently creaking bed and Dawn heard herself say, "You! when you can't do anything else you fuck, that's all you can do isn't it, fuck, just fuck, fuck, fuck like you aren't even a—a mind! You make me sick."

Vic froze, in the very act of entering her, forcing himself into her, he froze, just like that: like he'd been struck a blow to the head. Staring down at her like he'd never seen her before.

Then he was off her, off the bed. Slamming out of the room. Dawn heard him in the kitchen, slamming around there. She was scared what he might do—break something, dishes, a window? Throw a chair against a wall? What fury in him, you wouldn't want to laugh at him, a naked man, careening, dangerous in his kitchen at almost two o'clock in the morning. But there came the sound of the refrigerator door being opened, and slammed shut, hard. Another Coor's popped.

Make me sick. I hate you. Dawn lay in the tangled bedclothes, crying. Cupped her breasts in her hands, where they ached. No milk, never any milk but they'd ached. Upstairs, their neighbors were wide awake, and listening. Oh Christ. It left you so ashamed.

What time Vic came back to bed, after three o'clock probably, Dawn didn't want to know. Wasn't going to acknowledge even being awake though she'd gotten up to straighten the bed-clothes, tuck the sheets in neatly, adjust the pillows. Lying then stiff and straight beneath the covers waiting for him, and not waiting.

He crawled in beside her. Not a word. After one of their fights they could lie like this for hours, now stone cold sober, both of them sober, Dawn on her side of the bed and Vic on his, sprawled on his back, perspiring. He'd had how many beers she didn't know and didn't give a damn. His skin gave off a humid heat. His breathing was harsh, irregular, like something was caught in his throat. Toward dawn he might begin to snore, thinly at first, then louder. Then Dawn might nudge him, but they wouldn't speak. And she might fall asleep, too. By degrees. That thin headachey sleep like the hospital sleep, sedation like someone squatting on your chest so you can't breathe.

After a while, Vic would reach out to touch her—tentative, groping. Not a word. The last time, a few weeks ago, they'd lain like this, stiff and furious, mutually wounded, he'd so slowly slipped his fingers through hers it was like a boy slipping his fingers through a girl's—shy, but pushy, knowing what he wanted. And finally gripping Dawn's hand tight so it almost hurt and still he didn't say a word, nor did she, why should she, unless he did? Fuck him!

So. They were lying in bed, in full wakefulness, each bitterly aware of the other, but ignoring the other, when suddenly there came a scratching sound, loud enough to be in the room with them, and Vic sat up at once, saying, "Who's there?"—and Dawn sat up beside him, her heart knocking in her chest, staring into the dark, toward the window.

It was the little lost dog: not in the room with them, but at the window, outside, scratching its toenails frantically against the pane. It was yipping, not loudly, but rapidly, scarcely pausing for breath, as if it were in pain. Dawn knew that sound, that terrible sound that cuts you to the bone marrow. Somehow, the little dog had managed to leap up onto the window sill outside, which was at least five feet above the alley; it had managed to climb over the iron bars that curved over the lower half of the window, and to wedge itself inside, and squirm and wriggle down, head first, where, now, it was struggling to right itself, to wrench its head around and stand on its hind legs, muzzle smearing the glass, nails desperately clawing, peering in.

Michael Byers

SETTLED ON THE CRANBERRY COAST

Our lives in this town are slowly improving. When Trudi grew up, in the old reservation houses, the roads were dirt and the crab factory still wheezed along, ugly and reeking. In early summer the factory stayed open all night, and the damp dirty smell of the crab cooking in its steel vats blew off the ocean, all the way to Aberdeen, even beyond, for all I knew. I remember driving home from movies during my adolescence, the windows open; the sweet pulp-mill smell of Aberdeen was tinged with that distant damp cardboard of Tokeland's cooking crab.

But crab harvests withered fifteen years ago, the state jumped in with some money, and almost at once Tokeland plumped with antique stores and curiosity shops, and the old clapboard hotel became a registered landmark. The Indians, too, began prospering; three years ago, the local tribe sold their fishing rights to the Willapa and voted to put the money into CDs. Many have managed to live off the interest, and now buy fishing licenses like the rest of us. Their trawlers are easily the nicest, you'll notice them moored under the bridge in Aberdeen, the big sleek powerful monsters with aluminum hulls, blue-striped, the new nets, the new radar.

. . .

Neither Trudi nor I have ever been married. We went to high school together, years ago, but we didn't travel in the same crowds. She was from Tokeland, a half-breed Indian, and tended to hang with the toughs, surely tame by today's standards—the kids who wore leather jackets, the kids who smoked and overdid the hair gel. Trudi had long hair, unusually long, thick brown shiny hair that reached the middle of her back. Her crowd drove pickups instead of cars, and on Friday afternoons they'd motor out to the beach, pitching and hurtling over the dunes, then speeding down the long wide beach, big V-8s wide open.

I envied them, sort of, but didn't want to be them. Tokeland back then was not a good place to be from. It meant the clapboard shacks for the Indians, and outhouses, and pump wells instead of piped water, all of it on an open spit of land that caught the worst of the ocean winds. Winters, Trudi says, the wind would blow all day, all night, until it was a part of your soul, an extra function of your body, like your heart, or your breath.

I lost track of Trudi for a while after high school. I went off to college, then lived in the east for a few years with a woman I thought I would marry. When she left me, I decided to come home for a while to recover. I took a job teaching high school history and kept at it for twenty-seven years, fishing during the summers and doing some casual carpentry. Occasionally in the hardware store I'd see one of Trudi's rough old crowd, most of them prosperous fishermen now, having inherited their fathers' boats, now walking with the casual swagger of money, wearing designer blue jeans and monogrammed dress shirts. Some of these men make two hundred thousand dollars a year, I know; and they've always got the newest trucks, slim wives (in matching blue jeans) with tousled hair and high heels. They recognize me, most of them, and I hear them worry about their kids sleeping on the beach, the girlfriends and boyfriends, getting into this or that drug, trouble at school, and sometimes they ask me about their child, though I make it clear I am retired from teaching. I try to assure them that the kids will grow out of childhood, as they themselves have done, and privately I wonder why they can't see themselves in their children.

When I retired from teaching, packing my classroom with utter relief, handing in my teacher's editions for the last time, I found I was restless. Fishing wasn't enough to hold my attention all year round; I'd never married, had had no children. I had some good friends at the high school but I was afraid to linger there, afraid someone might call me a sad old man. On a whim I advertised myself as an independent carpenter and plumber. Most of my phone calls were just friends; they had recognized my name on the sign, they said, and had just called to see if it was really me. Oh, it's me, all right, I told them.

One day last summer I got a phone call from Trudi. She, too, had recognized my name, but she had a job for me. "I just bought a new house," she said. "It's a wreck, and I need someone to help me remodel."

"Trudi? I used to know you."

"Yes, you did." Her voice had become deep and raspy with cigarettes; but she had always had an expressive voice that she modulated well, low secret tones and high ones.

"Where's the house?" I asked.

"Just outside of Grayland. We're moving. I'm dumping my Tokeland house."

"So how have you been?" I asked.

"Oh, getting along. What about you? Married?"

"No."

"Divorced?"

"No, nothing. No kids," I said.

"I saw you retired from teaching last year. I saw you in the paper."

"I've gained a little weight since you knew me," I said. My picture had been on the inside front page: I was on stage, receiving a plaque from the principal and superintendent. My suit jacket had been open and my stomach loomed out in its striped shirt, my tie barely reaching to the third button. I had been shocked by the picture, unpleasantly, but strangely fascinated, too, as if I were seeing myself for the first time in years. "I'm on a diet now," I said. "All that cafeteria food." This was a lie. In twenty-seven years I hadn't eaten in the cafeteria once.

"We're none of us getting any younger. Do you want me to call you Mr. Thomas? You must be used to that."

"Ward is fine," I said.

"How about Frosty?"

I smiled. "Frosty's fine, too," I said. "You've got a good memory for someone you didn't really know."

"When can you start on my house?" she asked. "I've got my granddaughter living with me, so I need to get settled pretty fast."

"We can start tomorrow if you want. What do you need, a roof? New floors?" I pulled a note pad to me.

"Everything. There's nothing right with this house except the location."

"Where is it?" I asked. I wrote *everything* on the pad, then underlined it twice.

"Behind the post office, just over the bridge. I'll be there in the morning. I'll have a white pickup parked in the yard."

"All right," I said. "What time do you want me there?"

"Eight," she said. "Andrea's daycare starts at eight, and I've got work at nine."

"Where are you working?"

"The state park. I'm a ranger."

"A ranger? As in a park ranger?"

"Right."

"You wear one of those hats?"

Trudi laughed. "I'll have it on tomorrow."

"I can't wait. I never imagined you as the law enforcement type."

"Things change," she said.

"No kidding."

Twin Harbors State Park sits right on the main highways in and out of the area. It's got hundreds of campsites on both sides of the highway: one side is forested and mosquito-ridden, the other side is scrubby and dry, patches of sandy clearing among the scotch broom and shore pine. The campsites sit right alongside one another, children spilling through the campground, the four pit toilets hidden in the brush. Many years ago a friend of mine from college came out to visit me and insisted on camping there. I tried to dissuade him, but he was an Easterner, determined to experience the Pacific firsthand. When I picked him up the next morning, the camp was littered with beer cans and broken glass, and in the camp next to his there stood the blackened skeleton of a small pine tree, sooty dark, the soil around it burnt brown. This is where Trudi worked.

But I know, from working at the high school, that even the dirtiest and least engaging places can grow on you. The high school was a one-story yellow-brick building set down in a dirt field. The classrooms, unbelievably, had no windows—ostensibly to keep the kids from becoming distracted by the traffic going by on the highway. It was just an ugly place, institutional, unlandscaped, with pine trees around the edges of the athletic fields all dead of some sort of beetle blight, standing there for years, brown and dead, waiting to fall on the soccer players.

But the kids were usually interested and articulate, and they had mornings when they were thinking, their hands were raised, or I'd have a sweet kid in a certain period who always understood my jokes, or pretended to. In my fifth year there, a math teacher named Jack Patani, a little Italian guy, married one of his students. People were very understanding. I don't think I could have done it, but as a teacher I knew why *he* did. She was one of the sweet ones who adored him, and who, as he grew to know her, gave him good conversation and a nice young body. How can I blame him?

My house was about three minutes north of Trudi's, on the highway. As I drove, I felt my nerves rising. I've always dreaded reunions with old friends; they have something to compare you against, or they have grudges against you that you've forgotten.

Her house was just behind the post office, and her backyard border on a cranberry bog. She was standing in her yard, unloading lumber from her pickup. The first thing I noticed: her hair was cut short, like a boy's. She wore dark green work pants, like a mechanic's, a white tank top, and her face had deep wrinkles in it, I assumed from smoking. She stood straight and peered into my car. She had changed—but it was her, and her full smile I recognized. "Hello," I said, and we shook hands.

"Frosty! God! You look great!" She shook my hand firmly. Her voice was thick and raspy.

"Thanks, you too," I said, though I regretted the loss of her hair. "What have you been doing all this time?" I asked, and then winced, realizing this might sound as if I had expected more of her.

"Raising a daughter, working at the park. I've got my granddaughter with me now, I told you," she said. She smiled again and her eyes crinkled at the corner. Her face was weathered and sunbeaten, like an old man's, and her eyebrows were thick and black. "She's in the back, playing in the pool. I got the water hooked up today, and there's power, but I don't think the wiring's too reliable."

"A pool?"

"Oh, you know, a little wading pool, one of those plastic things you can buy. Come on back." We walked around the corner of the house. Trudi's arms were strong, her triceps bulging like a weight-lifter's. "I know, I know," she was saying. "It looks like a dump. But I could buy it for cash, and look—" she pointed over the back fence at the bog, misty and green. "That's a nice view. And the yard's big enough for Andrea to play in."

"I've seen a lot worse," I said.

Andrea was leaping in and out of a plastic wading pool. The pool was printed with alligators and hippos, and had maybe six inches of water in it. The little girl was wearing white underpants and was shirtless, so her belly hung out like a trucker's. She was four, maybe five, and had Trudi's thick grainy black hair. Trudi a grandmother? It would take some getting used to.

"Andrea, come say hello to Mr. Frosty. He's going to be helping us fix up our house."

Andrea stopped jumping, stepped carefully out of the pool, and walked over to us with the forthright gait of a topless dancer.

"Hello," I said.

"Hello," she said. I held out my hand to shake, and she plopped her hand solidly in mine—how small that hand was! It was wet and warm, like a little frog in my palm. She asked, "Is your real name Mr. Frosty?"

"That's what your grandmother calls me."

"Why?"

"When I was young, my hair turned gray, so I looked like I had frost in my hair."

"Oh." She looked a little uneasily at Trudi and padded back to the pool.

We went inside to check on the house. It was small—two bedrooms, a living room and a kitchen and bathroom. It had been built well, and from the look of the wiring and the moldings, it had probably been built in the twenties. The light fixtures had been replaced, probably after the originals were stolen, but the sink was definitely original equipment, a deep brown water stain under the hot tap. The tub, though handsome and claw-footed, had lost its enamel in spots, so sitting in it would be like sitting on sandpaper. The floor had a couple of rotten patches, but it was oak, a surprise. The ceiling was a total loss, sagging and stained—the whole thing would have to be replaced. "We're looking at four or five weeks here," I said. A tractor ran noisily along the fence, tending the bogs.

"That's not so bad. How much will it cost?"

This was difficult. She was technically a friend, and I didn't really need the money. "I'll need to price the materials before I can really know for sure."

"Well, roughly," she said. "I just want to know what I'm getting into." She was sweeping dust and nails out of one of the bedrooms. The nails pinged along the floor—you could see the ghost of a carpet.

I gave her a figure, a pretty low one, I thought, but I suppose she felt obligated to bargain me down. She said, "You're not a professional carpenter, now, are you?"

"I do it for money."

"Yeah."

"What I've given you is an estimate. The materials might come to more than that."

She shrugged. "Well, get me a list of the materials you'll need, and give me a work schedule. I want to do a bedroom first so Andrea and I can move in." She swept the nails into the dustpan and poured the mess into a plastic trash can. "I've got to go to work."

At her truck she pulled out a green ranger's shirt and buttoned it, tucked it into her pants, and then put on her ranger's hat. "The hat looks good," I said. She looked tough, not somebody I'd want to mess with if I were a kid shooting off fireworks on the beach.

"Thanks. I'll be home around six; you can bring the list by any time after that. Come on, Andrea, put your shirt on." She started her truck and waited while Andrea dressed slowly, stepped into salt-water sandals, then climbed into the truck. Andrea's wet underwear showed through her pants. They waved as they drove off, Trudi glancing behind her as she backed down the driveway.

My sister Jody has wanted me to get married for years. She's the principal of a high school in Raymond now, and every week or so I'll stop by and take her out to lunch. On her office door there's a bumper sticker that says, "As long as there are tests, there will always be prayer in school!" She is religious.

I have no way of explaining this—we weren't raised that way —other than to say she's always been an optimist. She started going to church in high school, perhaps at first as an excuse to dress up, but she came back glowing, just exploding with happiness. She'd pull the pins out of her hair, saying, "You've got to come, Frosty! It's so refreshing!" And I would gaze at her, and shake my head as a little brother does.

After I made the list of materials at Andy's Hardware (Andy, a big, horse-faced kid whom I taught, an unnerving person: he couldn't spell to save his life, but I'd glance at him in class, and he'd be shaking his head as if there were something I just didn't get), I drove down to Raymond to see my sister. She was ensconced behind her desk in her cinderblock office, plump, a new perm. On the wall hung a plaque: "Lord, give me patience . . . and I need it now!" "Hello," I said.

"Hey, Frosty. I've got one thing left to do before we go. Just a second." She held up a fat finger and dialed the phone.

"I'll be out here," I said.

I walked into the outer office, jingling my keys. I walked down one of the tiled halls. Scraggly worksheets were stapled onto bulletin boards—the kindergarten hall. A smell of pee from the bathroom. I peered through a window in a classroom door. Inside, I saw a young, blonde teacher sitting on the carpeted floor, leading a kindergarten class reciting days of the week. With each word, she moved her hands: clasped her fingers together for Tuesday, settled her hands on her shoulders for Wednesday, folded them over her breasts for Thursday. This woman couldn't have been more than twenty-three or twenty-four and the children's baby faces were set in earnest, their hands moving in grave imitation from shoulder to breast to cheek.

"Frosty?" Jody appeared in the hall, waving to me. "Ready?"

"Sure. Busy day?"

"Oh." She laughed. "The usual. Parents who don't think their kids should have homework."

"Should I come back tomorrow?"

"Oh, no, I'm happy to get out of here." We crossed the parking lot to her car.

"Do you remember a girl named Trudi?" I asked. "From Tokeland, sort of hung around with the Indian kids?"

"Sure. Her daughter came here to high school for a couple of years."

"Her daughter?"

"Yeah, Carolyn. She was in the math magnet program for the Indian kids. She dropped out after tenth grade."

"Trudi hired me to fix up her house."

"Really? Hired you?"

"Through my ad, you know." We swung down into her car and nosed out onto the highway into town. "She bought one of those old bungalows behind the post office."

"I'm trying to remember what happened to Carolyn," my sister said.

"I think she must have had a kid," I said. "Trudi's got a granddaughter living with her now."

"For some reason I want to say she went to California. I think she worked with the migrants for a while, just picking," she said. She shook her head, then laid two fingers on her temple. "I've got too many people up here. They're all starting to look like one another."

"Time to retire. Get the hell out of there."

Jody smiled. "People in town remember you," she said. "I introduce myself, and they'll mention you, and they'll start talking about you—your poster of Jane Fonda on the Harley?"

"That was a joke."

"Well, sure it was a joke! They loved it! God, those idiots up there didn't know what to make of you."

We drove in silence for a minute, then Jody asked, "Does Trudi ever hear from her?"

"From who?"

"Carolyn. Her daughter."

"I don't know. Why?"

"Just wondering." She pulled into the parking lot of the Lamplighter. "You don't have a problem with that?"

"With what?"

Jody said, "With Carolyn abandoning a little baby like that."

"Oh, Jody, come on."

Jody shrugged. I followed her into the air conditioning, the dark.

From Trudi that night I learned this: that Carolyn made it to California, just barely. Trudi tracked her down at a strawberry farm, where she was earning two dollars a flat with a two-year-old Andrea slung on her back in a blue shirt. Trudi brought Andrea home for the summer, then for the winter as well.

Carolyn didn't come back. She wrote twice from Mexico a year later, and on Andrea's fifth birthday, the mother was present only in her two letters tacked to Trudi's fridge, in one smiling photograph of her with Andrea on her back, and in Andrea herself, who when asked about her mother remembered only the heat and shady hats, the months of sunshine, and the easy dip and rise of Carolyn picking beans and fruit beneath her.

"This is you, isn't it?" Trudi pointed at a crowd picture, all banners and letter jackets.

I leaned over her shoulder, holding a half-sawed PVC pipe. "That's me. Pre-gut days."

"Can I see?" Andrea padded up to the card table, her feet swooshing in the grass.

"Sure, hon. That's Frosty."

Andrea took the big book in her arms and tilted it into the last of the light. She glanced back and forth a couple times. "How old are you?"

"Now? I'm fifty-two." I heard the tractor churning around the edges of the bog.

She lifted the book back to Trudi. "Where are you?" she asked.

"Here." Trudi hoisted Andrea onto her lap and began flipping the glossy pages. "Your grandmother was not a very good girl."

"What do you mean?"

"She didn't do her work in school."

"You didn't?"

"I thought it was more important to be with my friends." She glanced at me, then at the tractor coming toward the gate.

"Was Frosty one of your friends?"

"Sure he was," Trudi said.

I laughed and began picking up clutter—pipe elbows, nail bags, the netting off the bathroom tiles we'd put in that day.

"I knew Frosty pretty well," Trudi said.

The tractor stopped at the gate. The red-haired driver stood in the seat and waved, then sat down and gunned the engine. The sound was huge and rough, and Andrea cringed in Trudi's lap. "See what that guy wants," Trudi said.

I dumped the garbage in a steel can and walked up to the gate. "What do you want?" I called up to him.

"Open the gate!" His face was long and prognathic, his front teeth gapped.

"Why?"

"I have to get my mail!" he shouted.

I pushed up the latch and swung the gate back. The man gunned the tractor again, smiled, and rumbled through the gateway. Halfway to the road he stopped the tractor, stood, dropped his baggy jeans, and peed in a long yellow arc into Trudi's driveway. Then he sat down again and drove off.

"Oh, god," I said. "That asshole."

Trudi threw her head back and laughed, her leathery face wrinkling around her eyes. She put Andrea gently on the ground, still laughing, and walked to the driveway to kick dust over the mark. "That's the kind of thing I did in school, honey," she called across the yard, and I thought she might have been talking to either of us.

About three weeks into Trudi's job, we took a day off. I'd finished the roof, both bedrooms, and the wiring. We drove up to Grayland to watch the kite festival. This happens every summer, a friendly competition to pull in the tourists. The highway was lined with parked RVs, and a couple hundred people had gathered on the beach. Andrea gave a little gasp when she saw the kites, big fancy ones this year: tandem boxes, dual-stringed stunt kites, black and rippling, and my favorite, one long rainbow tube kite, huge and dignified, hanging in the wind like a blimp. "You like the kites, Andrea?" I asked.

She shifted uncomfortably toward Trudi and stared out the windshield. She's not used to having a man around, Trudi had said. She doesn't know what you're going to do. I don't know what I'm going to do, I'd replied.

"Look at the little black ones," Trudi said.

"I like the rainbow one," Andrea said.

"Good choice!" I tried to smile, not make any moves toward her. "Andrea, you and I agree on which kites are the prettiest." She just nodded seriously.

We parked by a hot dog stand. Merle Merrington, a retired deputy now working as a cook, was barbecuing the hot dogs, wearing an apron. "Hey, there, Frosty," he said. He had mustard in his mustache.

"Hey, Merle. Give me a couple dogs." I gestured behind me. "You know Trudi Fraser?"

"I think we've met a few times." He nodded at her. "Still working up at the park?"

"Yep."

Merle glanced down at Andrea. "Don't look now," he said to Trudi, "but I think you've got a big dog following you around."

Andrea giggled. "This is my granddaughter, Andrea," Trudi said.

"Looks like a big dog to me." he stared at her and barked, his boozy eyes red and haggard. Andrea barked back. "See?" he said. "And all this time you thought she was related to you. I bet you've been feeding her and everything."

"Nope," Andrea said.

"Ups! A dog that talks. Does the big dog want a hot dog?"

"Yes!" she barked.

"I thought so." He handed her a hot dog in a paper napkin; she took it boldly with both hands. This made me feel envious: the easy way he talked to her, and her smiling for him.

"Who's the guy with the tube kite?" I asked.

"Don't know. Some guy from out of town." Merle turned the hot dogs. "He's been here before."

We walked over to the man—short, bald, no more than thirty. His eyebrows were pale and bushy. "Nice kite," I said.

"Thanks." He held a plastic disk in his hand. Twelve plastic strings led to the kite.

"This little girl'd really love to try it," I said.

He glanced at us skeptically. "It's kind of difficult."

"I'll help her out."

He watched the kite.

"Just for a minute."

"Don't let go," he said. He handed me the disk, which tugged up and away from me. I knelt down and put my arms around Andrea from behind. She was sweaty and smelled like sun, and dirt, and meat. She grabbed where I told her, and we made the tube shiver and dive as it hung majestically above us, in place, like a dream animal.

Over the next couple of weeks the house got sturdier. I found some old oak boards in my shed and used them to patch the floor. I gutted the kitchen and put in a new fridge, new cupboards, a new window over the sink. I was proud of my work. It was quick, cheap, and somehow I didn't make any mistakes. The new wall in the kitchen was solid, stronger than the original.

Andrea became a little more comfortable around me. Trudi and I worked well into the evenings, the TV on in the living room as we put up plaster or spread joint compound. Sometimes we woke Andrea, who would then come toddling out of Trudi's room and watch us work. In the TV's late blue light her hair was steel gray. "Want to help?" I asked once. She wandered over, peered into the joint compound bucket, watched me spread the stuff back and forth. I took a fingerful and laid it on her palm. "Don't eat it," I said.

"I won't." She smelled it, then pinched it and rubbed it between her fingertips. "Feels like cookie dough," she said.

"That's right. We use it to hold pieces of the wall together."

"Like glue."

"That's right."

She wiped it back into the bucket. "How long till it's done?"

"The house? About a week. Seven days."

Jody came up one night during that last week with a bottle of wine and a twelve-pack of Henry's. We opened the gate to the cranberry bog and sat down on the grass. The cranberries were pale pink and small, hidden under the creeping leaves. "Here, have some of these with your wine," Trudi said, dropping a handful in my glass. "A touch of elegance."

"Fresh from the bog," I said, and drank deeply. The cranberries rolled around like ball bearings.

"So you're the principal," Trudi said.

"That's right."

"Look out, Andrea," Trudi said. "Frosty's sister is the boss of a school." Andrea said nothing, just crouched at the edge of the bog, collecting the brightest berries she could find.

"I like your house," Jody said.

"You may thank Frosty for that."

I said, "He *is* amazing."

"Yes, he is." Trudi patted my knee.

We drank the wine and began on the beer. A mist began wisping in from the ocean, squeezing through the pines and sliding past just about at eye level. Little tufts settled in the ditches, and scraps hung up in the trees like laundry. My sister said, "I taught your daughter, Carolyn." She was becoming drunk, and was making generous gestures. "No. Actually, no, I didn't. I didn't teach her. What am I saying? But I remember her."

"She didn't get too far," Trudi said.

"No, I remember that. A beautiful girl, though. Very pretty." Jody opened another beer.

"Thank you."

"You're welcome."

"I don't think we have to worry about seeing her around here any time soon," Trudi said.

Jody nodded.

"She is no longer a part of our lives," Trudi said, and something about the way she said *our* made us all glance over at Andrea, who now lay picking at the grass. I could imagine moving in with these two, sure, sleeping on the sofa at first—an urge to lend a hand, I suppose, to take on this little family—though they seemed whole and complete there at the edge of the bog, as if that *our* had sealed them off from me somehow. Trudi wore a strange expression, not of wonder, which you'll see on new mothers, but something closer to acceptance, and regret. But we don't live our lives so much as come to them, as different people and things collect mysteriously around us. I felt as if I were coming to Trudi and Andrea, easing my way toward them.

"Don't let it bother you," Trudi said, leaning toward me, her hand on my thigh. "She's not even something I think about any more. She's gone, gone, gone. And now here's Frosty for us." She kissed me on the cheek. "Am I drunk?" she asked. Her eyes were bright.

"Probably."

"Oh, good." She rubbed her face with her palm. "Mm. Don't even think about her," she said. "No point any more." I sat holding my beer. What was she imagining? The migrants' shacks, the mattresses that swelled with the dew and rain between seasons? "No point." Her lowered voice, the finality of it. I imagined the orchards hanging full of fruit, a faceless Carolyn lost in the trees.

I spent the night on Trudi's living room floor, and—as I do when I am hung over—woke up at dawn not nauseated but with the feeling that a wind was coursing through my head, that I had created a few vacancies upstairs. I made coffee and sat on the front porch, facing the back of the post office. The flagpole was still empty—no one had yet come in for work. I sat there, retired teacher, gut on my lap, plaster dust all over my pants from Trudi's floor.

After a while, Andrea walked out onto the porch with a bowl of cereal. "Good morning," I said.

"Morning."

"Want to go to Aberdeen with me today?" I asked. "I have to buy some radiators for your and your mom's bedroom."

"How long is that?"

"How long is the trip? About twenty minutes to get there. We won't be gone more than an hour. Want to come?" I noticed the delicate point of her chin, a trait she shared with Trudi.

"Okay," she said.

"Really? Good. Go ahead and get dressed. We'll go in about fifteen minutes."

I left a note for Trudi: *Gone for radiators with Big Dog. Back in an hour.* —F

Andrea climbed into my car having by herself put on corduroy pants and a white t-shirt. I leaned over to point out her seatbelt, but she grabbed the two ends herself—I could think of nothing to say. Her presence in the car was palpable, her thick meaty smell. We were both tense. "We could get you an ice cream cone there," I aid, and then remembered it was only eight in the morning. "Or maybe some pancakes."

She folded her hands in her lap and stared straight ahead, at the glove compartment.

"Remember where we're going?"

"Aberdeen."

"That's right. Good memory."

She closed her eyes and pretended to fall asleep, her hands clasped rigidly in her lap. I drove quickly, my window cracked open. What had Jack Patani said? He'd married her to give himself a few more good years. Still happy together, those two, and they'd had several good years. I admitted to myself, then, allowed myself to think for the first time, about marrying Trudi. I still hardly knew her at all.

Over the bridge in Aberdeen I nudged Andrea, who had fooled herself and really fallen asleep. She shifted a little in her seat. I walked around to the door, unbuckled her seatbelt, and lifted her against my shoulder. I carried her inside the shop. As we walked among the pipes, she spread her arms, her fat arms, to hold my neck; and as she rode I imagined that she remembered this strolling motion, and that more than any rocking could, or singing, this soothed her, and she let me hold her quietly in her sleep. I had the radiators loaded clanking in the trunk, and I sat on my hood, smoothing her hair with my hand, hearing her easy settled breathing.

David Gates

THE INTRUDER

1

They had the air conditioner on Hi Cool and the whole down-stairs smelled of roasting turkey. Friday afternoon. Finn sat in the blue armchair, which rested on Teflon wafers to protect the floor he'd finally gotten around to sanding and refinishing. With spar varnish, not that damnable polyurethane. He was reading, of all things, *Timon of Athens*, which he had remembered as be-ing much better. So this would probably be the last time in his life he would read *Timon of Athens;* that made it seem sad and precious, if not especially enjoyable. As he read, he also worried: that there would be too many leftovers, that Thanksgiving din-ner in July wasn't charming but simply outré, that none of the guests would know he'd been interested in American cooking before it had become fashionable, and that he had been boring James by saying so repeatedly.

James sat cross-legged in the maroon armchair with his ear-phones on. Among the few possessions he'd brought along when he moved in was his collection of books on tape. Lately he'd been reading—if that was the word—Edgar Allan Poe.

"Plugged-in and passive," he'd said. "I'm the first to admit it. The MTV generation. Before your very eyes." Affected deca-dence was one of James's comic turns.

"But *Poe?*" Finn had said.

"It's camp, what can I say?" said James. "I thought *all* faggots were into camp back in your day."

On the floor by his chair James had set a sweating glass of seltzer. He was forever setting his glass on the floor and Finn was forever nagging; today especially he should just bite his tongue. He'd invited Peter and Carolyn, of course, and some people from the Drama Department—Bill and Deborah Whitley, Byron Solomon—although he'd told no one it was an occasion. An anniversary, for James and Finn, could only be the anniversary of one thing, and Finn was—he called it considerate, James called it chickenshit—about shoving in people's faces what they didn't want to know. They'd decided to make today their anniversary, although it could also have been yesterday; by the time that had become important it was too late to pin it down. James had gone to the library and looked at the microfiche to check the movie ads in the paper that week. *Rebecca* and *Notorious* had been Wed-Thur, but they couldn't decide which it had been. For once Finn hadn't been teaching summer school and James said (his decadent routine again) that he hadn't cared what day of the week it was since the last time he'd held a job.

James's sister Carolyn lived on the next street, one house over from Finn's: their backyards touched at a single point. A year ago today—or yesterday—Finn had been out back taking down, at long last, the swing set that had been there when he'd bought the place. With a sledgehammer he'd pulverized the concrete plugs that anchored the thing in the ground; it lay on its side like a dog killed by a car, two stiff legs in the air. He was trying to decide whether it could be knocked apart with the hammer or whether he'd have to take a hacksaw to it when he noticed this —Finn hated the expression "young man"—dressed only in shorts and running shoes mowing the Sykes's lawn. Finn nodded and received a nod in return. Carolyn had forewarned him that her brother would be coming up to stay in the house for a few days while she and Peter were in Umbria, and encouraged him to go over and introduce himself. It seemed uncivil not to make use of this opportunity, but the brother's very good looks made Finn disinclined. That night, Wed or Thurs, he went to what he still thought of as the Central but was now called the Symposium: the musty, velvety old theater in town had become a revival house with air-popped popcorn and a beer-and-wine license, run by a graduate-school dropout convinced that civilized people were getting tired of VCRs. Ahead of him in the ticket line was the young man. When he turned away from the window with his ticket, he saw Finn, smiled and nodded, and walked over.

"I think you're Finn McCarthy," he said.

"Well, that makes one of us," said Finn. "However. Yes. And I think you're the person who was so diligently mowing the Sykes's lawn this afternoon."

"James Chase," said the young man. "Carolyn's brother."

"Yes, Carolyn had prepared me," said Finn. "Somewhat." Should he have? Well, it was said now. "I ought to have come over and said hello, but I was preoccupied."

"You did look kind of menacing with your sledgehammer," said the young man.

"That was my John Henry mode," said Finn. "Otherwise I'm harmless enough. So Peter and Carolyn euchred you into looking after the old homestead while they traipse around sunny Italy."

"It didn't take much euchring," said James Chase. "It was this or muggy Manhattan. Carolyn told me I should be sure and look you up."

"Ah," said Finn. "Here, why don't we go in?" Was he overreacting, or was this a bit gauche of Carolyn Sykes, to have steered this obviously gay boy in his direction when the first move, if any, ought to have been Finn's? On the other hand, he couldn't afford to think ill of Carolyn Sykes: except for poor Byron Solomon, and of course now the Whitleys, Peter and Carolyn were as close as Finn had to friends in this community. As Carolyn undoubtedly knew. Which was why she had taken such a liberty. Although she had surely meant well. (There: he was coming around already). And as to the boy's being obviously gay, would that have been so obvious to a less knowing eye? Did Carolyn herself know it? One's family had a gift for not knowing these things, or so it had been in Finn's family. This brother of Carolyn's was certainly presentable—whatever he meant by that—and obviously conversable.

When the lights came up at intermission, Finn turned to James

Chase and said, "I'm going to give *Rebecca* a miss, I think. I remember this as being the better of the two, and even this is starting to show its age. All this malarkey about how *magical* the two of them are together. Didn't seem so bloody magical to me. Ingrid Bergman reconciles me to living in the age of Julia Roberts."

"It really wasn't all that hot, was it?" said James Chase. "God, I feel like a heretic."

"Bracing, isn't it?" said Finn. "Tell you what. Since you're new in town. There happens to be quite a wonderful diner here. A lot of the old features pretty much *intacta*. And they make a mean rice pudding. And there's a jukebox thing in every booth, with all sorts of marvelous old songs. It still has 'Ring of Fire.' Do you know 'Ring of Fire'? Johnny Cash?"

"I must have heard it," said James Chase. "But, you know. I'm into Garth. Mr. Va Va Voom."

"Well then," said Finn. "We must educate you. Are you game?"

"Always," he said.

From the diner they went back to Finn's house, to hear "White Circle" by Kitty Wells, which Finn insisted was a minor masterpiece. He opened a bottle of wine, and soon he heard himself calling Willie Nelson a "nasty old bird," and was aware for the millionth goddamn time that he tended to sound like an old queen when he'd been drinking. And so to bed, a surprise to both of them. Finn had stopped doing this kind of thing years ago, and James, it turned out, had promised himself that he had not come up here to cruise. And he had sworn off older men.

Later that same night—actually it was beginning to turn gray outside the windows—when they got around to comparing stories, Finn's misgivings came back more sharply. James had been vague about his involvements in New York, but from what Finn could gather it was clear that he might really have been taking his life in his hands with this boy. But truly, wasn't AIDS simply the extreme, the mortal, instance of what had always been the case: that your new love's irrevocable past determined your future? But this James was his first adventure—was it possible?— since he'd moved here. Finn was so out of touch that he didn't even have a condom in the house. James, thank God, had come equipped (despite what he'd promised himself): he carried them in his wallet, like the flamboyantly heterosexual boys of Finn's high-school days.

Finn found James's coming-out story unsettling, too. His own announcement to his parents (he'd been forty; they'd been too old to hear it) had been like something out of a sensitive made-for-TV film: the father's anger, the mother's self-castigation. James had been in his last year of high school; he'd soaked the labels off of a Fibber McGee and Molly cassette and stuck them on a tape called *Top Sergeant* (which purported to be a recording of randy Marines in the barracks), then wrapped it and put it under the Christmas tree. As James told the story, his parents had waited to play it until his Aunt Alice showed up for Christmas dinner, and she had been so shocked that her dentures fell out. Finn suspected he'd invented at least part of this: Aunt Alice was clearly a stock character, a Margaret Dumont or an Edna May Oliver. And it may or may not have been true that his father's slapping him across the mouth had been the pretext for James's quitting school and moving to New York. But true or not, the story made Finn feel both excited and intimidated, the way he had felt as a child when Ricky Morrison had seduced him into playing with matches. From the can Finn's father had kept in the toolshed, Ricky had poured out a wide circle of gasoline onto McCarthy's lawn and tossed match after match until it roared up. It left a telltale ring of charred grass which Finn rubbed at in vain with the soles of his sneakers; he'd caught holy hell, named his accomplice and that was the end of his friendship with Ricky Morrison.

That first night, with Kitty Wells keening, it had been James who committed himself first: he took a deep breath, put a warm hand on the back of Finn's neck and pulled him close. Yet it had been James who had said, "I want to put this on you, can I?" So neither of them, Finn reminded himself, had all the power. That is, if you believed it was all about who fucked who.

James's Walkman gave a snap. Finn looked up from his book and saw him take off the earphones, stretch his arms up over his head and stand up. "The willies," he said. "So what time are people supposed to be arriving?"

Finn, still holding his book, rolled his wrist to check his watch. Ten after four, which of course had no bearing on the question. "I told 'em all six o'clock," he said. "I hate this malarkey where you have one coming at six o'clock and one at six-fifteen and so forth." It was endearing that anyone could still get the willies from Edgar Allan Poe.

"Six o'clock," said James. "Listen, if you don't mind I think I'm going to go up and nap for a little. Will you come wake me?"

Finn rested the open book against his stomach. "What time?" he said, hoping he didn't sound disapproving. He'd gotten up at three in the morning to take a piss; when he came downstairs for a swallow of wine from the refrigerator he'd found James in the study watching *Star 80*. The room had stunk of pot.

"I leave that," said James, "to your discretion."

Oh.

"Actually I might come up and join you," said Finn. "I'm pretty much at a stopping-place. Just let me baste Junior again."

"Don't feel obliged," said James.

"Now what's all *this*?" said Finn.

James shook his head.

"Nothing," said James. "I must be on the rag."

Oh fine, Finn thought. So now it was up to him whether to allow James to get in a jab for free or whether to turn this into another battle royale. Since there were guests due in a couple of hours he should just drop it. But. But but but.

"Am I being unreasonable?" said Finn. Like a damn fool. "To want to know what I'm being told?"

"You're never unreasonable," said James.

"And what is that supposed to mean?"

"What I said," said James. "You're never un*rea*sonable. *I* am unreasonable. As we all know."

Finn closed his eyes for a count of three and blew out his breath for James to hear.

"Now I've done it," said James. "Enter the Bickersons."

"*Why* are you doing it?" said Finn.

"What a reasonable question," said James. "Why doesn't James just go take his nap and wake up cheerful and refreshed? If there's anything the world doesn't need it's another scene with the bitchy *faggots* trying to keep it together in front of company."

"That's not what I'm concerned about," said Finn.

"Right," said James. He started up the stairs, then stopped and looked back. "Hey Finn?" he said. "You *would* be welcome to tuck me in."

Finn decided. "O.K.," he said. "Just let me deal with Junior."

James started up the stairs again. As his feet disappeared from sight he called back, "Don't be too long."

Finn closed *Timon of Athens,* not bothering to mark his place, and got up. Truly, that turkey smelled splendid. On his way into the kitchen he picked up James's Walkman from where he'd left it on the floor. Which story had given James the willies? Finn hit Eject and saw it wasn't the Poe at all, but just a tape tape. On the label someone had written "WORKOUT MUSIC/C. LAUPER ETC." The name seemed antiquated, even to Finn: wasn't she the Gracie Allen one? The writing was faded, and it wasn't James's.

2

Finn McCarthy was a maker of documentary films. Or had been until six years ago, when he was looking for a place to land and was approached by the college's Department of Communication Arts. That was the year his film about children's street games had been nominated for an Academy Award. He'd meant to show these children (filmed in Newark, Liverpool, Mexico City and Connecticut) as members of a savage tribe with alien customs and ceremonies; it had bothered him, therefore, that two of the three reviews he'd gotten had called it "sensitive." For whatever reason, he hadn't been able to get going on a new project since. It was his course load, his inability to travel. It was the too-comfortable life here: dinner parties with tolerant acquaintances in a tolerant college town. It was his house, the first he'd ever owned, which had needed everything done to it. It was James.

But at long last he did have a new project in mind. Which would damn well not be called "sensitive," either. And which would get him once and for all, at the age of fifty-two, out of the closet, not that he was truly *in* the closet. (James gave him guff about that, but that was just James.) Finn had ignored the whole

Stonewall business and everything thereafter; bully for them, of course, but. He was damned if he'd be ghettoized as a quote unquote gay filmmaker; his work was not political. Lately, though, he was beginning to wonder whether avoiding the subject of homosexuality in his films—well, not avoiding, just not obsessing—hadn't been a mistake. A mistake aesthetically. When he looked at his old work nowadays (which wasn't often) it felt impersonal to him. Put-together to a fare-thee-well, of course. But surely there was a way to get closer in without being either confessional or, God forbid, polemical. Assuming he wasn't too old to want to.

What he'd come up with was a film about the makers of gay porno films. Which, if it worked—if he could get the time and the funding and of course the access—would be a sort of oblique self-portrait in addition to whatever else. His films had always been about subcultures: American Indians who worked building skyscrapers, a leprosarium in what was then Southern Rhodesia, country-music fans. The children and their street games. But a subculture based on being homosexual and making films: how could this not end up being his best work? Or so he thought sometimes.

He'd gone so far as to begin collecting videos; he'd also written part of a first draft of an essay on the implicit formal conventions of pornography. If he could finish this and get it decently published—he'd try *Film Quarterly* first, obviously, then *Sight and Sound*—it might help with the funding. The biggest problem, aside from outright censorship—the Mapplethorpe business still had everybody running scared—was that these days such a subject could only be a downer: even safe-sex porn had a sort of *Masque of the Red Death* feel about it. Which was all to the good as far as the film was concerned. But it made the project a tougher sell, even with the Award nomination. If anyone still remembered it.

Another problem was that James was against it; it would set things back twenty years, he said. (Finn's first reaction was to be flattered that James thought a film of his could have any impact at all in the world.) "What if you were a black person?" James had said. "Would you make a movie about welfare cheats eating watermelon in their Cadillacs?"

"If I could get a grant from General Motors," said Finn. James looked at him. "It's not funny, man. You ever stop and think about where you *are?* You drive ten minutes outside this town, man, and you're in fucking Jesse *Helms* country. They don't *like* faggots out there, or haven't you heard?"

"You've lived in New York too long," said Finn. "I've never encountered the least—I mean I don't go to workingmen's *bars* on a Saturday *night,* but who in his right mind *does?*"

James was still looking at him. "You are so blind, man," he said. Finn had never seen him this exercised. And only once before had James called him "man."

That was when James had first moved in. He'd gone down to the city for a weekend to pick up the rest of his things and the weekend had lasted until Thursday. When Finn came to get him at the airport in Albany, James's explanation was so carelessly thin that Finn (who'd had a half-carafe of vile Paul Masson red wine while waiting in the lounge) had called him a slut.

"Listen, man," James had said, "this *slut* was good enough for you when you picked me up at the movies." James had had a gin and tonic on the plane.

"I picked *you* up?" said Finn.

"You don't know how lucky you are," said James. "You're getting a live-in slut all your own, man, complete with checkered past. Just don't push it."

This, of course, had been absolute malarkey. Finn knew what it was to be excited by beautiful bad boys, but at his age he also knew better than to let one move into his home. To take a lithe, treacherous animal to bed was one thing; to wake up next to one was something else again. James's good looks, in fact, had bothered Finn until he got used to them. (One thing that had helped humanize James was when Finn walked in on him spraying Right Guard into his running shoes.) In fact, after the first few days, Finn had been about to hint that it was getting time for James to go back to his sister's house. He changed his mind one afternoon when he came inside from mowing the lawn and found James in the darkened study. On the screen the little black girls from Newark were jumping double-dutch. James looked up, saw Finn in the doorway, thumbed the remote control and froze a little girl with her teeth clenched and one foot in the air.

"This is amazing," he said. "How did you get this to be so scary?"

Finn dropped into his Zen pedagogical manner. "Just by looking at it," he said.

"Gol-*ly*, professor," said James. He looked back at the frozen image. "I wonder how you look at me," he said. "I'd like to be looked at with kindness."

3

"Of course when I first saw it listed," Byron Solomon was saying, "I was quite humiliated."

"Why?" said Bill Whitley. "God, to be able to say you worked with John Ford."

"*Worked* flatters the case, I think," said Byron. "At any rate, I very nearly made a great fool of myself by calling them up and lacing into them about it. Jeannette, of course, talked me around. She said, 'Good heavens'—you remember—'Good heavens, how were *they* to know?' Because naturally for mere *movies* I never used Byron Solomon. Never sullied the great name." He laughed. It didn't sound bitter, and Finn wondered if that was even more depressing. "So she said, 'How were *they* to know, for heaven's sake.' You remember the way she was."

"I wish I could've known her," said Bill Whitley, apparently meaning it as a tactful reminder.

"God yes, I can hear her now," said Finn, throwing in a chuckle to boot, though in fact the imitation had sounded more like Marie Dressler than Jeannette; Byron Solomon, after all, hadn't been much of an actor. Bill Whitley, like the other newer faculty, tended to treat Byron as if he were senile, which was terribly unfair. It was true that he had slipped a bit since Jeannette died. But the man had to be sixty-five: who didn't slip? Really, Finn should have exerted himself more to find Byron a dinner partner. But one no longer worried about pairing people off for dinners, just as one no longer worried about going boy-girl-boy-girl at table, although Finn in fact had seated Carolyn between himself and Bill Whitley, and Deborah Whitley between himself and Peter Sykes.

"At any rate," said Byron, "my curiosity of course got the better of me, and down I went. And do you know, I thoroughly enjoyed myself? In *both* senses. I was on screen for *all* of three minutes, and let me tell you I was as bad a bad guy as ever chewed the scenery." Finn had heard Byron tell this story before, in exactly the same words. "And do you know what happened?" Finn knew. "A rousing cheer went up! The house lights came on! And there stood my entire class, applauding. Jeannette, it seems, had called one of my students—Finn, you remember her, a Susan somebody? Lovely girl—who had in turn called the fellow at the theater and arranged the whole thing. Jeannette had been prepared to drag me there bodily, if necessary, sick as she was. Well, let me tell you, it was like the 'Ed Sullivan Show.' *Toneet in air steeyewdio audience . . .*" Even Byron's Ed Sullivan was no good.

James was staring down at his plate for all of this, mixing together his turnips and mashed potatoes with his salad fork. Must he show his boredom so plainly? Finn had civilized him in some respects—he no longer drank Kahlua, for instance—but his table manners were still an embarrassment. Not just the elbows, but the face hanging over the plate and the clumsy business of having to switch his fork to his right hand after cutting a piece of meat because no one had ever taught him to use his silverware properly. That, of course, was a lost cause nowadays. James began mixing in his cranberries, turning the whole mess gray. Finn leaned over to Carolyn and said, "I think your brother's attention span has reached its limit. I should never have put him between Byron and Bill." Before Byron had gotten the floor, Bill Whitley had been holding forth on Simon Callow. Which Finn couldn't help but think punningly appropriate, though to say so later to James would be a cheap shot.

"But God help me," Byron Solomon was saying, "if there's a kinescope floating around of my episode of 'Judge Roy Bean.' Also pseudonymous. 'Law West of the Pecos.' Now that's one I do *not* care to have revealed."

"Edgar Buchanan!" cried Bill Whitley. Everyone but the Whitleys had heard about this, too.

"Suppose I mobilize him to help me clear," said Carolyn to Finn. "Meanwhile you can rescue poor Deborah."

Deborah Whitley, whom Finn had seated at his left, had her golden, mostly naked back to him, leaning into her conversation with Peter Sykes. Who had filled his and Deborah's wineglasses twice now, and was speaking too low for the rest of the table to hear. He made a fist, then stretched forth the fingers like a tenor hitting a high note. Muscles bulged in his forearm: Peter Sykes was a sculptor who'd spent the past three months working in an auto body shop to sharpen his welding skills. Deborah Whitley laughed.

Finn admired Carolyn for her civilized pretense that her husband was a bore, bending the unwilling ear of the large-breasted, precariously halter-topped Deborah Whitley. Carolyn's intelligence would probably get her through until her looks began to go. Good Christ, one's friends.

After dinner, Byron nodded off in Finn's chair; then his eyes flew open and he said he guessed he'd better toddle along. The Whitleys had brought him, but Bill looked so crestfallen—Finn was flattered that he was enjoying himself but appalled by his bad manners—that Peter Sykes offered to drive Byron home. This jogged Bill into a belated sense of the decencies, and that was it for the evening: one couldn't very well ask Peter and Carolyn to stay on with the Whitleys standing right there. Carolyn offered to help with the cleanup, but Finn wouldn't hear of it. She said she'd be glad to. Finn said they had things well in hand.

"Oh, don't be such a macho-man," she said. "You'll be up till all hours."

"Well . . ." said Finn.

"Shoo," said James. "No girls allowed."

"If you're sure," said Carolyn.

James rolled his eyes. "Ve vant," he stage-whispered, "to be alone."

Carolyn looked down at the beautiful wood floor.

After closing the door on all of them, Finn turned to James and said, "There was no need to be brutal. Couldn't you see she was upset?"

"What?" said James. "What are you talking about now?"

"Oh come," said Finn. "Even *you* couldn't have missed what was going on at dinner. I assure you your sister took note."

"What, Stanley Kowalski and Little Bo Peep?" he said. "Oh for God's sake. Parties are for flirting. That's what they're *about.* I mean when there's anybody there under *fifty.* Or wasn't it like that back in your day?"

"This was a social evening," said Finn, hating this tone he was being maneuvered into taking. "I don't regard that as giving people license to hurt other people's feelings."

"Ooh," said James. "Well I guess that tells *me.* The Queen of Feelings has spoken." He walked into the kitchen with that walk Finn hated. That goddamn faggot walk, where the shoulders didn't move. The fourth bottle of Montalcino—Finn also hated white wine—had just about that much left. He picked it up, glanced at the kitchen doorway, and polished it off. What would the Italian be for À *même la bouteille?* He carried the dead soldier into the kitchen, not even looking at James (who fetched a loud sigh as he bent over the dishwasher), and on through into the mud-room, where he dropped it, clank, in with the green glass. All this environmental malarkey was accomplishing exactly nothing—Was he the only one who noticed it hardly snowed up here in the winter anymore?—except to give a bunch of small people the power to tyrannize you when you went to the dump. Even grocery bags had turned self-righteous: "We Recycle," with the arrows going around. Finn hated that "we."

4

On Saturday morning the phone rang while Finn was standing at the refrigerator eating cold stuffing with his fingers. "Hi," said Carolyn. "I hope I'm not calling too early."

"No-no-no," said Finn, who'd just come in from the backyard. "I've been up since seven-thirty." He looked at his watch: eleven on the dot. "Didn't you see me out back with my trusty wheelbarrow? That bloody sandpile is finally going the way of the swing set. This time next year we'll have a civilized backyard, by Jesus." He hated saying "we" to Carolyn, but "I" would have been worse. "Did the Rinaldi children really play on that flimsy little swing set?"

"And every place else," said Carolyn. "*Four* of the little monsters. From sunup to sundown. Peter and I used to *pray* for a rainy day."

"Ah, but sure they were precious souls for Holy Mother Church," said Finn, breaking into his Oirish turn.

"Listen, Finn?" said Carolyn. "There's something—listen, James isn't standing right there, is he?"

"Christ no," said Finn. "Lazy son of a bitch is still asleep." The lumberjack mode, he felt, compensated for the *we*. "You want me to call him? It's about time he—"

"No," she said. "No, what I mean is, could I talk to you about something?"

"Of course," he said. He edged over to the kitchen table, watching the coils of the telephone cord stretch, and sat down. He put his hand to his shirt pocket as if pledging allegiance. Only the rattle of a matchbook.

"There was a message on the machine when we got home last night," said Carolyn. Finn was scanning the room: damn it, his cigarettes were over there on the counter, far out of reach. "My father went in for some tests a couple of weeks ago. And now they want him to go back and have some more done. And—you know, it just doesn't sound very good."

"Tests," said Finn.

"Well, he's had, you know, rectal bleeding. . . ."

"Right," said Finn.

"And I just thought James ought to be told."

"Right," said Finn. "Well, I agree. Do you want to, or shall I?"

"Well . . ." she said.

"I don't mind," he said. "I take it there's been very little contact?"

"Well, I guess it's been a little better since—you know, since he's been living up here," said Carolyn. "If anything, they're—"

"Would you excuse me a moment?" said Finn. He put the receiver down, wedging it between the heavy cut-glass flower vase and the diner-style metal napkin dispenser so the tension in the cord wouldn't pull it off onto the floor, went over and fetched his cigarettes.

"I'm back," he said, holding the receiver to his ear with his shoulder to strike the match. "Well, Carolyn, I'm very sorry to hear this about your father." He took a deep, welcome drag and considerately raised the mouthpiece as he blew out the smoke. "We'll hope it turns out to be nothing serious. And I will speak to James as soon as he comes down. Now are *you* all right?"

"Well," she said. "I'm just trying to, you know, wait to hear something concrete and not panic until there's actually something to panic about."

"Good girl," he said. "It's a harrowing thing, I know. I went through this with *my* father." Well, that was hardly a reassuring thing to say. "I can't honestly tell you that the waiting is the worst part"—Christ, he was getting in deeper—"but in your case I truly hope it will be." He had extricated himself by inspiration.

"So do I," she said. Then she said, "I'm sorry about your father."

"Oh this was years ago," he said. "So meanwhile. What do you recommend? Should James go down there, do you think? Are *you* planning to go down?"

"No," she said. "I think at this point all it would do is get everybody upset. You know, people showing up like . . ." Had she been going to say vultures? "Besides, Fort Myers isn't all that divine in July. But I do think that if he would call or write— I don't know, I just think it would mean a lot. If only for his own sake, you know? Like later on."

"Right," said Finn.

"I think he really is very ill. I just—something just tells me that."

"I'll go upstairs right now," he said. "And you'll let me know if there's anything further I can do."

"I will," she said. "Thank you."

"Ciao," he said, and stood up to put the receiver back in the cradle.

"So what's going on?" said James. Finn turned: James was standing, barefoot, in the archway leading to the dining room.

"I didn't realize you were up," said Finn. "That was Carolyn. It seems your father has gone in for some tests, and they're not certain at this point what if anything is wrong. But apparently your mother is quite upset, and your sister seems to think it sounds serious enough that she thinks you ought to get in touch with them."

"And say what?"

"I honestly don't know, Jamie," said Finn. "That would be up to you."

James went to the refrigerator, took out the carton of orange juice and drank from it. "Sort of tests are we talking about?"

"Again," said Finn, and spread his hands, palms up. A long ash fell off his cigarette and he saw it shatter softly on the floor. "It seems to be some sort of colo-rectal thing."

"That figures," said James. "So we're talking about cancer."

"Again," said Finn.

James said, "I want to talk to my sister."

The rest results weren't in until the following Saturday; on Sunday morning Finn drove James to Albany. He put James's ticket on his Discover card, and got him two hundred dollars, the daily limit, from a cash machine. After a goodbye hug at the gate, Finn walked back out to the car, sat on the front fender and watched the plane out of sight. Watched himself watch the plane out of sight.

5

The drive down to JFK used to take Finn four and a half hours; today it had taken five. He no longer had the energy—no, the foolhardiness—to roll seventy and seventy-five all the way. Even so, he was half an hour early, so he tried to get comfortable on the narrow aluminum ledge of a giant window near the security station, and to involve himself in the last act of *Timon of Athens*. He'd deliberately brought nothing else: damned if he would allow himself to get that far and not finish. But how was he to concentrate? About fifty other people were clustered here, including whole families with whining children; some sat against the wall, some paced, some just stood and shifted their weight from foot to foot. Only ticket-holders were being allowed to go through security and down to the gates where there were seats. And ordinary people, waiting for their loved ones, were denied a modicum of comfort all because—well, enough. It was unattractive to be querulous.

He'd driven all the way down here because James couldn't

find a direct flight. Getting to Albany would have involved shuttling from JFK to La Guardia, sitting at La Guardia for another two hours—ridiculous. If the lights started to bother Finn's eyes on the drive back, they could always stop and put up at a motel. He'd also driven all the way down here because he wanted to make another foray into Times Square.

James had seemed in fine fettle on the telephone, but now that it was certain the old man (he was five years older than Finn) had only months to live, God knows what buried feelings were bound to come out. Finn was truly sorry for James: he himself had been forty-five before he'd had to go through this. But he hoped that whatever James had to go through—and he was ashamed of how selfish this sounded—he hoped it would not be disruptive. During the week and a half James had been gone, Finn had written another three pages of his essay and had composed the covering letter. No doubt James would be upset that he intended to run an errand—particularly this errand—before going home. Damn: had he not taken so much wine last night, he would've been able to get up earlier, to finish picking up the house earlier, and to make his stop before coming to the airport. But if there had to be a showdown, then there would be a showdown. This was his only life, and there was only so much of it left.

He couldn't concentrate on *Timon of Athens*.

At last passengers with suitcases and garment bags began straggling down the long passage from the gates to the security station. No one had even bothered to announce the arrival: the slipshod way everything was run these days would make a saint querulous. Yet he mustn't visit this querulousness on James, who would need his support. And would find it unattractive. And there was James now, his canvas duffel bag slung from his shoulder, and in his other hand—what? A net bag of oranges.

Finn gave him a brotherly one-armed hug. James bent to lay the oranges on the floor, straightened up, gripped the back of Finn's neck and kissed him on the lips.

"This is New York City," said James. "Remember?"

"Forgive an old man," said Finn, giving his still-one-armed hug another pump. "When ye git my age, sonny . . ."

"If," said James.

Finn let go. James's tan, he noticed, was even deeper than when he'd left. So something more had been going on, apparently, than just the compulsive TV-watching and the silent family dinners he'd re-created so amusingly on the phone.

"Ah, nature's bounty," said Finn, bending to pick up the oranges.

"My mother insisted," said James. "She was very particular that they were for both of us."

"Well well well," said Finn. "God and sinners reconciled. But wouldn't pink grapefruit have been more appropriate?"

James began walking. The sight of his firm buttocks under his white shorts made Finn suddenly furious.

"Your tan looks splendid," he said, catching up. "So how are the beach girls down there? Really *stacked*, I'll bet."

James stopped. People went by on both sides, paying no attention.

"Hey Finn?" said James. "Why don't you give it a rest, O.K.? I'm just really not up to it. It's been a bad week."

"Yes, I can see it must have been hell," said Finn, appalled that he couldn't shut up.

"I don't believe this is happening," said James. "I've been off the plane for two minutes and already we're in one of these *things*."

"I'm sorry, Jamie," said Finn. "I don't know what the hell's wrong with me."

"Can we not stand here in the middle of all this?"

"Sorry. Here." He touched James's shoulder to guide him. "We're parked down this way."

They walked a few steps towards the escalator and James stopped again. "Look," he said, "would you rather I just took a cab into the city and got out of your life?"

"Jamie, I'm truly—"

"Because I don't seem to be making you very happy, and you're driving me out of my mind."

"You're shouting," said Finn.

"What, these people have never seen a pair of bickering *faggots* before?" Well, he was shouting now, at any rate.

"James," said Finn. "For Christ's sake."

"You want to know about my tan?" said James. "Well my parents have a *pool*, man. In their back*yard*. Which is where I sat for nine days, man, watching game shows with my mother. She keeps a TV out there so she can work on her *tan*. She looks like distressed leather. My father, meanwhile, sits in the den with the blinds closed watching, I kid you not, old Super Bowl games on his VCR. He's got tapes of all but four of however fucking many Super Bowls there are. And he's scared shitless and he eats so much Valium his flesh is turning to balsa wood."

"I'm so sorry," said Finn.

"Look," said James, "do you mind very much if we get out of here?"

In the parking garage, Finn unlocked the passenger door first. James in turn reached over and unlocked the driver's door, which Finn took as a sign of conciliation. He decided not to nag James about his seat belt. He reached over and stroked the back of James's head. James allowed it.

When they came out into the sunlight—it was still only five o'clock—Finn put on the air conditioning. James had taught him that it was more fun to keep the windows open when the air was on, even though it wasn't fuel-efficient. On the Grand Central, traffic in the other direction was motionless, but inbound it was moving right along.

"I hate to backseat-drive," said James, "but shouldn't we be in the other lane?"

"Ordinarily," said Finn. "But I need to make a quick stop-off in midtown."

"For what?"

Finn drew a long breath, let it out. "For something you don't approve of," he said.

"Oh," said James. He looked at his watch. "You know it's going to take *hours* to get in and out of Manhattan at this time of day. You couldn't have done this on your way?"

"I'm sorry," said Finn. "I'll make this as quick as I possibly can, but I get to the city so seldom that I really mustn't pass up the chance."

"So *this* is why you were so anxious to come down and pick me up," said James. "Tell me something. Do you ever think your tastes might be a little depraved?"

"We've been over this," said Finn.

"Well let me put it in another light for you," said James. "Did it ever occur to you that it might be insulting to *me?*"

They were caught behind a huge yellow school bus. The lanes on either side weren't moving any faster, but Finn cut to the left in front of a cab—the driver leaned on his horn—just to get behind something he could see past.

"You're not going to provoke me," he said. "We disagree about this project. I respect your view. I'm asking you to respect mine."

"Project?" said James. "What project? This isn't a *project,* for Christ's sake. It's one more old queen who likes to watch young dudes get it on. You can dignify it because you used to be some hot-shit filmmaker."

Finn looked over at him, this idle boy with his dirty blond hair blowing. Who made him waste his time and now held him in contempt for it. He had let himself become an aging man with no family, who no longer prepared before meeting his classes and whose taste for good wines was giving him broken veins in his nose. He was this young man's sugar daddy. He turned back in time to avoid ramming the BMW ahead of him by lifting his foot quickly from the gas pedal: to hit the brakes would call James's attention to his bad driving.

"For whatever reason," said Finn, his heart beginning to pound in delayed reaction, "I have done almost no work in the time I've known you. This is going to come to a screeching halt."

"You haven't done any work for five *years,* man," said James.

Seven, thought Finn.

"I'm not putting it off on you," he said. The pounding was now in his throat. "But I won't allow you to interfere with what I need to do." James said nothing. "And I might add that it might be time for you to start thinking about what you're going to do when *you* grow up. It's a waste of life, and it depresses me severely."

"Would you like me to go to night school," said James, "and study hairdressing?"

"That, my dear, is up to you," said Finn. "What I mean to do is to make a stop in midtown. For one hour, no longer. And then we'll be on our way. If you're coming."

"Finn," said James. "It's your car, it's your life. I don't really have anything to say about it."

"Now if you'd prefer," said Finn, "it *is* getting late-ish. We could have dinner in the city, leave when the traffic's thinned out, and maybe put up for the night somewhere along the way."

James didn't answer. Finn looked and saw that he was crying. Not sobbing, just letting the tears go down his face.

"Just please do what you're going to do," said James. "All I want is to get home."

6

James had been back almost a week before Finn had time to sit down and go through the videos he'd bought in Times Square. *Made* time, he corrected himself. But James had come down with a summer cold, Finn did have to nurse him, bring him ice cream and ginger ale and magazines, go to the drug store for cough syrup and Comtrex. And they did have to ask Peter and Carolyn over to hear James's report and to discuss what might have to be done in the time remaining. Which of course involved preparing a decent meal, and what with the shopping and the cooking that was *another* day shot to hell. And the lawn had needed another mowing: he'd neglected it the week before.

But now, at last, a quiet day. James, recovered, had borrowed the car for the afternoon. Acting mysterious about it, too. Perhaps out buying a thanks-for-taking-care-of-me gift, since before leaving he had—*mehercule!*—done the breakfast dishes and straightened up the bedroom. So Finn, having run out of distractions, sat alone in his study with a notepad, watching something called *Hellfire Club*. Two men lay side by side on a bed as cheap, nasty music went *wacka wacka wacka* on the sound track. One, with mustache and short hair, decked out in leather jacket, leather pants and motorcycle boots, was propped up on a pillow angrily puffing a cigarette. The other, with a platinum-dyed Mohawk, wore only a black leather collar with diamond-shaped silver studs. He lay face-down, his body a uniform dingy white; you could see the sores on his legs. (At least this film wasn't arty.) The leather one took a final drag, tapped off the final ash and stubbed his cigarette out on the Mohawk one's white buttock. The mohawk one twitched, then lay still again.

Finn suddenly felt sick to his stomach: these were only the

opening minutes of a sixty-minute film. He hit Stop and the screen went snowy. Was his discomfort a sign that here was something worth his attention? Had he needed to turn the thing off because it was too powerful? Or was it just ugly and frightening, period, without significance? Why did these films fascinate him? *Did* they fascinate him, or was he in fact burned out and desperately willing himself to be fascinated?

Well, good: simply to ask such questions was to work. Unless it was one more way *not* to work.

Perhaps the thing to do was to look at something less harrowing and allow his unconscious to process this.

He ejected *Hellfire Club,* put it back in its case, and looked through the rest of the new ones. Well, what about *Sean in Love?* If nothing else, it ought to be sensitive. Perhaps instead of films that were manifestly sordid, you wanted to look at the capital-S sensitive ones and spot the details that showed they were sordid, too. Or was that too easy? Probably that was too easy.

The premise of *Sean in Love* was that "Sean," a Wall Street type—there was some malarkey at the beginning about "mergers"—took an island vacation and kept falling for lifeguards, Rastas and what-not. He would gape at them, then the image would go wavy and dissolve (harp glissando on the sound track) to show that what followed was fantasy. In the third such fantasy he was in a sauna getting fucked by a Nautilus instructor—it seemed to Finn that the wooden bench must have been hell on his back and shoulders—when there was a cut to outside the door (through which their stagy moans could still be heard) where a third young man, in tight shorts, was reaching for the door handle. (This annoyed Finn: up to now the fantasies had been presented strictly from Sean's point of view.) "Oopsy-daisy," said the intruder—and Finn leaned forward. Cut from their surprised faces to the smiling face of the intruder: James, of course, of course, of course. Younger, but James. Finn had never been fool enough to think that particular smile had been turned on no one but him. He watched the scene through to the end, with its combinations and recombinations. All very predictable.

7

Finn was still sitting in his study when he heard the car pull in. He'd smoked all but one of the cigarettes that should have lasted him until sometime tomorrow, and he'd tossed the pack with the last cigarette inside it onto the floor just out of reach; that way he wouldn't smoke it until he really needed it. Well, now he would take the keys from James, saying as little as possible—he hoped James hadn't in fact brought a present—drive over to the Cumberland Farms for a fresh pack, and maybe by the time he got back he would have figured out what to do next. He heard the screen door slap and James calling "Hey, anybody home?"

He stood up and felt suddenly lightheaded. He'd been sitting there ever since—ever since. He opened the door and saw James coming through the kitchen. The living room between them, with its narrow glossy floorboards, looked as vast as a basketball court.

"So guess what?" said James.

"Suppose you just tell me," said Finn.

"I will," said James. He wasn't picking up Finn's mood at all. Or he was choosing not to pick it up, in order to make his own mood prevail. "You're looking at a productive citizen."

"A productive citizen," said Finn.

"Well, a soon-to-be productive citizen. I've got a job."

"Do you," said Finn. He remained standing in the doorway. James went over and sat down in the maroon armchair, draping one leg over the side and letting the foot swing.

"Well, aren't you curious?" said James.

Finn said nothing.

"I would've thought you'd be pleased," said James, who now seemed to be catching on.

Finn thought for a second. "I can understand that," he said.

"What's up?" said James. His foot stopped moving. "Oh Jesus," he said. "My dad."

"Say again?" said Finn. Then he remembered. "No," he said. "No, there's no news of your *dad*."

"Jesus," said James. "You scared the hell out of me. So listen, do you want to hear this or not?"

Finn stretched forth his hands as if supplicating and let them drop. "Fire away," he said.

"Well," said James, "there was an ad in the paper that they were looking for an assistant manager at the Symposium. So I went down and checked it out. You know, because I thought it would be like running the popcorn machine. But it's actually a serious job, like bookkeeping and shit. I *will* have to run the ticket window, but he said I'd have some input on the programming and I'll definitely be writing some of the little synopses in the schedule, and it's just—I think it's really going to be good."

"You've taken a job," said Finn.

"Assuming the reference I gave him checks out," he said, and laughed.

"Right," said Finn.

"So anyhow, I promise that every July I'll get them to run our Hitchcock movies again that we didn't like. God," he said, "I'm getting sentimental in my old age."

"Perhaps you could make it a triple feature," said Finn. "With *Sean in Love.*"

James cocked his head. "I don't get it."

"*Sean in Love,*" said Finn. "It's a video I picked up in Times Square. I think it would interest you greatly."

James took a deep breath and let it out.

"Oh," he said. "Always wondered what they ended up calling that thing."

"So what do they pay for work like that?" saidFinn.

"They paid *me* a hundred dollars. Which I needed very badly at the time. It was my first year in New York."

"A hundred dollars," said Finn. "Did you enjoy your work?"

"Did *you?*" said James. "What do you want me to tell you? That they were holding a gun to my head like Linda Lovelace? You know, I was eighteen, and this friend of mine asked me if I wanted to be with him in this movie—"

"Which friend was that?"

"He was supposed to be playing this exercise teacher or something," said James. "He actually *was* an exercise teacher. I used to go to his workout."

"I can imagine," said Finn.

"Maybe you ought to sit down," said James. "You look really pale."

Finn walked to the blue armchair—his footsteps seemed to echo and the journey seemed to take a long time—and sat down. Sparkles swam before his eyes.

"How many of these *friends* of yours," he said, wishing he had that last cigarette, "are dead?"

"How would I know?" said James. "This was one afternoon, like five years ago. Don't you think I think about it every day? Plus all the *other* stupid shit?" He reached into his jacket pocket and tossed Finn first a book of matches, then an unopened pack of cigarettes. "You know, everybody's got dead friends," he said. "Except you, right? Since you don't *have* friends."

Finn got the pack open, worked a cigarette out of it, lit it, took a first deep, wonderful drag and glanced around for an ashtray. The late afternoon sun glinted off the varnished floor. He became conscious of the faraway drone of somebody's lawnmower; for a second there he thought of nothing at all. Then he realized he was staring at the overlapping white rings by the side of James's chair.

"So," he said. "I suppose this explains why you were hellbent on getting me sidetracked from my project."

"One reason, yes," said James.

"Why didn't you simply tell me?"

"Because look at you," he said. "You know, I know about men who like naughty boys. And the bottom line is, that they don't like 'em to be too naughty. So." Quick shrug. "What? Would you like me to go over and stay at Carolyn's while I make other arrangements?"

Touching up just that little bit of floor, Finn thought, would be simplicity itself.

"I don't know *what* I would like at this point," he said. "I would like to believe that none of this really happened."

"Oh," said James. "Well if *that's* all. You can manage that O.K. Whether *I'm* around or not. I imagine you've already started."

Deborah Eisenberg

ACROSS THE LAKE

At first, what Rob saw from the back seat appeared to be projections of stone on the bluff just above—columns of lava, or basalt. Then the smoky morning split into gold rays, the black forms flickered human/mineral, human/mineral, and a shift of sun flashed against machetes, lighting up for one dazzling instant the kerchiefs tied over faces as masks, and the clothing—the wide, embroidered Indian trousers that Mick and Suky were headed toward the village to buy.

"Hoo hoo!" Mick said. "Worth the trip?" But his hand, extended for Suky's cigarette, was unsteady. How long, Rob wondered; how much longer until they reached the village?

When they arrived, he would eat something with Mick and Suky, maybe even check into the hotel, but he would look around for some way to get back to town immediately. There would be other tourists with cars, and there was supposed to be a boat, a little boat that carried mail across the lake, between town and the village to which they were going on the far side. In any case, he could hardly say it was Mick and Suky's fault that he had come; the fact was, he had knowingly—no, eagerly —given himself over to them, to these people he never would have dreamed of getting into a car with at home. And if something happened—if the guerrillas reappeared, or if there were robbers, or if he got sick, or if, most terrifying of all, they were stopped by the army—he would have only himself to blame.

Suky's small, tanned arm, draped across the seat, sparkled faintly. Her shoulder, the back of her neck . . . The car fishtailed and Rob turned his gaze to the steaming lake. Himself, himself to blame, himself, only himself. Perspiration—forming below the surface, squeezing its way up to collect in basins around each gold stalklet of a hair, in tiny, septic, bejewelling drops.

According to Mick, the crumbly, bunkerlike building they checked into was the village's premier hotel, the dirty pavilion where they sat now under a swarming thatch was the village's premier restaurant. "Only restaurant," Suky amended lazily. "Well, yeah, there's one other, but Mick got a wicked parasite there last year."

What difference did it make? Rob would be back on his way to town soon enough.

"Chicken everyone?" Mick said. "Always tasty, always safe." He put down the sticky menu and turned with a little bow to the child who was swinging idly against a chair, waiting to take their orders. *"Tres pollo."*

The child considered Mick before responding. *"Pollo no hay,"* he said impassively.

"Pués," Mick said. *"Pescado. Bien fresco."*

"Pescado no hay," the child said.

"Bueno—" Mick folded his arms and leveled a ferocious grin at the child. *"—Carne."*

The child stared back.

Suky yawned. *"Que hay?"* she said.

"Frijoles," the child said, already wandering off. Pleased, Rob wondered, because he could offer them beans, or because he could offer them nothing else?

The pavilion sat on a rise overlooking the muddy road, and beyond that, the lake. In front, just next to each of the poles that supported the thatch, a soldier stood, aiming a rifle at the shabby ladinos walking below, and the soundless Indians, in their elaborate, graceful, filthy textiles. From town, the lake had seemed blue, and the air over it tonic, a pure ether in which the volcanos and the hills presided, serene and picturesque. But on this side the air was green, heavy with a vegetal shedding, sliding, with a dull glint, like scales. The water, the volcano, the dense growth, and the crust of tin-roofed shacks that covered the hills all appeared to be discharging skeins of mist that made everything waver, as though they were under the lake, here, looking up.

"A gourmet paradise it may not be," Mick said. "But you've got to admit it's beautiful."

Incredible. Was Mick aware of his callousness? Even if you were to succumb to some claim of the dark and protean landscape, you could hardly ignore those soldiers. Their faces were smeared with anarchic black markings, and their eyes glittered red with exhaustion or hatred, or illness.

Of course, Rob was not unprepared for some kind of unpleasantness. The other day in town, when Mick had pointed across the lake to the village, Rob's insides had registered a violent but incoherent response. He'd heard vague but alluring mention of the area—its unparalleled weaving and embroidery, its ancient indigenous religions. He had the impression of an iridescence. But someone had referred to guerrillas, and someone else had told him about the people, Indian peasants, who had been untouched by centuries of change but who now, during planting and harvest seasons, were taken off to labor on the Eastern plantations under military guard. "It sounds really interesting," Rob had said politely to Mick.

"Interesting," Mick said. "It's sensational. Very dark, very magical."

Suky sighed then, Rob remembered. And he had said something about how he'd like to get there one day, and then Suky had said, "So why not come with us? We're going Wednesday."

Wednesday. Rob stared at her while she rooted around the bottom of her drink with her straw. "Why not?" she said. She looked up at him and pushed her drink aside. "This is a great time to go. Some general's up in the States, lobbying Congress for more aid, so the army's making kind of a point these days of not killing gringo tourist college boys." She had smiled then briefly, showing her funny little sharp, uneven teeth.

Shame (as though Rob were on the brink of doing or thinking

something unworthy) abruptly presented him with another memory: His parents, with boxes of slides, resulting from various travels, which they showed on a screen in the living room to himself and his sister, and sometimes to others in the community who were considering similar adventures. His parents were vigorous and inquiring—much more energetic, physically and intellectually, than he was. There had never been any place, as far as Rob knew, they hadn't wanted to go. And although they had made a show of disapproval about the casualness of Rob's plans this summer, Rob could feel their pride, their eagerness to see new places through his eyes. If only he had their stamina. Bad weather seemed only to intensify their interest in the way other people lived. And bad food, and bugs. Only two or three times, as Rob remembered, had their trips worked out badly. Their sunny temperaments seemed damaged on those occasions, when they had come home plaintive and baffled. Which trips had those been? Haiti? The Philippines? Rob was no longer sure —the slides had stayed in their boxes.

The infant waiter reappeared, shoving three plates of rice and beans onto the table and dropping a plate of tortillas into the center so that it buzzed. *"Dos más, Pablo,"* said a voice from over Rob's shoulder. Then, *"Welcome, welcome."*

The owner of the voice was probably no more than thirty, just a few years older than Mick and Suky, but his weighty graciousness insisted on a wide margin of seniority. He held one hand out to Mick, and with the other he decorously reached a chair for the sphinxlike Indian girl who accompanied him. *"Y Pablito,"* he called to the child, *"dos cervezas."*

Drugs, most likely, Rob thought. Rob had seen men like this in towns en route. But usually they kept to themselves, hanging around in clumps, or with various counterparts—burly, scarred Latins, or older good-for-nothings from the U.S., '60s casualties with greasy, faded ponytails, whose clattery frames and potbellies would have devolved from bodies as supple and powerful as this man's.

Rob started with dismay—his plate had been washed! A universe of disease trembled in a droplet of water on the rim. Think sick, get sick, was what Mick said, and that was probably true in some way, although the corollary—think healthy, stay healthy— seemed less of a sure thing.

"Rob, Suky, hey—" Mick was poking Rob on the arm, pointing to the beers Pablo was setting down in front of the newcomers. "Now this is smart. See what Kimball is doing?"

Kimball who? Who Kimball? Bad, Rob thought, not good—He had failed to control his attention. He channeled it now, with effort.

Despite the impression he made of size, this Kimball person was not tall, Rob saw—just rather broad, and well put together. Although his features were somewhat sharp and his dark blue eyes small, there was a suggestion of largesse, or costliness, possibly, about his creamy skin and loose black curls. And Mick had certainly fallen in behind him with disgusting alacrity. Astonishing, really. Lofty Mick, dignified Mick—but sensitivity to rank, evidently, was fundamental to this aristocracy of wanderers.

"People don't realize how easy it is to get dehydrated," Mick was saying showily to Rob. "Listen. The juice here is great. If you don't want to drink beer, you should have some juice, at least." But Kimball could obviously care less, Rob thought, who was a beer drinker and who was not; even though all the other tables were empty, he kept craning around as though he were expecting someone.

"I'm not thirsty," Rob said.

Suky's eyes were closed, though Rob thought he saw a mocking little smile flicker across her mouth. So what? He wasn't thirsty; he could wait—he had three safe bottles of water back at the hotel, in his pack, the weight of which had given Mick occasion to marvel, satirically, as they'd climbed into the car.

"Suky?" Mick said.

"Beer," she said.

"Well, I'mna have beer, and I'mna have juice," Mick said with infuriating cheer. "Pablo—" he called.

Was that really the child's name? Rob wondered. Or some demeaning generic business. And what was this Indian girl's name? Had she even been introduced? Her expression hadn't altered by a blink so far as Rob had observed, since she'd sat down. "*Señorita*," he said, "*vive usted aquí?*"

Kimball turned to contemplate Rob. "She don't speak Spanish," he said. He put his arm around the girl and said something into her ear in a language full of *sh* and *z* sounds. The girl laughed—a tiny, harsh glitter. "But, yeah—" Kimball turned back to gaze at Rob. "She wants you to know. She does live here."

The girl's eyes passed over Rob with a smoldering chill, like dry ice. She was even more terrifying, Rob thought, than Kimball. What was it about her? If only he'd asked Meredith along. She'd had the summer free; she'd hinted. And if she were here, she'd know what was upsetting him—she always did. Sometimes, as Meredith pointed out, it was nothing more than beauty. "Rob, that's *beautiful*, don't you see?" she would say. Or "that woman's not weird-looking, she's *beautiful*." Then Meredith would laugh and rub her head against his, and he would see: whatever it was, was only beautiful.

He sighed and put down his fork—he had tried to eat something, but both the rice and the beans had a scorched, compost taste. Suky glanced at his plate, at him. She took a sip of her beer, and stretched her arms high over her head. It was appalling, the way so many girls traveling around here dressed. With grimy bits of underwear showing, or worse, like Suky, with none, Rob observed as she adjusted the strap of her sluttish camisole, to show. What did people think about their country being turned into a private beach? What could the Indian girl, for example, be thinking? When Meredith traveled (Rob knew, though they had never yet traveled together) she took particular care to dress respectfully. Especially if she were going to some Third World country, where, as she'd said to Rob, the inhabitants had little to offer one another aside from courtesy.

Rob brought his mind to the table again, and found Mick entrenched in a boast-fest—the places he and Suky had gone hunting textiles to sell in the States, the foods they'd survived, the dangers they'd faced . . . Still, if he were to be honest with himself, Rob thought, he would have to admit that Mick and Suky had an effect on him even now. From the moment he'd met them, he'd contorted himself into all sorts of ridiculous postures—misrepresenting and stifling reactions, even exaggerating. And even now, when Mick was evidencing wormlike, sycophantic tendencies of his own, Rob couldn't control a desperation for their good opinion. Pathetic, but true.

He'd seen them as soon as he disembarked in town from the

bus. There they were, at a food stand, joking with the proprietor in Spanish far too advanced for Rob. They were clearly Americans, and he was pining for the sounds of American English, but really, it was something about their appearance that had stopped him—the way they looked together; their slightly feral, miniaturized quality, fastidious and carnal at once.

Although he'd been able to see from where he was standing the hotel recommended by his student guide book, he lingered near them, waiting to ask for their advice. When they finished their conversation, they directed him, without interest, to a hotel in the opposite direction from the one he was facing.

Their indifference had been disorienting. His sincerity, his good nature (and his looks, he conceded uncomfortably) generally made people attentive. But these two! It was hard to tell if they were even listening. *Most* people made an effort to show by their faces that they understood, were interested in, what one was saying. An unwelcome indignation branched quickly through Rob as he remembered this first encounter, clearing a path through which embarrassment then shot treacherously; he'd just been tricked by his *own brain* into thinking something distasteful—that the facial expressions displayed by most people, by himself, were social signals, like clothing.

The town was small, and over the next several days, Rob had seen Suky and Mick a number of times. They would nod from the sanctum of their unwashed majesty, and Rob was reminded, each time more keenly, that although they were the largest and most vivid figures in his small universe here, he was no more than a mote, for them, in this vast swarm of tourists.

But Sunday, they'd appeared at an overcrowded restaurant where Rob was sitting, and stood for a moment in the doorway. Rob gestured, more out of civility than hope, to the empty chairs next to him, but they made their way over and sat down without surprise or thanks. And when Mick put a leaf of lettuce and a slice of tomato—both virtually leaping with microbes—right onto his hamburger, Rob, giddy with happiness, had thrown caution to the winds and followed suit. How pure the lake had looked from that side, Rob thought again. He'd had a perfect view of it from their table, and had noted, he remembered, the way its surface reflected with such certainty the volcano and the little hills—the hills where he sat sweating, now.

Bali, blah blah blah—Mick was still going *on;* hill tribes, Panama, opium, blah blah—Rob had heard this all not three days before. Though no question Mick was a better performer for a worthier audience.

Worthier, but possibly less impressionable. Kimball merely rubbed his chin, frowning distantly. Only at one moment did his expression change. One of the soldiers had turned slightly; he seemed to be glancing up at Kimball. Did Kimball nod? It seemed to Rob he'd lowered his eyes a fraction of a second. Had something happened? No, there was only a young Indian walking quietly along the road below. Suky was squirming restlessly, her peculiar yellow eyes fixed on the lake, as she twisted a strand of her springy hair. Jealous, probably, Rob thought, for Mick's attention, and he was taken unawares by a harsh little clout of sympathy.

"We've come across a couple of times now," Mick was saying. "But we haven't had a whole lot of luck. Hard to find quality these days. Old stuff's in shit condition, new stuff's just plain shit . . ."

Kimball rested his fingertips together, indicating the Indian girl with a movement of his head, and Rob became fully aware of the fine, even stripe running through her clothing, the softness of the fabric, the yoke of her blouse, where flowers and jungle animals—jaguars, monkeys, snakes—bloomed and sported in a heavy embroidered wreath.

"I was noticing," Mick said.

"Made it herself," Kimball said.

Mick eyed the blouse sideways, then reached out and rubbed an edge of the fabric between his thumb and forefinger.

"Family does great work," Kimball said.

"Great piece," Mick said. "Yeah." He stared at the girl smokily.

Kimball leaned over to the girl and they spoke in low voices, as if, Rob thought, anyone else could possibly understand the preposterously arcane language they were speaking. "Listen," Kimball said. He pushed his empty plate aside. "She says when are you leaving? Because this is it—we could go check out her family's stuff, and then she and I could catch a ride with you back into town."

"Ideal," Mick said.

"Except we're sort of tight," Suky said.

"We can fit them," Mick objected. "No problem." He glanced at Rob.

"Sure," Rob said. "Of course."

"We've got a lot of luggage," Suky said, looking at Rob evenly. "Why don't you take the mail boat?" she said to Kimball. "It would probably be a lot more comfortable."

Rob felt himself flush. However comical Suky and Mick had found his pack, it would hardly prevent Kimball and the girl from sitting in the back seat with him.

Kimball was emitting a fog of absentmindedness. "Problem is," he said, "we got a business appointment—we got to get all the way to the capital by morning."

"See, so we couldn't help you out in that case," Suky said. "We're not going back to town until tomorrow."

"Huh," Kimball said. He reached over to the Indian girl's plate and wrapped a spoonful of her beans in one of the sour, hay-flavored tortillas. "Well, no sense our taking the boat anyhow," he said. "We'd get to town too late to go straight on. So we might as well spend one more night here, then squeeze in with you tomorrow."

"What about your appointment?" Suky said.

Kimball scooped up the remainder of the girl's meal. "Appointment'll just have to wait one day, because we're sure as shit not going to do the road from town to the capital after dark."

"After dark!" Mick said. "Hey, guess who we saw this morning. On *this* road. In broad daylight."

Kimball put his beer bottle down on the table and looked at Mick. "Who?" he said.

"The muchachos," Mick announced.

"You know this?" Kimball said, and only then did Mick appear to notice his unwavering stare.

"What he means," Mick said, turning to Rob as though it were Rob who'd committed some kind of faux pas, "is that around here you're never sure. Army dresses up like the guerrillas, guerrillas dress up like the army . . ."

Kimball was looking from one of them to another. "They didn't stop you?" he said.

"They were gone," Mick said. "They were there, and then they were gone, *vanished.*"

Really, Rob thought, there really couldn't be any question of who it had been, standing mere yards from them this morning. Oh, anyone could put kerchiefs over their faces, but who could learn to become invisible? Only people who had lived in the mountains. Only people who had been hunted in the mountains like animals. "See, look at Rob," Mick said. "He still looks like he saw a ghost."

Rob turned to Kimball, disregarding Mick's witticism. "Are they stopping people? You know, I heard they were, some places. I met a kid in San Cristobal who told me they stopped him, I don't know if it was here, really, and took his last fifty dollars. He said it was the worst experience he ever had. Not the money, obviously, but when he felt the gun, sort of rubbing against his hair, he said it was like a switch on his head, and everything lit up with this strange, glowy light and became completely lucid, like one of those little glass things." Rob remembered the kid's voice, his white, wondering face. "He said his life had always been all dark and confused, but right then he could see how it all fit together, and his whole life made perfect sense. And the sense it made—the sense it *made*—was that it was completely, totally pointless."

The others looked at him. Then Suky smiled and slid a cigarette out of her pack.

"Of course," Rob said, "he was glad it wasn't the army."

"Excuse me, dear," Kimball said to Suky. "You got extra?"

She inhaled luxuriantly, then handed Kimball her cigarette. "By the way," she said to him. "How did you happen to know we came by car?"

Kimball gazed at her in sorrow. "How else could you have gotten here before the mail boat came in?" he asked reasonably. "Besides," he added. "I saw you drive up."

"Hey, lookit," Mick said. "No soldiers." And in fact they had disappeared from in front of the restaurant.

Kimball squinted down at the lake. "Yup, and the mail boat's coming in," he said. He glanced at his watch—an incongruously expensive one, Rob saw. "On the dot, give or take."

"Fabulous," Suky said. "Hours of Pantsuits before we've got the place to ourselves again."

Kimball twisted around in his chair to look full at her. "You know what?" he mused. "You kids are nice kids. You got a sense of propriety, and that's something that appeals to me. So what I'm saying is, if you've *got* to stay over tonight, I want you to do me this favor. I want you to take care of yourselves, and stay inside."

"Can't," Suky said. "Rob and I have tickets for the opera."

Mick looked annoyed. "Very funny," he said. Kimball smiled indulgently. "Now *her* family—" he pointed at the Indian girl, "—barricades themselves in."

"No shit," Mick said. He pursed his lips and examined his juice glass. " 'Barricades.' "

"Hey, now," Kimball protested, as though Mick had maligned the girl's family. "These are good people."

Mick nodded gallantly at the immobile girl. "I don't doubt that for a second," he said. "But, what you're . . . I mean, if there's actual . . . *con*flict." He turned the glass in his hands. "What do you say, Suke?"

"Besides," Suky smiled sweetly. "Rob wants to stay, obviously. Rob wants to see conflict."

"No conflict," Kimball said. "Oh, sure, the odd incident, naturally, now and again, but the real problem around here," he lowered his voice, "is *brujos*. There was one recently, changed himself into a wild boar nights. Rampaged, was tearing up everyone's little plots of corn and beans, went after people whenever he got the chance." He studied Mick for a moment. "Now, Micky. We know that anybody who's out at night is up to mischief. I know that as well as you do. A person who's out at night is not a reliable human being. But things happen, and you got to take that into consideration. Someone's old lady gets sick, they have to get water from somewhere. A kid wanders out. You know how it is. And this *brujo* chewed up some folks something awful, they say, before they shot it one night in a cornfield. And in the morning? When the sun came up? The body turned into the sweetest old man you'd ever want to meet. One of our next-door neighbors." He sighed and shook his head. "But you know what?" He looked up as though surprised. "Rob— Suky— Are you listening? Because this is the interesting part, now. *Afterwards*, there were a lot of people who said that sweet old man and his wife were *guerrillas*."

Suky was looking at him thoughtfully. "No shit," she said, after a moment.

"No shit," he said. He stood, studying the empty spots where the soldiers had been, and hitched up his jeans. "Hey—" He whistled. "Pablito—"

"A buck fifty apiece," Mick said, when the bill was analyzed. "Can't beat that." He drained his juice, set the glass purposefully on the table, and stood. "Sure. We'll try to give you guys a hand, go back today if we do good business early—no real need to stay over, then. So, ready?"

"I think I'll just hang around," Rob said. "Explore."

Mick and Suky looked at him blankly.

"Okay, professor," Kimball said. "Explore away."

Now that Rob had succeeded in obtaining solitude, he found he had no idea what to do with it. The prospect of finding a ride back, which in the car had seemed so reasonable, was obviously absurd; he had noticed no other cars in the village. And who could he even ask? Pablo was at his elbow, staring at the little pile of money on the table. "*Sí.*" Rob nodded. "*Gracias.*" Pablo's eyes glinted as he seized it.

He could consult the man who had checked them in at the hotel, Rob thought. Though that didn't seem too promising. For a hotel keeper in a village to which few surely traveled, the man had been remarkably—not actually rude, Rob thought, but well . . . *preoccupied*.

There was one other party of guests at the hotel, Rob remembered. Three unsmiling button-faced blonds, of which one or two seemed to be boys. He could ask them. A good idea.

But when he imagined himself strolling back and finding them, a feeling of weakness overtook him. Their presence in the hotel's sunless courtyard earlier had been ghostly and forbidding. The hotel keeper had gestured to an enclosure beyond them—the shower, he explained. A shower! But Mick had been jittery and discouraging. "It'll be freezing, man. Let's go get some lunch—it'll warm up later." But Rob stood his ground— he'd earned the right, he felt, in the car. So Mick and Suky waited while he fetched the stiff little towel from his room—his cubicle—and disappeared into the shower stall. Instantly he was back in the courtyard, humiliated; the shower was *literally* unbearable. Mick had doubled up, and the blonds looked at him out of their button faces. But perhaps the blonds simply hadn't understood—they were foreigners. Well, foreigners, of course, but what he meant, he corrected himself, was, not American.

Rob gazed out at the watery sky, the cloudy lake. At the very worst, he'd only have to wait until late afternoon. Either Kimball would have succeeded in convincing Mick and Suky to return to town today, or he could take the mail boat by himself. Which was by far the more appealing alternative, actually—he was certainly in no hurry to be out on that road again. Anyhow, the urgency to leave had passed. There was something—well, something *correct* about being where he was. After all—the thought rose up dripping—it *was* where he was . . .

He had wanted to go, while he had the chance this summer before starting grad school, someplace very far away. Whenever his parents came home from their trips, they sparkled with things it was impossible to say. In fancy books of photographs you could see clues, hints, in the glossy pages, where boats rocked in the harbors of seaside towns, streetlamps spread a soft glamour through the rain of antique cities, where men and women of distant nationalities hunkered in the circle of the lens, enticing and resistant.

Since the beginning of summer he'd wound his way down and down and down, in buses throbbing with peasants and chickens. His heart had pounded at each blue and gold drop to the valley floors, at the crude white crosses marking death along the roads, at the shining, disinterested God-filled air, through which he had expected, at every moment, to plummet, along with his fellow passengers, bouncing in their tinny container from peak to peak. And he had felt, all the time, that he was following a trail of instructions that would lead him as far as it was possible to go.

Now here he was. As far as it was possible to go. The end of the trail, where the world trickled out into mud.

If Meredith were here, she would show him how to find the beauty of this place as though it were a photograph. Through her eyes, it would acquire coherence, meaning, intelligibility. The lake with its sudsy rolls of fog—Meredith would know facts about it: its size, its depth, its geological origin. She would have researched the social organization, the language, the economy of these silent, unreadable villagers. She would smile, now, and coax him to his feet.

Oh, if only he could just go back to the hotel and have his shower! But he imagined Meredith's bewilderment: *You got all the way there and didn't even see the market? Or the church?* She shook her thick gold-brown hair and laughed. *You just took a shower and went back?* No, she didn't laugh—her white smile dimmed when she saw his face.

All right. So, market, church, *then* shower and return. A few tourists were struggling up the hill—evidently Suky had overestimated the impending plague. They would be headed for the market themselves, Rob reasoned, as he lost sight of them in the thicket of tin roofs and little hills.

But despite the intricacy of paths and turnings, the market turned out to be no more than two minutes' walk from the restaurant. Indian clothing hung from stalls, and careful heaps of dwarfed and fly-specked mangos were displayed on crates.

Pale, smiling people, determined, apologetic, wearing squashy hats to protect them from the sun, aimed cameras at undersize children and their glowering mothers. Even worse was the dickering at the stalls. The scene had a sickening familiarity. It was like seeing as an adult one of those frenetic, meanspirited, sentimental TV shows Rob had watched as a child. "They want you to bargain, they expect you to. It's insulting if you don't," one woman was informing her shame-faced husband. "Twenty dollar," she said to the shop owner, believing herself, apparently, to be speaking a foreign language.

The shop owner was a large woman. Some automatic function was releasing rage evenly into her face. She held out for inspection a pair of trousers, embroidered with rich tiers of parrots and ice-cream cones while the customer deliberated—with shrewdness and forced gaiety—as though she were trying on hats in Paris.

It was a large, rusty stain on the side of the trousers that decided the matter. The shop owner was adamant. The stain would wash out, she insisted without a trace of credibility. The customer was knowing, regretful. As she walked away, strength of character lighting up her face, the shop owner hissed after her. The retreating customer's step did not quicken, though her expression toughened slightly. Rob, rooted to the spot, waited for her skin to blossom with hemorrhages, her flesh to turn to pulp, her hair and teeth to spring out onto the mud.

Why did he feel he must redress the imbalance between buyer and seller? It was a stupid and superstitious impulse, he told himself. Humanity everywhere was at ease with the barbarism of his countryfellows. And how not? It was simple—one had power and money on one's side; inevitably every act one committed was predicated on that fact. If he were to give in and buy something now, his transaction would be predicated on that fact as well.

It was true, he thought. He could buy or not buy; he could exercise his power and money or refrain from doing so, and that was the extent of his choice. But the notion only fanned the agitation threatening to rattle him like a dried gourd should he leave the market with nothing.

At the nearest stall he gathered up, roughly, like a criminal, several sashes and a pair of trousers, the inferior workmanship of which suggested a low price. He paid what was asked and left before the incredulous saleswoman could determine whether he ought to be addressed with mockery or with pity. Had his gesture alleviated in the least degree the disarray of his pulse, his breathing, his glands? No.

Mick had been right, he thought; he should have ordered some juice. His lightheadedness might well be dehydration, in part. But at least he'd managed to see the market already, and the church could not be far. He would take his dutiful glimpse, return to the hotel to drink some water and take his shower, and by that time Mick and Suky might be ready to leave. He tucked his purchases under his arm, noting that these new trousers of his were marred, too, by rusty stains. Should he deposit them by the side of the road? No point in that; whatever was on them was on him now, as well.

The church was not around the first turn he took, nor the second, nor the third. Around the fourth, little huts petered out into a foggy scrub. Figures were moving in the mist—women with water jugs on their heads and babies, wrapped in shawls, on their backs. Below, the gray lake and gray sky exchanged their vapors.

Something bulged from the scrub! No, only an old man, coming toward him. Sometimes these Indians looked a little pathetic, Rob thought, in their wide trousers, in all their loose, swaddling clothing. Clownish, almost, like patients. *"Señor,"* Rob called. *"Iglesia? Dónde está, por favor?"*

The old man approached Rob teeteringly. He held an old straw hat by the brim, and his expression was quizzical and humorous. Again, Rob asked where the church was, but the old man gave no sign of understanding, even of hearing, the question.

Moisture made his large black eyes radiant, his gaze penetrating but unspecific. His face was a patchwork with deep seams. His mouth had simply been left open, like a door, and inside, stumpy teeth tilted at random intervals. Yet the effect was pleasant, even soothing. Rob felt as though a thrumming sleep were beginning to enfold him as he watched the man approach. *"Iglesia,"* Rob said again. The word was a wooden ball, rolling on a wooden floor. It rolled toward the old man, who reached out, and Rob remembered, just in time, to retract his hand.

The old man paused in front of him, swaying. Drunk, Rob decided. In several places along the road this morning, they had seen figures sprawled out in the mud. "Drunk," Mick pronounced at the first. And at the third, "Shit, all of these drunks."

The man's face crinkled up, as though he and Rob were the oldest of friends. It wouldn't hurt to let him hang on to my sleeve, Rob chided himself. He couldn't stop looking at the man —it was as though he really had fallen asleep.

But the man had lost interest in the arm Rob now offered. His mouth moved, and the silky sounds of the language of the village were slipping around Rob. Yes, like patients, wandering around in the mist. *"No entiendo,"* Rob said, remembering that he was supposed to understand. The man smiled in agreement and nodded. They were both smiling, Rob observed with a mild, puzzled interest.

The old man pointed into the mist. "No," Rob said, smiling still, as the word breathed in and out—no, no—a sail, or wing, in front of him. But the old man beckoned, and retreated a few steps, looking at Rob.

Several yards off the path a cluster of freshly painted wooden crosses rose up from the mud. The man watched Rob, feeding out the silken cord of his language. *"No entiendo,"* Rob said again, smiling just the way the man was smiling. *"No entiendo . . ."*

Each declaration of Rob's ignorance seemed only to amuse the old man more. He nodded, held up a finger, then stood very still and bowed his head, as though he were preparing a recitation, or prayer. He looked up roguishly to check on Rob's attention, then bent over and picked up an imaginary bundle. Watching Rob playfully, he rocked the bundle in his arms, then replaced it on the ground.

He held his finger up again, waited for Rob to nod, then drew himself erect and saluted at someone beyond Rob. As Rob struggled with the thick air for breath, the old man aimed an imaginary gun at the spot where he had laid the bundle, and pulled its imaginary trigger. *"No entiendo,"* Rob said, as the performance began all over. "I don't—" but the old man persevered in his nightmarish repetitions. Behind him the crosses gleamed like bone, new and white, as Rob scrabbled in his pocket for small bills; when he thrust some at the old man, a handful of change fell twinkling in the mud.

One more turn and Rob was at the church. It was enormous, ludicrous. Inside, the streaked blue-green paint and distant ceiling made it seem the size of a stadium. Rob's empty gut kept turning slowly inside out, like a sock. He was covered with a chilling sweat.

Aromatic grasses and flowers were scattered on the vast, cracked concrete floor. Here and there groups of Indians squatted, chanting over smoking vessels. A child skittered by him, cawing and waving his arms in play flight, or mental illness. The chanting spiraled high, modal, nasal—looping back, around the new Spanish god who starved on the altar, looping forward into the dark future . . . Rob wiped the sweat that was leaking into his eyes. Good heavens—the three button-faced blonds from the hotel were parading far down the nave, one of them holding, in both arms, a monstrous pineapple. A *pineapple!* Saints, dressed in embroidered trousers and battered straw hats, looked lustfully down at it from their niches, the hunger in their plaster eyes exaggerated, Rob saw as he felt about for something

to lean on, by the kerchiefs—the guerrilla masks—the worship-
pers had tied across their saintly plaster noses and mouths.

His room faced the lake. The glass in the window was broken
and filthy, but that hardly mattered since the window could not
be closed, and from where Rob lay he could see clearly. Perhaps
the old man had only . . . There were a few shacks scattered
along the marshy strip between the hotel and the lake, and children played near the docked mail boat. Rob closed his eyes, and
the children's voices floated up to him, intimate and allusive,
like dreamed whispers in his ears. He had been lying there for
some time. Two hours? Three? It was impossible to guess; the
children's voices rose and fell, measuring nothing.

When Rob came in, he had slowly, carefully, drained one of
his three bottles of water. Then he'd gone back downstairs to the
shower stall, where no trickle, of any temperature, was to be
coaxed from the faucet. The hotel keeper was outside, at the
door, staring up into the hills. He waited courteously for Rob to
struggle through his question in Spanish. "Generator," the hotel
keeper answered in English, and made an unmistakable gesture
of termination before he returned to squinting up at the hills.

Graffiti were scratched into the dirt and old paint on Rob's
wall. *Hi,* one said. *My name is Bob I like this place I am American so
all here stinks The toilet doesn't work Too All here is disgusting I like
Indians I like* 😊   *I like most one good dead Indian The food here
in this place is disgusting All here is dirty dirty dirty Bye bye* 😊
Your Bob.

Rob stared at it stunned, then laughed. An American named
Bob! Oh, sure. Some German, more likely. And they had nerve
to talk. A *lot* of nerve. Besides, Rob thought, the toilet worked
perfectly. Or at least, he pointed out to himself, it had while the
generator was functioning.

His flat little pillow smelled of mildew. So did the shelf of
uncompromising lumps that was his bed. He tried to isolate the
strains of the odor, the ornate tangling of growth and decay; he
concentrated as his body dripped from the heat into the mattress
and plumes of gray light spread, confusing the water, the sky,
the volcano. Where were Suky and Mick? If only Suky and Mick
would walk in now, and they could all go back to town!

He closed his eyes and the village lay before him. For a moment the market stalls, the tin-roofed huts, the children looked pretty, and exotic—*beautiful.* But smells, rising up from the scanty heaps of rotting food set out for sale and from the tottering, fly-plagued animals, were saturating the glossy surface, causing it to decompose into a deep welter. The smells were making Rob soft, seeping into his body, allowing the chanting from the church to permeate him, too, and alter the codes of his cells with every tiny, insistent modulation.

He was now not merely dirty, he was contaminated. No, he was a crucible, originating poisons, spreading contaminants backward through his life. His parents appeared in their sunny kitchen. Rob drew himself in, but he could feel filth bleeding through his skin where his body pressed against the mattress.

Down below, a few tourists were drifting toward the dock. The children who had been playing were now harnessing themselves into work, begging caressingly for pencils. Rob could hear them: *Lápiz, lápiz,* in their sing-song Spanish, see them advance, surround, pull at sleeves, undeflected by the stony embarrassment of their prey. Obviously Mick had abandoned his prudent thought of attempting to return to town today, and Rob was actually going to have to get himself onto his feet, and go down to the boat.

In the kitchen, Meredith joined his mother and father. The sink was full of water. A pan bobbed up from under a merry mound of suds, and flashed. At home they hadn't yet noticed how the walls were beginning to stain, and buckle.

He turned over and curled himself around his pillow. Soap bubbles winked, breaking. He located one, and with great caution, introduced the tiny figures of his parents and Meredith into it—the soap vessel yielded and resealed around them. Then the bubble lifted and floated through the kitchen window. A little spasm jerked in his chest; he put his fingers to his eyes; his fingers came away wet and hot. "Knock knock," someone said.

"Who's there?" he said, sitting abruptly.

"Banana." Suky hovered in the doorway. "Listen—" She glanced away diplomatically. "—Two things. Number one: the generator's out. Number two: Mick's sick." Rob stared at her, waiting for the bits of speech to organize themselves into information. For a moment it seemed that she was going to come sit next to him on the bed.

A little bug was clambering insecurely over the strap of her camisole, making its way to the cupid's bow peak of her collarbone. She located it and let it board her finger, with which she conveyed it to the window. Her hands were fine and pliant, Rob noticed, her nails bitten savagely. A protracted shudder rose the length of his spine. "Sick, how?" he asked.

"Sick, plain old," Suky said. "I guess they put water in that juice this morning, huh." That was all she seemed to have to say. She stood aimlessly in the doorway.

Rob leaned over to sling his pack up on the bed. "I brought some clean water," he said.

"Clever," Suky said, unenthusiastically.

So, what more could he possibly do? "Did you have a good day?" he said.

"Yeah," Suky said. "Really great. And who knows—maybe Mick will stop throwing up eventually and we'll be able to go back tomorrow. I really look forward to the drive, don't you? Through guerrilla country with an informer in the car?"

"Army informer?" Rob stared at Suky. "Kimball?"

"Consultant, if you prefer," she said. "What did you think, he's an anthropologist?" She hugged herself despite the heat. "You and Mick, Jesus." Her hair curled like steam around her neck and temples, her camisole was spotted with damp. From the window past her, Rob saw the tourists assembling at the boat below. *Time to get up, time to get up*— He remembered his parents' cheerful morning voices; the way he had floated, waking from his night voyages, back into his own bed.

"But what we have to do now," Suky said, "is get some candles. The sun's going to set any minute."

"Candles," Rob said. "Candles . . . Oh, listen—better give these to Mick." He held out his two remaining bottles of water. "Before he gets dehydrated."

Suky watched him. "What about you?"

One of the dark blotches on her camisole seemed to be spreading slightly. Or possibly not. "The thing is," he said, "I've got to get down to the boat."

She took one of the bottles of water from him. "Great," she

said. Her skin gave off its faint sparkle, her face was expression-less, "So. Well. Bon voyage."

"Wait—" Rob said. "Is there—is there some way I could help?" But she was gone, and the stiffness and insincerity of his voice stopped him from calling after her.

Down at the dock the children clung to him, their eyes huge, their tiny hands searching for his pockets. A skinny monkey of a boatman with bare feet and torn, rolled-up pants was collecting the last fares. Rob squinted back at the village: green, fog, glints of tin. But he! Yes, they were all exposed down here at the dock, pinned behind the hidden crosshairs.

Across the lake a cluster of boxy buildings, all no bigger than his fingernail, floated in a disk of harsh blue. Hard to believe town was so close, that he and Suky and Mick had been there only this morning. Hard to believe that he was simply going back there now, to the loud, junky restaurants; to the strained, moribund, fever-pitch cheer of ladinos and gringos vacationing . . . *Time to get up, time to get up* . . .

He found Suky at the pavilion, sitting over another meal of rice and beans. "I brought a flashlight," he said. He took it from his pack, and held it out as an offering. "I thought you might need it."

She glanced up at him, then held out a sheaf of candles in answer.

A little girl, no more than six, arrived with a Coke for Suky. "*Dónde está Pablo?*" Rob asked. The girl stared at him.

"Reinforcements for the night crowd," Suky explained. "Pablo's in the kitchen, cooking."

Rob looked around; the restaurant was empty except for himself and Suky. "Mind if I sit with you?" Rob said, and waited until Suky shrugged.

Dusk was collecting rapidly, settling in heavy folds around the hills and shacks. All along the road, up and down the paths through the village, points of candles began to move at the stately pace of Indians. The volcano and the low vegetation appeared as a furze against the darkness; the sky and lake blended in a colorless sheen.

The little girl brought rice and beans for Rob. He ate a few bites—it was possible to eat, now that he was no longer hungry. Suky lit one of her candles and stuck it onto the table. The little girl drew close and gazed into the flame; she ran her finger sensuously along one of the other candles and looked at Suky, who shook her head no. The little girl leaned against Suky with a loud sigh, which turned into a yawn. *"Tienes hambre?"* Suky said.

"Hambre," the child agreed, and Suky picked her up. Settled in Suky's lap, the child finished Suky's meal, then Rob's, eating delicately with tortillas. When Suky stroked her glorious, filthy black hair, she responded with a snuffly little intake of breath, and they snuggled against each other, sated and filmy-eyed.

Pablo called from the kitchen; the little girl wriggled off Suky's lap. She picked up one of the candles and looked Challengingly at Suky. "All right." Suky sighed. *"Sí."*

"Y para Pablo?" the little girl said.

Suky rubbed her forehead. Was she crying? No, just fatigued, apparently. "Okay," she said, and child scampered off to the kitchen with her trophies.

The sky at the other side of the lake was still faintly blue; it had been clear the whole of the four, vanished days Rob had spent there; clear, he thought with tunneled reverberations of grief.

"I didn't take the boat," he said.

"Is that so," Suky said. She rubbed her forehead again.

"I didn't think I should leave you alone when Mick wasn't well," Rob said.

"Rob," she said, and he floundered in her amber stare. "Rob, let me clarify something, please: Fuck you."

Rob sighed. He passed his finger idly through the candle flame. It had fascinated him as a child—that you could do it and not feel heat; that any household object might disclose inexplicable gaps within a supposed sequence of events. *Was everything he said some sort of lie?*

A dog barked, began to bay. "Shit," Suky said. Candles blinked out one after the other, and night gushed over the village as two dogs, three dogs, joined in until a claxon sprang up in a ring around Rob and Suky. "Let me guess," Rob said. *"Brujos."*

Suky pinched out their candle, making the sky huge with moonlight, and Rob saw what she and the dogs had seen already: a line of black dots, small black shapes moving down the hills closer and closer, winding off a silent cog—a dark chain of soldiers, holding their rifles, descending into the village.

"It's okay—" Suky's quiet voice hovered within the wheeling frenzy of the dogs. "It happens every night. Someone we bought from let it slip to me and Mick today. Remember the guys we saw out front this morning? Every night they all come down. The whole unit. And they stay in the village all night and into the day. But while the mail boat's here they have to evaporate, right? So they go back up to their barracks to sleep while the tourists stumble around."

On the road below, a few late stragglers hurried past with candles, their faces abstract with purpose in the circle of illumination.

"The boat," Rob said. "The mail boat . . ."

"Uh huh," Suky said. "And now the tourists are gone."

The hotel keeper was still at the door. What was he always watching for, Rob wondered. Could he and Kimball discern one another through the blackness, across the hills, as clearly as if they were facing each other, inches apart? *I saw the village, I saw the market, I saw the church,* Rob insisted to himself, but all he could see now was a limitless dark, screened by the reflection of his own face, its expression of untested integrity, of convenient innocence.

Inside the courtyard the three blonds were feasting, fierce and ceremonial, on their pineapple. One of them hacked off a chunk of it with a long, shining knife, and held it out toward Suky. She paused. A troubling warmth floated off her. She shook her head, as though something had been denied, rather than offered to her. "Suky—" Rob said. She glanced at him, then turned away.

Tatters of shine lay on the center of the lake; the boat would have passed through them long before, and in the electric glare that was town, the tourists would just be tucking into steaks, ordering fancy mixed drinks, turning on the televisions in their hotel rooms. . . . But from town, this hotel, the whole village, in fact, would be invisible. Even from Rob's window, the shacks scattered just outside showed only as indeterminate patches of depthless black. Were soldiers, their rifles cocked, squatting there against barricaded doors? *Hi, my name is Bob,* Rob saw. He blew out his candle, but night covered the story that was unfolding below for no other witnesses.

He stretched out on his bed. The darkness around him rustled and whispered, and a satiny gleam from the moon and stars began to collect on his body. In country like this there were probably animals, all kinds of animals, jungly things. Not lions or elephants, of course, but snakes, certainly, and even monkeys, perhaps—the kind that screamed at night—and small nocturnal creatures that looked like big cats or rats and scampered through ruins of huts where people had recently lived. Just born, they would sleep for a few days in shaded hollows, and then one night, unlid their jewel-like eyes.

And when they opened their tiny new mouths, when their new little natures ordained that this one or that one would stretch the hinges of its sleek new jaws, what pleasures of discoveries there would be! The flickering tongue, the high-pitched howl, the needle-pointed teeth, whatever marvelous instrument it was, discovered anew by each new being, that was the special gift of its species. Yes. Rob's heart pounded as though he'd run to keep an appointment.

When the knock came, he waited for one luxurious moment; the gleam slid off him as he stood.

"Mick wants water," Suky said from the doorway. Rob cleared his throat. "How is Mick?" he asked. "Puking," she said. "As usual."

"Sit down," he said, breathless. "I've got that other bottle around here somewhere." Again, a long shudder ascended his spine.

Suky rested, propped up on one elbow while Rob pretended to search. When he could stand it no longer, he retrieved the bottle and a stack of styrofoam cups from their corner. "Here," he said.

Suky reached for the bottle, but he held it back. "Careful, careful," he said, experimentally. "It's all I've got left."

She looked at him sharply, before her face became opaque.

When she held out her hand again slowly, he relinquished the bottle.

Trembling, he disengaged two cups from the stack. Suky poured some water into each; the sound was deafening. "Cheers," he thought he heard her say, and their cups scraped together.

He struggled to restrain his uncoiling mind as he traced Suky's collarbone with his finger and blinked back the veil of terror that kept gathering across his eyes. Darkness was reaching out like creepers, unfolding into thick, oily petals, and distant sounds were becoming audible; Rob's thoughts were pattering here and there in darkness. "What's going on?" he whispered against Suky's throat, but her eyes narrowed, gleamed, dilated—already she was gliding off. Those distant cries—something waking now to the fragrance of blood? Levering the straps down from Suky's shoulders, Rob strained to hear, and waited.

Bernard Cooper

TRUTH SERUM

Every Tuesday at exactly three o'clock, the nurse would call my name and lead me into the examining room where I lay down on a padded table. Comfortable? she always asked, and always I said yes without conviction. I have no recollection of the woman's face, only her white, immaculate back, and the click of the door as it closed behind her. I'd be counting holes in the soundproof ceiling when Dr. Sward, my psychotherapist, would bound into the room. The man possessed an inexhaustible energy when it came to the task of psychic exploration, and I think he hoped some of his enthusiasm would rub off on his reticent clients. Dr. Sward prided himself on being a hale, contented fellow, a man able to overcome adversity. A former smoker, he'd had an operation to remove part of his larynx, and his voice, or what remained of it, was somnolent and gravelly. "Hello," he'd rasp. "Are we ready?" Dr. Sward took a seat in the room's only chair—vinyl exhaled under his weight—and removed a fountain pen and note pad from the breast pocket of his blazer. Pen poised, he beamed a broad and expectant grin, a lock of white hair falling onto his forehead.

Next entered Dr. Townsley, Dr. Sward's stout, mustachioed colleague, who swabbed my arm with alcohol and asked me to make a fist. I barely felt the injection, but serum rode into my vein like an intravenous hot toddy, and a primal, womb-worthy comfort seemed to radiate outward from the tip of the needle. Almost instantly my breathing deepened into rich, intoxicating troughs of air. I steeped in a heedless stew of sensation: release of rubber tied around my arm; small talk volleyed between the doctors; one shiny frond of a philodendron seemed like the greenest thing on earth. With the sudden candor of a drunk, I wanted to tell the doctors how happy I felt, but before the words could form, I heard the sound of what I thought was a receptionist typing in another room. Her typing would quicken— faster, manic, superhuman—and invariably I would think to myself, A million words per minute! What nimble fingers! The keys must be shooting sparks from friction! And then I'd realize it wasn't the sound of typing after all, but something more miraculous—chattering watts of light showered down from a bulb on the ceiling. Stirred to the verge of tears, I wanted to shout, "Hold everything, Doctors. I can hear light!" But my jaw went lax and my fist unclenched and I lost my grip on consciousness.

When I opened my eyes, the overhead lights were out. Dr. Townsley had gone, and Dr. Sward's voice emanated from somewhere near the wan glow of a table lamp. "How are you?" he asked.

I was eager to answer any question. I effervesced with things to say. I couldn't have lifted my head if I'd wanted to. "Good," I mumbled, trying to work the moisture back into my mouth. "Very good."

Dr. Sward believed that this experimental form of therapy would help me get to the root of my problem. His colleagues were having some success with the treatment, a combination of sodium pentathol, known during the Second World War as "truth serum," and Ritalin, a mild amphetamine which, given to hyperactive children, helps them gather their scattered thoughts. The sodium pentathol, he'd explained, would cause me to pass out, and the Ritalin would revive me. This paradoxical cocktail numbs a patient's inhibitions while at the same time enhancing their capacity for insight, its effect vanishing without a trace in about forty minutes. He suggested the drugs after I told him that talking to him for the past six months had done nothing to reduce the frequency or intensity of my sexual fantasies involving men. *Frequency, intensity:* those were the terms we used, as though the clinical distance they imposed was in itself an achievement, a way of dividing me from the heat and draw of desire. The final decision was up to me; no treatment could make me change if I didn't have a strong desire to do so, but I might, he felt, be resistant, and the drugs could break down my unconscious defenses and hasten our progress.

"How are things at home?" asked Dr. Sward.

I'd been living with a woman for three years, a woman whom I loved, and with whom I had a sex life both playful and pleasurable. I met Bia in art school in 1970. Passing her dorm room, I'd watch her cut bits of black and white photographs out of *Time* magazine with an X-acto blade, and then paste the fragments into long, hieroglyphic columns, giving current events a cryptic twist. In a circle of lamp light, she worked with the meticulous intensity of a jeweler, her concentration unaffected by the jazz blaring from her stereo. We began to eat dinner together at a local restaurant called The Happy Steak, and it was there, amid the faux cowhide upholstery and formica wood-grain tables, that we honed our love of the low-brow, discussing at length the soup cans and crushed cars of contemporary art. Budding conceptualists, we were indifferent to the *taste* of the steak, but delighted by the *idea* that our dinners were impaled with a plastic cow, its flank branded RARE, MEDIUM, or WELL. Instead of saying grace before we ate, we'd bow our heads, clasp our hands and recite, "Cows are happy when they cry/So we kick them in the eye."

I'm not sure at what point friendship turned to love—our relationship remained platonic for nearly a year—but I'm sure we would have had sex much earlier if both of us hadn't harbored longings for people of the same gender. My secret crushes included Robert Conrad, whose television show, "The Wild Wild West," had him stripped to the waist in almost every episode, his pectorals a lesson in advanced geometry, and Bill Medley of the Righteous Brothers, with whom I'd been smitten since junior high, romanticizing into satyr-hood his long, lean, horsey face. Bia, it turned out, was crazy for Greta Garbo, piqued by her high cheekbones, moist eyes, and the world-weary manner which suggested a womanhood rich in glamorous disappointments. We confided these guilty attractions late one night during a marathon conversation. Once they were aired, our admissions seemed less shameful, less significant, and I began to feel that sleeping with Bia was inevitable; who better to sleep with than the keeper of your secrets? Besides, as a side-effect of our heated discussions, her translucent skin and hazel eyes had begun to excite me.

The only word to describe our first sexual encounter is *premeditated*. We gave ourselves weeks to get used to the idea of sleeping with each other, to weigh the consequences—would physical intimacy jeopardize our friendship?—to prolong the delicious anticipation. Like a couple catering a large party, we tried to take into account every eventuality, every shift in the weather, every whim of appetite. Hers was the bed we'd use; it was the biggest, the most familiar; we'd sat on it for countless hours, smoking Marlboros, listening to jazz, watching TV with the sound turned down while improvising snappy patter. Intercourse, we decided, would be best in the late afternoon when the window shades turned Bia's room the color of butter. Afterward we'd shower together, and have a meal at The Happy Steak.

When the day we'd set aside finally arrived, we spent the morning at Descanso Gardens. Arms about each other, we were tender and nervous and telepathic, taking this path instead of that, staring at schools of darting koi, lingering before stands of cacti, awed by their bright, incongruous blossoms.

I had slept with only one person up to that point, a girl with whom I'd gone to high school. Alison whipped her long blonde hair from side to side, a semaphore of the feminine. Her arms and legs were hard and tan and she seemed, walking to class or sprawled on the lawn, all loose-limbed and eager, a living invitation. Alison loved sex. Got it as often and with as many boys as she could. Her flirtations had about them an ingenuous joy, a stark curiosity. The sexual revolution was in full swing, and Alison's hedonism gave her a certain cachet.

The night before I left for college on the east coast, I took her to a bar on the top floor of a high-rise in Hollywood. We shared fierce and slippery kisses in the elevator. Toasting each other at a tiny table, the city glittered below us. Men looked at her with lust and at me with envy; her company quelled my sexual doubts. I knew we wouldn't sleep together that night—she had to drive back home to Malibu before her parents returned from a trip—and this freed me from the performance anxiety that surely would have swamped me had sex been imminent. I helped her off with her coat, leafed through her hair, and paid the bill, playing my masculine role to the hilt because I knew there was no pressure to follow through. I'd carry with me to college the memory of our date, a talisman to ward off the fear that I might never escape my desire for men.

Imagine my surprise when, two months later, Alison showed up at my Brooklyn dormitory wearing a skimpy white dress in the middle of winter, an overnight bag slung over her shoulder. We hadn't seen or written to each other since our date. She'd been visiting her cousins on Long Island and wanted to surprise me. "You're hilarious," she said when I suggested she stay in the guest room off the lobby. She flopped onto my bed. Kicked off her shoes. Fixed me in her bright green gaze. Flipped her hair to and fro like a flag.

We batted her overnight bag off the bed and it skidded across the floor. Articles of clothing arced through the air. I tried, with brusque adjustments of my hips, to disguise any tentativeness when I entered her. It's now or never, I remember thinking. Her vagina was silky, warm, and capacious. It struck me that my penis might be too small to fill her in the way she wanted, and just when I thought that this tightening knot of self-consciousness might make the act impossible, she let out a yelp of unabashed pleasure. I plunged in deeper, single-minded as a salmon swimming upstream. My hands swept the slope of Alison's shoulders, the rise of her breasts. I didn't realize it until afterward, but I sucked her neck the entire time, fastened by my lips to a bucking girl. Alison's climax was so protracted, her moans so operatic, her nails so sharp as they raked my back, that when she sat up and felt her neck, I thought she was checking her pulse. Suddenly, she rose and ran to the bathroom, a swath of bed sheet trailing in her wake. "I told you," she shrieked, her voice resounding off the tile walls. She appeared in the doorway, legs in a wide, defiant stance, nipples erect. "I told you no hickies!"

"No you didn't."

"I said it right at the beginning."

"Then I didn't hear you, Alison."

She held her hand to her neck, Cleopatra bitten by an asp. "What am I going to do?" Her voice was about to break. "What am I going to tell my cousins?"

It was preposterous; she had come to Brooklyn to seduce me, and now Alison was mortified by the small, sanguine badge of our abandon. I said I was sorry.

" 'Sorry' isn't going to take it away."

"What about this," I said, turning to show her the marks I could feel scored into my back.

"Oh, great," she said. "Let's compare war wounds." She bent down and scooped up her white dress; it lay on the floor like a monstrous corsage. "You men," she said bitterly.

Forgive me, I was flattered. Placed at last in a class from which I'd felt barred.

I lit a cigarette, watching as she stood before the window and dragged a brush through her hair, the strokes punishing, relentless, and I began to see that Alison was angry at herself for the rapacious nature of her needs, and that her future, overpopulated with lonely men, would be one long, unresolved argument between ardor and regret. Or was I seeing my own fate in her?

An icy sky dimmed above the city. Alison shook her head at an offer of dinner. Her face, framed by sheaths of yellow hair, was pinched with the reflex to flee. "So," she sighed. She slipped into her shoes, stared through me and toward the door. "Give me a call someday." Her tone was clipped and bitter. Standing in my bathrobe, at a loss for what to say, I touched her shoulder and she shrugged me away, managing a weak and fleeting smile before she shut the door behind her.

When I turned around, night veiled the Brooklyn skyline. I tried not to think how far I was from home. Touching was futile; men or women, what did it matter? I crawled back into bed— the residue of Alison's odor rose from the pillow like a puff of dust—and fell into a dreamless sleep.

It would be a long time before I had sex again. All the while I told myself, with a sad resolve, that love-making was not one of my natural skills; all mixed-up when it came to desire, I'd have to depend on something other than sex for satisfaction. Somewhere I'd read that Picasso spent a lifetime channeling his libido into painting (this explained his prodigious output), and I secretly hoped that my erotic energy would be sublimated into art. Deprivation for the sake of art—the idea made me feel noble. It's no coincidence that during this period my class projects became huge and ornate, and although I hadn't the slightest understanding of, say, the mathematical principles behind my three-dimensional model of the Golden Rectangle, my efforts were often singled out for discussion by instructors impressed with the obsessive detail which had begun to characterize my work. One night, after too much to drink, this obsessiveness led me to paint my dorm room cobalt blue and glue dozens of Styrofoam cups to the ceiling, thinking they looked like stalactites. It took three coats of white latex to rectify the situation. Woozy from fumes, I began to understand sublimation's wild, excessive underside. Soon after that night, restless and homesick, I transferred to The California Institute of the Arts, where I met Bia.

Bia was still a virgin when we made our plans to sleep with each other, a fact I took into account when I clipped my toenails, conditioned my pubic hair with cream-rinse, and practically baptized myself with Brut before I walked into her room. My ablutions were not in vain; our sex was greedy, sweet-smelling teamwork. Spent as we were in the aftermath, we radiated fresh contentment. I rested my head on Bia's breast, grateful for my good luck and the buttery light. That afternoon we began to live together, devotion a knot we'd tied with our bodies.

As for our homosexual yearnings, once we became a couple, we didn't bring them up again out of affection and deference; like the foundation of a house, they remained present but unseen, the trust that prompted such confidences the basis of our relationship. Both of us, I think, wanted to believe that we were embarking on the grand adventure of heterosexuality, and that the fear of ostracism with which we had lived so much of our lives could be shucked off at last like a pair of tight shoes. We were relieved, those first few years of living together, to see our love reflected back from movies and billboards and books. Never taking for granted the privilege of public touching, we kissed in cars and markets and parks. But there persisted for me this unavoidable fact: regardless how gratifying I found sex with Bia, I wanted to have a man.

"Knock, knock. Is anybody there?" joked Dr. Sward. "I was asking what's new."

In the first few seconds of every session, consciousness was something I tried on for size like a huge droopy hat. Then I'd blurt a forbidden thought. *The Armenian who works the steampress machine at the dry cleaners was wearing a T-shirt and I swear I could feel the fur on his forearms from across the room.* Usually, Dr. Sward greeted my disclosures with a bromide. Once, I told him that every masturbatory fantasy I'd ever had involved a man, and that I'd gotten to the point where I frankly didn't see how psychotherapy, no matter how probing, enhanced by drugs or not, could alter an impulse etched into my brain by years of unrelenting lust. Dr. Sward laughed his hearty laugh. I thought I heard him lean forward in his chair. He suggested I substitute the image of a woman for the image of a man the second before I ejaculated. I considered telling him that if I had to concentrate on his advice I'd never be able to come, but his casual tone made change seem so easy, like using a giant vaudeville hook to yank an awful act off stage.

Despite the fact that his advice was often facile, I continued to visit Dr. Sward once a week. He was sincere in his efforts to change me; I was the ambivalent party, riveted by the bodies of men, yet tired of grappling with secret lust. I blamed myself for the inability to reform, chalked it up to a failure of will, and would have tried just about anything that promised relief from confusion and shame. Determined to spend my life with Bia— she was my ally in art; there was no one with whom I had more fun—I thought it might be worth enduring my frustrations with therapy in order to ensure the longevity of our relationship. Perhaps there would come a point where my sexual impulses would be simplified, a straight line where there once had been all the twists and turns of a French curve. I knew few gay men, and to some extent still believed that homosexuals were doomed to a life of unhappiness; I never entirely exorcised the images of homosexuality that figured into the rumors and hearsay of my childhood, images of gloomy, clandestine encounters, trench coats and candy the recurrent motifs. I suppose I understood that no behavioral modification, no psychological revelation would take away my desire for men, but in the end, I went back to Dr. Sward's office because—this is the hardest confession of all—because I wanted to hear the light.

The terrible power of that sound. When I tried to describe it to Bia, I resorted to the phrase: The Music of the Spheres. How lazy and inadequate! The universe seemed to be shuddering, seized by a vast, empathic spasm, crying out in a tremulous voice. I don't mean only visible stuff—chairs and cars and buildings and trees—but microcosmic tremblings, too—pollen and protons and cosmic dust. The sum of matter had been struck like a tuning fork, and one vital, cacophonous chord issued from a lightbulb screwed into the ceiling of a room where I lay on a padded table and tried to revise my life. Compared to that sound, all the doctor's concern, all my apprehension, all the rules governing who touches whom, were muffled to a feeble squeak. The glory of it left me breathless.

Now I would never claim that the sound was a panacea, but it became an extremely beneficial aspect of therapy, given the way it trivialized my problems with it's big aural blast. Dr. Sward believed that my desire for men could be broken down into a set of constituent griefs: lack of paternal love; envy toward other men for their sexual certainty; a need for identification confused with a drive for physical contact. And then, one day, the blare of the light still ringing in my ears, I asked the doctor if heterosexual desire wasn't also a muddled, complex matter, fraught with the very same helplessness and hurt he attributed to my particular case. Didn't he, for example, ever seek his wife's maternal attentions, or envy her sexual receptivity, or yearn to burrow into her flesh, his nerves alert and bordering on anguish? Without a dose of desperation, or the aches and pains left over from one's past, what would sex between two people be? A pat on the back?

All the things I believed to be true pushed from behind like a harried crowd; it was the sodium pentathol talking. The silence that followed embarrassed us both. Worried that my challenge to his authority had upset him, I back-peddled a bit. "I'm just thinking out loud, you know, trying to fit the pieces together."

"Of course," said Dr. Sward. "Of course. But after all, we're not here to talk about me."

. . .

I saw Dr. Sward for another six months before I announced, emboldened by an especially heady dose of serum, that I felt it was time for me to terminate therapy. He offered no argument for my staying. In fact, he was surprisingly willing to see me leave, and I couldn't help but think my visits had become for him a source of professional, if not personal, disappointment. For the past year Dr. Sward had insisted that, since I lived with a woman and enjoyed with her a passionate sex life, I was, ipso facto, heterosexual—a conclusion which struck me as absurd, like thinking that, when Charles Laughton plays Henry VIII, he is actually King of England. During our final sessions, however, Dr. Sward seemed resigned to my conflict, more respectful of the obstinate, wayward power of human want.

"Would you say," he asked rather pensively at the end of our final session, "that the nature of your homosexual fantasies has changed at all during the course of our working together?"

"They've changed a little," I said to placate him, meaning they occurred with even greater frequency.

"Will you attempt a hetero- or homosexual life after you leave this office?"

"Don't know," I lied, sliding off the table and shaking his hand. We sighed and wished each other luck.

What I did know was that, as far as the outcome of sodium pentathol therapy was concerned, the one truth that mattered to me now was the electrifying strength of lust. Still, I made no effort to leave Bia for months after I quit seeing Dr. Sward. I was frightened of uncertainty, of exile to a shapeless fate, and the closer I came to a life without her, the more her company soothed me.

When I finally did tell her I wanted to move out and test my feelings for men, we were sitting side by side at Kennedy Airport, waiting to board a plane back to Los Angeles after a vacation. Destinations echoed over the loudspeaker. Travelers checked their boarding passes, gathered at gates. All that rush and flux, all those strangers embarking on journeys, made urgent and keen my sense of departure. I turned to Bia and, before I knew what I was doing, mumbled there was something I had to say. I kept protesting my affection, my helplessness. I wanted desperately to take her hand, to hold her to me, but fought it

down as a hypocritical impulse. She stared at me, uncomprehending, as though I were pleading in a foreign language.
Then the dawning of fury and hurt as she understood.

Once on the plane, our steady, defeated weeping was disguised by the roar of the engines. Every time I turned to face
her, at a loss for what to say, I glimpsed our reflections in the
airplane window, vague and straying above the earth.

It wasn't until long after I'd moved out, after Bia found a
woman and I found a man, that I mustered the courage to tell
her what had happened in New York. We'd spent the afternoon
at opposite ends of Manhattan, she uptown, having lunch with a
friend, and me in Soho, visiting galleries. Walking back to our
midtown hotel, I cut through the West Village. It was hot and
humid and overcast, the dark air charged with impending rain.
Men congregated on the sidewalk or shared tables at outdoor
cafes, their sleeves rolled up, shirts unbuttoned, talk and gestures intent. A few of them turned to watch me pass. Self-con-
scious as I was, I actually believed for a moment that they were
straight men who thought I was gay, and I regretted wearing
the gauzy Indian shirt I'd bought at an import shop, and which
now felt as insubstantial as lingerie. I began to walk faster, as
though I might outstrip the realization of what and where I was.

A salvo of thunder, a blanching flash of light, and there began
a heavy, tepid rain. People ran for cover in doorways, gathered
under awnings drummed by the rain. My shirt was drenched in
seconds, patches of my bare skin seeping through the fabric like
stains. I kept tugging the cloth away from my body, but the wet
shirt clung and flesh bloomed through. Dressed yet exposed in
the middle of the city, arms folded across my chest, I froze as
though in an anxious dream. Then I dashed into the nearest
doorway where another man stood, waiting out the rain. He had
a round, guileless face and brown hair beaded with drops of
water. "You're positively soaked," he said. We eyed each other
nervously, then peered up at the sluggish clouds. Neither especially handsome nor interesting, his small talk—he knew where
I could buy an umbrella, hoped he had closed his apartment
windows—calmed me. His weathered neck, encircled by a gold
chain, made me wonder how old he was and if he spent long
hours in the sun on a balcony somewhere in the city, with

friends perhaps, or the man with whom he lived, and I glimpsed, as if through the window of his skin, a life more solid and settled than my own. He was, I decided, a man who'd adapted to his own desires; I envied him his sexual certainty, and so bore out, although in reverse, one of Dr. Sward's theories. I would have had sex with that talkative, innocuous stranger in an instant, would have gladly given him the burden of releasing me from ambivalence. And just when it occurred to me that it might be possible to seduce him, just as I wrestled with a proposition, the rain let up, he wished me luck, and dashed down the street.

I walked aimlessly, for hours, till the pale sun made my shirt opaque.

That night, when Bia reached out in her sleep to touch me, she touched a man on the edge of action, shedding the skin of his former life. I tossed and turned. The hotel bed felt hard and unfamiliar. I didn't know then that Bia and I would remain lifelong friends, or that by never again falling in love with someone of the opposite sex, we'd preserve the exception of who we once were. I knew only that impatience outweighed my remorse. Over and over, I replayed my encounter with the man in the doorway; in fantasy, I lived on my own, and when he asked me if I had a place, I told him yes, I had a place.

Edward J. Delaney

THE DROWNING

My father came from the old country in middle age, and to his last he instilled in me the peculiarities of his native tongue. Even now, at the age of seventy, I am left with his manners of speech, his inflections and growls. He left me with his sayings, and I recall one in particular, his favorite, a half-comic shout of equal parts exasperation and petition: "Help me, Father Alphonsus!"

Most often this was uttered in moments of high disgust. My father worked as a hod carrier until he was seventy, a job that condemned him through all those years to being eternally strong and eternally exhausted. At night, sitting in his chair in the parlor of our tenement, he would brood over the five of us, his children, as we bickered over one thing or another—the last scrap of the night's loaf, a new toy pilfered from a classmate— and he would take on the resigned look of a condemned man, and invoke the name of this priest, a man he had known long ago. And then, if my mother didn't rush from the kitchen to herd us from danger, my father would often hit one of us.

Even late in life he had ridged muscles along his chest and back. His face was etched with a sunburned and skeptical squint. When we were young, he hit hard. When he sat down again, walled in now by the wails of a child, he'd rub the sting from his cracked hands and fall into a black mood. "Forgive me,

Father Alphonsus," he'd mumble. The meaning always seemed clear. My father was a man of weakness and vices, and he made no apologies. He prayed for strength in the face of us. Much later in life I found myself praying aloud to Father Alphonsus a time or two, such as when my own son stole a car. The matter was quietly settled in the office of a police-department captain, with the victim of the theft staring at me from across the table and my son quietly sobbing. Father Alphonsus, the faceless man of grace, hovered ethereally over the proceedings.

Alphonsus, my father told us, was the most well-intentioned man he had ever known, "if such things should count for anything." Alphonsus was a near relation, the keeper of faith in Fenagh, the hamlet on Lough Ree where my father was born.

"He was a man who knew nothing but to offer the best he could," my father said. "I have neither his patience nor his benevolence." My father wasn't cruel, but he lived a life of bricks on his back, the stabbing workday sun, and day's-end liquor bought with the desire for the most liquid at the lowest negotiable rate. He'd drink and play our battered phonograph, closing his eyes and giving himself over to the crackling arias. Though he often invoked the name of his old village priest, he found no priest here to be worthy, and he fell away from the Church despite my mother's prodding. When I was seventeen and was offered a scholarship to Boston College, he complained bitterly that I could do better than to deal with Jesuits, insincere bastards that they were. I suspected that my father could have done much better than his dire life, but he seemed not to want to, couldn't fully engage in the way things were. It didn't seem unusual that a hod carrier would prize his books, his Greek classics and sweeping histories. He was Irish, and illegal. He could not become lace-curtain Irish, and my father had nothing good to say about those who were. He maintained through his life the sidelong glance he had learned when he first came off the boat, before he found my mother and married her.

This Father Alphonsus was one of the few people mentioned from my father's youth. I had no sense of what the man was like, his look or manner. At times I wondered if he was real. But one day, late in his life, my father came to feel a desperate need to tell me a story.

This would have been 1952. My father was about the same age as I am now, but he was much closer to death than I assume myself to be. A resolute smoker of filterless Camel cigarettes, he was in the advanced stages of cancer of the larynx, which at the time was virtually incurable. In the nursing home, in a wicker wheelchair, he talked compulsively despite the ongoing strangulation of his voice box. He'd take a deep breath and then release it in long, rattling phrases, and I would sit and listen to monologues about his job and friends and enemies and crooks and aces. Later, in his yellow-walled hospital room, he'd go on and on while I watched the rectangle of sunlight glide imperceptibly across the waxed floors and then fade and die. I sensed in all this talk a spiraling movement toward something central. He had, he told me, things he needed to say. Important things. What happened on Father Alphonsus's final day was one.

Alphonsus had been the youngest of six, born six weeks after his father's death by pneumonia, and from the moment of his birth his mother had unshakable plans for him. Alphonsus would be her last chance, and she was the kind of woman who felt that producing a priest was a fitting and necessary act of completion to her maternal career. From the earliest age Alphonsus was groomed for sacred duty. She made him tiny knitted vestments and pasteboard altars as playthings, enlisting his older brothers, rougher boys, to encourage Alphonsus to believe that he was different. Alphonsus's mother spoke to him nightly about the duties he would assume, bedtime tales about faith and good works. His oldest brother, Eamon, explained to him about celibacy, and none too charitably. But Alphonsus listened and nodded. The details Eamon so eagerly shared, using examples of his own sordid exploits as proof of what Alphonsus would miss, horrified the younger boy. Eamon waited then for a response. Alphonsus's nightly sessions with his mother allowed him to apply the appropriate word: *sacrifice.* "Good lad," Eamon said. Alphonsus, even as a child, was looking forward to the priest's solitary life. His heroes were the Irish hermits of the Middle Ages. He read stories of their lives on the rocky islands off the west Irish coast, lives of gray skies and gray seas. These stories filled him with awe for the heroism embodied in shunning the world.

Sacrifice did not define the process of Alphonsus's rise to the priesthood. He slid through seminary and took up his works back at St. Enda's in Fenagh, his boyhood church. When his superior, the aged Father O'Donnell, passed away on the night after Christmas, 1906, the twenty-six-year-old Alphonsus became his village's spiritual leader.

Nights, standing in his bedroom as rain washed the windows of the drafty stone rectory, he thought that he didn't regret what he had become but that he wouldn't ultimately measure up. The feeling wasn't new. He had completed his studies with neither distinction nor exceptional difficulty. He had never considered himself brilliant, but he had enough intelligence to see his own utter lack of intuition. Could a priest, confronted with the fluid nature of reality, afford not to rely heavily on hunches and inspiration? In his small room in the seminary he prayed long and searchingly, believing that a sudden feeling of enlightenment or resolve might be transmitted from the Creator. But when he finished with his prayers, he felt nothing.

In the first dozen years or so after ordination things went relatively well. His posting to the village seemed clear notice that not much was expected of him from his superiors. Alphonsus presided over the reassuring cycle of dawn masses, funerals, and weddings; he taught catechism and organized a football team of the younger boys. These were the things Alphonsus had imagined himself doing effectively. He'd stand at the edge of a rain-softened field, the winds off the lough making the edges of his cassock snap and tighten around his legs, and he'd watch the boys, some playing barefoot, as they kicked the ball about. He felt like a giant then, affecting a sternness he recalled in O'Donnell. He hoped to instill in them the fear he'd held of the old man. But at the same time, he felt small and weak in the face of the unanticipated crisis. It had not yet happened, but he knew its inevitability, if not its form. He felt that these things could be seen by the shrewd among his parishioners: His stammering uncertainty when faced with the difficulty of a pregnant girl, Amanda Flynn, asking to be quietly married, even though half the town had already heard whispered dispatches of her condition. Or the town's thieves and adulterers and his sheeplike acceptance of them sitting in the front pews, their faces masks of haughty and false devotion. He would meet their eyes briefly and then look away.

One day, after years of this stoic service, Alphonsus awakened early to a knocking on the door. This tapping was light but relentless, on and on until he had let his eyes adjust and find the phosphorescent hands of his clock. It was three o'clock. An early riser, Alphonsus was surprised to be rolled out of bed, and the insistent softness of the knocks as he descended the stairs indicated to him a call for last rites, perhaps for the elder John Flanagan, who'd been kicked shoeing a horse and was not expected to recover. At the door he found a boy, perhaps ten years old, shivering.

"Father, you have to hear a confession," the boy said.

"Pardon?"

"A confession. You hear confessions, don't you?"

"Well, I thought you were . . ." Alphonsus felt a twinge of anger. "Of course I hear confessions. But I generally don't find children on my doorstep at odd hours. Now, get inside here. We'll do it in the study, and it had better be good."

"It's not I who needs to," the boy said. "The person is waiting inside the church."

What was this? Alphonsus made the boy stand in the entry while he ascended the stairs to change clothes. The oddity of this demanded confession made him suspicious. For a shaky moment he worried that this would be a robbery. He sat at the edge of the bed, still in his underclothing, his cassock across his knees. He tried to place the boy's face. The child was not one of his footballers; the face was reminiscent of the O'Neals, a family of beggars who lived in a beaten-down mud cottage outside the town, near the lough shore. Alphonsus heard the door below open and then shut. The thought of what might be afoot—being lured out by the boy and then thrashed for his pocket watch—made him wary. Alphonsus went to the bedroom window and looked out. The boy had left the house and now stood on the dark lawn with a man. They were shadowy forms, but he could see that they were looking up at him. The man raised his arm and waved. Alphonsus waved back and then held out a raised index finger: *one moment*. The man nodded.

When Alphonsus came out the door, he felt the glassy cold cutting through his sweater. The man and boy moved forward to meet him, in the steam from their own breathing. The man, his face hidden by the pulled-down front of his cap, was staring at the ground.

"The boy said you'd gone inside the church," Alphonsus said.

"No, Father. He's right inside the confessional."

They stayed in the yard while Alphonsus went in. He fumbled for a candle at the back of the nave, still half waiting for hands to seize at him from the dark. But in the weak light the church was still. He entered the confessional, snuffed the candle, and slid back his screen.

"Are you there?" Alphonsus said.

"Aye, Father."

"Then go ahead."

The voice began its mumbled recitations, and as he waited, Alphonsus rubbed his eyes of sleep and wondered about the elder John Flanagan and whether he had lived through the night. Alphonsus was feeling light and electric, not quite anchored in the dark. He realized that the man had stopped talking.

"Go ahead," Alphonsus said.

"Father, I've breached the Fifth Commandment."

Alphonsus was silent. He was sure the man was confused. "Do you mean adultery, then?" he said.

"No."

"Tell me the Fifth Commandment."

"Thou shalt not kill."

Alphonsus felt strangely calm. This was the first time he'd encountered such an infraction. A killer! He silently recalled the seminary lessons: *Forgiveness is the priest's task, punishment the law's.*

"Who?" Alphonsus said.

"I don't know his name."

"Who knows about this?"

"No one, Father."

"Not your friends outside?"

"Not even them. Only you."

"And where is the dead man?"

"In the woods near the lough."

"Is that where you killed him?"

"That's where I did him, Father."

Alphonsus leaned back against his bench. He told himself to go slow.

"And while you were standing over his body there in the woods, were you feeling remorse for your act?"

"I felt sorry I had to breach a commandment."

"Was it self-defense?"

"In a manner of speaking."

"What manner was that?"

"That we are all in danger, Father."

"Some men, to prove their remorse, might turn themselves in."

"Aye," the voice said. "Some might."

"And why not you?"

"Others will be involved. Others who don't deserve such troubles."

"How so? Troubles from whom?"

"From the Black and Tans."

"Oh, my," Alphonsus said. He ran his fingers along the starched smoothness of his collar. Matters had taken on a more troubling dimension. He now understood that the dead man was a policeman from the RIC, the Royal Irish Constabulary. Four years had passed since the Easter Rising in Dublin, and in this four years of undeclared civil war the RICs, seen by many as agents of British rule, had often been targets. The RICs were Irishmen, but more and more the younger men had left the ranks, some openly disavowing their ties, others simply slipping out, often to England. Those who remained were the older hands, who after years of service were not sure whether to be more afraid of the Irish Republican Army or of a lost pension. But with each new death of a constable came more recrimination and violence.

The Black and Tans, since they'd been brought in from England, had begun a policy of retribution that was as simple as it was vicious. When a policeman was killed, the Tans generally burned the village nearest the killing. Alphonsus did not need to calculate the distance to the shores of Lough Ree: as a sport fisherman, he knew the lough, a landlocked elbow of water a mile wide and eleven long.

"Father . . . ?"

"Yes."

"My penance?"

Good God! Was this how simple it should be? Alphonsus was speechless. Penance? He sat for a long time, thinking, wondering whether he could somehow find a way to consult with someone. What was the penance for such an act?

"I can grant no penance yet," Alphonsus said. "I want you to return here at the same time tomorrow night. I want you to do nothing except pray. Take no action. Now, where is this body?"

"Father, I don't know if . . ."

"Good Lord, man! Tell me where this poor lad is, so he can receive the sacrament due him!"

"Do you know the path to the rock formations on the east side of the lough?"

"I do."

"He's twenty or thirty yards north of the path, about a quarter mile up from the shore."

"How did he get there?"

"He was answering a call for help."

The man fell silent. Alphonsus could hear his breathing. "Father?" he said. "Father, I thought you had to grant penance."

"Not in the case of the Fifth Commandment," Alphonsus said. "Most people have no experience in this." He quivered at his own lie, but his voice remained firm.

As Alphonsus sat in the confessional, listening to the receding footsteps and then the slam of the church door, he rubbed his hands on his knees, trying to calm himself. Indeed, he was thinking of the town of Balbriggan, which had burned a few weeks before at the hands of the Black and Tans.

But, Alphonsus wondered, could this man who had spoken to him in the confessional truly be repentant, having known what his actions would lead to? Alphonsus thought not. But he had, from his training, clear guidelines: as much as he wanted this man to turn himself in, he could not require it. And doing so probably wouldn't help, once the dead man was discovered. The Black and Tans, so called because of their odd makeshift uniforms of khaki army trousers and black RIC tunics, were men in whom the cruelty of war had become ingrained. They were being paid ten shillings a day, good money, but still they often sought as payment the suffering of those they saw as enemies, which was nearly anyone Irish.

Alphonsus relit his candle. The movement of the shadows in the boxed closeness of the confessional made him think of the lick of flames. The Black and Tans' terror felt close at hand. Why should anyone be absolved?

In the morning he offered sunrise service to a handful of sleepy elders and then returned to the rectory for breakfast. The housekeeper, Mrs. Toole, had brought in a two-day-old copy of *The Irish Times*, and over his toast he went through it slowly, looking for news on the Troubles. In the village he had heard talk of how the Black and Tans had taken to roaring down Dublin streets on a lorry, wildly firing their weapons; in Kiltartan a woman was dead, hit by stray shots with a child in her arms. But in the *Times* he found no mention.

He changed into his gardening clothes. His flower beds faced the woods, and at the edge of the trees he had vegetables. He spent hours here, for the priesthood had not proved to be excessively demanding. Many days he stood at his fence, watching the movements of the drawn carts and of his parishioners, the cottiers coming from the clodded potato fields. Far off, on an open meadow, unfurled bolts of linen bleached in the sun, long white bars against the hard green. Today, in the garden, he contemplated the early-morning confession, and the meeting that night. He felt ludicrous standing here in the garden, but at the same time he wanted to be nowhere else, for he was alone.

Down the rutted lane that curved behind the near cottages he saw Sean Flynn, the retired schoolteacher, walking his dog. The animal, runty and of no clear breed, dug at a rabbit hole. Flynn, leaning on his cane and softly cursing the dog, saw Alphonsus, and ambled up.

"Father!"

"Mr. Flynn."

"Have we been fishing this week, Father?"

"I confess I haven't. But soon."

"Father, the weather's turning cold."

"I know, I know. It's pitiful that I haven't."

"Today, then."

"No, I have some matters."

"Father, clear your mind."

"Perhaps."

"You really should."

"I think I will, Mr. Flynn. Really."

"Today."

"Yes, today."

It would be his reason, then, to go to the lough. In the house, packing his equipment, he slipped in his stole and oils. He put on a clean cassock and adjusted his biretta, his priest's crown with its hard sides and pompon. Mrs. Toole was down below, dusting in the dining room, and he went to the kitchen to pack a jam sandwich.

"I'll be off fishing now," he said.

"Today?" she said.

"Why not?"

"With Mr. Flanagan on his deathbed from that horse kicking him?"

"Um, well, I'll be back by midafternoon. I heard he's doing better."

"Really? Who told you?"

"Mr. Flynn. We were just talking outside."

Mrs. Toole went back to dusting the china cabinet. "You and the fishing," she said.

"Every chance I get," Alphonsus said.

"Father?"

"Yes?"

"You're fishing dressed like that?"

"If anyone does need last rites, I don't want to do it in my fishing clothes. I shan't be long, anyway."

The row from his usual fishing spot to the shoreline edge of the path was longer than he was used to. After pulling his boat onto the rocks, he walked up and down the path several times, first making sure no one was near, and then beginning to scan the thick woods for any sign of the body. The killing had been in the dark, he assumed, so perhaps the instructions were confused. The day had become brilliantly crisp, and he couldn't see anything human amid the play of shadows and light. Alphonsus stepped off the path and walked broad circles, searching, pulling up the hem of the cassock so he wouldn't get muddy. He kept his eye on the path, too, in case someone came. He wouldn't have an answer if asked what he was doing.

After an hour he sat. He unfolded his sandwich from its greased paper and ate, thinking. He had, in his estimation, covered nearly every possible spot where a body might be. He wondered if this was a hoax. He was too exhausted and tense to fish, and the winds beyond the woods seemed to be picking up. Had he been fishing, he might have been in dangerous waters. He wished he didn't have to return to the village, to the confessional. Bad things were to happen, and he had no idea how to stop them. If he didn't find the body, someone else would: the absence of this constable would eventually become known. Though some constables deserted, slipping away to the north or across to Britain, Alphonsus reasoned that only proof of a desertion would curb the Black and Tans' impulse for destruction.

His calling was powerful, but an unwillingness to absolve the man in the confessional was stronger, a mixture of revenge and principle he couldn't shake free of. He didn't know if that man had been an O'Neal, but he was certain the man was like the O'Neals, someone embittered with his lot and perhaps too willing to blame everything on the British. But he had to absolve, to heed his vows. When his sandwich was gone, he walked down to the lough and drank at water's edge from cupped hands. Back up the path, but now not as far from shore, he plunged into the woods, again searching.

The body was half hidden with wet leaves, the accumulation on the windward side like dunes overtaking a pyramid. Alphonsus knelt, put his hand on the shoulder, and gently rolled the man on his back.

"Hello, Thomas," Alphonsus said.

He hadn't considered the possibility that he would know the deceased. The body was that of Thomas Shanahan, a royal constable stationed at the RIC barracks on the other side of the lough. Thomas had from time to time come to mass at Alphonsus's church. Alphonsus had made a point of welcoming him, for he believed that all were equal in the eyes of God. Thomas was also a fisherman, and after mass they had often talked of their favorite spots. Thomas's face was clean, his clothes neatly straight. He wasn't in uniform but in thick wool trousers and shirt, as if off duty. Alphonsus turned him again, and now saw the crust of hardened blood on the back of his head. As he removed his oils and stole from his fishing kit, Alphonsus scanned the trees, ready to become prone should he hear footsteps.

Thomas was middle-aged, a bachelor who, Alphonsus sensed, was as private a person as he. Thomas lived in the RIC barracks, but in his conversations with Alphonsus never spoke of any of his mates. But of course one couldn't, in the same way that Alphonsus understood he would hear no mention of the Black and Tans and their tactics. Alphonsus, as he daubed the oils upon the cold face, assumed that Thomas had deplored all this, and Alphonsus didn't care to know different.

When he finished the last rites, Alphonsus sat for some time on a rock, looking at the body. How had Thomas come here? Had he been ambushed fishing? No rod or kit lay nearby, but those might have been spoils for the killer. He could go on speculating, but he couldn't avoid what he now planned to do. From his own bag Alphonsus extracted his trowel, the best he had been able to manage without being noticed. He walked in a circle around Thomas, looking for the softest and highest ground, and then knelt and began digging.

This act, he knew, transformed him. He had no business doing this. The dirt did not give way as easily as he'd imagined; he'd felt, coming out in the boat, that he could be back at the rectory by dusk. But the soil was choked with rocks. Hours into it, he stood back and looked at the pitiful rut he'd clawed out, and he laughed in despair.

"Tommy," he said to the body, "I damned well don't know what to do with you. This just isn't Christian, is it?" Tommy, on his side, stared out onto the lough.

Alphonsus peered up through the trees, not able to shed the sense that he was being watched. He had the feeling that the killer might come back, to see that the body was still there. The IRA wanted the body to be found, surely, so that a bloody raid by the Tans was inevitable. The killing of a fellow Irishman like Tommy would create doubt and ambivalence unless it was followed by the necessary retribution by the Brits. Was he being used in this? Did someone expect that Alphonsus himself was going to report the death? Or would the killer return, having thought things over, to put Tommy in a more conspicuous place?

His plan had been to bury Tommy, but Alphonsus now saw that he wasn't capable of finishing the job. The hole was barely two feet deep. Alphonsus recalled his grandfather's stories of the Famine, of skeletal men burying cloth-shrouded friends as packs of starving dogs gathered at the periphery, yelping with hunger and bloodlust, set to dig as soon as the living moved on.

"Forgive me, Tommy, but I can barely move now," Alphonsus said. "I thought my gardening had made me fit enough to undertake this."

A wind was picking up on the lough, making the water choppy and whitecapped. The row back would be dangerous if he didn't go soon. He felt a rising panic. He would have to drop Tommy into the deep waters—he saw this. He'd not be back until well after dark, but his midnight confession awaited. He'd have to be there or the killer would certainly have suspicions.

Down by the water he searched for a way to weight the body. Rocks were all around, but no means of attachment. His fishing kit could be loaded with them, but the top was loose and the ballast might fall out as the package sank. Alphonsus saw one way to do what he needed to do. Standing above the body, he removed his cassock, and then pulled off Thomas's pants and shirt.

Getting the cassock onto the body was easy. Thomas was a bigger man than he, but the cassock was loose. Alphonsus adjusted the braces of Thomas's pants and rolled up the pants and shirt cuffs so that he was clothed for the stealthy trip back to the rectory. In a pocket was a purse with Thomas's papers and a sizable bit of money. Alphonsus was surprised that this hadn't been taken.

The boat rode low on the water with two men in it, the dead one loaded down with stones, the live one weighted by the terror of being caught. Alphonsus had used his fishing line to bind the bottom of the cassock around Thomas's ankles to hold the rocks; the collar was snug at the neck. The last trace of sunlight was nearly gone. Alphonsus stroked hard against the winds, slicing out toward the rough middle of the lough.

He was a sinner now—he could see that. He would dump a dead man into the cold waters as if he were a load of garbage, would grant penance to a murderer. He would return to his rectory, slip past Mrs. Toole so that she wouldn't notice his inexplicable change of clothing, and spend the rest of his life trying to live with this. And all he wanted was for no one to be hurt. So be it. If this body somehow resurfaced or washed to shore, with a cracked skull and wrapped in a cassock, so be it. Or if the Tans correctly interpreted Tommy Shanahan's disappearance and overran Fenagh anyway, so be it. "So be it, Tom," Alphonsus said. "A week will pass and you won't turn up, and they'll know, they'll know."

He stopped rowing. The moon shone through a break in the clouds, giving definition to the far edges of the lough. To say a prayer at a moment like this seemed crude and sacrilegious, desperate and artificial. But he prayed now anyway, prayed for guidance.

Nothing came to him. He felt that matters were on an inevitable course and he could do nothing but send Tommy to the bottom and then go home. "Do as we must do," he said to the body.

He grabbed the shoulders of the cassock. He crouched in the boat, the balance becoming uncertain, and then he lurched and Tom hit the gunwale. The boat was listing. Water was pouring in. He had imagined a noiseless letting-go of the body, but now Alphonsus was in a fight, and in his panic he wasn't sure whether he was trying to shove the body away or pull it back on board. But neither was happening and now he was underwater, the coldness and dark shockingly sudden. He looked up and could see only a single blurred spot of weak light. He wanted to reach for it, that moon in the sky over on the other side of the surface. His hands were still clenched to the bunched fabric of his own cassock, now weighted with death, and he let go of it, and the solid block that was Thomas grazed his leg and ankle and then was gone.

Alphonsus had been hanging on to the side of the overturned boat for some minutes when he decided that he would not return to Fenagh. That he would survive was not a given; the water was cold enough and his arms were tired enough from the digging that he felt almost nothing, except for the dull pain of the thick muscles along his neck. But he clung on, the wind and waves rocking him in crests and swells, until he was desperate enough to push away from the boat and swim for shore.

His thought, as he crawled out of the water on his hands and knees, was of his hat, his black biretta, floating like an ornate ship far out of reach, its black pompon now a keel. He had seen it from the boat, puffed by the wind and etched by moonlight, unwilling to sink with the cassock. The boat, too, would be found, far off on the lough, known by those fishermen who knew him.

In the woods he undressed, squeezed water from his clothing. He considered trying to light a fire. Naked in the cold air, he plunged into the water again to clean himself, and then dressed in the wet woolen shirt and trousers. His black brogans squished loudly when he walked, but he was moving quickly. In no time he was well up the path and along the rutted highway toward Dublin. By dawn he would find a ride in a chicken lorry, and by that evening he would use Tommy Shanahan's wet money to get a room over a public house by the docks. Three days later, his clothes dry and black stubble making his face lose its delicacy of appearance, he would bribe a dock worker to get him into the steerage of the first ship leaving Ireland. The dock worker would ask, "Why are you going?" The answer would be this: that the stowaway was a royal constable from near Fenagh, that he was running away, and that he hoped no one would find out. And when these words were out, the dock worker's face would be twisted with revulsion and the story of his flight would be common knowledge in Fenagh in a few days' time.

My father, telling this story thirty-two years later in a wheelchair in the rest home where he would die, told me that this is how he came to be a man born in middle age, with a name picked from a city directory. He told me he felt the need to unburden himself, that my mother never knew, and that he was for that reason glad she had preceded him into death. He said this without a hint of expectation that I would say anything to console him, and I didn't. I couldn't. I was in my twenties then, leaning over the man who had hit me so hard and so frequently that I had gone to bed many nights wishing to be someone else, a different child. I should have said something. But I stared at him until a nurse came to us and said he needed to eat.

A few years ago I went to Ireland, for the simple reason that I am a devout Boston College football fan and that year they played a game in Dublin against West Point. I boarded an Aer Lingus 747 packed with alumni, and we sang drinking songs high over the Atlantic. Only on the day after the football game did I think to rent a car and take a drive. Asking in Dublin, I found no one who'd heard of Fenagh, but I set out toward Lough Ree, and on its eastern shore I got directions to the town. There I parked, and walked the length of its primary streets, and stood for a while in front of St. Enda's Church, without going in. At a small shop I talked to the keeper, a man older than I, and he told me he had a niece in Boston he sometimes went to visit. I told him I'd had a relative here, a Father Alphonsus.

"Of course," he said. "I've seen the plaque." He pointed me down the road toward a knoll overlooking the water. There, behind some overgrown brambles, I found an engraved plate, the size of an envelope maybe, mounted on a rock.

"Father Alphonsus Kelly, RIP. Drowned November 5, 1920." I stood on the knoll and looked at the harsh waters where this man had lost his life and become someone else. He was a man who became old and could not aspire to the better part of himself he believed he had squandered—who had come to find, I think, that in his exile he couldn't bring himself to try to be like Alphonsus, who indeed was a specter that floated over all our lives. Standing at the edge of the lough, I said a prayer for my father. I petitioned that he might be delivered from a purgatory of which I had been part.

Alison Baker

LOVING WANDA BEAVER

Oleander Joy could not have said which she loved more, detasseling corn or Wanda Beaver. Most girls detasseled for a few summers during high school and then went on to other jobs, but Oleander kept going back. She loved easing through the cornstalks under the summer sun, sliding her hand up toward the tip of tassel after tassel and then yanking sharply so that the tassel came off intact in her palm. Watching it fall from her hand to the ground, she imagined the millions of nascent corn germs that were torn away, never to reach the silk of their own developing ears, banished so that the alien corn planted in every other row could fertilize the entire field unchallenged. Thousands of tassels lay unspent in the field, trampled by detasselers, drying up uselessly, to be turned under by huge heartless machines in the late summer after the mature ears of hybrid corn were harvested.

But Wanda Beaver, her crew boss, was just as much a delight. The thrill of catching a glimpse of Wanda's skinny, brown, barely clothed frame here and there among the cornstalks! The wave of heat that rippled through Oleander, from her face down through her body and on to her knees, when Wanda now and then bared her huge white front teeth in a smile aimed in Oleander's direction! Life in the summer was an uninterrupted anticipation of the pleasure to be felt every ten seconds in the palm of Oleander's hand, and at scattered and irregular times in Oleander's heart.

She had been longing for Wanda Beaver so long that she had lost any other goals in her life. Even her elderly mother, out in the Vercingetorix Nursing Home, worried about her, when she remembered who she was.

"When are you going to forget this Beaver business?" old Mrs. Joy would say. "Look what Nikki's accomplished."

Nikki Joy, Oleander's travel agent sister, lived comfortably in a condominium in Indianapolis. She rarely visited old Mrs. Joy. "What would be the use?" she said to Oleander on the phone.

"You could call before you came to see if she was lucid," Oleander said.

"By the time I got there she'd forget me again," Nikki said. "It's pointless. Besides, she thinks I'm there, and that's just as good."

It was true that old Mrs. Joy believed that Nikki spent her afternoons sitting in the next bed, knitting. "Nikki and I watched 'Edge of Night' today," she'd say to Oleander. She turned to the next bed, which was often empty, and frowned. "Now where'd she go to? I suppose she went to the toilet. Oleander, you think you could sneak in some cigs?"

Oleander had a vision of the future for herself and Wanda Beaver. She and Wanda would get off the bus after a long day of detasseling and head home together to a big old house, not unlike the house old Mrs. Joy had grown up in in Tell City, which Oleander had loved to visit as a child. Oleander would open cans of smoked oysters, and she and Wanda Beaver would sit on the back steps eating oysters and drinking cherry Cokes as the fireflies came out and the trees vibrated with the droning of the cicadas and a hot blanket of night dropped over the town.

If it were up to Oleander, she would spend all year in the fields tugging off corn tassels, as long as Wanda Beaver appeared to her now and then and said, "Nice rows, Oleander."

"Why, Wanda, thank you," Oleander would reply. "But you'll catch your death in that bikini. Here. Take my—" and she would quickly slip out of her own shirt, or sweatshirt, or down jacket, depending on the weather, and drape it over Wanda's goose-bumpled golden shoulders. The jacket would hang to her knees, loose and big as a tent.

"Why, Oleander," Wanda would say, looking at her as if for the first time. "You're absolutely right. I *was* cold." And she would continue on down the row, humming the tune Oleander had been humming when she arrived.

But detasseling was a purely seasonal job, lasting only a few weeks, and then Oleander went back to her full-time position at the Institute for the Study of American Sexual Appetite, where she worked in the Library of Desire. She was the Processing Clerk; every acquisition passed through her hands. She accessioned, stamped, measured, and recorded it all, and entered into the computer the descriptions that the cataloger scrawled on the accompanying forms.

The cataloger was a pale man named Will Middleton, who was an acknowledged expert on sexual models and paraphernalia, not only among the library staff but among the scientific staff of the Institute, and it was not unusual for visiting sexologists to be brought into the cataloging department to discuss the provenance or proper usage of newly identified sexual objects. Will Middleton had completed all the coursework for a PhD, and even written a dissertation entitled "Nuances in the Recording of Sexual Idiosyncrasy: A Vision of Realia," but in the end he had been unable to face his orals board; he had never gotten his degree, but the Administration had let him keep his job anyway.

During the seventies the Library had been a hotbed of activity, with new material in every conceivable medium flowing in at a steady pace. During the eighties, though, a precipitous drop in Federal funding had coincided with decreasing academic interest in sexual activity, and every department had been forced to lay off not only support staff but professionals. Now, as the nineties slouched toward the millennium, Oleander Joy and Will Middleton were the only employees in Cataloging.

Will Middleton never talked about his life outside the Library, but he paid keen attention when Oleander came back after summer vacation and spoke of hers. He would take a bite of sandwich and then sit very still as Oleander described the busload of chattering teenage girls, the raw-silk texture of a corn tassel, the weight of the midsummer sun on her shoulders, and the sun's slow slide over Wanda Beaver's long bikini-clad body. When Oleander blinked and came out of her dream of Wanda Beaver, she realized that Will Middleton had finished his entire sandwich without chewing.

"Oleander," he said now, "you're not getting any younger. What are you going to do about Wanda Beaver?"

A piece of Oleander's own sandwich stuck in her throat at his words, and she coughed for a while and had a long drink of water before she was able to speak. "Will," she said, "I'm not one to rush into things."

"It's all very well to laugh," he said, "but a lifetime of inaction is hardly worth the time, is it?"

"It's more like a lifetime of devotion, Will. Something quite different," Oleander said slowly.

Will leaned forward, shaking his head. "Are you going to hang there in suspended animation for the rest of your life?"

Oleander imagined herself dangling like an oversized piñata from the ceiling of the reference room, turning slowly in the infinitesimal breeze from the fans inside the computers, gazing helplessly down at the professors of sex who were tapping away at the keyboards of the on-line catalog. Probably no one would ever look up. She could bob gently above them forever.

She realized that Will was waiting for her answer, staring at her, his eyes huge and pale behind his plastic spectacles. "What?" she said.

Will sighed and sat back. "It's a good thing we're the best of friends, Oleander," he said. "Otherwise it would be very hard for me to work with you."

"I know," she said. "I would have trouble too."

But she had been faking distraction: Will's words had lodged in her brain. "Will," she said later that afternoon, "I think you are like the pot calling the kettle black."

Will Middleton looked up from the incunabulum he was examining. "Have you ever thought that perhaps the pot has a certain insight into the quality of blackness?"

"Are you saying," Oleander said, after pondering this for a moment, "that you live an empty life?"

Will gazed out the window behind her, where a ginkgo tree glowed in the afternoon sun. "Perhaps I'm saying," he said, so softly that Oleander had to lean toward him to catch the words, "that I have spent my life in a condition of unrequited longing."

"Why, Will," Oleander said, "I had no idea."

"Of course not," he said. "You're obsessed, and that's the nature of obsession. To be caught up so deeply that nothing but the object of the obsession exists for you. It's a disease."

"Love is not a disease," Oleander said.

"Love takes many forms," he said. "If it didn't, we'd be out of work."

They *were* the best of friends, but only within the walls of the Library of Desire. Oleander had never seen Will Middleton in the outside world; she had never imagined that there might be more to his story than met the eye. That afternoon as she unpacked boxes of books and plastic models and videotapes and magazines and piled them on the cart beside Will Middleton's desk, she watched him pick up each object, assign a classification number to it, and move on to the next one. He handled everything with the same detachment; nothing really caught his interest. He was so very pale, and his glasses were so thick! Surely a person like Will Middleton could never experience the same sort of longing that Oleander felt for Wanda Beaver.

Old Mrs. Joy used to tell her daughters that time went faster as a woman aged. "It seems just yesterday," Mrs. Joy would say, "that the two of you were babies, in your little blond pigtails and little smocked dresses." Nikki and Oleander would roll their eyes at each other behind their mother's back, and sigh, and go on watching television, or eating, or doing each other's nails.

Over the years, though, the maternal mutterings had sunk in, and Oleander had fully expected time to begin to pass more swiftly, the world to spin more rapidly on its axis, and winters to pass in the blink of an eye. But what Mrs. Joy had not made clear was that only selected pieces of time rushed by. It was the summers in the corn that were gone before they had gotten well started. The rest of the year—the long autumnal dying, the colorless, lifeless winter, the spring that crawled out of the frozen earth at a snail's pace—went on and on and on as if time had been stretched beyond human imagination.

By early winter the ginkgo trees had lost their golden leaves and stood denuded outside the Library of Desire, glistening in the cold gray rain. This was the time of year when Oleander felt most hopeless. The next detasseling season was months ahead in an uncertain future, and the last was fast receding into the past. Now she had to go into the stacks and stand perfectly still, close her eyes, and hold her breath before she could summon up the beads of sweat on Wanda Beaver's forehead, the little prickles of dark stubble on her shaved thighs, the gap where her prominent hips held her bikini bottom away from the tan skin of her stomach. Then, with the total Wanda Beaver spread-eagled against her eyelids, Oleander breathed deeply and could almost feel the hard dry clods of earth underfoot and hear the sinister drone of flies from a nearby hogpen.

But she couldn't maintain it for long; a distant door would slam, or a student would wheel a truck of books into her aisle and start shoving them onto the shelves, or a sex researcher would sidle past, the soles of her boots making just enough noise that she jolted Oleander out of the past and drove Wanda Beaver further into it. Then Oleander would sigh and clomp back down the corridor to her office, with such a dark, cold hand of despair clutching at her heart that she was sure she would die before detasseling season rolled around again.

At such times Will Middleton would watch her closely as he pretended to analyze a newly acquired film on the VCR, and when she sat down at her desk and stared listlessly out the window, he would ask, with what might have been sympathy, "Thinking about the Beave again?"

Oleander sighed and nodded.

Will Middleton leaned back in his chair and crossed his arms. "How much do you know about this person, anyway?"

"I know enough," Oleander said.

"Is she married?" Will said. "Does she have children? What does she do in the winter?"

"These are superficial concerns," Oleander said.

Will Middleton leaned forward, his eyes large and wavery through his lenses. "Supposing," he said, "she were to fall in love?"

"With whom?" Oleander said.

"Anyone," he said. "Some man."

Oleander considered this. Wanda Beaver was so attractive, it *was* surprising that she hadn't ever married. Before Oleander's reluctant eyes there appeared the image of Wanda Beaver married to one of the detasseling foremen, or to someone who worked out at the steel recycling plant, someone with plenty of money and a hairy chest.

"Sure, baby, you can have anything your skinny little heart desires," the unknown man drooled over Wanda Beaver's bare shoulders. "Sure, you can have that run-down ol' place in Tell City. We'll fix it up real nice."

And there they were, the hairy man and Wanda Beaver, packed like Okies into the man's old Chevrolet, driving out of town on Route 142, looking straight ahead down the road toward Tell City. When they got there, they got out of the car and walked right up the steps of old Mrs. Joy's house, with old Mrs. Joy as a little girl still sitting there in a pinafore. Hairy walked right into the house and began to live there with Wanda Beaver, when it was Oleander who should have been doing it instead.

She felt as if she had stepped into another dimension, where she could see things from an entirely different angle than she ever had before. Wanda Beaver could marry a hairy man at any time.

"Will," she said, "what should I do?"

He reached over and tapped the INTERRUPT button, leaving the video to flicker impotently on the screen. "Oleander," he said, "what is it you want?"

Oleander stared helplessly at him, trying to think of a way to phrase it. It had to do with the nature of desire itself, and the condition of completion. When she saw Wanda in the corn, her protuberant teeth gleaming in the sun, it was as if Oleander's skin went suddenly empty, the way a papier-mâché sculpture is suddenly empty when the balloon inside it is pricked by a pin. Just as a sculpture hardens into the shape of the balloon, her skin had taken on the shape of her desire; and the knowledge that there was no way of fulfilling her desire filled her with both ecstasy and despair.

But Will's words had made her realize that she was in danger of losing everything. So long as her imagination had lived within definite boundaries, she had been full of a certain kind of hope, an elation at the limitlessness of possibility. Now the suggestion of an alternate reality had torn a jagged, dangerous hole in the thin membrane around her life. Her condition had changed. She could hope, but she could not pretend.

"I just want to be happy," she said.

Will Middleton stood up and began to pace back and forth across the office. "Happiness is a byproduct," he said. "An accident. A result." He looked sideways at her. "You don't want happiness, you want Wanda Beaver."

"It's the same thing," Oleander said.

"Oh, Oleander," he said, "after all these years here, haven't you figured it out? The difference between passion and happiness, desire and fulfillment, the object and the pursuit?"

She put her hands over her ears. "I don't know what you're talking about," she said. "I'm not an intellectual." And she closed her eyes and sat hunched over as his voice droned on.

What did he know about love? All he loved was his cataloging work; he was as far removed from reality as it was possible to be. He spent his days categorizing love into erotica or sexuality or lust, describing it in rigidly defined terms, and popping it into a computer database. Why, Will Middleton spent his time trying to objectify love, and make it mean the same thing to everyone, which led to its meaning nothing to anyone.

I'm not the one living in a dreamworld, Oleander thought, and she smiled as she imagined herself floating high over a cornfield in late July, gazing down at herself among the teenage girls working the rows, their smooth-muscled arms reaching overhead to pluck the tassel from each stalk. There was nothing more real than the weight of the Midwestern sun on your back in late July, or even the helpless, defeated feeling that filled you as you inched your way through rows of wet corn after a week of thunderstorms, the mud sucking hungrily at your sneakers, drops of cold water and small, sticky specks of corn germ shaking off and sticking to your skin and your glasses when you reached up for a tassel. Nothing more real than, in the middle of such a dismal day, the sudden stab of pleasure in your heart at the sight of a dripping Wanda Beaver at the end of the row.

. . .

"I won't last forever," old Mrs. Joy had often said, and as winter turned the corner toward spring, it became all too clear that her words had been prophetic. She became vaguer and vaguer, until at last it was evident that she would never again remember who Oleander was.

"It's as if she's already gone," Oleander said to Nikki on the telephone.

"She's been gone for years," Nikki said.

"But she's always *been* there," Oleander said. "Sundays and Wednesdays, she was always waiting for me."

Nikki snorted. "She didn't care if you were there or not."

"How do you know?" Oleander said. "You never bothered to visit her."

"If she's happy in a dreamworld, leave her there. I've got better things to do than force people to face reality."

"That's not the point," Oleander said.

Nikki sighed. "You're just like her."

"I am?" Oleander said.

"Take this Wanda Beaver," Nikki said. "She's a figment of your imagination. You've never even spoken to her."

"Of course I have." Oleander glared at the telephone. "When we're out in the fields, we talk all the time."

"Okay, okay," Nikki said. "Just remember, you're not a spring chicken. And that library's a dead end too."

"It's an important research institution," Oleander said.

"Sure," Nikki said. "Those who can't do, teach; and those who can't teach, do research."

"You don't know what you're talking about," Oleander said. "They're world-renowned experts."

"Expert shmexpert," Nikki said. "Take my advice. Get out into the real world before it's too late." Oleander heard her puffing on her cigarette, and could almost smell the smoke drifting through the receiver. "Let's just hope she doesn't use up our inheritance in hospital bills. I'd like to get to Paris for once in my life."

As her mother faded, Oleander at times felt strangely light-hearted, as if the string that had tethered her to earth all her life was fraying, and once it snapped nothing would remain to keep her from soaring away. But at other times the threat of freedom hung heavy on her heart. Day after day she plodded along the streets through the melting snow and down the steps of the Library of Desire, and she felt that no one in the world would notice or care if she went in the door and never came out again.

Walking along, she thought deeply about what Nikki had said. Maybe Will Middleton was a cataloger in the Library of Desire because he couldn't function in the real world. If those who couldn't do research did cataloging, what did that say about those who just processed item after item, connecting to nothing at all?

For so long she had thought that she was working in the Library of Desire just so she could afford to spend her summer vacation in her real life, in the cornfields with Wanda Beaver. Was she fooling herself? Could it be that the truth was something else—that she stayed in the Library because she was afraid to plunge into the fields of life wholeheartedly?

What could she do? If she approached Wanda Beaver—if she *spoke* to her—she risked losing not just her detasseling job, but the life she had built around it. If only there were something that would give her the answer, tell her what to do. Nothing or something? That's what it boiled down to. Either way the risk was the same.

She was so deep in thought that she walked right into Ruthie Cline. The impact knocked her to the ground.

"Are you all *right?*" Ruthie shrieked. "Have you broken a *hip?*"

"Ruthie, I just turned forty, for God's sake," Oleander said, letting Ruthie help her up.

"I'm not concerned with your age," Ruthie said. "Oh my God, is that you, Oleander?"

"Who did you think it was, Noam Chomsky?" Oleander said crossly. She shook off Ruthie's clutching hand.

"I thought it was some poor old soul who couldn't get up," Ruthie said. "If you didn't want any help, you should have stood up."

"Thank you, Ruthie," Oleander said. "What are you up to these days, anyway?"

"About five-five," Ruthie said. "Ha-ha. Remember, I was such a jokester in school? I still am, Oleander. I don't think people really change much, do you?"

Oleander shrugged. "But you didn't recognize *me*."

"Well, you weren't always lying on the sidewalk," Ruthie said. "And Oleander, pardon me for saying this, but you have put on a little weight, haven't you?"

"I really don't know," Oleander said. "It's not something I pay much attention to."

"Same old Oleander," Ruthie said. "Lost in a daydream. Still detasseling with Wanda Beaver? Ha-ha."

Oleander frowned. "As a matter of fact, I am."

Ruthie shook her head. "Oleander," she said, "what would you do with Wanda Beaver if you had her?"

And Oleander began to tell Ruthie Cline about the house in Tell City where her mother, old Mrs. Joy, had grown up, and where Oleander and her sister Nikki had spent so many summer vacations before their grandparents died and the house was sold. She told her about the wide front porch with the lattice where brilliant red roses had climbed; about the peeling white paint; about the dim hallway that smelled of dust and cats and lilacs as you stood just inside the door waiting for your eyes to adjust to the dark; about the huge, sparsely furnished rooms with no reading lamps where she and Nikki wandered while their mother sat on the porch drinking gin and lemonade with *her* mother.

And she told her of her dream: that she would take Wanda Beaver to live in the old house, and they would lie out in the yard on summer afternoons letting their skin darken and burn, and as the sun finally began to drop behind the snowball bushes and shadows slowly crept toward them across the lawn, they would go inside, take ice-cold bottles of beer from the refrigerator, and stand together in the dim kitchen chugging the beer, which would trickle over Wanda Beaver's upturned chin and down her neck, mingling with the sweat that stood in the little hollow between her clavicles, and drip down her chest into the dark space in the center of her bikini top and out again on the other side.

Ruthie closed her mouth. "That's all?"

Oleander opened her eyes. "Isn't that enough?"

"It seems quite innocent," Ruthie said.

Oleander sighed. "Maybe it wouldn't be enough for her."

"If it's enough for you," Ruthie said, "it might very well be enough for her."

In later years Oleander could not pinpoint the exact moment when she decided to act, or exactly what pushed her over the edge toward action. It might have been Will Middleton's prodding; it might have been her mother's gradual slide toward death; it might have been Nikki Joy's harsh remarks about the lack of substance in Oleander's life.

Or it might have been the miraculous encounter with Ruthie Cline. For as she stood there staring at her, Ruthie fished a business card out of her pocketbook. "I'm in real estate now, Oleander. Tell City's out of my territory, but there are some real nice manufactured homes out in South Towne Village."

Oleander stared at the card Ruthie had thrust at her.

"Interest rates are terrific these days," Ruthie said, shrewdly watching Oleander's face. "But they could go up any day."

Oleander looked from the card to Ruthie's face. "I don't have a down payment yet," she said, "but I might have at any time."

Ruthie nodded. "It's the American dream," she said. "It's what everyone wants in her heart of hearts."

And as if there *were* miracles, it was spring. The pale days stretched out longer and longer, flocks of migrating songbirds stopped to rest in the flowering ginkgo trees, and business picked up in the Library of Desire as researchers ventured out of their offices, excited once again at the concept of love.

All winter the image of Wanda Beaver had shrunk and grown fainter, and Oleander had squinted and concentrated hard just to picture her smile; but now, in spring, she had only to blink and Wanda Beaver grinned at her. She smelled her suntan lotion in the shower, she heard her voice as she walked to work, and all day she caught glimpses of Wanda Beaver in the Library of Desire, leaning over the reference copy of the *Kama Sutra*, disappearing into the locked stacks of Early American Erotica, flickering across a TV screen in the wet carrel where a social work student was watching a clinical video.

As spring turned to summer, and the corn in the fields out-side of town shot skyward, Oleander's heart rose to a spot high in her chest, just below her neck, where it lay swollen, pounding irregularly, cutting off the air to her lungs. She had trouble con-centrating on her work; several times Will Middleton had to ask her to reenter data she had mistyped, or relabel the rubber Vic-torian appliances a wealthy benefactress had left to the Library.

"I just hope I'm doing the right thing," Oleander said as she cleaned off her desk the day before her vacation started.

"It's better to have loved and lost, than never to have loved at all," Will said.

"Oh, for heaven's sake," she said, "I *do* love. I don't need to lose."

"You love," he said softly, "but until you *are* loved in return, you have no idea what love can be."

She looked over at him and saw that he had taken off his glasses, and that the thick lashes surrounding his violet eyes were the color of ripening peaches. She felt a rush of affection for him, poor Will Middleton, her good friend, who had pa-tiently listened to her and advised her for so many years. A man with nothing and no one, who had not exactly *failed* in life, but had sort of given up, and settled into a safe little slot, and spent his days classifying the experiences of the world around him, never daring to have any of his own.

"Will," she said, "you once said that you were full of unre-quited longing. What for?"

It might have been the moment Will Middleton had been waiting for. At her words a light might have gone on in his pale eyes, and his breath begun to come a little faster in his thin and hairless chest, as his own unspoken hopes and deeply concealed desires began to edge toward the light of day.

But as he looked at Oleander, he saw that her thoughts had already skipped beyond him, beyond the walls of the Library of Desire, and out to the cornfield where Wanda Beaver waited. "A PhD," he said, and he was not surprised when she didn't even hear him.

At five-thirty in the morning, Oleander climbed onto the bus with the other detasselers. She listened idly to the giggling teen-agers, and gazed out the window as the bus passed the familiar schools and houses, the Institute where Will Middleton would soon be hard at work, the Vercingetorix Nursing Home where her mother lay unaware of what would happen to her daughter today. The sun was behind the trees and its light was still kind, its heat tender, and a sweet haze lay on the fields of tall, lush corn. She wished that the ride would never end. She wished the bus would eternally travel through the morning light along a two-lane road, between endless fields of corn, and that starlings would soar in great unmolested swarms over the fields forever.

But the bus rolled into someone's barnyard and stopped in front of a gleaming steel barn. Oleander moved with the teenagers down the steps and saw Wanda Beaver, in shorts and a tee shirt, standing with the other crew bosses, talking to the farmer. Wanda was nodding, her hands on her hips, her eyes now and then drifting away from the faces of the people she stood with and out over the field into which the detasselers would soon plunge.

Oleander started toward her, but she thought better of it and made her way to the far side of the group of teenagers. When Wanda started sending the girls into the field, one per row, Oleander was the last to be assigned.

"Okay, Oleander," Wanda Beaver said. "Go for it."

Now or never, Oleander thought; and with a pounding heart she took her life in her hands and bravely said, "Wanda?"

"Yo," Wanda Beaver said, looking at her as if she had never really noticed her before.

Oleander knew that this was the moment she had been moving inevitably toward for forty years. Everything she knew of love was gathered there at the edge of the cornfield. All that she had learned, everything she had experienced, had prepared her for this moment; and yet she felt so unprepared. She wasn't ready. How to begin? I love you? Howsabout shacking up? You are the most miraculous thing in my life, and I want to live with you?

"Do you own your home?" Oleander said.

Wanda Beaver snickered. "You think I'm made of money or what?"

"It's the American dream," Oleander said, "and my dream too."

Wanda Beaver looked at her watch. "My cousin's in real estate," she said. "I'll tell her to give you a call."

"Oh," Oleander said, a little disconcerted. "But not just that." She took a deep breath and stepped forward. "I have something to tell you."

Wanda Beaver felt an entirely new sensation in her solar plexus as Oleander came toward her. "Jiminy," she said.

Afterwards, it was this moment that Oleander would put on personal reserve in the Library of Desire, to be checked out, carried off into the dark stacks on the third floor, and perused again and again: the oil glistening on Wanda Beaver's body, its sweet coconut fragrance rising like steam from her thighs; the morning sunlight, thick with promised heat, that coated the heavy green leaves of corn; the weightless little white clouds skipping across the sky, the black shape of a hawk circling slowly beneath them; the thin, bright light of understanding that had begun to dawn in Wanda Beaver's eyes; and the fragile, frightening possibility that the next soft, brown tassel that Oleander touched would hold the love she had been seeking for so long.

John Updike

THE BLACK ROOM

"I don't *want* to go," said Lee's mother, though she had already agreed to go, in the too bright, teal-blue silk dress that had come out of the cedar closet where it had hung for all the years in which she had been too fat to wear it. Her weight loss was not a good sign, Lee felt, though as a boy and then as a man and then as a middle-aged man he had hoped for it. Less of a mother, he had thought, would be more—more chic, more manageable. But now that she was in her eighties and her clothes hung loose on her and her skin hung loose above her elbows, he was frightened. He wanted her bulk back.

He tried joking: "It's the chance of a lifetime." She didn't smile, so he tried backing out: "You don't have to go. I'm the one who cares, so I'll go alone."

Yet it had been her idea. She had heard that their old house in the city of Alton was being sold; the then-young couple who had bought it, Marine Lieutenant Jessup and his wife, had enlisted in a retirement community and placed the house on the market. Embarrassingly, Lee felt, his mother had phoned the Jessups and explained how much it would mean to her son if he, on one of his monthly visits from New York City, might come by. Neither she nor he had entered the house since that drizzly November day forty-seven years ago when the movers had cleared out their furniture, damaging the cane-backed sofa and breaking two plates of Philadelphia blueware in the process. The family, which had numbered five then, climbed into a newly bought secondhand Chevrolet and drove twenty miles in the rain to the unimproved farmhouse that Lee's mother had settled on as the site of her long-deferred self-fulfillment.

She said now, "That Alton house nearly killed me and I swore I'd never set foot in it again."

"You've made your point. Forty-seven years is as good as never. You've put the house in its place, Mother."

"Your grandfather was always convinced that Jessup had slipped Jake Oberholz a fifty, to persuade us to accept the eight thousand." Lee had heard it all before: Oberholz had been their real-estate agent, and Jessup had been fresh out of the Marines, a quiet war hero, slim and blond and tall in Lee's memory of him, and in a white dress uniform. Lee had seen him once, in the front hall, from the height of a twelve-year-old, while the sale was still being negotiated. The whole thing had gone on over Lee's head.

"Well, you didn't want the place," he pointed out. "Jessup did. Come on. We can't not go now, after you've got us invited. You shouldn't have set this up if you didn't want to go."

"I was trying," she said primly, "to please my only child."

They maneuvered themselves out of the back door of the sandstone farmhouse, and were halfway across the yard to Lee's BMW, with its blue-and-white New York plates. His mother's car, with its blue-and-orange Pennsylvania plates, was stored in the barn. Her cardiologist had forbidden her to drive, though she occasionally did, to the 7-Eleven at a crossroads two miles away, "to keep the engine from seizing up," she said. They moved slowly, her hand heavy on his arm; even a little exertion left her short of breath, though she didn't stop talking: "I don't know why you always spite me by loving that house so."

"I don't say I love it. I was born there, is all."

"It was too much house—my father's vanity made itself a monument the day he bought it. He bought it when I was off at college, without even telling me. I never could feel at home there. Neither could Mother. We weren't city people. It nearly killed her, trying to keep it clean, up to city standards. It had a peculiar dust in it, that clung everywhere."

He had heard this before, too, but its implausibility still made him laugh. "Well, you showed it," he told her. "You escaped its clutches."

"I don't know why you've always resented our moving. Honest to goodness, Lee, I added years to all of our lives by getting us out of Alton. The only city person among us was your father."

Everyone had been sick that first winter in the little farmhouse, which had been heated by fireplaces, with an outhouse at the bottom of the yard. There was no heat at all upstairs. It had snowed from November to March. Their water came from a pump on the back porch, up from the icy earth. There had been no electricity. Lee and his father had gamely participated in the first wave of renovations but gradually spent more and more time in the family car together, prolonging errands, running back to Alton.

"I was just a child, Mother. I was in no position to resent anything. I'm still not."

But was she right? Had he loved the house, all these years, just to spite her? It was a long, narrow-faced brick house on a wider lot than most along the street. In his childhood the bricks had been painted pale yellow and the trim dark green. There was a front porch, a side porch, and an upstairs porch, and the yard had held cherry trees, a walnut tree, a birdbath, a bed of lilies of the valley, and a vegetable garden that his grandfather turned with a shovel every spring.

"I can take it or leave it, seeing the house," he said. "This trip wasn't my idea, remember." They were skimming along a highway lined with ranch houses, which had been a winding asphalt road the first time he had travelled it, with an occasional dirt lane leading off to a barn, a silo, a square stone farmhouse just like theirs.

"I had to, seeing as it was our last chance. They were always inviting us, those first years. On every Christmas card. Then they stopped asking. I thought I'd get through life without ever having to see those rooms again. I like your idea, of you going in alone. You could drop me off at Weisbach's Drug Store for half an hour."

His mother's fanciful distortions and quick little visions had always struck him as a higher form of truth. This trip *was* his idea; she had read his mind and arranged it to please him. He said, truthfully, "Without you, Mother, it'd be no fun."

"I could sit at the counter and have a sundae. You have to say this for Luther Weisbach—he didn't stint on the butterscotch."

"Mother, I don't think it's still called Weisbach's. And drugstores don't have counters any more."

The road surface wore a moist shine. It was a soft late-September day, the sunshine golden and the trees misty. A barn whose red side had said "Jesus Saves" in fading letters year after year was suddenly gone, replaced by a Japanese-style building with wide eaves and redwood shingles—a golf-course clubhouse.

"You weren't such a child," his mother said, picking up another thread of her mental web. "You were thirteen. If we'd stayed there you'd still think of yourself as a child. That house made everybody in it childish. As long as I was in that house, I was just my parents' daughter."

The Depression had thrown them all together. The Crash took his grandfather's savings, and then his father had been laid off from his job in Pittsburgh. Lee had been born into this nest of disappointment, and had been a happy child. All four adults had conspired to make him happy, as if his happiness might yet reverse their fortunes. They had scraped by, with various jobs. The war had come along and helped. With their modest war profits, his mother had finagled the change of houses, moving them to what his father had called "the sticks." Now, with his grandparents and father long dead, the sticks—raspberry canes and sumac and wild grape and poison ivy—were moving ever closer to the little farmhouse, as his mother's strength waned. For decades she had wielded the clippers and scythe like a man, and had ridden the power mower hour after hour, bouncing in widening circles around the lawn. Now reluctant teen-agers did the mowing, when they could be recruited from the countryside. His mother's house smelled of dust balls and mouse droppings; the plumbing and heating, brand-new in 1946, had become antique. Yet she insisted, "That Alton house was never healthy. The coal furnace made a gas that sat on my chest whenever I'd lie down."

Lee laughed again, for they had reached the far end of his old street, and he was heading home.

. . .

This neck of Alton had a small-town quality, many of the houses freestanding on lots adorned by hydrangeas and rhododendron bushes, and even the semidetached houses solid and well kept up. The vacant lots of Lee's childhood had been filled in, and the street had been widened at the expense of a row of sycamores whose blotched bark and buttony seed pods had seemed oddly toylike to him, as if God were an invisible playmate. On the uphill side, a tall row of semidetacheds held fascinating little guttered spaces between them, passageways sexual in their intimacy, with a thin slice of sky at the top. Even widened, Franklin Street from its far end had a contained, narrowing look. In the side of Lee's vision his mother's hand fumbled in her black pocketbook and darted one of her nitroglycerin pills into her mouth. "Don't be nervous," he said.

Over her teal-blue dress she had donned, though the day was unseasonably warm, an old-fashioned wool overcoat in a broad plaid, with a fox-fur collar. Her thick head of chestnut hair had been one of her youthful glories; Lee remembered from childhood the witchy, dripping tent her hair made after she had washed it, a towel worn over her shoulders as it dried. Now this hair, gone in the last decade from iron-gray to a gauzy white, let pink scalp show through, and she wore indoors and out a round knit cap on her head, bigger than a beanie but not quite a beret. Her ankles and feet were so swollen she could no longer squeeze her feet into anything but running shoes; even for these, she had chosen a vivid, several-striped pattern. From the days when she had been a young beauty and her father had still had money, she retained a taste for attention-getting clothes. Lee tried to repress his embarrassment, as he had when he was an adolescent and she was a vivacious, overweight, countrified woman, her sun-reddened hands and forearms scored by the scratches of raspberry and greenbrier thorns. "Why would I be nervous?" she asked testily.

It was he who was nervous. Parking the car, he rubbed the tires against the curb, which the street improvement had left higher and whiter than it had been. Getting out of the car, Lee seemed eerily tall in this setting of his earliest days. The houses across the street, with their trees and telephone poles, presented the same silhouettes, though on this side the sunshine struck down strangely through the absence of sycamores, and the Jessups had taken away the waist-high box hedge that had shielded the front yard from sidewalk traffic. Sidewalk traffic, of course, was a thing of the past; it belonged to the Depression, and to door-to-door salesmen walking on foot, and people running to catch clanging trolley cars. The new concrete curb of the widened street was so high that his mother couldn't get the door of the BMW to swing open, and he had to repark it, his stomach nervously pinching. Entering this house again, this paradise at the far end of his life, seemed a trespass.

The brick front walk, with little ant cities of mounds like coffee grains between the bricks, had become glaring concrete. The distance across the porch to the front door, which he remembered as large and full of peril—for the porch had thick brick walls which might conceal a crouching beast—had dwindled to two strides. The door, with its letter-slot lid saying "MAIL" and its bevelled-glass window, had been replaced by an opaque panelled door, though the leaded sidelights and tinted fanlight holding the house number, 303, remained above. Jessup, who greeted them inside the door, had grown shorter than Lee, but his hair was still close-cropped and blond, and his figure had a military trimness. Mrs. Jessup, whom Lee had never met, was like a bride on a wedding cake, perfect of her kind, though grown plump and white-haired. She had dimples and bifocals, and cheeks as round and pink as if rouged. The Jessups greeted Lee cordially, but saved their real ardor of welcome for his mother, whose shrunken figure seemed, to him, engulfed by their courteous bodies. His eyes were darting about, desperate to light on something familiar and cherished.

"What a *nice* idea this is," said the former marine. "I must say, you folks have waited to the very last minute."

"Well, my father used to tell me, 'Don't be so impatient, Lucy. Good things keep.' "

Her charm—Lee tended to forget that about his mother. When pulled out of the sticks and put to the test of social encounter, she rose to the challenge. "I love your yellow wallpaper," she told the elderly couple. "This was always such a dark hall, with the two big gloomy radiators. I never knew why there had to be *two;* on winter days it was the warmest spot in the house. Lee used to lie on the floor, drawing, where we all had to step over him.''

The flattened texture and faded brown of the carpet that had lain at the edge of his drawing pad returned to his mind's eye out of the past, along with the diagonal beams of dust-laden light that came in the sun-parlor windows and broke on the wide oak arms of his grandfather's favorite chair. The sun parlor was gone, swallowed up by an office; Jessup had used the G.I. Bill to become an attorney. Lee was tempted to open the office door on the chance that his grandfather was still sitting there, in the slant of sunlight, his head tilted back in that ostentatiously resigned way he had, and his hands, frail and brown as onion-skin, folded across the buttons of his gray sweater as he waited for the mailman or the afternoon paper boy to bring him word of the world. His grandfather had exuded an air of quiet defeat that the boy found endearing.

"Everything is so *right,*" his mother was saying. "When we were here, everything was slightly *wrong.*"

Lee knew, as the Jessups did not, that his mother distrusted rightness, in this bourgeois sense—felt herself rather above it, in fact. As her breathy voice flirted behind him, in and out of the Jessups' catering voices, he felt freed to walk ahead, looking for traces of the house he remembered. There were almost none. Renovations had come in and washed everything away, even the old touches of elegance like the elaborate spindlework headers above the wide doorways into the living room, and the fluted wooden pillars beside these. The ceilings, plastered in tidily overlapping semicircles, seemed lower. Instead of their old Oriental rug with its mazy border and the cane-back settee and its companion chairs—their brown cushions holding that musty, oystery scent country parlors have—there was fat modern furniture in pastel shades surrounding a glass table supported on wrought-iron scrolls. A semi-tropical Floridian luxuriance had crept into Pennsylvania interiors since the forties. Where their Christmas tree had annually stood, between the two front windows from which Lee would watch, beyond the porch wall, the coal sliding thunderously down the chute that telescoped out from the truck, now stood a blond-stained wood cabinet holding souvenirs of the Jessups' foreign travels—beaten copper, carved ivory, Mexican pottery, New Mexican turquoise.

The "piano room" held not the old upright Chickering piano but a large-screen television set and a cabinet of hi-fi components. Down the dark hall that had once seemed perilously shadowy and long, beside the flight of stairs his grandfather had called "the wooden hill," the dining room quickly appeared, minus the Tiffany lampshade that had hung from the center of the ceiling, and the mahogany-veneered sideboard with the cloudy mirror, and the stained-pine corner cabinet that had held their good china, including the Philadelphia blue-ware whose broken plates had been one of the costs of the move from Alton. In this room, on a strip of wooden floor between the figured rug and the doors that led out to the side porch, Lee used to bowl, with rubber Disney dolls—Mickey Mouse and Pluto, Donald Duck and Ferdinand—for tenpins. Now wall-to-wall carpet covered the space. Staring down, trying to picture the concealed floorboards, he was overtaken for a moment by a sensation of being in a cave—a sheltered sense of great things going on above him, where the Second World War merged with Walt Disney's busy kingdom, while he set up his battered rubber creatures and bowled them down again with a lopsided softball.

The house was quickly traversed; next came the kitchen, which he had not expected to find unchanged. Even the plumbing had been moved about, so that in place of the slate sink with its long-nosed copper faucets now bulked an electric stove with a black-faced microwave, and where the old gas stove had poured forth X-patterns of blue flame a modern stainless-steel sink had appeared, the dishwasher and trash compactor installed to one side. Rose-colored cabinets matched a giant double-doored refrigerator; the little walnut icebox, the blackened tin toaster that had sat on a gas burner like a tiny house full of chinks, the food-grinder that had clamped to the edge of the kitchen table were so thoroughly, irrevocably carted away by time that Lee could scarcely imagine the boy who used to reach up on tiptoe to the red-and-white recipe box on top of the icebox. The family kept its meagre cash in the tin recipe box, and he was entitled, at schoolday lunchtimes, to buy a Tastykake to eat on the walk back to elementary school.

"So Mr. Oberholz came to us," his mother was saying behind him, "and said, 'It was an eight-thousand-dollar house when you bought it in 1925, and it's still an eight-thousand-dollar house in 1945.' My dad, he was such a trusting man, he believed him, just like he believed all those shysters who unloaded their stock off on him before the Crash, but me, I had a bit of the devil in me I guess, I couldn't believe it hadn't gone up in value *at all* in twenty years. Now I read in the paper that you're asking over two hundred thousand. I still have friends in town who send me such clippings in the mail. If you can call them friends."

Lee tried to intervene. "Mother, it's only since the nineteen-fifties that people expect to make money off of real estate. And now they're losing it again."

But Mrs. Jessup could defend herself. She had already gained a first-name basis with the older woman. Her cheeks aglow with a pretty blush of indignation, she said, "Lucy, we really couldn't have paid a penny more. Even so, we went into debt, so Hank was working nights as a watchman as well as going to law school. Those were hard times."

"It's been a kind house to us," Jessup said, in a soothing lawyer's voice, putting the done deal behind them. "We raised three beautiful children in it."

Back in the dining room, Lee at last found a survival of the house of his own childhood: the windows. They were still tall, gaunt four-pane windows, and the panes were still the old glass whose waveriness and oval bubbles had fascinated him as a child. He would stand and move his head and watch the lines of their neighbors' house undulate, as in the underwater scenes in *Pinocchio*. The oval bubbles, like immortal microbes, were still there, in the glass, though combination storm windows dulled the outlook, and the neighbors' house was a different, closer house, filling the vacant lot where Lee as a boy had played fungo and kick-the-can with Doug Rickenbach and Shorty Heister and the neighborhood girls, who lived in the sexy row houses across the street and whose parents would call them home from their rickety high porches in the summer twilights, as the fireflies came out.

The tour of the downstairs completed, Mrs. Jessup politely asked, in the narrow hallway, "Would you like to see the upstairs? We moved some walls about, to accommodate the children; I doubt you would recognize much."

"I'd love to see it," Lee said. Upstairs had been the enchanted realm of sleep, of days home sick in bed, of his parents in their underwear, of his grandparents muttering behind their closed door. Ultimate realities had resided upstairs.

"Lucy, there was something I've always wanted to ask you about," Mrs. Jessup said, drawing close enough to touch the older woman on the shoulder, next to the prickly fox fur. "When we moved in, there were two little rooms out back, above the kitchen, looking into the back yard."

"Yes. The one on the right was Lee's room, looking toward the vacant lot."

"And the other, the one with only the one window, was painted black."

"Oh, no! Was it really?"

"Yes, and we couldn't figure out what it had been used for. Had it been a darkroom, maybe, for your husband's photography?"

"Norman never took a picture in his life. I was the family photographer, with this old Kodak that had lost its viewfinder. You paced off the yards and hoped for the best."

Mrs. Jessup persisted. "It must have been for storage, then."

"Yes, we kept a few things in it. Mother's ironing board, her Singer sewing machine, an old sleigh-bed headboard and footboard that had been *her* mother's . . . but I don't remember that room as *black.*"

"Well, it was. We were quite struck and puzzled, I remember, at the time."

Sensing an impasse, Lee asked, "Mother, do you want to come upstairs?"

"No," she said. "No, I don't."

"Really? Why not?" He darted a look at her; her face, fallen into creases with her loss of weight, seemed pale, stricken by some internal development. He felt the effort with which she kept up the charm.

"You-all go," she said, "and I'll spare myself the stairs and just sit and admire how bright and cheerful the Jessups have made our dreary old living room."

"Then I'll stay right with you," Mrs. Jessup said. "We'll have a good chat. Shall I make us a cup of tea?"

For much of his life, Lee had seen other people his age, attracted by his mother's charm, draw close; but in the end, only he could follow her twists and turns. Sometimes he wondered if his personality hadn't been so exactly fitted to pleasing his mother that it was not much good for pleasing anyone else.

"Tea? To tell the truth, I never developed the taste for tea. I was a coffee drinker, up to a dozen cups a day, and now the doctors say I shouldn't drink even decaf. Coffee and ice cream and apple pie were my sins, and now I'm paying for them. Norman always used to say to me, 'You're the last person in the world, Lucy, who thinks there's such a thing as a free lunch.' "

While Mrs. Jessup coped with this pronouncement, her husband took Lee upstairs. In passing, Jessup touched the newel post, with its round knob. "Bet you recognize this."

"Yes." But in fact the knob, with its equator of beaded grooves, had seemed an unpleasant presence to Lee—an eyeless head, a possible Martian.

"I asked that it be left," Jessup said, with what seemed shy pride, "though Dorothy thought it didn't go with the new décor."

At the head of the stairs, one little flight of three steps had led to a hall that went past Grampy and Grammy's bedroom, on to the guest bedroom, which overlooked the street. Another short set of steps had led the other way, to his parents' bedroom and his own, and a third set had gone up to the communal bathroom. In this windowless landing they had gathered, sitting on the steps, during air-raid drills, while Lee's father strode around the darkened neighborhood in his air-raid warden's armband and helmet. Now this awkward architecture had been smoothed into a parade of bright bedrooms and adjacent baths to accommodate, in the Jessups' prime, the couple and three growing children. Lee's grandparents' room, which even through a closed door had smelled powerfully to his childish nostrils of countrified must, of old shoes and old bodies and mothballed blankets and bottles of pungent liniment, had become the Jessups' daughter's room; it was still decorated with her school pennants, a single, relatively demure, rock poster, her frilly bed coverlet, some stuffed animals, and framed photographs of herself as a child, as an adolescent with braces, as a graduating senior, as a bride, and as a mother posing with two small children in what Jessup told Lee was a back yard in Colorado, where she now lived with her husband, an Air Force pilot. "Born ten years later, she'd have been a pilot herself," her father boasted.

The guest bedroom, where his mother would go for her naps when she needed to get away from them all, and where Lee, when sick, would recline in a litter of picture books and cough-drop boxes, had been expanded outward, into a massive master bedroom, swallowing the hall window, whose sill had always held a potted geranium. At the back of the house, other walls had vanished as his little room with its stained and varnished wainscoting had been merged with the mysterious one next to it, and his parents' bedroom had been carved up to accommodate a spacious bathroom that the Jessup sons could share. The boys' bedrooms still held racing-car posters and traces of extensive electronic equipment. "Well," Lee said to his host, by way of termination, and in response to a certain unstated expectancy of congratulation, "I'd say you spent your years here very well."

"It was a happy house for us."

"Good. For me, too." No longer child and young veteran, they had become two aged men who had loved the same object. One had won and one had lost, but now the winner was surrendering the prize also. Lee looked around a last time and couldn't find himself, even in the shape of the windows. A hurricane of time had swept through this house, leaving nothing undamaged. His parents' bedroom had opened onto a side porch like the one below, with jigsawed balusters holding up the wooden, green-painted rail. The present railing was ornamental ironwork, as if they were in New Orleans.

Downstairs, a glance told him that his mother was in trouble. She had slumped to one side on the sofa, and was resting a bony hand upon her chest, as if to quiet something within it. Yet her face still bore a listening smile, as Mrs. Jessup finished saying, presumably of a son, "Now he's in corporate finance in Wilmington, with this wonderful Bank of Delaware."

"Mother," Lee announced, by way of rescue, "you missed a grand tour up there. They knocked out the wall between the guest bedroom and the hall and made a master suite! Grammy and Grampy's old room is full of pennants and teddy bears!"

"Dorothy was saying," she responded, "that she agreed with me—this house is hard on its women." She spoke in little hurried skips, struggling for breath. When she stood, she staggered one sideways step, and leaned heavily on Lee in heading to the front door. She had never taken off her plaid overcoat.

"Can't we get you anything?" Mrs. Jessup asked, her eyes and cheeks brighter with alarm. "Even a glass of water?"

"You've done . . . everything," was the answer. "I get . . . these spells, where my chest . . . doesn't seem to have any *depth*. It was lovely of you to let us . . . see what all you've done. You've done . . . wonders."

The porch, as Lee escorted his mother across it, seemed as wide as he remembered it from childhood. The concrete walk glared under their shoes as they shuffled to the curb. She allowed herself to be folded into the passenger's seat, and lifted a hand and waved it in response to the Jessups' cheery, worried farewells. As he drove down the street, in the direction in which he used to walk to elementary school eating his Tastykake, past Weisbach's Drug Store, she struggled to breathe, in intense, sharp sips; her body shook as if some invisible predator had it by the nape of the neck.

Lee asked, "Shall we go home or straight to the Alton Hospital?"

"Home." The syllable seemed all she could manage.

As he made the turn to circle the block, her hand in the side of his vision fed a pill into her mouth.

"That house," she explained. "I needed . . . to get out."

"Just like always." Her retreating into ill health irritated him. "Well," he announced, driving parallel to Franklin Street, "you won't have to see that house ever again."

"That room was never black."

"What?"

"That's what upset me. That room was never black. Why would anybody in their right mind . . . paint a room black?"

"That's what they said they were wondering."

"They imagined it. The walls had old cream-colored paper, with silver florets, and the wainscoting was pine, stained walnut. Mother used to do her sewing in that room, before her eyesight went."

"They couldn't have just imagined it, they must have had some basis, Mother. She was very definite."

"Yes, about everything. Maybe it was a joke. That's how those Alton people are. That's the way they were when I was a girl. Sly. Always poking fun. It made me feel bad. It made me feel crazy. That they would think we would have had a black room."

"How's your chest?"

"A little better. Don't you remember how the room was?"

"I don't remember ever looking in, Mother. That room frightened me. When I would go to sleep in my bed, I remember, I would turn to face that wall so that if something came through the wall I could grab it before it grabbed me."

"Oh, my. And here we all thought you were such a happy child."

As Alton fell away behind them and the country roads sang beneath their tires, her spirits lifted. She helped him make their dinner, directing the cooking from her chair at the kitchen table, where she sat with all her pill bottles at her elbow. He fried a big slice of ham, boiled up some frozen succotash, and baked two potatoes in the crusty old oven: the kind of meal she used to devour, with a heaping of ice cream to top it off. She ate half, trying to please him, and he finished her plate, which made him feel unpleasantly full. During the night, he heard her moving about in her room, clearing her throat and gasping, on the other side of the wall. It was still dark, before dawn. He thought of going in to her, but fell asleep instead.

In the morning, the smell of coffee rose up the stairs—the smell of life. His mother was downstairs ahead of him, in her quilted purple bathrobe, with a tent of white hair worn loose over her shoulders. "Isn't coffee verboten?" he asked.

"Not to you, yet. I had a cup myself. I don't know why that woman offering me tea made me so mad."

"You were determined something would," he told her. Lee had to leave right after breakfast, since it was a good three hours back to New York and he had promised to take his younger daughter to her riding lesson in Central Park while his wife went to a Sunday matinée of *Jelly's Last Jam*. His mother came outside with him and shuffled along as far as the sandstone walk allowed. She was dressed in wool-lined suède slippers, and the uncut lawn was lank and drenched with dew. Beyond the house, the sumac was turning red here and there, and the poplars showed a yellow tinge. Fall was on the way, with winter behind. What would she do, alone? They should have discussed it last night, after dinner, instead of watching television: "Golden Girls" followed by "Empty Nest." She had become an unreality addict.

"Wouldn't you like it," Lee asked, "if we could get somebody to stay in the house with you this winter?"

"The Jessups, maybe," she said. "They could call this their retirement home. They could clean out all my cobwebs and put in wall-to-wall polyester."

In the low morning sunshine, the eastward house wall was the warm brown of fresh toast. Lee was conscious of the wet lawn, the wild raspberry canes, the towering trees beyond as a tightening net of interwoven, ruthless nature. The house seemed as perilously small as his mother. From the pitying look on her face, he knew she was viewing him as a child, having one of his nervous stomach cramps. "It's a real problem, Mother," he weakly insisted. "It worries me. You shouldn't be alone."

She had taken to wearing her glasses less and less. The absence of frames gave her face a startled, naked look, even now, when she assumed her teasing expression. She asked, "Why would you want to kill me, making me live with somebody else? I just barely survived living with your father all those years."

He was content to be dismissed, yet couldn't make himself move off the sandstone walk, the ten yards or so to where the car was parked. This September day was beginning with high clouds, a few ribs of cirrus arched in the stratospheric cold. Some birds made a sudden flurry of noise in the old, half-dead pear tree. There was a buzzing in the air, a constant eating. The truck traffic on the Jersey Turnpike would be at its height. "Think about it. About, you know, more ideal arrangements."

"Lee, this house *is* my ideal arrangement. Now don't make

Jenny late for her lesson. Girls love horses. That was why I resented my father's moving us to town—it meant I couldn't ride anymore. Here. Let's see if I can make it to the road." Holding on to his shoulder, she kicked off her slippers and stepped off the last stone barefoot. The chill of the wet grass sprang a delighted laugh; she hobbled with him to the side of his car. Her blue-veined feet were puffy on top, like a baby's feet. "Now, I'll be fine," she recited, when they had stopped walking and she could get her breath. "I'll take my pills and try to eat more and get some strength back. I'm sorry I let those city folk get the better of me yesterday. I had wanted so *not* to act up."

She disentangled her weightless, onion-skin hand from his arm and found a footing on the uneven lawn which held her upright while he got into his BMW and started the engine. Seen through the open car window, in the morning light, her face looked defenseless around the eyes, the delicate skin owlish. "I'm sorry," she told him, "I let myself be so frightened."

"You mean of the room that they—?"

She was startlingly quick to touch his arm again with her hand, to stop his mouth. "Don't even *say* it!"

Anne Whitney Pierce

STAR BOX

I never did much like the sound of that Mr. Primavera, so when he invites me for tea after the fact—the fact of Esther's being dead and buried, that is—I can only be offended. I remember Esther saying, with quicksilver wistfulness in her voice, that he was a bit of a Don Juan. She'd heard them on the stairs, seen them in glimpses through her door—women of all ages and sizes, coming and going at all hours of the day and night with the smell of tea. She'd heard them thumping above her in Mr. Primavera's apartment doing heaven knows what, as the music went round and round on his Victrola, though she didn't seem old enough to use the word.

Esther's husband, Avery Brubaker, was the dart champion at the Medford Pub and won a tropical vacation once on a quiz show he traded in for cash. "Long as the man pays his rent," he said of Mr. Primavera, "whose business is it how many broads he's slamming?" Avery spoke his mind, Esther said, and never mind what was in it.

They seemed an unlikely couple, Avery and Esther. I suppose there are no other kinds. Avery worked for a chemical plant out on Route 128, taking often to the road for long stretches in an enormous cylindrical truck with danger signs posted all over it. He was a slight, arched man, thin shoulders dropping into a

long waist and bowed legs. A coarse orange fuzz sprang out at
the tops of his V-neck T-shirts, matting his arms from shoulder
to wrist. Avery looked like a great, grisly caterpillar, gone upright and given a small bit of wit and language to abuse.

And Esther—soft, worried Esther, with the curly hair. She'd
been pretty once, but had never known it. She buttoned her
shirts high and religiously; I'd never once seen her bare collarbone. She worried about the little things—someone had to, she
said—the color of hothouse tomatoes and finding the right
length shoelaces, the life of a lightbulb, books out of place on a
shelf. She'd worked in a nursery before she married Avery,
tending the plants and flowers in a warm damp greenhouse she
loved. But Avery hadn't wanted a wife who worked, and why
take a husband, Esther said, who was unhappy from the start?

I met Esther on a hot day last June, in a park up on Powder-
house Hill, surrounding the old fort. We used to take our dogs
for an evening stroll and land on our favorite benches, which
happened to rest side by side. Esther was a big woman, and her
legs were bad, but in those days they still got her around. We'd
sit and chat and watch the children play and the clouds pass
overhead. Our dogs, both since dead, lay low on their paws and
growled at one another. Esther wore a brown cardigan sweater.
Mine was a dull green, almost identical in style, with braiding
and a beaded collar. Sometimes, when I looked at Esther, I saw
myself in thirty years—maybe even twenty—and the glimpse
into time alarmed me as much as it gave comfort. The park was
filled with pale, dying light, and children, and echoing noise,
full of everything Esther had lost, and I was still waiting to
have.

Esther had children—a son and a daughter—both grown and
childless and far away. "I'm afraid you wouldn't like them all
that well," she once told me. They turned out to be rather cold,
selfish people, she wasn't sure why, though she blamed herself
for all their distances and shortcomings.

"Course Avery and I were too young to start a family," Esther
said. We exchanged bits and pieces of our lives in the park, passing them back and forth like neighborly cups of sugar. "Too
young and too poor. Still, the children got their baths. They got
their teeth fixed and they got a good education. It seemed like a
miracle sometimes."

"Children don't raise themselves," I told her. "Children are helpless."

"Mine never were," she said. "What was your home like, Elaine?"

"Home?" Esther would toss the conversation over to me, intent on her knitting needles, always busy making things for other people's grandchildren. Catching the ball with shaky hands, I began to tell Esther things I'd never told anyone else. "My house was very . . . hot," I remembered. "I had to wear a woolen nightgown, even in the summer. The itching drove me crazy. I vowed when I grew up I'd sleep naked every night."

"And do you, dear?"

"Not often," I said, thinking of Rufus.

"That's always the way isn't it? Witch hazel's good for the itch."

Esther's fingers spun rectangles of lavender and blue. "You had brothers and sisters?"

"Two older brothers. They were in league." A popsicle melted into an orange puddle at my feet.

"Not against you, I hope."

"No." I drank fizzy water from a bottle and bit the corners of my nails. "Just against the world. They got away with murder, my brothers."

"Your mother must have been so pleased to finally have a little girl to dress up."

"She would have liked such a little girl," I said. "But I didn't like dresses. I liked to dig for bones."

"Of course you did," Esther said soothingly, no judgement passed, no statement made.

"Do you know what my mother said when I told her I wanted to be a geologist?" I asked Esther. "She said, 'Fine, Elaine. You can start by digging out the rocks in your head.'"

"Sounds like your mother had a sense of humor."

"No," I said. "She didn't have any at all."

It was just six months ago, as the December winds blew into our collars in the park, that Esther told me, "Well, Avery's gone."

"Where's he off to this time?" I asked her.

"Heaven, I hope," Esther said. "I wouldn't call Avery a bad man."

"Heaven?"

Avery died the way people can in his profession, in an accident where the chemicals exploded on impact and set his truck on fire, killing him somewhere on an interstate in Pennsylvania —instantly, painlessly, Esther was assured by another widow at a coffee-and-sympathy party down at the chemical plant. Esther made finger foods and a Jell-O mold and spared everyone her sorrow by not bringing any along. Esther didn't see Avery's death as tragedy. She had no religion, but she did have faith. Avery had his spot reserved in heaven, in the corral where brave men go to lasso the wild horses that bucked them on earth, to tell slightly tall tales of their wild rides, to smoke cigars and down frothy beers forever after.

Soon after Avery died, Esther asked me for dinner one night. She liked to try out the Recipes of the Stars on the back page of the *TV Guide*. She watched the soaps in the afternoon, making love chains on a neat chart. Angela loved Brad who pretended to love Kelly who seduced Amber who jilted Antoine, who two-timed with the twins, Francesca and Nicole, one of whose baby was born blind, the other kidnapped from the maternity ward by Angela, who loved Brad, who pretended to love Kelly. . . .

Sandwiches cut in diamond shapes with walnuts and cream cheese were a Sammy Davis offering. Mary Tyler Moore's weight watcher special was cut-up pineapple served on its skin with cottage cheese and cinnamon sprinkled on top. Johnny Carson made a chicken with lemon sauce, though I found it hard to believe Johnny Carson had, in recent years, touched the naked, bumpy skin of a raw chicken.

"Isn't it nice the stars find time to cook?" Esther's thoughts were as generous as mine were niggardly. "Such wholesome foods, too. I would have thought they lived on caviar and champagne. How's the Joan Rivers Meatloaf, dear?"

In those dark winter days, I'd come for dinner after work, once, sometimes twice a week. Esther would shake out my coat of cold and snow and drape it over Avery's armchair. She'd light a candle for Avery and set it on the table. I didn't know she was counting time. I think she planned to be gone by April, not because Avery had been a good excuse for living, but because she suspected she'd been left with no other. Avery's memory

grew dim in the flickering candlelight as we dipped potato chips
into Bob Hope's Cheddar Cheese Spread and watched the city
moon rise.

A month or so after Avery died, the talk turned to Mr. Primavera, the neighbor. He wasn't entirely well, Esther thought.
He'd gotten a haircut; he'd had a cold. He'd been cooking something that smelled Chinesey. One of his women visitors had
thrown something down the stairs and Mr. Primavera rushed
down after it. The women still came and went. Esther didn't
want to be nosy; it was no concern of hers. After all, Mr. Primavera had very kindly been bringing up her mail, Avery's old
task, knowing her legs were bad on the stairs. Mr. Primavera
had a receding hairline; however, he was not going bald. He
brought her a photograph of himself as a child as proof. He had
a full mustache, and wasn't as young as one might think at first
glance. He was very polite, very pleasant. All in all, Esther
thought, he was a fine man. But whatever could he be doing
with all those women?

I'm sure this Mr. Primavera is neither Casanova nor sinner. If I
have tea with him, I will make quick reference to Rufus, lest he
misunderstand why I am what I look like—a thin, bookish
woman who likes to live alone. "When Rufus and I went to the
Roxy," I will say. No, that would be a lie. Movies were out, even
slapstick or subtitles. "When Rufus and I were on our way back
from the grocery store." Yes. Only lovers buy morning milk and
eggs together.

Mr. Primavera doesn't have to know I have pried myself
away from Rufus. I have loved Rufus in some more than ordinary way. But maybe that is only because Rufus is not ordinary,
because Rufus is deaf. He has never heard anything—water
dripping or typewriters clacking or a children's song or the hiss
and rumble before the tea kettle roars, or anything at all except
what I imagine to be a ceaseless, screeching hum in his head.
After a while, this great gap of sound and rhythm was simply
too colossal and frightening to cross. There are too many things
Rufus and I couldn't do—take naps or go on vacation or to the
symphony, not so much because he was deaf, but because life
for Rufus was just too serious to include such frivolities. When I

was with him, I found myself in constant self-reproach for not being grateful or hardworking or happy enough, although I always before felt enough of all three. It was too hard and too exhausting to find replacements for the most ordinary of human events, too late to rearrange my own self, so long and hard in the making.

A deaf silence is not golden, but a watery grey. Rufus and I tried to flop and jibe, to ebb and flow and swoop and pout and fly as other people who think they might love each other for a good long while will do. I took a sign class at the Adult Center; he studied hieroglyphics. I once dragged him outside in a summer shower and broke into an off-tune Billy Holliday song. Rufus stared. I unbuttoned my shirt, caught raindrops with my tongue, fell off my pirouettes onto the cement sidewalk, saw smoke swirl out of my laughter. I tugged his arm, pleaded. He would only move the top half of his body, eyes on the lookout for witnesses to my folly, fingers wiggling his innocence, his embarrassment.

"Lighten up, will you, Rufus?" I was mad and tried to say so in sign, drawing a lightbulb in the air, but of course Rufus did not understand. "Just . . . have . . . some fun!" I slapped two fingers end to end and played the clown—making faces, making fun, making eyes. Rufus just kept staring—disdainful, incredulous, uncomprehending—in the end they were all the same. My dance grew stiff, the dance of a sci-fi creature on a leaden planet with gravity to spare, and the song became no more than a mournful plaint, making light of the rain, without which we would all perish. I quieted myself, buttoned up my shirt, led the way inside. We dried ourselves solemnly, blew our noses, rubbed our wrinkled feet, got ready to make penance love. *You win, Rufus.* I signed, draped in a towel, shivering, reaching out to touch his blue lips. *You're deaf, Rufus.*

I am deaf, Rufus said, finger to ear, then to mouth. He pulled the towel from me and stared at my body with the steady, impassive gaze of a bird of prey. He shook his head and swung his hands together, heavy in a cradle of dead air. *But nobody wins.*

Sex for Rufus had nothing to do with passion or lust or fun. It was mission. Catharsis. For both of us, it was need. Sex with Rufus was like floating down a cool river. I don't know how much of my pleasure he shared. In bed, our thin bodies slid and turned in rhythm. The silence was vast and limp, the sweat hot and cleansing. Our bodies slid and crunched; we felt each other's bony fingers, reveled in our spare selves, our plainness, our indentations. We knew no inhibitions, none of our usual fears. We found the pools in our collarbones and the arches in our feet, the Vs in our ribcages. We were both left-handed and knew the periodic table by heart. We were generally clumsy and fond of figs. We fit. I used to wake Rufus from twitching, deaf sleep with a finger down the line of hair to his navel. He'd turn to me and fuck me with solemnity, approaching the task before him like all others, with a fierce commitment to succeed.

How was it? Rufus asked this with his eyes alone. Never again would *was it good for you?* do.

G-o-o-d! I'd sign the letters on his boy-smooth chest with that same finger as we lay, barely damp, untangled, in the sheets, dotting the exclamation point low. *You're so good.* I'd bring my hand from mouth to palm and try to explain all the meanings of the word. But Rufus took all them as insults.

By the autumn after the raw spring we met, I began to feel both selfish and neglected. I could not go on taking so much from Rufus and giving back so little. I could not go on giving so much and getting so little back. I'd go to work at the museum and make myself forget Rufus for days at a time, until I found myself back in my car, on my way to school for the deaf, wondering if men cruising for a whore felt the same driven, toe-tapping, devil-be-damned way. *It's over,* I finally tried out the words one night in clumsy sign just around the time Avery died, flinging my clumsy fingers to the wind. *I'm no good for you, Rufus.*

Rufus misunderstood again, signing back, swaggering, proud. *I can be better.*

"No," I said out loud, collapsing. "You are better. I'm the crumb."

I couldn't make him understand the word, over and over crumbling imaginary bread in my hands and letting the pieces fall, then dropping down on all fours to play the mouse who nibbled away at them, because this was the word that had come to me, the one I wanted to use. Rufus got down on his knees with a grudging smile beside me. *All right, Elaine,* he was telling me. *We'll play.*

No, I said. *This is not a game.* I lifted my fingers and made them speak—flopping, waving, tapping my palms. *Get up. Good-bye.* I pushed my thumbs forward into time. *Forever.*

I left us both feeling foolish, and angry, no longer man and woman, mice that we'd become.

Please come to tea on Thursday at five fifteen. Mr. Primavera's invitation comes in a plain white envelope, typed on an old typewriter with a faint ribbon and clogged O's. I take the note out again and again at the museum, putting aside the pieces of an early primate vertebra recently found by a Dutch tourist in Indonesia. I feel the note, sniffing it, studying it under my light box, trying to put it into some context, get some sense of something from it, some smell, some feel, some aura, as I would a relic from the earth. But the note is timeless, unexceptional, odorless. It is no more than a summons, really. And I am not a sucker for *pleases*, having been raised by a mother who gave pennies to reward them.

I decide to go. For Esther's sake. In memory of Esther, who caught me in my slow tumble from the planet Rufus, who asked for nothing in return but my so-so company, who made me Carol Burnett's Veal Verdiccio and recommended a good shampoo for wispy hair, who up and died out of the blue. She would have urged me to go for tea with Mr. Primavera, to get out a bit more, not to end up like that boy Jack, all work and no play. Afterwards, were she alive, she would smile and pluck the details from me one by one as she fed me fluorescent orange macaroni and pale green celery stalks—the color of his bedspread, the feel of his sofa, the fruit in his fruitbowl—don't leave anything out, dear—were his socks matching? How strong did he take his tea? Did you see any of the women? What were they wearing, or not wearing? Esther would not flinch. She really would want to know.

"Don't mind the cats," Mr. Primavera tells me at the door. Three appear at his ankles and start to rub against his legs. "They get more uppity every day. You must be Elaine."

"I am Elaine." I step inside, bolstered by that fact. The rays of gleaming yellow eyes fall upon me. Slowly, one by one, the cats come to life, eyelids lifting, tails twitching, backs arching, mouths yawn. One licks its paw on the couch; one eats from a bowl; one stretches on the windowsill. "Esther never mentioned you had cats," I say.

"I'm not sure she knew," Mr. Primavera says. He is small, big-eared, clean—an urban elf in a *Beethoven Was One of the Boyz* T-shirt. "Please sit down." I sit down in one of two mismatched armchairs, placed side by side in what is virtually an empty room, save the cats and one large, worn, Oriental rug. "Salada okay?" he asks.

"What?" A bust of Beethoven stares with plaster brows down at me from its perch on the shelf next to the record player.

He says, "I like having my fortune told by a tea bag."

"Fine, anything," I say. "As long as it's caffeinated. I've got to go back to work later tonight."

"Esther said you were a nervous person."

"She did?" I swing my head around to catch Mr. Primavera's eye near the lit stove-top, feeling instantly betrayed. It is one thing for Esther to have told me about Mr. Primavera's hairline. For we are both women, and she spoke of it with nothing but reverence. "I work long hours at the museum," I said. "I'm . . . busy."

"What did Esther have to say about me?" Mr. Primavera asks, rolling his head my way as the tea kettle whistles.

"She said you were . . . very . . . neat." I tug at my hair with a dark look and try to make it sound like an accusation.

"Neat?" he says, looking around the room as he hands me my tea. "Not much to it. Avery called it the feline flophouse."

"Did you know Avery well?" I take my tea bag out of my cup and wind the string around the spoon. My fortune on the tag reads *Life is what happens while you're making other plans.* A stream of sunlight catches one of my fingers and warps it.

"I worked with him down at the plant for a while," Mr. Primavera says.

"You drove those trucks?"

"Me?" Mr. Primavera laughed. "Good god, no. I worked in the shipping office. It takes a certain kind of person to do road work."

"Dead, you mean?" Mr. Primavera has brought out the sarcastic in me, a side I don't know well.

Mr. Primavera shakes his head. "Not dead," he says.

"Brave?" I say, although I know this is not what he means.

"No," he says. "Brave people swallow their fear. Avery had none."

"Why did he call this the feline flophouse?"

"I take them in," Mr. Primavera says. "Strays, sick, maimed, blind. I had an epileptic cat once. She had her last seizure right there on the couch. I buried her down by the river."

"Very generous," I say. "Esther was the same way."

"She made that man a pie every night," he says.

"You make her sound like Betty Crocker," I say. The hot tea fills the pit of my stomach. I have lost all the weight Esther gained for me.

"Betty Crocker is my idol," Mr. Primavera says, raising his eyebrows and one palm. "Seriously."

"Look," I say. I lean forward and plant my elbows on my knees. "Esther wasn't stupid. She was very independent. I think she saw Avery for exactly what he was." I am strangely comfortable here, free to uncross my legs and speak my mind.

"What was he?" Mr. Primavera asks me.

"I only met him once or twice," I say, "but I would have said he was sort of a boor."

"Bore?"

"Boor."

Mr. Primavera shrugs. "Esther seemed happy enough."

"If she were happy," I say, "I don't think she would have died that way."

"What way?"

"Of nothing in particular. No one dies of old age anymore."

"No one ever really did," Mr. Primavera says. "They only told us that."

We sip our tea. The doorbell rings and Mr. Primavera looks at his watch. "Must be Marjorie," he says.

"Marjorie?" I slip my shoes back on and straighten up in the sagging chair. "I've stayed too long," I say, though it hasn't been long at all. "Thanks for the tea." I get my coat and open the door. Behind it stands Marjorie, wrapped up too warmly for late spring in bright, striped clothes—scarf and turtleneck and thick makeup. A big dog sits on a leash beside her, all eyes and not enough hair for its bulk, panting from its run up the stairs. The three cats appear at the door and start to hiss. Mr. Primavera hisses back at them and they retreat. He smiles and ushers Marjorie and the dog inside as I leave. The smells of damp dogs and humans mingle. The dog turns around and barks at me. She looks a little bit like me, I think, a little bit like Esther. Marjorie, that is.

From Mr. Primavera's I go to visit Rufus at the school for the deaf where he teaches gym and is an assistant math teacher. In the dusk, the school looks like a pleasant enough place—a rambling, shingled old house in good repair, with a modern addition tastefully placed behind. The woman at the front desk smiles at me. "Haven't seen you in a while," she says. It's 6:15. I consult the chalkboard at the main door. Pink letters tell me the leisure hour has just begun. The movie of the evening is *The Pink Panther*. Rufus often stays late on Fridays to work out in the gym. I sign my name in the visitor book and head down the corridor. The gym is empty. I find Rufus in the math room, sitting at a desk, a pile of papers before him, looking out into space, his mouth dropped open. He is wearing his teacher clothes—rumpled corduroy and flannel, the knot of his tie yanked free. It pains me to find Rufus this way at an unappointed moment—unoccupied, unengaged, a dull look in his eyes that cannot define itself. Rufus has never had the luxury of knowing what it means to be bored; rest is laborious, a void. He is resting because the chalkboard says it is time, and he obeys the chalkboard, not because he is ruled by it, but because it brings order to his life.

When Rufus sees me, he jumps up with startling strength, bringing that tightening to my stomach that for so long I mistook for fear, then *learned* to be sex. Rufus is a mismatch of flesh and age, just as Mr. Primavera is. The face is far too old for its twenty-six years, a face that might have kissed the brows of a thousand dead children for all its pain. His body is strong, unscathed, a body you'd expect to be hurling a discus or raising high the roof beams. I robbed the cradle; I am thirty-two. But Rufus has long been older than I will ever be.

"Elaine!" A soft croaking noise I've come to recognize as my name slips from his lips. His mind races to consider why I've

come, how he'll treat me, as leper or long lost lover. How un-
wise of me to appear at this moment, how unfair, after all this
time, after tea with Mr. Primavera, elusive and unsure. Rufus
has the edge and knows it.

He starts up from his chair with a twisted smile, but when he
remembers we no longer touch, he sits back down, slowly tipping his chair back and forth against the blackboard, letting me
watch him as he knows I've come to do, as a movie star does for
a camera, the thrill of adoration paled, resigned to a performance instead of a real show. He twirls a pencil in his fingers
and gestures to a child's desk. I sit down, bumping my knees.
Rufus gets up and writes slowly, in sprawling letters on the
blackboard, *What do you want?*

I give Rufus the shrug I've been practicing for so long, the
shrug of a lifetime, the one that will explain I am only out of
sorts, not out of reach, out of touch, not necessarily out of love—
that most of all I am just scared.

I first met Rufus a little over a year ago, in April, when I took a
group from the Institute for the Deaf on a fossil dig at Pilgrim's
Hill. I stood in the damp forest watching the deaf people dig,
feeling the world slipping away, the senses leaving me one by
one—first hearing, then smell, then touch, and finally vision as
the new greens and browns fell into a cool black void. Rufus
was the most possessed of them all to unearth something, the
most reverent of the things the earth reluctantly coughed up to
him. He pawed at the ground with his slender hands, scooping
out handfuls of dirt and caressing each thing he found, bringing
it to me for identification and admiration, never disappointed by
just a twig or a stone or a dead bug or a clump of moss. Nothing
in that forest, in that small highway-bound, trash-littered clump
of the newly-thawed 20th-century earth, was going to disap-
point him. It was the way Rufus touched those things of the
earth that made it impossible, when he asked me later on the
bus ride home, if I would take him on another dig, to say no.
Impossible, when his hand first touched me across the cracked
green leather seat of the bus, not to want it, tell it to wander, to
explore. To dig.

. . .

There is a knock at the classroom door. A tall boy enters. He reads the writing on the board and nods to me with a quick jerk of his head. This is greeting. This is Billy. Billy is young, maybe nineteen. His hands move constantly. He lost his hearing in a construction accident working alongside his father, two years ago, two nights before the prom. The echoes of the things he's heard keep him mad, keep him moving, ever stalking the sounds he knows he's missing, that may be trailing him, taunting him, lurking in dark corners—his mother's nagging, race cars revving, fights brewing, prom music playing, sweet groans from a parked car on a midsummer's night.

Billy shoots an invisible basketball into a hoop with a silent pop of the lips, gesturing towards the gym.

Later, Rufus signs lifting his arms. *Fly away, Billy.*

Billy gives me the evil eye on his way out, dribbling an invisible basketball all the way. *There is no later*, he signs.

Rufus and I sit desk to desk and sign a simple conversation about the weather and work, the snippets of talk that have always before been but a slight prelude to lovemaking, but now must constitute the whole of our connection. A light rain is falling. We can't stroll the grounds. *Come on*, Rufus signs. We take a walk around the building. The common room is filled with people, playing cards, some just sitting, some watching "Jeopardy." They jump up to sign the questions, *What is Athens? What is rutabega? What is an aphid?* The only other sounds are the rhythmic, hollow bouncing of the ping-pong ball on a green table and the rain hitting the skylights. Rufus and I buy Snickers bars at the canteen, and walk down the halls, our sneakers squeaking on a floor that would have made even my mother's look dingy.

How is your friend? Rufus signs.

Which friend? I ask.

The knitter. His hands get busy; he purses his lips.

She died. I close my eyes and lay my head on prayer-ready hands, more dramatic than the deaf would ever have it.

Dead? His palms meet, one up, one down, and flip quickly as his eyebrows rise. *When?* He circles one index finger around the other in time.

March. I spell it, letter by letter, shocked to discover how long it's been since I've been to visit Rufus. But he is not surprised that I come and go and say things I don't mean, that summer is almost here, that someone has died.

I'm sorry. Rufus' fist rubs his chest in sympathy, but not sorrow. He comes near me. Like the push of the Squiggle Z button on my computer that negates the last command, his touch on my arm erases my goodbye. I feel his breath on my face. His palm rolls us toward the door. *Let's go.*

Once off the grounds, Rufus slides into the driver's seat of my car and takes the wheel with a nearly wicked smile. Like Esther, he is strangely pure, excited by the tiniest of demons inside him. Rufus drives fast along the river, grinding the fragile gears. I want to touch him as he drives, his leg or his arm, but instead count the strokes of the windshield wipers, and the blotchy sycamore trees along the river.

Back at my apartment, we ride up in the rickety elevator, backs pressed against opposite sides, eyes locked. We undress and go to bed and stay there into the night, rolling in and out of love and sleep, relieved to have each other back as jars, receptacles for our spillings. After we make love, once, twice, and then again, we hold on to one another uncharacteristically, draped in the dark, dozing on and off. Sometime in the night, Rufus makes omelettes with scallions and cream cheese, which our bellies can't hold. We drown it with black coffee and sleep soundly at last. In the morning, I mend Rufus' shirt while he does sit-ups on the floor. And then I drive him back to the school for the deaf.

A few days later, I go back to re-push the Squiggle Z button, to undo the mistake, to unlapse the lapse. It is still raining. Rufus is playing basketball in the gym with five or six boys. He's been expecting me. There is only readiness in his eyes. He slings a towel around his neck and signs to Billy to take over, barrelling the ball into the boy's belly, stealing his wind. We walk the barren halls again, fast, and I strain to keep up with him. Rufus pulls me into a supply closet and closes the door, pulling me to him, half of a demon's smile rising on his face. I push him away and tell him the other night was just a dip into a pool, that I hope we are still friends, I just came to talk. Sure, he says, a sneer lifting his sagging face. He couples his first fingers, switches them back and forth. *Friends.* His hands line up edge to edge, thumbs in, moving back and forth like a saw. His mouth moves blah, blah, blah; his legs cross in anger. *So go ahead, Elaine. Talk.*

I tell Rufus a bit about Mr. Primavera in clumsy, makeshift sign. The light in Rufus' eyes dies. I tell him about the cats and the bust of Beethoven and women on the stairs, thinking it will make a good story, but Rufus is not interested in anything that even faintly resembles fantasy.

How much do you like him? Rufus asks.

I don't even think I do like him, I try to explain, bumping up against the locks of a mop.

Do you love him? The fists cross across his chest and a thumb points to a shapeless, noosed him, dangling in space.

No.

Do you love him? Rufus reins the thumb back in and jabs in against his chest, the fists still crossed, still pressing.

I can only nod my head yes. And shake my head no. And nod and shake and nod. "What do we do with the silence, Rufus?" I ask out loud.

Rufus sticks up his middle finger and is gone. He leaves me in the supply closet with stacks of paper brown towels and toilet paper and cleaning fluids. I am shocked, not because Rufus is angry. I've been expecting that, waiting for its relief, as I used to be when I finally found the spiders my brothers let loose in my bed and squished them dead with my shoe. I am shocked because Rufus' middle finger has just screamed at me and the sound has been deafening. If we have anything left to say to one another, we will have to learn how to speak all over again.

The next week, two traveling lectures and one drizzly dig later, I'm a bit under the weather. I stay home from work one day and put on the vaporizer and soak my feet and read old *National Geographic* magazines. Women on a tiny island in the Pacific have a life expectancy of eighty years, and half the body fat of the average American woman. I am not really as sick as I hoped to be. By the time Mr. Primavera calls in the afternoon, I've used three Kleenexes, barely, and I'm hungry, with no food in the house.

"A cup of hot tea might do you good," he says.

"Why are we doing this?" I ask him the most tactful of my burning questions—why his voice trembles and what women see in him will have to wait.

"Why do we need a reason?" he says.

Why do we need a reason for anything that seems interesting, possible, harmless? I change my shirt and slip wool socks over my wrinkled feet. I wear beaded Chinese slippers and leave my hair hanging loose instead of winding it up into a bun and stuffing the end tips into the coil I usually do. Taking a glance in the mirror, I see an odd and mythic creature—part empress, part sea dragon, part bag lady. Today, though, I have achieved some sort of softness, I think, some kind of grace. I am my most beautiful in profile, in mid-reach, the leans and stretches of me, sunk in a strange man's chair.

"You don't look very sick," Mr. Primavera says at the door.

"Sick is maybe too strong a word, Mr. Primavera."

"Come on. Make it Anthony. Have some tea."

Count Dracula was a vein man, reads my fortune. I laugh. Anthony pours himself a cup and joins me on the couch. I get up and turn Ludwig's angry face around. The Victrola sits silent. I have not moved Mr. Primavera to music, it seems.

"I wonder when Esther and Avery's marriage went sour," Anthony says out of the blue.

"I didn't know it had." I cough on too quick a gulp of tea, instantly glad Esther and Avery have taken their secrets to the grave, that there will never be any proof that what Mr. Primavera is about to tell me is true.

"Before the mistress, or after." The green rises in Anthony's eyes like floodwater. "Did Esther know?"

"She must have," I say carefully, swallowing my surprise.

"Avery and I used to talk out on the stoop," he says. " 'Just find a woman who understands you, Anthony,' he'd tell me. 'Don't listen to your body. It'll screw you up. Find a greasy spoon, if you have to, maybe a waitress.' Then he'd always say Esther didn't turn out to be the woman he thought she was."

"Who ever does?" I picture Rufus on that first day on the dig, so lively and full of smiles, so unlike himself. "Esther made the best of Avery," I say. "He could have done the same."

"I think he tried," Anthony says, rubbing a striped kitten with a white patch over one eye. "But she made him crazy."

"Maybe he already was."

"Maybe." Anthony fiddles with his spoon. "What do you do, Elaine?"

"I'm a paleontologist."

"Come again?"

"I'm a geologist. Fossil and bone racket."

"You put together pieces of the past?"

"That's a grand way of putting it, I guess."

The doorbell rings. Anthony puts the kettle back on. "That must be Alice," he says.

Laughing, I tip my head back and swallow the last sip of cold tea. I've become one of Mr. Primavera's tea ladies in spite of myself. "What do you do, Anthony?" I ask him as I put on my coat. "Besides drink tea and rescue cats?"

"Right now," he says. "I'm recuperating."

I am polite because my mother told me rude little girls, along with little girls who pick their scabs, never get husbands—never get happy. And so I don't ask Anthony, from what? Alice is solemn, with lots of thick, reddish hair, come with a limp and a violin case, as she does every Tuesday at six. I stand out on the sidewalk, looking up at Anthony's curtains. After a while, I hear the sweet desperate wail of the violin, and I understand for one cragged, flashing second, what Rufus misses.

The next day, I get a call from Esther's daughter Camille in Chicago, asking me to sort through her mother's things. "You mean that hasn't been done yet?" I imagine with horror the sour milk in Esther's refrigerator, the moldy shower cap, maybe even Esther herself, decaying, slumped over in some chair, her teeth gleaming, her fingernails grown into curling claws.

"I had to rush off on business right after Mother died," Camille says. I met her at the funeral. Small and slick like an otter, she bore no resemblance to Esther. "I'm in the thick of things just now, and my little brother is useless at this sort of thing."

"Your mother was very kind to me," I tell her, "but I really don't think I'm the one . . ."

"It was so sudden. She spoke of you so often, Eleanor."

"Elaine."

"Please, Elaine." Her voice self-corrects, stuck in a hard place between a plea and a command. "You'd be doing us a favor. I'm sure my mother would've wanted it that way."

Camille, I remember Esther saying, was used to having the last word.

The next day, I sit in Esther's apartment on the floor of her living room with a pile of papers I've taken from her desk. Even Esther has not been able to die cleanly, without a trace. I find the usual leftover business of dead people—some unpaid bills and receipts, and a few lists. One reads, *Ajax, cottage cheese, catfood.* Esther had no cats, only the dog that died. Another list must have been older; one of the items is *underwear for Avery.* The thought of Avery dying in saggy, grey underwear drums up the nervous, slightly hysterical laugh of the living trying to grasp the dead, a laugh that used to burst from my throat at some of the worst misunderstandings Rufus and I had—a laugh that rose up in me unbidden, shivered, dry and fishy tasting on the roof of my mouth before it spilled forth, a chute of dusty coal, making Rufus furious, misreading lips, fingers, scowls—socks for soul, headache for brainstorm, fuck for luck.

The lists are the most intimate things I come upon, the most revealing. Otherwise I am struck by the Jane Doe nature of Esther's things. There are no pictures, no souvenirs of trips, no matches from a favorite restaurant, nothing but generic aspirin and twenty-year-old Epsom salts in the medicine chest, nothing to color it Esther's home except for the metal file box labeled *Star Box,* filled with the recipes of the stars. I replace the yellow tape that holds the label in place and wish, maybe even pray, to a tiny wizened god I once saw in a tomb in Mexico, a mere box of bones, that the star box needed organizing. But it doesn't. Nothing here does. Without Esther, this is just a moldy, public place.

Midway through the pile of Esther's papers, I see the wavy fringe of an old photograph. I expect it to show two smiling children or Avery at the wheel of his truck, a young Esther in a wedding gown. But it is Anthony Primavera's face that stares out at me, Anthony at the age of fifteen or so, a terribly thin boy standing on a shore, his lanky hair windblown, the head already too heavy a burden for his thin neck. And it is there, the receding hairline, odd on a boy odd-looking to begin with. On the back are scribbled some words in Italian. I slip the picture into my pocket.

When the desk is orderly, I put on one of Esther's frilly aprons with bitten cherries on it, get ready to clean. The apartment is covered with a thin layer of grime. I look for the Ajax Esther never got around to buying. I scrub as best I can with an old sponge and dish soap. I water Esther's parched plants, pick off the shriveled leaves and mist those that are left. I sweep all the cobwebs and dead flies from the bay window. Out on the grate of the fire escape, I find a cat dish, encrusted with bits of dry food. I wash the cat dish, put some tuna out on the grate as night falls, and lock the door. And the next day, when I come back to Esther's apartment to finish up the cleaning, there is a knock at the door.

"I heard footsteps," Anthony says. "What are you doing here?"

"Cleaning," I say.

"Why?"

"Esther's daughter called. She wanted someone to take care of things."

"Things as in what *things?*" I have made Anthony nervous.

"Everything. As in all things."

"Big job." Anthony looks at me strangely, maybe because I'm wearing a dress, one of several I've bought to wear to work— waisted, open-necked things with indescribable shapes and colors on them, soft, shimmery dresses that shift on my shoulders and show the shapes of my breasts. We had a visit today from a visiting Egyptian dignitary. After I gave him a tour of the museum, I took him to lunch. It is another me who performs these acts, not the digger in me, but the pleaser, the me who orders chicken salad and pays the check, makes transatlantic calls, smiles and gently removes the hand from my arm without offending the mind that has moved the hand, the one who locks the doors of the museum at the end of a day.

"You look different today," Anthony says. "May I come in?" But he is already over the threshold, taking everything in, touching things, hands sliding over surfaces and objects. "It never did feel like Avery's house."

"It's strange being here without Esther," I say. In the cupboards, I find no tea. "Will coffee do?" I ask him.

"Just some water," he says, sitting himself down in a hardbacked chair. "Coffee has its way with me."

I pour Anthony some water and start on my third cup of coffee. "Esther talked about you a lot in the end."

Anthony sips at his water. "She made a movie character out of me, I think."

I nod. "Half saint, half pimp."

"Pimp?" He looks up at me in surprise.

"Who are all the women, Anthony?"

"Friends. Friends of friends."

"No men friends?"

"A few."

"Avery?"

"Avery was a friend."

"Do you collect women?" I ask him.

He shakes his head. "Collectors are hoarders. Finders keepers. They clean their finds and sort them and put them under glass. They are usually afraid of something. My father collected beer bottle caps. I wasn't allowed to touch them, the things that cut your fingers and littered the streets. He hit me when he drank, but he lay those bottle caps on velvet. I could never understand why you collect the dead and beat the living." Anthony points to the row of fossils and bone pieces arranged along the windowsill, things I used to bring Esther as offerings for her company and her star food. "You are a collector," he says.

"You can touch them," I say. "Go ahead."

Anthony gets up and picks up a seagull bone and runs his finger along its ridge. "I just never understood," he says. "What's the point of a collection after it's been collected?"

"Crossing lines," I say. "Time zones, date lines, dimensions, going from one world to another. What about the cats?" I say. "You collect them, don't you? You feed them, brush them. You like their company."

"We tolerate each other," Anthony says. "They come and go as they please."

"The women, too?"

"Ha, ha. Of course."

"They come to depend on you," I say. "For food and warmth. Bottle caps and bones aren't beholden."

"It's their choice," he says. "Cats aren't stupid."

"If you don't hold onto anything," I say. "Then you have no past." I gesture around the empty apartment, puzzled. "She left nothing. I'm having trouble remembering her."

"Who should she have left anything for?" Anthony says.

"Her children. Her friends. Posterity."

"You met those children," Anthony said. "Posterity is just as greedy. And you were only an acquaintance really, weren't you?"

"Why didn't you ever ask Esther up for tea?" I ask him. I want to get past the angry feeling I have for him, move onto something else—indifference, annoyance, even lust will do. "It would've meant a lot to her."

"I did," he says. "After Avery died, we met on Wednesdays. Her legs couldn't manage the stairs, so I came here instead. We watched the soaps together. She had a crush on that vampire, Dr. Cranshaw, and I had a thing for . . . well, never mind."

"What did you talk about?" I ask him.

Anthony thinks. "Teenage pigeons. Where they hang out. Why you never see them." Pause. "Swollen ankles." Pause. "The nurses' uniforms on 'General Hospital.' The hemlines haven't changed. They've stayed the same mini all these years, back in 1966. I should've done the same."

Collectors live day to day and call it sensible, gathering bits and pieces as they go, as gestures of time's goodwill, of apology. But they distinguish always between a past and a deep past. I look to the dark ages because my own short history reveals so little. I sidestep the future and ask it for promises it can't keep. Rufus holds the past to nothing and expects nothing of the future, understanding they are one in the same, separated only by the dotted line of consciousness. Rufus will not be collected. He will not live in a glass case or be scrutinized in any other than natural sunlight. He will not be placed on velvet nor led willingly into the rain. He will accept no labels, not even deaf. But unlike me and Anthony, he will take chances.

Anthony and I commit to nothing. I know why the women climb his stairs, and why they climb back down again. They bring no valuables here; they take no risks. Anthony takes nothing from them. He is the tea man, a gentle devil's advocate, the man in the black booth, the man with no childhood, no sex drive, no hair on his chin, no intentions. Curiosity may or may not have killed a few cats; it certainly is not enough, in the end, to keep people alive. Survival has to involve something that at least approximates love, and whatever that is, it is not easy or amenable. It comes neither in pieces nor in one fell swoop. Rufus takes blood every time I see him, and I from him. We do not need more words, only more time to consider the ones we've already flung at one another.

"What are you recuperating from?" I ask Anthony softly.

"Call it whatever you like. A crisis, an illness. A lover spurned. A razor blade misused. Avery found me in my room. He bound me up and took me to the hospital. Afterwards, he sat with me out on the stoop and checked my arms, every night until he died. He was my healer, the man on the stoop. I prayed for him when he was on the road. Now, I feel shaky some days."

I cannot touch Avery, so I say, "I'm sorry."

"If he'd known the real truth about me," Anthony says, taking the last sip of his water, "he probably would have let me bleed."

"Esther would've mopped you up," I say.

"She wanted to find me a nice girl," Anthony says.

"Not really," I say. I take the photograph out of the pocket of my dress and hand it to Anthony. He looks at it silently, without expression. "That was my father," he says. "In Italy. His family moved here soon after. My grandfather died when I was four. After that, everything changed." Anthony's hand shakes ever so slightly as he slides the photograph into his shirt pocket, more like a shiver. We sit in silence on Esther's sofa. What Esther thought we might offer one another, what we once shared—bits and pieces of the Brubakers—their food, their conversation, their comfort, is gone. Anthony rises, uncomfortable as guest, cold without hot tea. He must be going. It is Wednesday, 4:30, and Meryl will be coming soon. Meryl is a botanist. I might like her, scientist to scientist. She's bringing an herb-and-shrub cure for his sinuses.

When Anthony's gone, I turn on Esther's TV and sit back down onto the couch with the seagull bone and Esther's star box. A woman on "Merv" has proof there is life after death. Sure enough, the couch pillows sink low and Esther is suddenly beside me.

"Turn to Channel 5, Elaine," she says. "It's a big day on 'Eden's End.' " Lo and behold, Deidre has just found out her husband's brother is the father of her sister's baby and her mother's lover to boot, and knowing Deidre, Esther says, one of them will be dead or crippled or in a coma before the week is through. I flip back to "Merv," and look in the star recipe box under G for Griffin, to see what Merv may have had to offer Esther. Under G, there is only Jane Goodall's Banana Delight.

"Oh, come on," I tell Esther. "It's got to be a gimmick. Jane Goodall would never write on a recipe card from her hut in Africa, an ape at each side, *Dear CBS: Peel three bananas; rub together two sticks.*"

"Don't be such a cynic, dear," Esther says. "They're people, just like you and me. Don't you think Jane Goodall ever had bad dreams in that hut, a craving for peanut butter, a hankering for 'I Love Lucy' any regrets at all?"

Esther takes out her knitting needles. I lean my head back and close my eyes. I smell Lucille Ball's Fried Halibut Supreme and am suddenly starving. But it is not quite dinnertime, not yet time to do anything but sit beside Esther in the musty twilight and think—think lascivious and murderous thoughts with Deidre—plot, plan, keep busy, eyes wide, pulses, thumping, chase Anthony to the health food store, wolf down the pack of oyster crackers I save from lunch, push Rufus back into that supply closet and lock the door.

The woman on "Merv" swears she was a reptile in another life, eons ago, when the dinosaurs lumbered and ice masses flowed. She ate leaves and bugs. To this day, she is a protein lover, a big woman. Life as a dinosaur was better. She had a new lover every year, and no taxes. The children left the nest early. There was only hot and cold, big and small. Not good or bad, no deadlines, no PMS, no addictions, TV, no offense, Merv. Merv laughs into his doubling chin. Esther's knitting needles click. By five o'clock, I'm dozing, the TV murmurs turning to the chatter of dreams.

I have only this life, I tell myself, fighting sleep, and I will not rest except for this one moment. Rufus knows about time. He tried to tell me with his middle finger. Figure, at the Institute for the Deaf, the echo of Billy's basketball flings itself against a gym wall, and the leisure hour is not due for another hour and a half.

Charles Baxter

KISS AWAY

The house had an upstairs sleeping porch, and she first saw the young man from up there, limping through the alley and carrying a ripped orange-and-yellow Chinese kite. He had a dog with him, also with a limp, and both the dog and the man had an air of scruffy unseriousness. From the look of it, no project these two got involved with could last longer than ten minutes. That was the first thing she liked about them.

Mid-morning, mid-week, mid-summer: even teenagers were working, and in this flat July heat no one with any sense was trying to fly kites. No one but a fool would fly a kite in this weather.

The young man threw the ball of string and the torn cloth into the alley's trash bin while the dog watched him. Then the dog sat down and with an expression of pained concentration scratched violently behind its ear. It looked around for something else to be interested in, barked at a cat on a window ledge, then gave up the effort and scratched its ear again.

From the upstairs sleeping porch, the young man looked exactly like the fool in the tarot pack—shaggy and loose-limbed, a songster at the edge of cliffs—and the dog looked like the fool's dog, a frisky yellow mutt. Dogs tended to like fools. They had an affinity. Fools always gave dogs plenty to do. Considering this, the woman near the window felt her heart pound twice. Her heart was precise. It was like a doorbell.

She, too, was unemployed. She had been out of college for a year, hadn't been able to find a job she could tolerate for more than a few days, and with the last of her savings had rented the second floor of this house in Minneapolis, which included an old-fashioned sleeping porch facing east with a sloping wood floor and white slatted blinds. She slept out here, and then in the mornings she sat in a hard-backed chair reading books from the library, drinking coffee, and listening to classical music on the public radio station. Right now they were playing the *Goyescas* of Enrique Granados. She was running out of money and trying to stay calm about it, and the music helped her. The music seemed to say that she could sit like this all morning, and no one would punish her. It was very Spanish.

She put on her shoes and threw her keys into the pocket of her jeans. She raised the slatted blinds. "Hey!" she yelled down into the alley.

"Hey, yourself," the young man yelled back. He smiled at her and squinted. Apparently he couldn't see her clearly. That was the second thing she liked about him.

"You can't throw that kite in there," she said. "That dumpster's only for people who live in this building." She shaded her eyes against the sun to see him better. The fool's dog was now standing and wagging its tail.

"Okay," he said. "I'll take it out," and when she told him not to and that she'd be down in a second and he should just wait there, she knew he would do what she asked. What she hadn't expected was that he would smile enormously at her and, when she appeared, give her a hug—they were strangers after all—right out of the blue, bizarre in its affection only because he didn't know her. She pushed him away but could not manage to get angry at him. Then she felt the dog's tongue slurping on her fingers, as if she'd spilled sauce on them and needed some cleaning.

He offered to buy her coffee, and he explained himself as they walked. He had once had good prospects, he said, and a future about which he could boast. He had been accepted into the

Wayne State University Medical School eighteen months ago but had come down with a combination of mononucleosis and bacterial pneumonia, and after recuperating, he had lost all his interest in great plans. The two illnesses—one virus and one bacteria—had taken the starch out of him, he said. He actually used expressions like that. He had a handsome face when you saw him up close, but as soon as you walked a few feet away something went wrong with his appearance; it degenerated somehow.

His name was Walton Tyner Ross, but he liked to be called Glaze because of his taste for doughnuts and for his habitual faraway expression. She didn't think someone whose nickname was Glaze was ever likely to become a successful practitioner of medicine, but in a certain light in the morning he was the finest thing she had seen in some time, especially when viewed from a few inches away, as they walked down Hennepin Avenue for breakfast.

Stopping under a tree that gave them both a moment of shade, he told her that if she wanted him to, he would show up regularly in the morning from now on. They would project themselves into the world, he said. She agreed, and on the next few mornings he appeared in the alley, his dog, Einstein, a few feet behind him. He called up to her, and the dog barked in chorus. She didn't think it was very gallant, his yelling up at her like that, but she had had her phone disconnected, and his passion for her company pleased and moved her.

They would walk down Hennepin Avenue past what he called The Church of the Holy Oil Can—because of its unbecoming disproportionate spire—to one of several greasy smoky restaurants with plate glass front windows and red-and-white checkered café curtains and front counters with stools. They always sat at the stools because Walton liked to watch the grill. The first time he bought Jodie a breakfast of scrambled eggs and a biscuit and orange juice. As the breakfast went on, he became more assertive. Outside, Einstein sat near a lamppost and watched the passing pedestrians with an expression of studied insolence.

Walton Tyner Ross—looking very much like a fool as he spilled his breakfast on his shirt—was a Roman candle of theories and ideas, and Jodie admired his idea that unemployment was like a virus. This virus was spreading and was contagious. The middle class was developing a positive taste for sloth. One person's unemployment could infect anyone else. "Take you," he said. "Take us." He wolfed down his toast slathered with jam. "We shouldn't feel guilty over not working. It's like a flu we've both got. We're infected with indifference. We didn't ask to get it. We inhaled it, or someone sneezed it on us."

"I don't know," she said. In front of her, the fry cook, a skinny African-American kid with half-steamed glasses, was sweating and wiping his brow on his shirtsleeve. The restaurant had the smell of morning ambition and resolution: coffee and cigarette smoke and maple syrup and cheap after-shave and hair spray. "Maybe you're right," she said. "But maybe we're both just kind of lazy. My sister says I'm lazy. I think it's more complicated than that. I once had plans, too," Jodie said, indicating with a flick of her wrist the small importance of these plans.

"Like what? What sort of plans?"

She was watching the fry cook and could hardly remember. "Oh," she said. "What I wanted was an office job. Keeping accounts and books. Something modest, a job that would leave the rest of my life alone and not eat up my resources." She waited a moment and touched her cheek with her finger. "In those days —I mean, a few months ago—my big project was love. I always wanted big love. I wanted a small job and huge love, like a bouquet. A bouquet so large you couldn't pick it up with a truck."

He nodded. "But so far all the love you've gotten has been small."

She looked at him and shrugged. "Maybe it's the times. Maybe I'm not pretty enough."

He leaned back and grinned at her to dispute this.

"No, I mean it," she said. "I can say all this to you because we don't know each other. Anyway, I was once almost engaged and everything. The guy was nice, and I guess he meant well, and my parents liked him, but almost as soon as he became serious about me, he was taking everything for granted. It's hard to explain," she said, pushing her scrambled eggs around on the plate and eyeing the ketchup bottle. "It wasn't his fault, exactly.

He couldn't do it. He couldn't play me." She gave up and poured some ketchup on her eggs. "You don't have to play me all the time, but if you're going to get married, you should be played *sometimes*. You should play him, he should play you. With him, there was no tune coming out of me. Just prose. You know, Walton," she said suddenly, "you sometimes look like the fool illustration on the tarot pack. No offense. You just do."

"Sure, I do," he said, and when he turned, she could see that his ears were pierced, two crease incisions on each lobe. "Okay, look. Here's what's going to happen. You and me, we're going to go out together in the morning and look for work. Then in the afternoon we'll drive around, a treasure hunt. Then I don't know what we're going to do in the evening. You can decide that." He explained that good fortune had put them together but that maybe they should at least try to fight the virus of sloth.

She noticed a fat balding man with hideous yellow-green eyes sitting on Walton's other side, staring at her. "Okay," she said. "I'll think about it."

The next morning, he was there in the hot dusty alley with his morning paper and his dog and his limp, and she came down to him without his having to call up to her. She wasn't totally presentable—she was wearing the same jeans as the day before, and a hand-me-down shirt from her sister—but she had put on a little silver bracelet for him and a glass pin in the shape of a palm tree near her collar, and as they walked to the restaurant he complimented her on her pleasant sexiness. He told her that in the moments that she had descended the back steps, his heart had been stirred. He was immune from self-embarrassment.

Limping with her toward the café, Einstein trotting behind them and snapping at flies, he said that today they would scan the want ads and would calculate their prospects. In the late morning they would go to his apartment—he had a phone—and make a few calls. They would be active and brisk and aggressive. Walking with him, enjoying his optimism, Jodie felt a passing impulse to take Walton's arm: he was gazing straight ahead, not glazed at all, and his shirtsleeves were rolled up, and she briefly admired his arms and the tinsel sunlight on the bright gold hairs.

In the restaurant, at the counter spotted with dried jam and brown gravy, where the waitress said, "Hiya, Glaze," and poured him his coffee without being asked, Jodie felt a pleasant shiver of jealousy. So many people seemed to know and to like this unremarkable but handsome limping guy; he, or something about him, was infectious. The thought occurred to her that he might change her life. By the time her Belgian waffle arrived, Jodie had circled six want ads for temp secretaries with extensive computer experience. She knew and understood computers backwards and forwards and hated them all, but they were like family members and she could work with them if she had to. She didn't really want the jobs—she wanted to sit on the sleeping porch and listen to the piano music of Granados and watch things going by in the alley—but the atmosphere of early morning ambition in the café was beginning to move her to action. She had even brought along a pen.

She felt a nudge in her ribs.

She turned to her left and saw the same fat balding man with horrible yellow-green eyes sitting next to her whom she had seen the day before. His breath smelled of gin and graham crackers. He was smiling at her unpleasantly. He was quite a package. " 'Scuse me, Miss," he said. "Hate to bother you. I'm short bus fare. You got seventy-five cents?" His speech wore the clothes of an obscure untraceable Eastern European accent.

"Sure," she said without thinking. She fished out three quarters from her pocket and gave the money to him. "Here." She turned back to the want ads.

"Oboy," he said, scooping it up. "Are you lucky."

"Am I?" she asked.

"You got that right," he said. He rose unsteadily and his yellow-green eyes leered at her, and for a moment Jodie thought that he might topple over, covering her underneath his untucked shirt and soiled beltless trousers. "I," he announced to the restaurant, although no one was paying any attention to him, "am the Genie of the Magic Lamp." No one even looked up.

The fat man bent down toward her. "Come back tomorrow," he said in a ghoulish whisper. Now he smelled of fireplace ash. "You get your prize." After a moment, he staggered out of the

restaurant in a series of forward-and-sideways lurching motions,
almost knocking over on the way a stainless steel coatrack. The
waitress behind the counter watched him go with an expression
on her face of irritated indifference made more explicit by her
hand on her hip and a pink bubble almost the color of blood
expanding from her lips; bubble gum was shockingly effective at
expressing contempt, Jodie thought. All the best waitresses
chewed gum.

"Who was that?" she asked Walton.

He shook his head like a spring-loaded toy on the back shelf
of a car. As usual, he smiled before answering. "I don't know,"
he said. "Some guy. Tad or Tadeusz or like that. He always asks
people for money. No one ever gives it. You're the first. The
absolute first. Come on. We're going to my place to make some
phone calls. Then we'll go on a treasure hunt."

When they came out to the sidewalk, Einstein cried and shivered with happiness to see them, barking twice as a greeting.
Walton loosened her from a bicycle stand to which she had been
tethered, while Jodie breathed in the hot summer air and said,
"By the way, Walton: where did you get that limp?"

He turned and smiled at her. Her heart started thumping
again. She couldn't imagine why men didn't smile more often
than they did. It was the most effective action they knew how to
take, but they were always amateurs at it. Jodie thought that
maybe she hadn't been smiled upon that much in her life. Perhaps that was it.

"Fascists," Walton said, getting up. "My dog and I fought the
fascists."

Walton's apartment was upstairs from an ice cream parlor, and
it smelled of fudge and heavy cream. Although the apartment
had a small study area with bookshelves and a desk, and a bedroom where the bed was neatly made and where even the dog's
rubber squeak toys were kept in the corner, the effect of the
neatness was offset by a quality of gloom characteristic of places
where sunlight had never penetrated. It was like Bluebeard's
castle. The only unobstructed windows faced north. All the
other windows faced brick or stone walls, so that no matter
what time of day it was, the lights had to be kept on.

They went through the circled want ads, made some telephone calls, and arranged for two interviews, one for Jodie as a receptionist at a discount brokerage house, and one for Walton as a shipping clerk.

Having finished that task, Jodie dropped herself onto one of the floor pillows and examined a photograph on the wall over the desk, showing a young couple, both smiling. Wearing a flowery summer dress, the woman sat on a swing, and the man stood behind her, about to give her a push.

"That's my father," Walton said, standing behind Jodie.

"It's your mother, too."

"I know it. I know it's my mother, too. But it's mostly my father. Maybe you'll meet him. He always likes to meet my girlfriends."

"I'm not your girlfriend, Walton," she said. "I hardly know you."

He was quiet for a moment. "Want a beer?" he asked. "For lunch?"

He said unemployed people should always seek out treasures and that was what they would do during the afternoon, but just as they were about to go out to his car, he fell asleep in his chair, his dog at his feet, her front paws crossed.

Jodie sat where she was for a moment, painfully resisting the impulse to go rummaging through Walton's medicine cabinet and desk and dresser drawers. Instead, she brought a chair over next to him, sat down on it, and studied his face. Although it wasn't an unusual face, at this distance certain features about it were certainly notable. The line where the beard began on his cheek—he was clean-shaven—was so straight that it seemed to have been implanted there with a ruler. He had two tiny, almost microscopic, pieces of dandruff in his eyebrows. His lashes were rather long, for a man. His lower lip was also rather full, but his upper lip was so small and flat at the bottom that you might not notice it unless you looked carefully. When he exhaled, his breath came in two puffs: it sounded like *hurr hurr*. He had a thin nose, and his left cheek appeared to have the remnant of an acne scar, a little blossom of reddening just beneath the skin like a truffle. With his head leaning forward, his hair in back fell halfway to his shoulders; these shoulders seemed to her to be about average width for a man of his height and weight. Even in sleep, his forehead was creased as if in thought. His hair had a wavy back and forth directionality, and it reminded Jodie of corrugated tin roofing. She found wavy hair mysterious; her own was quite straight. She reached up to touch his hair, being careful not to touch his scalp. That would wake him. She liked the feeling of his hair in her fingers. It was like managing a small profit after two quarters of losses.

She was sitting again on the floor pillow when he woke up five minutes later. He shook his head and rubbed his face with his hands. He looked over to where Jodie was sitting. "Hi," he said.

"Here's 'hi' comin' back at you," she said. She waved all the fingers of her right hand at him.

That evening she went to a pay telephone and called her older sister, the married and employed success story. Her older sister told Jodie to take her time, to buy some nice clothes on her credit card, and to watch and wait to see what would happen. Sit tight, she said. Jodie thought the advice was ironic because that kind of sitting was the only sort her sister knew how to do. She told Jodie to have her phone reconnected; it wouldn't cost that much, and after all, telephones were a necessity for a working girl in whom a man was taking an interest. She asked if Jodie needed a loan, and Jodie said no.

Her best friend gave Jodie the same advice, except with more happy laughter and enthusiasm. Wait and see, go for it, she said. What's the difference? It'll be fun either way. Come over. Let's talk.

Soon, Jodie said. We'll see each other soon.

Her dreams that night were packs of lies, lies piled on lies, an exhibit of lies. Mayhem, penises on parade, angels in seersucker suits, that sort of thing. She woke up on the sleeping porch ashamed of her unconscious life. She hated the vulgarity and silliness of her own dreams, their subtle unstated untruths.

· · ·

Her job interview was scheduled for eleven o'clock the following morning, and after Walton had called up to her and taken her to the café, she stared down into her third cup of coffee and considered how she might make the best impresson on her potential employers. She had worn a rather formal white ruffled blouse with the palm tree pin, and a dark blue skirt, and she had a semi-matching blue purse, at the sight of which Walton had announced that Jodie had "starched notions of elegance," a phrase he didn't care to explain. He told her that at the interview she should be eager and honest and self-possessed. "It's a brokerage house," he said. "They like possession in places like that, especially self-possession. If you're straightforward, they'll notice and take to you right away. Just be yourself, within limits."

But she wasn't convinced. At the moment, the idea of drifting like a broken twig on the surface of a muddy river was much more appealing. All through college she had worked at a clothing store as a checkout clerk, and the experience had filled her with bitter wisdom about the compromises of tedium and the hard bloody edge of necessity. She had had a gun pointed at her during a holdup her fourth day on the job. On two other occasions, the assistant manager had propositioned her in the stockroom. When she turned him down, she expected to be fired, but for some reason she had been kept on.

"There you are." A voice: her left ear: a phlegm rumble.

Jodie turned on her stool and saw the fat man with yellow-green eyes staring at her. "Yes," she said.

"I hadda get things in order," he said, grinning and snorting. He pulled out a handkerchief speckled with excretions and blew his nose into it. "I hadda get my ducks in a row. So. Here we are again. What's your three wishes?"

"Excuse me?"

"Just ignore the guy," Walton said, pouring some cream into his coffee. "Just ignore the guy."

"If I was you," the fat man said, "I'd ignore *him*. They don't call him Glaze for nothing. So what's your three wishes? I am the Genie of the Magic Lamp, like I said. You did me a favor, I do you a favor." Jodie noticed that the fat man's voice was hollow, as if it had emerged out of an echo chamber. Also, she had the momentary perception that the fat man's limbs were attached to the rest of his body with safety pins.

"I don't have three wishes," Jodie said, studying her coffee cup.

"Everybody's got three wishes," the fat man said. "There's nobody on Earth that doesn't have three wishes."

"Listen, Tad," Walton said, turning himself toward the fat man and spreading himself a bit wider at the shoulders; he was beginning, Jodie noticed, a slow threatening male dancelike sway back and forth, the formal prelude to a fight. "Leave the lady alone."

"All I'm asking her for is three wishes," the fat man said. "That's not much." He ran his dirty fingers through his thinning hair. "You can whisper them if you want," he said. "There's some people that prefer that."

"All right, all right," Jodie said. She leaned toward him and lowered her voice. She just wanted to get this over with. She wanted to be left in peace, or at least left in peace with Walton. She wanted to finish her coffee. "I want a job," she said softly, so that only the fat man could hear, "and I want that guy sitting next to me to love me, and I'd like a better radio when I listen to music in the morning."

"*That's it?*" The fat man stood up, a look of outrage on his face. "I give you three wishes and you kiss them away like that? What's the matter with you? Give an American three wishes, and what do they do? Kiss them away! That's the trouble with this country. No imagination! All right, lady, you got it." And he dropped his dirty handkerchief in her lap. When she picked it up to remove it, she felt something travel up her arm—the electricity of disgust. The fat man rose and waddled out of the restaurant.

"What was that?" Jodie said. She was shaking.

"That," Walton said, "was a typical incident at Clara's Country Kitchen Café. The last time Tad gave someone three wishes, it was because someone'd bought him a cup of coffee, and a tornado hit the lucky guy's garage a couple of weeks later. That's the kind of luck Tad passes on. What'd you ask for?"

She turned to look out the front plate glass window and saw Walton's dog gazing straight back at her.

"I asked for a job, and a better radio, and a million dollars."

"Then what was all that stuff about 'kiss away'?"

"I don't think he liked the radio part."

"No, I know," Walton said. "It's that Rolling Stones tune. It's on an early album. *Gimme Shelter*, I think." He raised his head to sing.

> "*Love, sister, is just a kiss away,*
> *Kiss away, kiss away, kiss away.*"

"I don't think that's what he meant," Jodie said.

Walton leaned forward and gave her a little peck on the cheek. "Who knows?" he said. "Maybe it was. Anyhow, just think of him as a placebo-person. He doesn't grant you the wish, but he could put you in the right frame of mind."

"I liked how you defended me," Jodie said. "Getting all male and everything."

"No problem," Walton said. "I like fights."

She thought that she had interviewed well, but she wasn't offered the job she had applied for that day. They called her a week later—she had finally had a phone installed—and told her that they had given the position to someone else but that they had been impressed by her qualities and might call her again soon if another position opened up. Having expected the woman who was relaying this displeasing information to sound formal and officious, Jodie was surprised that she was warm, almost friendly. Jodie felt that she herself had very poor judgment about people's voices in telephone conversations and was often given to embarrassed speechless pauses.

She and Walton continued their job-and-treasure hunt, and it was Walton who found a job first, at the loading dock of a retailer in the suburbs, a twenty-four hour discount store, known internationally for shoddy merchandise. The job went from midnight to eight a.m.

She thought he wasn't quite physically robust enough for such work, but he claimed that he was stronger than he appeared. "It's all down here," he said, pointing to his lower back. "This is where you need it."

She didn't ask him what he was referring to, the muscles or the vertebrae or the cartilage. She had never seen his lower back. On the passenger side of his car, she considered the swinging fuzzy dice and the intricately woven twigs of a bird's nest perched on the dashboard as he drove her to her various job interviews. His conversation was sprinkled with references to local geology, and puzzles in physics and math. He was interested in most observable phenomena, and the car reflected his interests. She liked this car. She had become accustomed to its ratty disarray and to the happy panting of Einstein, who always sat in the backseat, monitoring other dogs in other cars at intersections.

At one job interview in a glass building so sterile she thought she should wear surgery-room snoods over her shoes, she was asked about her computer skills; at another, about what hobbies she liked to fill her spare time. She didn't think that the personnel director had any business asking her such questions and said so. He said it *was* indeed his business. She didn't get that job. But at a wholesale supplier of office furniture and stationery, she was offered a position on the spot by a man whose suit was so wrinkled that it was prideful and emblematic. As it turned out, he owned the business. She was being asked to help them work on a program for inventory control. She would have other tasks. She sighed—those fucking computers again—but she took what they offered her. If she hadn't met Walton, if Walton and Einstein hadn't escorted her to the interview, she wouldn't have.

To celebrate, she and Walton decided to escape the August heat by hiking down Minnehaha Creek to its mouth at the Mississippi River across from Saint Paul. He didn't have to be at work for another four hours. Walton had brought his fishing pole and tackle box, and while he cast his line into the water, his dog sitting behind him in the shade of a gnarled cottonwood, Jodie walked down the river, looking, but not looking for anything, exactly, just looking without a goal, for which she felt she had a talent. She found a bowling ball in good condition and several unrusting beer cans that she did not touch.

She walked back along the river to Walton, carrying the bowling ball. On her face she had constructed an expression of delight. She was feeling hot and momentarily beautiful.

"See what I've found?" She hoisted up the ball.

"Hey, great," he said, casting her a smile. "See what I've caught?" And he held up an imaginary line of invisible prize-winning fish.

"Congratulations," she said. She saw that he was studying her with an expression that mixed longing and appreciation. She knew that, when he had thought she wouldn't notice, he had been gazing at her in a prolonged way. From the middle of the river came the double blast of a boat horn. Another boat passed, pulling a water-skier with a strangely unhappy look on her face. The clock stopped; the moment paused: when he said he loved her, that he was so lovesick for her that he couldn't finish his meals, she almost didn't hear it. In the midst of this heat and distraction, there he was, five feet away, the sweat standing out on his forehead and the waves from the Mississippi splashing periodically at their feet. He held out a white rose to her; God knows where he got it from. With the air infected with haze and choler, the cold river water felt wonderful, an elemental relief. She threw the bowling ball out as far she she could into the river and rushed forward slowly in his direction, taking her time. When he kissed her, she put her hands in his hair—she was as tall as he was—and the thought occurred to her that if you waited long enough, the things you wanted to do in secret could be done consciously, overtly, in public.

"Happy days," she said, taking a breath. "Happy days."

He had wanted to come up to her apartment, and this time she let him. She made him some iced tea, but when she came out to her tiny living room, Walton was still standing up, pretending to count his change. Einstein had found a corner where she was panting with her eyes closed. Jodie handed Walton the glass of iced tea, but instead of drinking from it, he raised the cold glass to her forehead. She was trembling and doing her level best not to show it. Back and forth the glass rolled on her skin. "Please," he said.

She took him by the hand and led him out onto the sleeping porch. His body was cool everywhere except for his face, where the skin was feverish. But she herself was quite warm, and he warmed her up further, heated her up to just under a boil, and when she called out, not knowing whom she was calling for, she discovered that it was Walton's name she was calling. What she hadn't considered until now was that fools probably made the best lovers. They were devotees of passing pleasures, connoisseurs of them, and this, being the best of the passing pleasures, was the one at which they were most adept. Or maybe this particular skill was characteristic only of Walton. "Look at me," she said, as she was about to come, and he looked up at her with that same grin on his face, pleased as could be.

"So. Happy ever after?"

Walton was asleep after a night's work, and Jodie had gone down to Clara's Country Kitchen Café by herself. This morning the fat man with yellow-green eyes was full of mirthless merriment, and he seemed to be spilling over the counter stool on all sides. If anything, he was twice as big as before. Jodie had been in the middle of her second cup of coffee and her scrambled eggs with ketchup when he sat down next to her. It was hard to imagine someone who could be more deliberately disgusting than this gentleman. He had a rare talent, Jodie thought, for inspiring revulsion, as if the possible images of the Family of Humankind did not somehow include him. He sat there shoveling an omelet and sausages into his mouth, only occasionally chewing.

"Happy enough," she said.

He nodded and appeared to snort. " 'Happy enough.' " Sounds of swallowing and digestion made their way toward her. "I give you a wish and you ask for a radio. There you have it." His accent was even more obscure and curious this morning.

"Where are you from?" Jodie asked. She had to angle her left leg away from his because his took up so much space under the counter. "You're not from here."

"No," he said. "I'm not really from anywhere. I was imported from Venice. A beautiful city, Venice. And aromatic. You ever been there?"

"Yes," she said, although she had not been. But she did love history and all its stories. "Lagoons, the Bridge of Sighs, and typhoid. Yeah, I've been there." She put her money down on the counter, and when she stood up, she felt a faint throbbing, almost a soreness but not quite that, Walton's desire, his physical trace, still inside her. "I have to go."

He resumed eating. "You didn't even thank me," the fat man said. "You smell of love and you didn't even thank me."

"All right. Thank you." She was hurrying out.

When she saw him in the mirror behind the cash register, he was tipping an imaginary hat. "You're welcome," she heard him say, before she pushed herself out into the morning's unfocused August oppression. She had seen some quality behind his yellow-green eyes, a moment's flash, and she didn't know what to call it, whatever it was being a mixture of malice and sorrow and wisdom; but as soon as she was out on the sidewalk, under the café's faded orange awning, she thought about Walton, how she wanted to see him immediately and touch him, and she headed for the crosswalk, all thoughts of the fat man dispersing and vanishing like smoke.

On the way back, she saw a thimble in the gutter and deposited it in her purse; and then a fountain pen, left on the brick ledge of a storefront income tax service, gleamed toward her in the cottony hazy heat, and she took that, too. Walton had given her the habit of appreciating foundlings. When she walked onto the sleeping porch, she took off her shoes. She still felt ceremonial with him. She gave him her treasures, and he rewarded her, as she thought he might. Although their time was short, she had her desire, and then she had to dress herself again and catch the bus. Einstein groaned in her sleep as Jodie passed her in the hallway. The dog, Jodie thought, was probably jealous.

A woman in love is usually visible on a city bus. Jodie hummed, smiled privately, and looked at everyone else with politeness but no special interest. Her love was a power that could attract and charm. She had luck; everyone could see it.

Through the window she spotted a flock of geese in a V-pattern flying east and then suddenly veering south.

From time to time, at work—where she was bringing people rapidly into her orbit thanks to her aura of good fortune—she

would think of her happiness and try to hide it. She would remember not to speak of it, good luck having a tendency to turn
to its opposite when spoken of.

She considered the future with joyful wonderment and split-
seconds of apprehension. She called her sister and her mother,
both of whom wanted to meet Walton as soon as possible. Her
best friend, Marge, came over one stormy afternoon in a visit of
planned spontaneity and was so impressed by Walton Tyner
Ross that she took off her glasses and sang for him, thunder and
lightning crashing outside and the electric lights flickering, before going home. She'd once been a vocalist in a band called
Leaping Salmon. It was her only life-adventure, and she always
mentioned it in conversations to people she had just met and
wanted to impress.

I have a lover, Jodie thought. Most people have lovers without
paying any attention to the matter. They don't care; they don't
even notice. But it's what I want, and it's what I have. Odd: this
luck.

She couldn't wait to see him when she returned from work.
Every time she came into the room, his face seemed reanimated.
Sometimes, just thinking about him, she could feel a tightening,
a prickling, all over her body. She was so in love and her skin so
sensitive that she had to wear soft clothes. The whole enterprise
of love, now that she had it, seemed a bit old-fashioned and
retrograde, and she was half-amused by her infatuation with
Walton, and his with her, but it alarmed her, too. When she was
alarmed, she took down the tarot pack.

Using the Celtic method of divination in the book of instructions, she would set down the cards.

This covers me.

This crosses me.

This crowns me, this is beneath me, this is behind me, this is
before me, this is myself.

These are my hopes and fears.

The cards kept turning up peculiarly. Instead of the cards
promising blessings and fruitfulness, she found herself staring at
the autumn and winter cards, the coins and the swords. This is
before me: the nine of swords, whose illustration is that of a
woman waking at night with her face in her hands.

She had also been unnerved by the repeated appearance of the Chariot in reverse, a sign described in the guidebooks as "failure in carrying out a project, riot, litigation."

Propped up in her living room chair, she had been dozing after dinner when the phone rang. She answered it in a stupor. She barely managed a whispered "Hello." The ringing of a telephone in the midst of sleep had always caused her heart to clutch.

She could make out the voice, but it seemed to come from the tomb, it was so faint. It belonged to a woman and it had some business to transact, but Jodie couldn't make out what the business was. "What?" she asked. "What did you say?"

"I said we should talk," the woman told her in a voice barely above a whisper, but still rich in wounded private authority. "We could meet. I know I shouldn't intrude like this, but I feel that I could tell you things. About Glaze. I know you know him."

"Who are you? Are you seeing him?"

"Oh no no no," the woman said. "It isn't that." Then she said her name was Glynnis or Glenna—something odd and possibly resistant to spelling. "You don't know anything about him, do you?" The woman waited a moment. "His past, I mean."

"Not much," Jodie admitted.

"I can fill you in. Look," she said, "I hate to do this, I hate sounding like this and I hate being like this, but I just think there are some facts you should know. These are facts I have. I'm just . . . I don't know what I am. Maybe I'm just trying to help."

"All right," Jodie said. She uncrossed her legs and put her feet on the floor and tried to clear her mind. "I get off work at five. The office is near downtown." She named a bar where her friends sometimes went in the late afternoons.

"Oh, there?" the woman asked, her voice rising with just a trace of curiosity, or, it might be, pity. "It's . . . well, it's not easy for me to take." When Jodie didn't respond, the woman said, "The smoke in there makes me cough. I have allergies. Quite a few allergies." She suggested another restaurant, an expensive outdoor-and-indoor Italian place with wrought iron furniture on the terrace and its name above the door in leaded glass. Jodie agreed to it, although she hadn't liked it the one

time she'd been there. However, she didn't want to prolong
these negotiations for another minute. "And don't tell Glaze I
called," the woman said.

When Jodie hung up, she felt so uneasy that she began to
chew her thumbnail. Until she glanced up and saw her reflection in a window, she wasn't aware that she was falling back
into that old, bad habit.

She was seated in what she considered a good spot near a window in the non-smoking section when the woman entered the
restaurant and was directed by the headwaiter in Jodie's direction. She was twelve minutes late. As the woman made her
progress toward the table, Jodie attempted a smile. The stranger
was pregnant and was walking with a slightly prideful sway, as
if she herself were the china shop. Although she was sporting a
beautiful watercolor-hued peacock blue maternity blouse, she
was also wearing shorts and sandals, apparently to show off her
legs. The ensemble didn't quite fit together, but it compelled
attention. Her hair was carefully messed up, and she wore two
opal earrings that went with the blouse, and she was pretty
enough, but it was the sort of prettiness that Jodie distrusted
because there was nothing friendly about it, nothing settled or
calm. She was the sort of woman whom other women instinctively didn't like. She looked like an aging groupie, and she had
the deadest eyes Jodie had ever seen, pale gray and icy.

"You must be Jodie," the woman said, putting one hand over
her stomach and thrusting the other hand out. "I'm Gleinya
Roberts." She laughed twice, as if her name was, itself, a witty
remark. When she stopped laughing, her mouth stayed open,
and her face froze momentarily, as more soundless laughter continued to emerge from her. Jodie found everything about her
disconcerting, though she couldn't say why. "May I sit down?"
the woman asked.

Feeling that she had been indeliberately rude, Jodie nodded
and waved her hand toward the chair with the good view. The
question had struck her as either preposterous or injured, and
because she felt off-balance, she didn't remember to introduce
herself until the right moment had passed. "I'm Jodie Sklar,"
she said.

"Well, I know *that*," Gleinya Roberts said, settling herself delicately into her chair. "You must be wondering if this baby is Glaze's, and I can assure you that it's not," she said with an absolutely frozen half-grin, a grin that seemed preserved in ice. The thought of the baby's father hadn't occurred to Jodie. "I'm in my fifth month," the woman continued, "and the Little Furnace is certainly heating me up these days. Bad timing! It's much better to be pregnant in Minnesota in the winter. You can keep yourself warm that way. You don't have any children yourself, Jodie, do you?"

Jodie was so taken aback by the woman's prying and familiarity that she just smiled and shook her head. All the same, she felt it was time to establish some boundaries. "No, not yet," she said. "Maybe someday." She paused for a second to take a psychic breath and then said, "You know, I'm pleased to meet you and everything, but you must know that I'm curious about why you're here. Why'd you call me?"

"Oh, in a minute, in a minute," Gleinya Roberts said, tipping her head and staring with her dead eyes at Jodie's hair. "I just wanted to establish a friendly basis." She opened her mouth and her face froze again as soundless laughter rattled its way in Jodie's direction. "Jodie, I just can't take my eyes off your hair. You have such beautiful black hair. Men must love it. Where do you get it from?"

"Well," Jodie said, obscurely feeling that it was none of the woman's business, "my father had dark hair. It was quite glossy. It shone sometimes."

"Oh," the woman said. "I don't think women get their hair from their fathers. I don't think that's where that gene comes from. It's the mother, I believe. I'm a zoologist, an ornithologist, actually, so I'm not up on hair. But I do know you don't get much from your father except trouble. Sklar. Isn't that a Jewish name? Jewish people have such beautiful black hair."

Before Jodie could answer, the waitress appeared and asked for their order. Gleinya Roberts reached for the menu, and while Jodie ordered a beer, the woman opposite her—Jodie could see the traffic outside reflected on the woman's reading glasses—scanned the bill of fare with eyes slitted with skepticism and one eyebrow partially raised. "I'd like wine," Gleinya Roberts said, and just as the waitress was about to ask what kind, she continued, "but I can't have any because of the baby. What I would like is sparkling water but with no flavoring, no ice, and no sliced lemon or lime, please." The waitress wrote this down. "Are you ordering anything to eat?" Gleinya Roberts asked Jodie. "I am. Perhaps a salad. Do your salads have croutons?" The waitress said that they did. "Well, please take them out for me. I can't eat them. They're treated." She asked for the Caesar salad, explaining that she positively lived on Caesar salad these days. "But no additives of any kind, please," she said, after the waitress had already turned to leave. Apparently the waitress hadn't heard because she didn't stop or turn around. If Jodie had been that waitress, she believed that she wouldn't have turned around, either. "I'm afraid I'm terribly picky," Gleinya Roberts announced. "You have to be, these days. It's the Age of Additives."

"I eat anything," Jodie said, rather aggressively. "I've always eaten anything." Gleinya Roberts patted her stomach and smiled sadly at Jodie but said nothing. "Now, Gleinya," she pressed on, "perhaps you can tell me why we're here."

Gleinya held her left hand out with the fingers straight and examined her wedding ring. It was a quick gesture but it was not lost on Jodie. "It's about Glaze, of course," she said. "Maybe you can guess that I used to be with him. It ended two years ago, but we still talk from time to time." She took a long sip of her water, and while she did, Jodie allowed herself to wonder who called whom. And when: it was probably late at night. "Anyway," she went on, "that's how I know about you." She put down her water glass and smiled unpleasantly. "That's how I know about your sleeping porch. He's terribly in love with you." she said. "You're just *all* he thinks about."

Jodie moved back in her chair, sat up straight, and said, "He's a wonderful guy."

"Yes," the other woman said, rather slowly, to affirm that Jodie had said what she had in fact said but not to agree to it. Suddenly, and quite unexpectedly, Gleinya Roberts half stood up, then sat down again and settled herself, flinging her elbows out, and before Jodie could ask why she had done so, though at this point the inquiry did seem rather pointless, Gleinya Roberts said, "It's so hard to get comfortable in your second term. All those little infant kicks." She patted her stomach again.

"They don't seem to have hurt you, exactly," Jodie said.

"No, but you have to be careful." She touched the base of her neck with the third finger of her right hand, tapping the skin thoughtfully. "You have to try to keep your looks up. You have to try to keep yourself up. Of course, my husband, Jerry, says I'm still pretty, 'prettier than ever,' he says, a sweet lie, though I don't mind hearing it. He just says that to please me. It's just a love-lie. Still, I try to believe him when he says those things."

I bet you do, Jodie thought. I bet it's no effort at all. "You were going to tell me about Walton."

"Yes, I was," she said. The waitress reappeared, placed Jodie's glass of beer, gowned in frost, in front of her, and Jodie took a long comforting gulp from it. All at once Gleinya Roberts' voice changed, going up half an octave. She had leaned forward, and her face was inflected with old grudges and hatreds. "Jodie," she said, "I have to warn you. I just have to do this, woman to woman. I want you to protect yourself. I know it's suspicious, coming from an old girlfriend like this, and I know that it must look like sour grapes, but I have to tell you that what I'm saying is true, and I wouldn't say it unless I was worried for your sake, unless I was *afraid*. He likes fights. He likes fighting. You've seen his limp, haven't you?"

Jodie swallowed but could not bring herself to nod.

"He got it in a bar fight. Somebody kicked him in the ankle and shattered the bone. I mean, that's all right, men get into fights, but what you have to know is that he used to beat *me* up. He'd get drunk and coked up and start in on me. Sometimes he did it carefully so it wouldn't show—"

"—He doesn't drink," Jodie said, her mouth instantly dry.

"Maybe he doesn't drink *now*," Gleinya Roberts said, smiling for a microsecond and patting the tablecloth with little grace-note gestures. "But he has and probably will again. His sweet side is so sweet that it's hard to figure the other side. He just explodes. It's like the Fourth of July, except in a nightmare. And it's abusive. It's so abusive. He waits until you're really, really happy, and then he explodes. Once, months and months and months ago, I told him that someday I wanted to go out to the West Coast and sit on the banks of the Pacific Ocean and go whale watching. You know, see the whales spouting by, on their migrations. We both had a vacation around the same time—"

"—I don't think it's the 'banks' of the Pacific Ocean. That's for rivers. I think you mean 'shore,' " Jodie said.

Gleinya Roberts shrugged. "All right. 'Shore.' Anyway, we both had a vacation around the same time, and we drove out there . . . no, we flew . . . and then we rented a car. . . ."

She put her hand over her mouth, appearing to remember, but instead her eyes began to fill with tears, and at that moment Jodie felt a conviction as powerful as any that she had ever experienced, that this woman was lying, and was still probably in love with Walton.

"We rented a car," she was saying, "and we drove up from San Francisco toward Arcata, along there, along that coast. There are redwood forests a few miles back from the coastline, those big old trees. We'd stay in motels, and I'd make a picnic in the morning, and we'd go out, and Glaze would start drinking after breakfast, and by mid-afternoon he'd be silent and surly—he'd stop speaking to me—and by the time we got back to our motel, he'd be muttering, and I'd try to talk about what we had seen that day. I mean usually when you go whale watching there aren't any whales. But there are always seals. You can hear the seals barking. I'd ask him if he didn't think the cliffs were beautiful or the wildflowers or the birds or whatever I had pointed out to him. But I always said something wrong. Something that was like a lighted match. And he'd blow up. And he'd start in on me. Have you even been hit in the face?"

Jodie had turned so that she could see the sidewalk through the window. She was getting herself ready. It wasn't going to take much more.

"It comes out of nowhere," Gleinya Roberts was saying, "and it takes you by surprise so much that you're not ready for it when the second one arrives. The first blow gives permission to the second blow. The first beating gives permission to the second beating, and the third, and the fourth. You don't expect it. Why should you? He broke two of my ribs. I had a shoulder separation from him. He got very practiced in the ways of apology and remorse. He has a genius for remorse. You don't believe me, do you?"

Jodie said nothing.

"I don't blame you. I wouldn't believe it either. I thought he

was Prince Charming, too. Just like you. Believe me, I had to
kiss a lot of frogs before I found the right guy. But he won't tell
you. *He* won't tell you about himself," she repeated. "Ask his
father, though. His father will tell you. Well maybe he'll tell you.
You haven't met his father, have you?"

She speared a piece of her Caesar salad, chewed thoughtfully,
then put down her fork.

"A woman has to tell another woman," she said, "in the case
of a man like this. I wanted to help you. I wouldn't want you to
be on daytime TV, one of those afternoon talk shows, in a body
cast on stage, warning other women about men like this. Jodie,
you can look in my eyes and see that what I'm telling you is
true."

Jodie looked. The eyes she saw were gray and blank, and for a
moment they reminded her of the blankness of the surface of the
ocean, and then the waters parted, and she saw a seemingly
endless landscape of rancor, a desert of gray rocks and black
ashy flowers. Demons lived there. Then, just as quickly as it had
appeared, the desert was covered over again, and Jodie knew
that she had been right not to believe her.

"You're lying to me," Jodie said. She hadn't meant to say it,
only to think it, but it had come out, and there it was.

Gleinya Roberts nodded, acknowledging her own implausibility. "You're just denying. You're gaga over him. Just as I was.
Sunk in adoration. That sweet side. Playing the fool."

"What?"

"I said, 'Playing the fool.' "

"I thought that was what you said."

Jodie, her head buzzing, and most of her cells on fire, found
herself standing up. "You come in here," she said, "with your
trophy wedding ring, and your trophy pregnancy, and your
husband who says you're still pretty, and you tell me this, about
Walton, spoiling the first happiness I've had in I don't know
how long?" Gleinya Roberts tilted her head, considering this
accusation. Her face was unaccountably radiant. "I don't have to
listen to you," Jodie said. "I don't have to listen to *this*."

Her hands shaking, she reached into her purse for some
money for the beer, and she heard Gleinya Roberts say, "Oh, I'll
pay for it," while Jodie found a ten dollar bill and flung it on the

table. She saw that Gleinya Roberts' face was paralyzed into that attitude of soundless laughter—maybe it was just strain—and Jodie was stricken to see that the woman's teeth were perfect and white and symmetrical, and her tongue—her tongue!—was dark red and sensual. She leaned forward to tip over her beer in Gleinya Roberts' direction, careful to give the action the clear appearance of accident.

What was left of the beer made its dull way over to the other side of the table.

"He's beautiful," Jodie said quietly, as the other woman gathered the cloth napkins to sop up the beer, "and he makes sense to me, and I don't have to listen to you now."

"No, you don't," she said. "You go live with Glaze. Glaze is like the kea. A beautiful bright green New Zealand bird. It's known for its playfulness and mischievousness. But it's a sheep-killer and will pick out their eyes. Just remember the kea. And take this." From somewhere underneath the table she grasped for and then handed Jodie an audio cassette. "It's a predator tape. Used for attracting hawks and coyotes. It used to be his favorite listening. It fascinated him. It'll surprise you. Women don't know about men. Men don't let them."

Jodie had taken the tape, but she was now halfway out of the restaurant. Still, she heard behind her that voice coming after her. "Men don't want us to know. Jodie, they don't!"

In a purely distanced and distracted state she took a bus over to Minnehaha Creek and walked down the path alongside the flowing waters to the bank of the Mississippi River. The air smelled rotten and dreary. Underneath a bush she found two bottle caps and a tuna fish can. She left them there.

Sitting on the bus toward home, she tried to lean into the love she felt for Walton, and the love he said he felt for her, but instead of solid ground and rock just underneath the soil, and rock cliffs that comprised a wall where a human being could prop herself and stand, there was nothing: stone gave way to sand, and sand gave way to water, and the water drained away into darkness and emptiness. Into this emptiness, from a broken crack in a wall she could not see, poured violence: the violence of the kea, Walton's violence, Gleinya Roberts' violence, and finally her own. She traced every inch of her consciousness for a place on which she might set her foot against doubt, and she could not find it. Inside her was the impulse, as clear as blue sky on a fine summer morning, to acquire a pistol and shoot Gleinya Roberts through her heart. But it was not a solution, though for a split-second it felt like one; it was instead the problem giving rebirth to itself. Her mind raced through the maze she had constructed, that Gleinya Roberts had constructed for her, and she could not find the way in or the way out.

Gleinya Roberts had lied to her. Of that she was certain.

But it didn't matter. She was in fear of being struck. Although she had never been beaten by anyone, ever, in her life, the prospect frightened her so deeply that she felt parts of herself—a portion here, a tiny measure of her soul there—turning to stone. Other women might not be frightened. Others were beaten and survived. But she was not them; she was herself, a woman mortally afraid of being violated.

Three blocks from her apartment with the upstairs sleeping porch, she bought, in a drugstore, a better radio with a cassette player in it, and she took it with her, upstairs; and in the living room she plugged it in and placed it on the coffee table, next to Walton's latest found treasures: a pleasantly shaped rock with streaks of red, probably jasper; a squirt gun; and a little ring through which was placed a ballpoint pen.

She dropped the predator tape Gleinya Roberts had given her into the machine, and she pushed the PLAY button.

From the speaker came the scream of a rabbit. Whoever had made this tape had probably snapped the serrated metal jaws of a trap on the rabbit's leg and then turned on the recorder. It wasn't a tape loop: the rabbit's screams were varied, no two alike. Although the screams had a certain sameness, the clarifying monotony of terror, there was a range of internal variety. Terror gave way to pain, pain made room for terror. The soul of the animal was audibly ripped apart, and out of its mouth came this shrieking. Jodie felt herself getting sick and dizzy. The screams continued. They went on and on. In the forests of the night these screams rose with predictable regularity once darkness fell. Though wordless, they had supreme eloquence and a

huge claim upon truth. Jodie was weeping now, her palms to
her eyes, the heels of her hands dug into her cheekbones. The
screams did not cease. They rose in frequency and intensity. The
tape almost academically laid out at disarming length the necessity of terror. All things innocent and forsaken had their moment of expression, as the strong, following their nature,
crushed themselves into their prey but not before enjoying the
nonmusical noises coming out of the mouths of their victims,
the grunts and screams fearfully symmetric, sickening, following an obscure law, a pattern of sorts. Still it went on, this
bloody fluting. Apparently it was not to be stopped.

Jodie reached out and pressed the PAUSE button. She was shaking now, shivering. She felt herself dying, and when she looked
up, she saw Walton standing near the door—he had a key by
now—with Einstein wagging her tail next to him, and he was
carrying his daily gift, this time a birdhouse, and he said, "She
found you, didn't she?"

He puts down the birdhouse and squats near her. From this
position, he drops to his knees. Kneeling before her, he tries to
smile, and his eyes have that pleasant fool quality they have
always had, and his dog Einstein pants behind him, like a back-
up singer emphasizing and reasserting that what the lead singer
has just said is perfectly true. Walton's hands start at her hair
and then slowly descend to her shoulders and arms. Before she
can stop him, he has taken her into his embrace.

He is murmuring. Yes, he knew Gleinya Roberts, and, yes,
they did own a predator tape *she* had found somewhere, but, no,
he did not listen to it more than once. Yes, he had lived with her
for a while, but she was insane, and insanely jealous, hysterical,
actually, and given to lies and lying, habitual lies, lies about
whether the milk was spoiled, lies about how many stamps
were still in the drawer, lies about trivial matters and large ones,
a cornucopia of lies, a feast of untruth.

He is what he seems, he says. A modest man who loves Jodie,
who will love her forever. Did she tell you that I beat her up?
Do you really think I am what that woman says I am? Do you
really think so? It's her delusion. If it was true, would this dog
be here with me?

Jodie looks at Walton and at his dog. Then she says, Raise

your hand fast, above Einstein's head. Look at her and raise your hand.

When he does what he is asked to do, Einstein neither cringes nor cowers. She watches Walton with her usual impassive interest, her tail still wagging. She has what seems to be a dog-smile on her face. She approaches him, panting. She wants to play. She sits down next to where he kneels. She looks at Walton—there is no mistaking this look—with straightforward dog love.

Jodie believes this dog. She believes the dog more than the woman.

Let me explain something, Walton is saying. You're beautiful. I started with that the first time I saw you. He does a little inventory: you lick your fingers after opening tin cans, you wear hats at a jaunty angle, you have a quick laugh like a bark, you move like a dancer, you're funny, you're great in bed, you love my dog, you're thoughtful, you have opinions. It's the whole package. How can I not love you?

And if I ever do to you what that woman said I did, you can just walk.

One day he will present her with an engagement ring, pretending that he found it in an ashtray at Clara's Country Kitchen Café. The ring will fit her finger, and it will be a seemingly perfect ring, with two tiny sapphires and one tiny diamond, probably all flawed, but flawless from a distance and when not viewed through a magnifying glass. They will be walking under a bridge on the south end of Lake of the Isles in Minneapolis, and when they are halfway under the bridge, Walton will ask Jodie to marry him.

She will then sit for a few more weeks on the sleeping porch, considering this man. She won't be able to help it that when he moves suddenly, she will flinch. She will be distracted, but with the new radio on, she will from time to time do her best to read some of the books she never got around to reading before. Literature, however, will not help her in this instance. She will take out her tarot cards and place them in their proper order on the floor.

This covers him.

This crosses him.

This crowns him.

This is beneath him.

This is behind him.

But the future will not unveil itself. The newspapers of the future are all blank. She will in exasperation throw the tarot cards into the dumpster. She will stop being a believer in the eloquence of the future before it arrives.

Once upon a time, happily ever after. She will look occasionally for the hideous fat man at the breakfast counter on Hennepin Avenue, but of course he will have vanished. When you are awarded a wish, you must specify the conditions under which it is granted. Everyone knows that. The fat man could have told her this simple truth, but he did not. Women are supposed to know such things. They are supposed to arm themselves against the infidelities of the future.

She will feel herself ready to leap.

And just before she does, she will buy a recording of Granados' piano suite *Goyescas*. Again and again she will listen to the fourth of the pieces, "Quejas ó la Maja y el Ruiseñor," the story in music of a maiden singing to her nightingale. Probably the bird is caged. In any case, it sings her questions back to her from its perch behind or before the bars. Jodie will listen to this piece, out on the sleeping porch, as if it holds the answer to her secret. She will have a question, a question for the maiden's nightingale, but will not know how to ask it.

One Sunday night around one o'clock she will hear the distant sound of gunshots, or perhaps a car backfiring. She will then hear voices raised in anger and agitation. Sirens, glass breaking, the clatter of a garbage can rolled on pavement: city sounds. She will fall back to sleep easily, her hands tucked under her pillow, as calm as a child.

Robin Bradford

IF THIS LETTER WERE A BEADED OBJECT

I am sitting in the darkness under the stairs in my house in Galveston, Texas, while the waves rearrange the shoreline. Perhaps you don't remember me: Nan Evans (née Johnson), Forest School class of 1961. I roomed with a girl named Sophie who used to fall out of her bed at night and you were our house mother, Miss Ella. Do you recall that evening you spoke to us in chapel on your travels in Japan? You were wearing a lovely embroidered coat. As you gave your presentation, you seemed to hover above us, vases and carvings of women and swans in jade and alabaster brought from the Orient trailing behind. Your voice hung like mist and drifted into our clean, curved ivory ears. Your coat was made of silk the color of rain, with threads of red-orange and gold.

Do you remember me?

Try. Out of the quiet, gray morning air girls emerge, long lines of them, hundreds, with pink faces and shiny hair, dressed in blue and yellow. A breeze blows across your soft cheek, but does not muss the hair of the girls in the line. Susanna, Margaret, Elena, Jane. You wonder: Where is that girl who lived with Sophie who used to fall out of bed at night?

I never expected I'd live in Texas. I never considered living alone. Now, I am like the Japanese doll on your shelf living in a glass case trimmed with black wood. Her hair fell in a neat line across her forehead, her dress twinkled with gold vines. Red fringe hung from her wrists and headdress. Open it, you said. And I untied the braid that encircled the case and reached inside to straighten the fringe, soft as bird feathers.

Two days ago a tropical storm whirled across the map and into the gaping arms of the Gulf of Mexico like a wedding bouquet spinning streamers through the air. Batteries, bread, and water have evaporated from the earth. A parade of cars crawls over the bridge and down the highway lined with pink oleander. I have had the thought of writing you before, the way one does at certain times in one's life, wishing to reconnect old ties, but only today have I begun.

I am listening to the radio, softly, and eating cheese sandwiches, drinking bottled water, reading *Moby-Dick*, and writing to you, while the storm named Gilbert thrashes his sinewy arms against the sea.

Have you remembered me yet? In your 1961 scrapbook mine is the page with the dried yellow cellophane tape sliding off the paper and onto the carpet. I drew a long-legged snout-nosed horse and a little dog. Then I taped in a bit of my own reddish hair where the horse's mane would be, and added several wisps of black on the head of the dog. (Sophie's hair was black.) In the lower right-hand corner I pasted my own small face, trimmed from my body and the surrounding landscape.

Maybe, Miss Ella, you'll know me right away. As the girl who sat in the gold light of her window, looking down on you and Miss Julie, the senior English teacher, in the garden. As I tried to picture in my mind the sharp edges of Horace's Golden Mean or the gentle hand of a character of James as it rested on a marble mantle, I watched you. Seated as you were next to each other, the hems of your skirts in the grass met like overgrown petals, a basket of trowels nearby. I wished I could hear you, for I hoped you were talking of me.

When you described the quiet gardens of Japan the figure of Christ, slim as a girl, hung above you from a strong invisible thread. The statue must hang there still. Human life is more capricious. Could your foot have slipped in the rain? Could some weakness have drilled its way into every organ of your long, willowy body? Maybe you are forgetful of everything that has happened before and wake each morning as if it is your first. Do you lie in your bed silent as a letter in an envelope? Are you sleeping underground like the root of a felled tree?

Under the stairs is the safest place to be. It is the center of the house and the point at which there is the least stress. I stretch out my legs and take inventory. The mink jacket which Jack gave me for our twentieth anniversary hangs above my head. The silver service hides in its burrow of purple velvet. I am using one of several scrapbooks for a table top. The boxes contain certificates of swimming, birth, and graduation; lace, bibs, and misshapen velvety animals whose names have not been forgotten.

Have you traveled the world, Miss Ella, the way you planned to when you retired, with your portable easel and smooth wooden case of paints tucked under your arm? Did you send postcards to Miss Julie which read, "Another great day of painting. What they say about the light is true. Up early tomorrow as I leave the next. Today I looked up and thought you had come"?

Bored, I remove all the silver from its chest and arrange the pieces on the carpet before me. With the knives I form an arc, blades fanning outward, like a setting sun. Then I place the two sizes of forks inside, alternating with the teaspoons and tablespoons, then the smooth, blunt butter knives. The serving pieces form rays in my design. I am noting (on a separate page) that three spoons are moderately to severely scratched and that one dinner fork is missing. I'm also short one engraved napkin ring.

Love is like a bowl, brimming with fruit salad, hot soup, floating flower petals. Or completely empty and put aside. Do you remember Jack Evans? He lettered in football and track at Stonebury. He was my husband for twenty-three years; in what would have been our twenty-fourth year he married someone else.

The summer after graduation Sophie and I took a trip. On the way to her parents' house we stopped so that she could see her boyfriend who was working as a lifeguard at a resort in the Catskills. She said they were just going for a drive, and got into

his car with its round, innocent headlights. Alone in our n.
room, I read a magazine, listening for the car to bring her back.
Instead I heard the radio of the people next door. Cars pulled in
and out, doors slammed, farther down. The phone rang while I
took a bath but when I answered no one was there. At 11:30 I
turned down the sheets which were wrinkled. I found a hair,
not too long, but black, next to my pillow. I saw the coin box for
the Magic Fingers, which we had found so funny, and shut my
eyes.

Right next to the highway, but hidden from view, was a wa-
terfall, mossy and tall, lined with ferns. Sophie and I spread out
a blanket and laid out food from a basket we'd brought. A fine
mist rose from below. She pinned back her black hair. The water
seeped from the rock, pelted the fern, and trickled through our
ears. When I turned on the light it was the ceiling leaking. It was
three in the morning.

Until I got up at 6:15 the sound of someone walking was constant and heavy above my head. But the leaking stopped. I left
in the chill air for the diner up the road, leaving a note on the
door and a towel over the wet carpet. I smoked and drank coffee
until she came and then got sick on the edge of the highway, as I
wasn't used to smoking. I want to say that when she came for
me she looked beautiful—unwashed, but beautiful.

Dearest Ella, hours have passed during which I drank one cup
of water, ate a large chunk of cheese, and read 112 pages of
Moby-Dick. And how still it is outside. I hear the air conditioner
click on and off. I hear the wind like a distant airplane passing.
The radio says that on the coast the tides are at record highs and
the surfers haven't slept in two days. When Ishmael visits the
fishermen's chapel I am reminded of our class trip to Westport.
Hundreds of twinkling white stone plaques, which read "Lost
At Sea" and "Hope," covered the walls.

I have imagined your adventures. You traveled for days in a
boat so big that on your tiny bed, sounding out the phonetics of
the native language from a guidebook, you forgot you were on
the undulating sea. The only hotel on the island looked out over
twenty fishing boats. You spent your days mostly alone, draw-

; what you would paint. One morning, at dawn, ⌐ster from one of the men, for you and her to . When she arrived, if she was not too tired, you to the place where Ariadne had been left. It is a nderstood. After she gave him the ball of string and the ⌐nd to her finger, and after his boat weaved a golden design across the sea and safely back, why did he let his end go?

While you sketched, she walked along the water's edge in billowy pants bought just for this purpose. And with the meal you drank a wine you had come to love. Then a try at loving ouzo. She spit it out into the sea, licorice-sweet saliva running down her chin. The sun set like a red leaf floating on the water.

That night, sunburned and slightly drunk, you both undressed. The bones of her shoulders and back moved delicately as she closed the wooden shutters. Her skin was as beautiful as you remembered it. She wore the thinnest white cotton against the heat. Her hair, brown stroked with gray, fell from her pillow onto yours. Against your cheek. Dear? you said.

In case of disaster, I can swim. My older brother taught me when I was twelve by throwing me in over and over until I had the idea. The water closed around me like another skin. If I fought, panic overcame me and the water burned like fire in my nose and throat. But if you give yourself over to it, you find that your body is naturally buoyant.

And I can row a boat. If I have to. Set the oars in the locks and lean way back. The blades urge aside the water and the boat moves backward, which is the direction I am heading. The blades skim across the surface and plunk in again.

I slept. Fallen from a cruise ship, wearing a lovely black evening gown, I was knocked unconscious so that I woke in the plush insides of a whale. What a funny sort of life it was! It wasn't as slippery and loathsome as one might think. There were lots of cozy places to sit and somehow I lit a torch and began writing a letter to my husband to let him know how to find me. Suddenly another man appeared who was quite handsome. He wore a white turtleneck and had slick black hair. He offered to cook for me and do the dishes until I adjusted to living there. So I threw away the letter and began to look around. I found the world around me interesting enough to draw. The structures of the whale were quite complex and challenging to render.

Every two hours I allow myself to go out into the hallway and stretch. I duck into the bathroom or to the kitchen to get something I've remembered. The digital clocks flash red. Outside the sky is bottle green; the blades of grass shiver. All the birds are gone. Dogs are barking. I am not near enough to the sea to know how it has changed.

But with my hand on the page, the words form smooth as beads, easy as a necklace between my fingers.

Her lips, soft, the color of melon. The freckles along her collarbone. Do you want to do this? You wanted to ask but were afraid of the answer. So you held your hand cupped over hers.

If the water comes roiling all around me, I can grab the doorframe, the window ledge, a waiting tree limb. Clutching the radio, the flashlight, the notebook and the pen, safe, just in time, in plastic bags saved just for this purpose, I will continue to write.

She was willing. You touched her hair now lying like a tree root between you. You lifted aside the edge of her gown. She closed her eyes when you kissed the place above her breasts. Making little sounds, she tasted like salt. As if she had been lost in the ocean and dredged up on the sand to lie beneath the sun for days, not just one day. She moved her heels rhythmically against the mattress. She was willing.

Until a certain, still, immeasurable moment.

In the morning she put everything, her billowy pants, her cotton nightgown, her hairbrush, back into her bag. At breakfast her eyes were red and beautiful. *Don't*, she said and ordered her bread and coffee herself, in English. The boats don't come out here every day, the waiter answered her in perfect American English. They come when they wish. So it was another whole day of sketching and watercolor studies farther up the coast. She scooped water over her shoulders far down the beach. She rode in the front seat of the hired car on the way back to town and you rode in the back. The sun was a red hole ripping apart the seams.

I imagine a tidy, well-supplied boat. I pull the cord and it starts right up. I go slowly so my wake will not lap up over someone's doorway. I imagine a family on an island except the island turns out to be a roof. They don't speak any English, and they are crying. Besides the parents, there are two children and one baby with fuzzy black hair. I can hear the baby crying over the churning of the water. A tree limb breaks and is swept off. There is not enough room for all of us. The mother and father are calling to me. Is that Spanish they are speaking? What will I do?

Moby-Dick—halfway through, I am bored with the story. I have been thinking that real wisdom belongs to the dark-skinned peoples. Queequeg with his tattoos. I have read of Tarahumara Indians in Mexico who live in tiny houses less complex than their granaries. That is because every time someone dies the house is burned down. And Zulu Indian maidens send messages to their men in the form of beaded trinkets. Green is for the trampled thin body, like a blade of grass, which is alone. Black is for the rafters that you stare at as you lie in bed thinking of his other lover.

If this letter were a beaded object, I think it would be long and slim as a belt, with a complex and colorful, unimaginable design. I would sit for weeks close to the light pushing my needle through tiny glass beads, creating the pattern as I went. My thick fingers would grow thin.

The wind is like a whale now, snapping at the house. A wedding occurs across town, despite the weather, because the flowers and the food are already paid for. Everyone will remember this day. Especially the silent girl with a mane of black hair who has never had a date but who told her mother that when the bride throws the flowers over her shoulder she will catch them. Indeed, they fly beneath the ceiling right into her cupped hands.

Ella, I would like to visit you. I have been saving for so long for the right place and time and hope the airport is not destroyed by this storm. I would like to ask you: all sorts of things. Will I see Miss Julie? If you don't remember me, then make up answers that you think are possibilities. Confuse me with someone else, if you must. In any case, write soon.

I can smell the water, have been smelling rain in this closet for days. Inland, rivers are rising; the sea has lost its sense. I have rescued the Ziploc bags from the kitchen and soon will begin taking measures to keep the important things dry.

That beautiful coat from Japan, do you still have it? Do you still wear it when you go out for special evenings? When I think of you, that is what you are wearing, and if no one told you then I will: that evening when you spoke in chapel, you were enchanting.

Perri Klass

CITY SIDEWALKS

Claire is in a hurry, running for the bus. As usual. The day-care center had asked, since it's Christmas Eve, if everyone could pick up by four today, and Claire's boss had assured her that she could leave early, but then at the last minute one of his research assistants discovered that the lab would be completely out of some very important enzyme preparation by Monday, and it had to be reordered at once, and now Claire doesn't think she'll make it by four. So she'll be late again to pick up her daughter, and on Christmas Eve. She hurries out of the lab building and takes the shortcut through the hospital, even though it means going in a door marked Do Not Enter and then racing through the lobby, where the homeless people are already gathering for the night, taking their places among the sick.

It seems to Claire that her life is made of apologies and excuses. I'm sorry, Dr. Fergus, I wish I could stay and finish typing this, but I do have to pick up my three-year-old at her day-care center. I'm sorry, Lynnette, I know I'm late to pick up Thea, but the bus didn't come. I'm sorry, Thea, I know I'm the very last mommy.

Out the automatic sliding doors and then only half a block more, and maybe if the bus comes right away she'll be on time. And Thea will be glad to see her, not woebegone and worried at being left till last, and Lynnette will smile, and everyone will wish each other Merry Christmas. Merry cold snowless New England Christmas. Claire pulls her coat closed but doesn't break stride to zip it, then glances over at the windowless graffitied wall of the hospital and suddenly does break stride, veers off course, kneels down on the sidewalk. A bundle of rags, tucked right up against the wall—but she heard it cry, and though she said to herself, Maybe a kitten, she knew perfectly well that no kitten sounds like that. And no bundle of rags, either. Her hand is shaking slightly as she peels away first one, then another shabby blanket: Under them, securely zipped into a green snowsuit, there is a baby. Red face contorted, really howling now. A baby lying on the sidewalk.

What should she do? What the hell are you supposed to do? Take the baby back into the hospital lobby and hand it to someone? Call the police—she looks around, but of course there are no police in sight. They pull up frequently enough to the emergency room, bringing in people who have been hurt; this hospital, in this bad neighborhood, is widely known as the place to go if you've been shot or stabbed. How can she run into that waiting room and try to hand a baby to someone who won't understand what's going on? Then, with an unmistakable clank and a whoosh of exhaust, her bus pulls up behind her. Without really thinking about it, Claire grabs the baby up out of the blankets and runs for the bus stop. She makes it, she's on the bus, she'll be at the day-care center on time, and as she drops into an empty seat, with the unexpected weight of this strange baby in her lap, she smiles down in triumph. The baby, who has evidently enjoyed the jolting run for the bus, smiles back at her, a big, adorable, gummy smile: Well, here we are.

All the way to the day-care center, Claire wonders what she should have done, what she should do, and rocks the baby gently on her lap. Boy or girl, she wonders, and guesses, somehow, boy; there is something about this face that is distinctly different from Thea's well-remembered baby face. Age, she guesses, somewhere around six months. What the hell kind of crazy person leaves a six-month-old baby lying out on the street in December? Though perhaps some people might wonder, What the hell kind of crazy person picks up a baby off the street and goes running for a bus? The baby *looks* healthy. But why not leave a baby somewhere warm if you're going to leave a baby— but who would leave a baby?

There are tears in Claire's eyes as she makes her way off the bus and into the day-care center. Thea is out in the hallway, sitting on the low red bench with a couple of other children and one of the teachers. "Oh!" Thea screams. "Oh! Mama, we got a new baby for Christmas?" And she comes running up to grab at Claire's legs, to pull on the baby, demanding let me see, let me see, what kind of baby is it, where did you get it, what's its name? Everyone in the hallway is watching.

Yes, indeed, Thea has been asking for a baby. In her room at the day-care center, there are three children who have recently acquired younger brothers or sisters, and two more have siblings on the way. Thea asks often when she can have her own little sister or brother.

"Come on, Thea," Claire says. "Get your coat on, let's go."

Lynnette, Thea's teacher, brings over Thea's red winter coat.

Thea yells, "Lynnette, we got a baby for Christmas!"

"Thea, the baby is just visiting us," Claire says softly.

"Just for Christmas?"

"We'll see," Claire says, eager to get home and put this heavy baby down, and pick up her own beautiful, perplexed daughter, tell her some story or other, never tell her, never even hint, that someone threw a baby away, left it on the street. This desperate need to wrap herself around Thea's perfect, strong, graham-cracker-scented body, she suddenly realizes, has been building in her ever since she found the baby. "Come on," she says, as gaily as she can, "let's take this baby back to our house!"

"Yeah!" shouts Thea, all confusion gone. "Lynnette, we're going to take this baby back to our house!"

"Merry Christmas," Lynnette says quietly to Claire, who suddenly feels a wave of grateful affection for this cheerful, energetic woman who teaches photography all morning and then works the afternoon shift at the day-care center. What a nice, kind woman Lynnette is, her long, fair hair straggling loose from her braids, her face all smiling and discreet, as she helps Thea zip her coat and asks no questions of Claire.

"Merry Christmas, Lynnette. I hope it's a good one." And

they leave the day-care center together, Claire and Thea and the strange, still, amiable baby, and soon they are home. The very first thing Claire does, before taking off the baby's snowsuit and looking to see if there is any identification, or if the baby has been hurt in any way, or even finding out if it's a boy or a girl— before doing any of these things, she kneels and puts the baby gently down on the rug in the crowded little living room, and then, still on her knees, she turns and takes Thea in her arms and kisses both cold red cheeks, kisses her tangled black curls, rubs her up and down her straight little back. The scent of cold comes off Thea's body like vapor, but she is already struggling within her mother's embrace, struggling to see the baby, up close, face to face.

Claire spent many years of her life thinking of herself as, well, maybe not beautiful but definitely attractive, definitely sexy, definitely someone men responded to. Tall, with long legs and a lot of curly black hair, and also, she knew perfectly well, that edge, that special kind of nerve that lets you be the first one dancing, or even the only one. She had fun in college, and right after, with a succession of boys, and married Marvin, Thea's father, partly because he was so very serious, so inexperienced at having any kind of fun at all, that it touched her. He was in medical school when she married him, and he helped her find the job in the lab building, working for Dr. Fergus. She actually liked working there, liked the techs and the secretaries and the young scientists much better than she had liked the people at the insurance office where she had been working.

But she and Marvin didn't do very well together, especially not when medical school was over and his internship began, and they had the same fights over and over again. That he took her for granted and used her as a convenience and paid no attention to her. That she didn't understand the pressures he was under. That he had only married her to have someone to support him financially and do his laundry. That he was tired, please leave him alone, he was exhausted. Marvin now has a girlfriend who is a doctor and presumably understands all the pressures.

But it would be wrong to leap to the conclusion that Claire is

one of those wives ditched along the path to doctorhood, one of
those hardworking first wives who get dumped for someone
younger or classier by their newly certified husbands. There are
such women around the hospital, and maybe Dr. Fergus and
some other people assume that's Claire's story too, but Claire
knows better. It was she who ended the marriage, she who told
him, I would rather live alone than live with you, I would rather
sleep with no one than sleep with someone who is never here
and doesn't notice me when he is. And then, two weeks after he
moved out, she realized she was pregnant.

In all fairness, and Claire tries to be fair, Marvin has behaved
pretty well. He pays child support, he spends time with Thea
every other weekend except when he's on call. His parents, who
have no other grandchild, are obviously uncomfortable with the
situation, but they see Thea whenever they come to Boston,
they send her funny greeting cards with checks tucked inside,
and they never forget her birthday. In fact, the two biggest pack-
ages under the tree are from Grandma and Grandpa. In fact,
when Claire thinks about Marvin remarrying, as he surely will,
what hurts her is the idea of Thea losing her grandparents,
when they turn their doting to new, less disconcerting grandchildren. Even though they will still conscientiously send birthday presents to Thea, she will have become a peripheral, odd
grandchild. And Claire's own parents are dead, and her sister
lives two thousand miles away and disapproves of her, of Thea,
of everything.

Claire still looks fine, she's still tall and long-legged, though
her hair is cut short. But surprisingly, or maybe not so surprisingly, what changed most after she had a baby was her face. Her
stomach came back almost exactly as it had been, but her face is
now an older woman's face, a serious face, a sometimes haggard, sometimes remarkable face, but certainly not a face full of
fun. Did that happen with pregnancy, or did it happen over the
first year of living alone with an infant and almost no money, up
in the morning and off to the day-care center and then on to
work after nights interrupted three or four times by Thea, a hungry and willful baby, dragging herself and the baby home in the
evening to make supper and play on the floor till bath time?
And worry: Would they be able to stay in their apartment, or

would the building go condo? Would she lose her job? Would she be asked to leave the day-care center if she kept showing up late? These were her three most cosmic worries; her prayer had been, Just let me keep the apartment, the job, the day care. And she had kept them.

It's so different now, coming home. Thea walking, even dancing along, taking off her own coat, eager to help make dinner, her favorite evening activity. She can mold hamburgers or meatballs, pour barbecue sauce onto chicken, even cut certain carefully selected vegetables with a butter knife. She's actually good company. And after supper, when Claire sprawls on the couch exhausted, Thea bangs her tambourine and dances, entertains her tired mother with endless versions of her favorite numbers: the little-girl-named-Thea dance, the spinning-round-and-round dance, the taking-off-my-clothes dance, the wearing-Mama's-scarves dance.

But today, coming home has a weird echo of that hard first year. The tiredness in her shoulders from carrying the baby, a weight that you carry tightly, and with great care, especially on icy sidewalks. And now the sound of the baby starting to cry. Claire goes over, kneels beside the baby, and takes off his snowsuit. Yes, it's a he. Under the snowsuit are faded and tattered stretch pajamas, dimly printed with bunnies, and under the pajamas is a very sodden diaper.

And thank heaven, Claire realizes, they have diapers. She doesn't have to set out with two children to find a drugstore open on Christmas Eve. Thank heaven Thea isn't fully toilet trained. Actually, this has been a point of some conflict, since Thea has been perfectly toilet trained at day care for the past four months but completely unwilling to cooperate at home. And now she seems delighted to go fetch one of her diapers for the baby, and stands at her mother's side, watching the changing process. Her diaper is of course much too big, but Claire folds down the top and tapes it to overlap around the baby's waist. And while she's changing him, she looks him up and down, wondering, worrying, Maybe someone has hurt him. But his rosy skin is without a blemish; even his bottom is pink and smooth, without diaper rash.

He's a beautiful baby. Silky brown hair, big blue-green eyes, long long lashes. This little boy is a fair, pink angel, like some Victorian Christmas card of a child.

Oh, well, it's time to do something about him, time to alert the authorities. After all, she still wants to read a Christmas story to Thea, and play the Rudolph tape a couple of times and help her hang a stocking. And supper. And bath time. And then, when she finally gets Thea to bed, there will still be some presents to wrap and the stocking to fill. Claire frowns—there is very little money this year, and the fact is that what she has been able to buy will undoubtedly pale beside the gifts from Marvin, from his parents. Will Thea understand that that is not because Claire doesn't love her? What nonsense, she tells herself. Last year Thea was more interested in the ribbons and wrapping paper than she was in the gifts; this year will she know the dollar value of everything under the tree?

The tree itself is small; she got it only two days ago, after Thea had asked every day for weeks. On her way to the phone, Claire switches on the blinking blue lights, thinking they may distract the baby. Dry and wide awake now, he lies on his back and looks around him, and Claire is astonished to find that this feeling, too, is familiar: that vague sense of triumph at having gotten the baby home safely on a cold day, having changed him and settled him in a warm and comfortable room.

So, what should she do? Dial 911? Hello, this is an emergency, an hour ago I found a baby but I didn't have a chance to call? The baby, as if amused, brings his fist up to his mouth and smiles, as if he is pleasantly surprised to find that old familiar fist here in this new room. Instead of calling 911, Claire dials the local precinct, gets switched from person to person and finally disconnected. She calls back and this time finds her way to a man who wants to know the details, and with a sense of great relief she gives him her name and address—I'm a responsible citizen, doing my duty. But after she finishes her explanation, he tells her that the baby needs to be reported to the precinct in which he was found, not to the precinct in which she lives. He says this kindly, not as if he is giving her the runaround but as if he is trying to save her time and trouble, and Claire finds herself encouraged by his tone to ask another question.

"What happens to him—to the baby—after I report this?"

"Well, they'll probably send out a squad car and pick him up, then they'll deliver him to the department of social service, they'll call the twenty-four-hour hot line, and they'll get him settled in a foster home. That is, if there is any department of social service left after the last round of budget cuts. We're lucky there are still a few policemen."

Claire wishes him a Merry Christmas and hangs up. And then sits for a moment or two. A few feet away, Thea is talking quietly to the baby, telling him in great detail which of her toys she will let him play with and which ones he can't play with because he is only a baby.

Budget cuts; they have hit the hospital hard. Budget cuts are part of the reason she was so scared about losing her job—still is scared.

Claire flips through the phone book, through the government agencies listed in the front. There's the department of social service twenty-four-hour hot line. Maybe she'll just call that first, find out what they're going to do with this baby, rather than handing him over to some unknown policeman. She'd like to be sure there's a foster home waiting.

There isn't. The man who answers the phone at the department of social service is once again very nice. His name is Harry Friedman, and at first he sounds tired and discouraged, a man who maybe doesn't want to listen and doesn't want to talk. But then, when Claire tells him the story of how she found the baby, thrown away, he makes a shocked noise. Whatever he sees in his job has not left him invulnerable, and Claire likes him for that.

"Well," Harry Friedman says ruefully when Claire stops talking, when she asks him what happens next, "well, that's a very good question. What happens next, I'm afraid, is that we let the police know so they can try to find the kid's family, and meantime I get busy and try to find an emergency foster-home situation. The problem is, we keep a list of these homes, ready to take a kid on no notice and keep him for a couple of days—but earlier this afternoon there was a bad fire that burned out one of our regular long-term foster homes. Terrible thing, nicest people you'd ever want to know."

"I hope no one was hurt," Claire says, and it seems to her that

she means this more sincerely than he can possibly know; she
feels suddenly exposed to all the sadness and risk and loss of
the city.

"No one was hurt," he says. "But they lost pretty much everything they had. And the thing is, they had five foster kids in
that house, three of them special-needs kids. Like I said, they
were our regulars. So I've just been placing those kids, used up
all our emergency spaces. I just got the last kid placed ten minutes ago. So now I'll start working on your baby."

Your baby. Hearing it said like that gives Claire the courage to
ask the question she had no intention of asking. Thea is bringing
her stuffed animals out of her bedroom, one by one, and arranging them in a circle around the baby. "Listen," Claire says to
Harry Friedman, "since it's Christmas Eve and all—since you
don't have any emergency places—what I mean is, would you
even consider—I don't have to work tomorrow, of course, and
the next day's Saturday—would it be possible for the baby to
stay here? With me? Just over Christmas, I mean."

There's a pause; he's obviously thinking about it. Thinking
about how to tell her that's out of the question; after all, he
doesn't know who she is, or where she lives, or what she's like.

"In certain cases," he says slowly, "in special cases—the hot
line supervisor does have the power to make out-of-the-ordi-
nary decisions about emergency placements—"

"Please," Claire says, cutting him off, shocking herself. "Listen, my daughter is playing with him right now, introducing
him to all her stuffed animals. Look, I don't pretend to know
what could make someone throw a baby away, but don't you
think after whatever he's been through, he might as well spend
the holiday here, where we want him?"

"We would need to do a background check on you," he says,
somewhat apologetically.

"You mean, with the police?"

"Well, I'll call the police now anyway and report the baby, let
them know we're involved, and check for criminal records on
any adults in your home—but what I'll personally need to do is
check department of social service files, make sure there have
never been any problems about children in your care—I hope
that would be okay with you."

"There's only me and my daughter, Thea, and you can check anything you want," Claire says, thinking suddenly of Thea's old yellow plastic baby bathtub. That's what they'll do, she and Thea, they'll give the baby a bath together, and soap all the dirt and any memory of the sidewalk away. It occurs to her to try to give herself a little more respectability, and she tells Harry Friedman that she works at the hospital, even names Dr. Fergus, tells him where Thea goes to day care. Go ahead, check us out, she thinks, we're poor but we're honest.

Harry Friedman is thinking, talking slowly again in his considering half-sentences. "I don't mind telling you—" he says, and then pauses, as if he does in fact mind telling her. "It would certainly make things simple—I mean, finding a place on Christmas Eve when we've used up all the ones we had—and with the budget cuts and all it's harder than ever—and then you're right, it seems sad for him to get squeezed in someplace where they don't really want him."

"Please," Claire says. "My little girl will think it's a Christmas present."

"Listen, what I'll need to do is send someone around later this evening to meet you, get a look at where you live. But if everything checks out—well, I don't mind telling you it might be best for everyone." Now he's talking fast, convincing himself.

"I'll be here," Claire tells him. "We aren't going anywhere."

By the time the doorbell rings two hours later, Claire and Thea have bathed the baby in Thea's old tub. They have also named him. Claire was ready for her daughter to insist on Rudolph, or maybe even Frosty, but in fact, when asked what they should call the baby, Thea said with certainty, "Robbie," which is the name of her best friend at day care, a three-year-old boy who seems to be completely in her thrall and follows her around all day, playing the games she chooses and obeying her orders. Presumably, this is exactly the disposition she wants to see in a younger sibling or any other child who comes into her home. So Robbie it is, and Claire has packed his pajamas and snowsuit away in a grocery bag and dressed him in a red velour romper that Thea's grandparents sent her years ago; it's a little too big for him but very much in the holiday spirit. Thea, who enjoyed the bathing process as much as Robbie did himself and who squidged baby shampoo around on his little head with so much glee that you'd never think getting her own hair washed usually involved a screaming fit, has been allowed to button up the romper and to help towel-dry that soft little head. Robbie has been gurgling and smiling throughout, so much so that Claire has begun to wonder whether all this care and attention is new to him, is an unexpected delight.

And we're so well equipped for this, Claire thinks, settling Robbie in Thea's old infant seat. Why has she saved all this equipment, all these clothes, for heaven's sake? Why this closet full of stuff, packed neatly away as if she really did plan to have another baby, just the way Thea wants? But at least when Thea asks anxiously if Santa will know to bring presents for Robbie or if he'll have to share hers, Claire can promise that there will be special presents for Robbie waiting under the tree. In that closet, she thinks, are plenty of jumpsuits, certainly a rattle or two, nothing Thea will recognize or resent or want. She'll wrap them tonight when she wraps Thea's presents.

By the time the doorbell rings, Robbie is happily eating mashed banana out of Thea's plastic baby spoon, and Thea, chewing absently on her chicken drumstick, is watching Claire feed him like it's some kind of magic show. Every time he spits out food, Thea laughs aloud, amused, but also slightly anxious; she needs to hear Claire say, each and every time, That's okay, that's just how babies eat. When the doorbell rings, Thea has just asked, Is that why you don't want to keep him, because he's so messy? And Claire, running to get the door, hears behind that question all the anxiety of a child who sometimes senses her mother's despair at the unending mess of keeping their life moving along, maybe a child who is already old enough to wonder, Why did my father leave?

The man at the door is Harry Friedman himself, short and round with thinning brown hair combed straight back from his forehead. Buttoned into a trench coat that's a little too tight around his middle, lugging an enormous sack. Claire makes him welcome in the kitchen, offers him tea, and then, seeing the side-long looks he is taking at Thea's drumstick, she offers him some cheese and crackers, and he sheepishly tells her, I wouldn't say no. Good, she thinks. After he's eaten her cheese and crackers, he can hardly decide she's a dangerous incompetent. In the end, she makes him a can of Thea's astronoodle beef soup as well, and Thea decides to have a small bowl herself. Claire tips the last bits out of the pan into her daughter's bowl, and as a noodle squiggles out onto the table, Thea gives a shriek of victorious delight: Mama made a mess! And Robbie, in response, gives a loud baby gurgle, his face tracked with mashed banana, a gurgle and a smile so infectious that both adults start to laugh.

Claire sits down in a kitchen chair, shocked to realize she's crying. That laughing baby. Someone left him on the sidewalk. A crack in the sidewalk, she thinks, he's slipping through the cracks. And she's crying, maybe for the baby, maybe because these are the very fears she sometimes has for herself and Thea, slipping through the cracks, left unprotected in a cold, dark world. She covers her face with her hands and takes a deep, gasping breath. Feeling a hand on her shoulder, she looks up to see that Harry Friedman has come to stand behind her.

"What a world," she says to him, shaking her head.

He looks into her eyes, very serious. "You do what you can," he tells her, "you take care of the people you can take care of."

Thea comes wriggling onto her mother's lap, checking out her face to see if she's still crying, elbowing her way into a scene of adult emotion that clearly unsettles her. Claire folds her daughter up in her arms, holds her hard, while Harry sits back down, finishes his soup.

"So," he says calmly, as if everything were clear and obvious, "you'll keep this little fellow over Christmas, then Saturday we'll come around and collect him. I'll find him a good place to go, I promise."

He is tousling Thea's curly dark head, patting Robbie on the belly. Belting on his tight trench coat, picking up his sack. Thea, of course, wants to know what's in the sack, and Harry actually blushes as he tells her it's toys, Christmas presents for some kids he knows. "The ones who were in the f-i-r-e," he tells Claire. "Lost all the stuff they were going to get. I just thought—that's where I'm going now, to drop these off."

He holds out his hand and Claire shakes it. She feels she is waiting for some other piece of information from him, some word of advice that will give the world a little more sense. He approves of her, he thinks this is a good, warm place for a lost baby; will he perhaps tell her that before he goes? He doesn't, though, just the handshake and a Merry Christmas addressed to Thea, who is eyeing his sack with intent three-year-old possessiveness, and then he is gone.

Claire sponges Robbie's face clean, wipes the banana off his fingers, carries him into the living room. The tree is still blinking, blue flashes across the worn but comfortable old couch. Claire sits down, holding Robbie on her lap; his body feels different now that he is getting sleepy, his weight sags against her a little bit, though he keeps his eyes open and fixed on the tree.

"Can Robbie stay here and sleep in my house?" Thea asks.

"Robbie can stay tomorrow, but the next day he has to go to a new home," Claire tells her. "But we're lucky, because we get to have him for Christmas." We're lucky, she thinks. Maybe this baby will be a little luckier too, from now on. And when he leaves, the day after Christmas, he'll leave with a good supply of baby clothes and a stuffed animal or two. He won't go empty-handed to his new home.

"We're lucky," Thea repeats. Maybe she's a little relieved to hear the baby isn't staying for good; surely it has been a little disconcerting to see her mother paying so much attention to another child all evening. The important presents, Claire thinks, the big new toys, those will all be for Thea. And Thea and I, she thinks, we are going to be okay.

"Maybe you'll dance for us?" Claire suggests. "Robbie's getting tired, I think he's going to fall asleep soon—could you do a dance to help him go to sleep?"

Thea gets her tambourine, holds out her arms, and gets ready to spin. "Okay," she says, smiling that on-the-edge sparkling smile. "This is the Christmas Eve Robbie-go-to-sleep dance." She spins and swoops, utterly confident in the blinking blue lights. She stomps in a circle, lifts up her shirt, and bangs out a rhythm with the tambourine on her plump little belly; she bends forward at the waist and shakes her head crazily so her curls whip back and forth. And all the time she is giggling with glee at her own performance, and Claire laughs too, sitting on the couch and holding the baby, holding him the way you hold something precious, some remarkably important gift, even if it isn't really yours.

BIOGRAPHIES
and Some Comments
by the Authors

Alice Adams lives in San Francisco. Her most recent book of short stories is *After You've Gone* (Knopf), her most recent novel *Almost Perfect* (Knopf).

" 'The Haunted Beach' is, like most of my stories and novels, a mix of memory and invention. I did, in fact, go back to a Mexican beach town —where a blue flight bag was stolen, containing only my room key, and I did have just such an encounter with an old man, whose wild pirate's face I will never forget. I also have a fondness for a certain kind of cheap Mexican ring, with lovely (perhaps fake) opals. As usual, then, I attached my own adventures to quite other people."

Alison Baker lives with her husband in Ruch, Oregon. Her first collection of stories, *How I Came West, and Why I Stayed*, was published by Chronicle Books in 1993.

"I am aware of two things that led me to write 'Loving Wanda Beaver.' As a teenager I detasseled corn in the summer to earn money for contact lenses, and the memory of that hot, sweaty, underpaid work has stayed with me for a quarter of a century. Just as some adolescent girls fall in love with horses, a Hoosier girl may become obsessed with detasseling corn, and spend her free time dreaming about the corn, the rough tassels, the hot sun, the fragrance of hogs in nearby pens. As with horses, most girls outgrow their love of detasseling; but my story is about Oleander Joy, a woman who never overcomes her obsession.

"I spent many years as a medical librarian, and I once found a copy of the *Kama Sutra* hidden in the reference collection behind Goodman & Gilman's *Pharmacological Basis of Therapeutics*. A decade of musing on this led me at last through the doors of the Library of Desire; and I'll be darned if it wasn't Oleander Joy, working there in the cataloging department."

Charles Baxter is the author of three books of stories, most recently *A Relative Stranger* (Norton), and two novels, *First Light* (Viking Penguin) and *Shadow Play* (Norton). He teaches at the University of Michigan and lives in Ann Arbor.

"My parents once owned a house in Minneapolis with an upstairs sleeping porch facing the garage and the alley. 'Kiss Away' begins on that porch and then moves into a greasy spoon of the imagination. A friend's apartment in Buffalo, New York, that reminded me of Bluebeard's Castle found its way into the story, as did another friend's description of a predator tape. Her account of it brought back to me a memory that we once had neighbors, decades ago, who listened to one of these recordings as twilight came on."

Robin Bradford was born in Japan and grew up in Tulsa and Houston. She received her M.A. in creative writing from Brown University in 1988. Her stories have appeared in *Central Park, Chelsea, Fiction,* and *Tyuonyi.* She lives in Austin, Texas, with her husband.

"I began writing 'If This Letter Were a Beaded Object' when I moved back to Texas from Providence. I felt very isolated with all my friends far away. For my birthday my best friend, Marina, also a writer, sent a scrapbook she found at a flea market. It had been made in 1954 as a gift for a woman who was retiring from her job as a nurse at Pembroke College. The pages were filled with drawings, photographs, and poems that told a hundred stories. First, I wrote 'Beaded Object' in a 'Q & A' form that I copied from Donald Barthelme. Later, I chose a letter form instead. I decided writing letters to people connected to your old life was a form of survival. At the time, I was writing very long and frequent letters myself. For five years I tinkered with the story and it was rejected eighteen times! Once, a friend was writing to Guy Davenport and we decided to enclose 'Beaded Object.' He wrote a delightful note back, so that renewed my faith in this strange story I thought only I would ever love."

Michael Byers grew up in Seattle and attended Oberlin College. He is now in the writing program at the University of Michigan.

"This story takes place on a sad little stretch of beach on the Washington coast; we spent vacations there when I was a kid. It's a gray and boring place, by and large, but I do find myself writing about it fairly often—probably because I know almost no one there and can populate it as I need to. The story, which went through several drafts, expanded and contracted for a few months before settling at this length."

Peter Cameron is the author of the story collections *One Way or Another* and *Far-Flung* and the novels *Leap Year* and *The Weekend*. His fiction has appeared in *The New Yorker*, *The Paris Review*, *Rolling Stone*, and other publications. He has taught fiction writing at Oberlin College and Columbia University. He lives in New York City, where he works for Lambda Legal Defense and Education Fund.

" 'Departing' was written first as a story, and went through many drafts and titles. Somewhere in that process I began to sense that there was more going on with these characters than the perimeters of the story would allow. And so I wrote a novel, *The Weekend*, which explores this same territory, but in a different, slower way. I wanted to reveal what lay beneath the surface of the story. I'd never felt the need to do this before: to recast a story as a novel. I was somewhat bothered by this formalistic indecision, as I used to believe that real distinctions existed between stories and novels, and that a writer should know, instinctively, which form an idea should take. I think I realize now that there are a lot of ways to tell a story. And some are not necessarily better—or more correct—than others."

John J. Clayton teaches creative writing and modern fiction at the University of Massachusetts, Amherst. He has published a novel, *What Are Friends For?* and a collection of short fiction, *Bodies of the Rich*. His stories have appeared in a variety of periodicals, have been reprinted in *Prize Stories: The O. Henry Awards* and *Best American Short Stories*, and have often been anthologized. He has been fiction editor of *Agni* and editor of an anthology, *The D. C. Heath Introduction to Fiction*.

" 'Talking to Charlie' is deeply autobiographical *emotionally*, though hardly at all autobiographical in literal fact. I found myself moved by the spiritual longings and essential fatherly tenderness of the character. And that feeling in myself made the story a risk—it would have been so easy to write yet one more self-indulgent, sentimental story of midlife crisis. The 'war' between the voice of the 'writer' and the story he's telling—saves it, I hope, from being banal.

" 'Talking to Charlie' is like the condensation of a novel; my favorite contemporary short story writer is Alice Munro, and while I make no claim to comparable mastery, I love it when I'm able in my stories to encompass a comparable complexity of emotional life and social realities. I love the feeling of a story flowing over its boundaries, hinting at life beyond the form, chancing too-muchness."

Bernard Cooper is the author of *A Year Of Rhymes* and *Maps to Anywhere,* which received the 1991 PEN/USA Ernest Hemingway Award (both from Penguin). "Truth Serum" is the title piece from a collection to be published by Viking. He teaches in Los Angeles where he lives with his partner of eleven years, Brian Miller, a psychotherapist.

"I am often told that my memoirs read like short stories. Perhaps this is because time and distance lend a certain writerly shape to the sprawl of recollected experience. Furthermore, I have no qualms about improvising a few facts in order to get closer to the truth.

"In the case of this particular story, for years I'd been haunted by the sound that emanated from the light fixture in Dr. Sward's office. But what exactly had I heard, and what had those doses of truth serum shown me about my own nature? To find a way out of the labyrinth of social assumptions, to try to come to terms with one's sexuality is no small matter, and this story is only the fragment of a picture so large and complex, I will never perceive it in its entirety.

"An off-kilter pun—to hear the light—lies at the center of this story. Dr. Sward had hoped to mend me and, in an oblique and unexpected way, he had. To write this narrative was to revive a set of emotional and sexual reckonings, and to grapple again with the unruly power of longing and love."

Edward J. Delaney was born in 1957 in Fall River, Massachusetts. He began his career as a journalist, and has written for the *Denver Post,* the *Chicago Tribune Magazine, The National,* and other publications. He began writing fiction in 1990 and has published in *The Atlantic Monthly, The Greensboro Review, Carolina Quarterly,* and other magazines. He lives in Fall River with his wife, Lisa, and their children, Kieran and Caitlin.

"I received the acceptance of the story from C. Michael Curtis of *The Atlantic* hours after my car was stolen from in front of the house and wrecked a few miles away, which fits perfectly the Irish superstition that no good luck goes unpunished and no bad luck goes unredeemed. This story took shape over an autumn, and this version emerged from an earlier story set in contemporary times and more-familiar terrain. It was the third try on a theme that interests me greatly, which is when sense of moral duty bumps up against a sense of commitment to a pledge. The first-person narrator was simply a way to make the story link with the present, but the story-within-a-story approach seemed to interest readers more than I anticipated."

Deborah Eisenberg: "I was born in 1945 and started writing over thirty years later. New York is where I live, but I usually work (teach) else-where—these days at the University of Virginia. I've written two collections of short fiction—*Transactions in a Foreign Currency* and *Under the 82nd Airborne.* 'Across the Lake' will appear, I suppose, in an eventual third collection. It's one of a series of stories I wrote set in Latin America. And I suppose all of these stories could be described as angles of entry into riddles of power and powerlessness, and the relationships— mutable and immutable—between those who have power and those who don't.

"Even though it takes me a long time to write a story I tend to re-member very little about the process. I do remember that this was a story I was eager to write; that is, I started with many more elements than I usually do. I had the setting—a very real town, lake, and village, which I just couldn't get off my mind—and I knew the story was to contain several characters from the population that drifts around the world. But despite the fact that I knew all this from the beginning whereas I usually have no more to start with than a phrase or an image or a feeling, it took me just as many months and drafts and discarded notebooks as it usually takes me before a story begins to budge—before it comes alive and begins to move on its own."

David Gates writes about books and popular music for *Newsweek.* His stories have appeared in *Esquire, Gentleman's Quarterly, Grand Street, Ploughshares, TriQuarterly,* and *Best American Short Stories 1994.* His first novel, *Jernigan* (Knopf), was published in 1991; he's now completing a second.

" 'The Intruder' is a story I used to haul out, rewrite and resubmit every few years; it's so old that in its earliest version the central charac-ters, two gay men, gave not a thought to AIDS. It got its share of rejec-tions (including a form letter from *TriQuarterly,* which published it years later); one agent hesitated to circulate it out of sexual-political unease. Will Blythe at *Esquire* talked me into actually *writing* the dinner party scene, rather than cutting straight from the preparations to the morning after; it would be a poorer story if not for his help, though *Esquire* ended up bouncing it, too.

"Two other acknowledgments. Reg Gibbons at *TriQuarterly* suggested that 'The Intruder' ended too abruptly, prompting me to shoehorn in an extra beat (if you can shoehorn a beat) before the final two lines of dialogue. And Jorge Luis Borges beat me to that title by years and years. His 'La Intrusa' wasn't a model for my story, but his notion of a lover as an intruder certainly went into the hopper."

Ellen Gilchrist is the author of twelve books. In 1984 she won the National Book Award for a book of stories called *Victory over Japan*. She lives in Fayetteville, Arkansas.

"I always have children in my life. Their perceptions are dazzling, their coping skills are godlike, the beauty of their faces and hands always calls me back to the beauty of the world. If this story is 'good' or 'interesting' or 'useful' it is because it is told from a child's perspective. There is a narrator but the narrator is influenced by Teddy's perceptions. I was lucky to imagine it and lucky to get to write it down. There is a lot of work to writing. Perhaps the work makes the luck. Maybe the luck just decides to visit one of us every now and then. It was with me when I was writing this one long, cold, February night."

Allegra Goodman: "I live in Boston, where I am writing short fiction, a novel, and a Ph.D. dissertation on Shakespeare.

" 'Sarah' is part of a series about the Markowitz family published in *Commentary* and *The New Yorker*. The collection will be published next year by Farrar, Straus & Giroux. Sarah Markowitz appears in many of the Markowitz stories. The warm response she provoked from readers —particularly from women—encouraged me to write a story focusing on her. I decided to structure the story on Sarah's struggles to manage her class and to deal with Rose. I wanted to show her in her professional as well as her familial role. I began by writing her students' creative writing compositions in longhand. The students and all the dialogue in Sarah's class grew out of these imagined compositions.

"Despite the fact that Sarah is almost twenty-five years older than I am, I find a great deal of myself in her. It was not difficult to write about her, because I felt how much we shared. It is not our dreams that are so different, but our opportunities."

Elizabeth Hardwick: "I was born and grew up in Lexington, Kentucky. After the University there I went to graduate school at Columbia and thus became, I guess, a New Yorker. I've lived in various places, but mostly in New York and there I am still. I began my writing life with short stories and I remember what a fateful excitement it was when the first was accepted in *The New Mexico Quarterly*—long, long ago. I say 'fateful' because the first acceptance seems to say, Yes, it can be done. But, of course, every time you face the page again, you wonder. And it is a disappointment that writing does not get easier, but harder.

"I published more stories, three novels, and three books of literary and cultural essays. Recently, I thought of collecting my stories—if I could find them—and I thought I would use those set in New York, purging, as it were, some of the earlier ones. I found, to my distress, that one story, printed in various anthologies, did not take place in New York, as I had imagined, but in Chicago, a city I know nothing about except for a visit at the time of the Democratic Convention in 1968, a 'happening' much later than the composition of the story. Almost in a mood of repentance, I wrote the present title, 'Shot: A New York Story,' and I am honored to have it in the O. Henry volume. This honor makes me wish to write another and another, but, alas, it is ever again proving difficult to be a member of our strange profession, writing."

Perri Klass is a pediatrician at a neighborhood health center in Boston, and co-director of the Reach Out and Read program at Boston City Hospital, a program that integrates books and literacy counseling into pediatric practice. She has published several books, most recently *Baby Doctor: A Pediatrician's Training*, and *Other Women's Children*, a novel.

"This story grew out of my experience working at a city hospital, out of walking through the parking lot past residents of a homeless shelter —out of the general sense that for many, many people in the city today, the margin of survival is narrow and precarious. I started to wonder what would happen if someone gave up, if that strange-looking bundle next to the chain-link fence turned out to contain a child, left without explanation. I was interested, I think, in the way that modern urban reality can suddenly veer toward all that is most Dickensian, outcasts picking up their living on the streets, children fending for themselves in the city—and what could be more Dickensian, after all, than an abandoned baby at Christmastime?

"When I was actually writing the story, I really did call the Department of Social Services, just to make sure I knew what their actual policy would be in such a situation. I identified myself by name and medical title, explained in detail why I was asking this hypothetical question—and then, after the man had answered all my questions very patiently, he cleared his throat and asked me, 'So, *have* you found a baby on the street, ma'am?' He didn't seem to think it was at all un-likely."

Elliot Krieger: "I was born in 1948, and was raised in West Orange, New Jersey. I graduated from Johns Hopkins University, and I have a doctorate in English from SUNY Buffalo. I taught English for five years in colleges in Boston, and published numerous scholarly articles and a book on Shakespeare's comedies—then left academe for newspapers. For the past fifteen years I have been at the Providence (R.I.) *Journal-Bulletin,* where I am the editor of *The Rhode Islander Magazine.* 'Cantor Pepper' is my first and so far only published fiction; before its accep-tance at the *Rio Grande Review,* it had been rejected fourteen times— which perhaps may encourage other writers who believe in their stories to keep trying.

" 'Cantor Pepper' is based on fact, although the events in the story are entirely fictional. The rabbi, the old cantor, the temple itself—these I recalled from my childhood. Cantor Wilson Wyatt, however, is my in-vention, as is everything that follows once he steps into the rabbi's study. Because the people, the setting, and the social conditions were so clear in my mind, I was able to let the story unfold and invent itself as it went along. The writing went slowly, as it usually does for me—no more than a paragraph or so a night. Often I find that my stories move down a lot of false paths, and I have to backtrack to get the story going in the right direction. That wasn't the case here; I pretty much wrote the story straight through without revision, but when I finished I did go back to develop the climactic meeting between the rabbi and Wyatt."

Cornelia Nixon was born in Boston, Massachusetts, grew up mainly in Northern California, and now teaches at Indiana University. She has published a book on D. H. Lawrence and a novel-in-stories, *Now You See It,* which won the Carl Sandburg Award in 1991. She lives with her husband, poet Dean Young.

"This story is about three young women raised in the fifties and early sixties, who (despite certain intellectual pretensions) were tutored in placid virginity on the model of Grace Kelly, with the assumption that all of life's essential questions would be answered by the arrival of a prince; they are only seventeen when sexual and social revolution reaches them in 1969 and 1970. They earnestly protest the bombing of North Vietnam and Cambodia, and are open to sexual experiences their mothers scarcely knew about—open enough to try them, that is, if not to live with them. A decade or two later, the story of Ann and Rachel might have come out differently, as would perhaps in some ways that of Margy and Henry. I have been interested in Margy's life since 'Risk,' which appeared in *Prize Stories 1993: The O. Henry Awards*, and the story continues in a novel about her and her future husband, which I hope to finish in 1995."

Joyce Carol Oates: " 'You Petted Me, and I Followed You Home' is one of a number of stories of mine that evolve over a period of time, discontinuous and unpredictable. The little lost dog is 'real'—the image, the memory, of a dog like this dog, following us one day in the street, in a now-forgotten city, continues to haunt. And the strange title—these words, part-reproachful, with an undercurrent of passion and possessiveness, were once spoken to me, and have haunted me through the years. *You petted me, and I followed you home*—the refrain runs through my mind at odd, unexpected times, apparently lodged deep in my memory. A virtual incantation, a curse, a prophecy!—I must have believed that writing this story would erase the phrase from my interior life, but it has not done so.

"The story itself was written swiftly, in longhand, on a number of sheets of paper, my usual not-very-practical method. Scenes were then reordered, and some were excised, in the rewriting and revising, which, for me, is the more pleasurable aspect of writing. In the first phase, there is anxiety and tension and a sense that however swiftly I write, I won't get everything down, much will be lost; in the second, much longer phase, there is a sense of slow-growing but usually reliable satisfaction, as the chaos of 'feeling' is subordinated to an aesthetic structure. When I reread early versions of a story, I sometimes wonder if I haven't pared too much back; I think perhaps 'You Petted Me, and I Followed You Home' in its final published form is rather too pared back, more 'minimalist' than it might have been. I knew the woman and the man much more intimately than I'd indicated, the woman especially—but there seemed not enough space, given the restrictions I'd set for myself, to accommodate this knowledge.

"In any case, the dog completes the story, obliterates the human beings, in an action terrifying to me, as I'd understood from the outset it would.

("Having written this piece, I subsequently revised 'You Petted Me, and I Followed You Home.' The version published here is a new one.")

Anne Whitney Pierce is a lifelong resident of Cambridge, Massachusetts, where she lives with her three daughters and their father, Alex Slive. Her short story collection, *Galaxy Girls: Wonder Women,* won the 1993 Willa Cather Fiction Prize and was just published by Helicon Nine Editions. Her stories have appeared in numerous literary magazines.

"I began 'Star Box' soon after the last of my three daughters was born. My life was mainly set in a two-bedroom apartment in the company of children under the age of five. Home was a chaotic, joyful, sleepless place, a place of great refuge and yet great isolation. Outside the family time warp, real time flew by. People close to the fold began to die. This story began with a death and some thinking about how we go about filling in the holes of loss. I considered what might happen when two mutual, but unacquainted, friends of a dead person come together after the friend is gone—cautiously, sadly, perhaps defensively —what kind of connection they might form and how the spirit of the dead person might intervene. Also at work in this story are the notions of sound and speech, how we stumble to get through to one another, how well we manage sometimes, how miserably we can fail. I wrote this story as I listened to the noises of my cluttered home—babble, song, rhyme and whine—as I listened to the silences of fear, hurt, secrets, sleep. I considered a world where the middle finger shooting up from the hand of a deaf man in anger could as forcefully shatter an uneasy silence as a cry leaping out from the deepest reaches of a child's nightmare."

Padgett Powell: "The geneses of this story are three: (1) Shortly after a man told me of being seduced by the mayor of Fredericksburg, Virginia's, wife after he mowed her lawn, I (2) met a woman married happily some twenty years and enraged about it, and (3) well before any of this as a horny child I mowed many lawns, many of them for women, *praying* something like what happens in this story would happen to me. It never did. There was a basketball player for Michigan, I think, some time ago named Jimmy Keith whose name I misheard as Teeth.

"I teach, or try to, fiction writing at the University of Florida. My books are *Edisto, A Woman Named Drown,* and *Typical.*"

John Updike was born in 1932, in Shillington, Pennsylvania, and graduated from Harvard College in 1954. After a year at an English art school and a stint as a Talk of the Town reporter for *The New Yorker*, he has lived in Massachusetts as a free-lance writer. He is the author of sixteen novels and ten collections of short stories, of which the most recent is *The Afterlife and Other Stories.*

" 'The Black Room' is based on my mother's last months and gave me considerable comfort to write, some years after she was dead. I kept fiddling with the prose, trying to tune it exactly to the pitch of a unique personality; there are a number of small differences between the version reprinted here and that printed in my 1994 collection, *The Afterlife.* Several readers wrote me after its magazine publication asking me what it meant, which made me worry that I had failed to be clear. But, as the story suggests, none of us wants to be told that the house of life holds a black room."

MAGAZINES CONSULTED

Agni, Boston University, Creative Writing Program, 236 Bay State Road, Boston, Mass. 02215

Alaska Quarterly Review, College of Arts and Sciences, 3211 Providence Drive, Anchorage, Ak. 99508

American Short Fiction, Parlin 108, Department of English, University of Texas, Austin, Tex. 78712-1164

Antaeus, 100 West Broad Street, Hopewell, N.J. 08525

Antietam Review, 7 West Franklin Street, Hagerstown, Md. 21740

The Antioch Review, P.O. Box 148, Yellow Springs, Oh. 45387

The Apalachee Quarterly, P.O. Box 20106, Tallahassee, Fla. 32316

Arizona Quarterly, University of Arizona, Tucson, Ariz. 85721

Ascent, P.O. Box 967, Urbana, Ill. 61801

The Atlantic Monthly, 745 Boylston Street, Boston, Mass. 02116

Boulevard, P.O. Box 30386, Philadelphia, Pa. 19103

Buffalo Spree, 4511 Harlem Road, P.O. Box 38, Buffalo, N.Y. 14226

California Quarterly, 100 Sproul Hall, University of California, Davis, Calif. 95616

Canadian Fiction Magazine, P.O. Box 1061, Kingston, Ontario, Canada K71 4Y5

The Chariton Review, The Division of Language and Literature, Northeast Missouri State University, Kirksville, Mo. 63501

The Chattahoochee Review, DeKalb Community College, North Campus, 2101 Womack Road, Dunwoody, Ga. 30338-4497

Chelsea, P.O. Box 5880, Grand Central Station, New York, N.Y. 10163

Chicago Review, 5801 S. Kenwood, Chicago, Ill. 60637

Christopher Street, 28 West 25th Street, New York, N.Y. 10010

Cimarron Review, 205 Morill Hall, Oklahoma State University, Stillwater, Okla. 74078-0135

Colorado Review, 360 Eddy Building, Colorado State University, Fort Collins, Colo. 80523

Columbia, 404 Dodge Hall, Columbia University, New York, N.Y. 10027

Commentary, 165 East 56th Street, New York, N.Y. 10022

Confrontation, Department of English, C.W. Post College of Long Island University, Brookville, N.Y. 11548

The Cream City Review, University of Wisconsin-Milwaukee, P.O. Box 413, Milwaukee, Wis. 53201

Crescent Review, 1445 Old Town Road, Winston-Salem, N.C. 27106-3143

Crosscurrents, 2200 Glastonbury Rd., Westlake Village, Calif. 91361

Denver Quarterly, Department of English, University of Denver, Denver, Colo. 80210

Epoch, 251 Goldwin Smith Hall, Cornell University, Ithaca, N.Y. 14853-3201

Esquire, 1790 Broadway, New York, N.Y. 10019

Farmer's Market, P.O. Box 1272, Galesburg, Ill. 61402

Fiction, Department of English, The City College of New York, N.Y. 10031

Fiction International, Department of English, St. Lawrence University, Canton, N.Y. 13617

The Fiddlehead, UNB, P.O. Box 4400, Fredericton, New Brunswick, Canada, E3B 5A3

First for Women, 270 Sylvan Avenue, Englewood Cliffs, N.J. 07632

The Florida Review, Department of English, University of Central Florida, Orlando, Fla. 32816

Four Quarters, La Salle College, Philadelphia, Pa. 19141

Gentleman's Quarterly, 350 Madison Avenue, New York, N.Y. 10017

The Georgia Review, University of Georgia, Athens, Ga. 30602

The Gettysburg Review, Gettysburg College, Gettysburg, Pa. 17325-1491

Glimmer Train, 812 SW Washington Street, Suite 1205, Portland, Oreg. 97205-3216

Global City Review, Rifkind Center for the Humanities, City College, 138th and Convent Avenue, New York, N.Y. 10031

Grain, Box 1154, Regina, Saskatchewan, Canada S4P 3B4

Grand Street, 131 Varick Street, #906, New York, N.Y. 10013

The Greensboro Review, Department of English, University of North Carolina, Greensboro, N.C. 27412

Harper's, 666 Broadway, New York, N.Y. 10012

Hawaii Review, Department of English, University of Hawaii, 1733 Donaghho Road, Honolulu, Ha. 96822

High Plains Literary Review, 180 Adams Street, Suite 250, Denver, Colo. 80206

The Hudson Review, 684 Park Avenue, New York, N.Y. 10021

Indiana Review, 316 N. Jordan, Bloomington, Ind. 47405

Iowa Review, 308 EPB, University of Iowa, Iowa City, Ia. 52242

Iowa Woman, P.O. Box 680, Iowa City, Ia. 52244-0680

Kalliope, a Journal of Women's Art, Florida Community College at Jacksonville, 3939 Roosevelt Boulevard, Jacksonville, Fla. 32205-8989

Kansas Quarterly, Department of English, Denison Hall, Kansas State University, Manhattan, Kan. 66506-0703

The Kenyon Review, Kenyon College, Gambier, Oh. 43022

Ladies' Home Journal, 100 Park Avenue, New York, N.Y. 10017

The Literary Review, Fairleigh Dickinson University, 285 Madison Ave., Madison, N.J. 07940

Magic Realism, Box 620, Orem, Ut. 84054-0620

Manoa, English Department, University of Hawaii, Honolulu, Ha. 96822

The Massachusetts Review, Memorial Hall, University of Massachusetts, Amherst, Mass. 01002

Matrix, c.p. 100 Ste-Anne-de-Bellevue, Quebec, Canada H9X 3L4

McCall's, 110 Fifth Avenue, New York, N.Y. 10011

Michigan Quarterly Review, 3032 Rackham Building, University of Michigan, Ann Arbor, Mich. 48109

Mid-American Review, 106 Hanna Hall, Bowling Green State University, Bowling Green, Oh. 43403

Midstream, 110 East 59th Street, 4th Floor, New York, N.Y. 10022

The Missouri Review, 1507 Hillcrest Hall, University of Missouri, Columbia, Mo. 65211

Mother Jones, 731 Market Street, San Francisco, Calif. 94103

Nantucket Journal, 7 Sea Street, Nantucket, Mass. 02554

Nassau Review, Nassau Community College, One Education Drive, Garden City, N.Y. 11530-6793

New Directions, 80 Eighth Avenue, New York, N.Y. 10011

New England Review, Middlebury College, Middlebury, Vt. 05753

New Letters, University of Missouri-Kansas City, 5100 Rockhill Road, Kansas City, Mo. 64110

The New Renaissance, 9 Heath Road, Arlington, Mass. 02174

The New Yorker, 20 West 43rd Street, New York, N.Y. 10036

The North American Review, University of Northern Iowa, 1227 West 27th Street, Cedar Falls, Ia. 50614

North Atlantic Review, 15 Arbutus Lane, Stony Brook, N.Y. 11790-1408

North Dakota Quarterly, University of North Dakota, Grand Forks, N.D. 58202-7209

The Ohio Review, Ellis Hall, Ohio University, Athens, Oh. 45701-2979

OMNI, 1965 Broadway, New York, N.Y. 10012

The Ontario Review, 9 Honey Brook Drive, Princeton, N.J. 08540

Other Voices, The University of Illinois at Chicago, Department of English (M/C 162), 601 South Morgan Street, Chicago, Ill. 60680-7120

Pangolin Papers, Box 241, Nordland, Wash. 98358

The Paris Review, Box S, 541 East 72nd Street, New York, N.Y. 10021

The Partisan Review, 236 Bay State Road, Boston, Mass. 02215

Phoebe, Women's City Program, State University of New York, Oneonta, N.Y. 13820

Playboy, 680 North Lake Shore Drive, Chicago, Ill. 60611

Ploughshares, Emerson College, 100 Beacon Street, Boston, Mass. 02116

Prairie Schooner, Andrews Hall, University of Nebraska, Lincoln, Neb. 68588

Puerto del Sol, College of Arts & Sciences, Box 3E, New Mexico State University, Las Cruces, N.M. 88003

RaJah, 411 Mason Hall, University of Michigan, Ann Arbor, Mich. 48109

Raritan, 31 Mine Street, New Brunswick, N.J. 08903

Redbook, 224 West 57th Street, New York, N.Y. 10019

River Oak Review, P.O. Box 3127, Oak Park, Ill. 60303

Rio Grande Review, Hudspeth Hall, U.T.–El Paso, El Paso, Tex. 79968

Sailing, 125 E. Main Street, P.O. Box 248, Port Washington, Wis. 53074

Salamagundi, Skidmore College, Saratoga Springs, N.Y. 12866

Santa Monica Review, Center for the Humanities at Santa Monica College, 1900 Pico Boulevard, Santa Monica, Calif. 90405

Sequoia, Storke Student Publications Building, Stanford, Calif. 94305

Seventeen, 850 Third Avenue, New York, N.Y. 10022

The Sewanee Review, University of the South, Sewanee, Tenn. 37375

Shenandoah, Box 722, Lexington, Va. 24405

Short Fiction by Women, Box 1276, Stuyvesant Station, New York, N.Y. 10009

Snake Nation Review, 110 #2 West Force Street, Valdosta, Ga. 31601

Sonora Review, Department of English, University of Arizona, Tucson, Ariz. 85721

South Carolina Review, Department of English, Clemson University, Clemson, S.C. 29634-1503

South Dakota Review, Box 111, University Exchange, Vermillion, S.D. 57069

Southern Humanities Review, 9088 Haley Center, Auburn University, Auburn, Ala. 36849

The Southern Review, Drawer D, University Station, Baton Rouge, La. 70803

Southwest Review, Southern Methodist University, Dallas, Tex. 75275

Stanford Humanities Review, Stanford Humanities Center, Stanford University, Stanford, Calif. 94305

Stories, Box Number 1467, East Arlington, Mass. 02174-0022

Story, 1507 Dana Avenue, Cincinnati, Oh. 45207

Story Quarterly, P.O. Box 1416, Northbrook, Ill. 60065

The Sun, 107 North Robertson Street, Chapel Hill, N.C. 27516

Tampa Review, Box 135F, University of Tampa, Tampa, Fla. 33606

The Threepenny Review, P.O. Box 9131, Berkeley, Calif. 94709

Tikkun, Institute of Labor and Mental Health, 5100 Leona Street, Oakland, Calif. 94619

TriQuarterly 2020 Ridge Avenue, Evanston, Ill. 60208

Urbanus, P.O. Box 192561, San Francisco, Calif. 94119

The Village Voice Literary Supplement, 36 Cooper Square, New York, N.Y. 10003

The Virginia Quarterly Review, University of Virginia, 1 West Range, Charlottesville, Va. 22903

Vogue, 350 Madison Avenue, New York, N.Y. 10017

Washington Review, Box 50132, Washington, D.C. 20091

Webster Review, Webster University, 470 E. Lockwood, Webster Groves, Mo. 63119

West Coast Review, Simon Fraser University, Burnaby, British Columbia, Canada V5A 1S6

Western Humanities Review, University of Utah, Salt Lake City, Ut. 84112

Whetstone, P.O. Box 1266, Barrington, Ill. 60011

Wind, RFD Route 1, Box 809K, Pikeville, Ky. 41501

Witness, Oakland Community College, Orchard Ridge Campus, 27055 Orchard Lake Rd., Farmington Hills, Mich. 48334

Yale Review, P.O. Box 208243, New Haven, Ct. 06520

Yankee, Main Street, Dublin, N.H. 03444

Zyzzyva, 41 Sutter Street, Suite 1400, San Francisco, Calif. 94104